Untamed Feelings

Rutuja Naik

Invincible Publishers

First published in India in 2016 by Invincible Publishers

ISBN: 978-93-86148-25-4

Invincible Publishers
F-55, Sushant Lok II, Hong Kong Bazar Lane Sector 57,
Gurgaon-122003

Opposite Kasturba Ashram, Radaur Distt Yamuna Nagar, Haryana-
135133

Acknowledgement

Many people have helped me through the journey of writing this book.

I would like to thank Wattpad community for providing me with a platform to share my stories with thousands of readers world wide.

All my Wattpad readers Shriya Gupta, Alice Singh, Shiksha Sharma for their meaningful and positive comments that encouraged me to complete the story.

My Wattpad friends Anika Upadhayay, Amore Schmidt, Shreya Shah and all the Wattpad group members for their help and support.

Ajay Setia of Invincible publishers and all the team for selecting my book. Malvika for helping me in the process of editing and Sneha for the beatiful book cover.

My college friends Neha Kasar, Heena Kudu, Bhoomika Naik, Sharayu Kole, my cousins Asmita Patil and Isha Naik, my brother Jayesh Naik for their love and support.

To the one guy who inspired me, the guy of my dreams I would like to thank him without him the book would have never being completed.

Last but not the least my parents and God for their love and blessings .

* * *

Chapter 1- "First day of hell"

"Jenny, get out of your fucking bed now!" My bonkers of a friend, Beth screamed at the top of her lungs.

I need to confess something to you guys before anything. I do love my sexy friend but it comes with a price which I am not willing to sacrifice.

The price is being a morning person. This would never happen at all. Even if sun starts rising few hours early I would still sleep late. So getting up Early is out of the question for me.

"Get out before before I am forced to do something you will hate." She threatened.

You might be wondering, with all the screams of my friend, Beth, I would have got used to being a morning person. Matter of fact, no, I cherish my sleep way too much for that. Bloody hell, I sleep more than a new born baby, which cuts to the fact that I am erratic, admit it, even Beth admits this to some extent she just tortures me by screaming on purpose.

What a great friend, Right?

I always, imagine her being the wicked witch of the west. Pure evil, I know.

Rising up to the infuriating sound of my friend, my lifeless eyes decide to give my room a glance before heading back to bed. I looked at my phone, it read 7:00, way too early meaning much more time for sleep my mind happily stated.

I laid back in my slumber.

After a while, I heard another scream from Beth, this time, she is literally dragging me out of bed, which is worst, my eyes suddenly opened by the sudden touch, man I was going to kill this girl.

"It is eight already, Jennifer, have some manners and get your ass going. You would not want to be late for High school I hope." She screamed again.

High School, crap. I frantically did get my ass moving in a fuss, heading straight to the washroom, not knowing how the bloody hell will I get to my destination in twenty minutes. My conscience cursed me, for sleeping like some dead corpse and seeing wrong time and for not being aware of my responsibilities. But then it happens every time so probably now my conscience also knows that I am made this way.

Exiting my washroom, I went straight to my bed, where I keep my quickest outfits ready if, in case I was late, which never happens right. Note the sarcasm.

I stole a look at myself in the mirror; my outfit was passable and decent, I was wearing ripped black jeans topped up with a red checkered t-shirt which I adore to life and my black Dr. Martins boots. But once my eyes reached my face, I gasped at the state of my awful face.

Oh my Gosh! My eyes are all puffy again! I thought to myself.

This is what I never get though I oversleep all the time I still get puffy Eyes, which makes me look like I haven't slept for years

I mentally cursed myself again; and decided to wake up early tomorrow, like that was ever going to happen my conscience said doubting me.

Hurriedly, I applied some concealer to hide the puffiness underneath my eyes. Once, I was satisfied with my look I headed out. I am not a beauty, to be straight, I am just decent. But at school, everyone is just extraordinarily beautiful than me.

Heading down stairs, I ambled in to the kitchen; I could literally feel Beth's ears boiling on either side of her with anger.

What a wonderful way to start your morning, Jenny! My conscience sarcastically said. I mentally patted my back proudly as I was faster than usual but still late. I grabbed an apple before walking my ass to school and kissing my parents a goodbye for their lovely day because I surely know mine isn't going to be. Being lazy has its peak because of which Beth is giving me a ride.

Did you really think a lazy piece of shit such as myself would walk to school, no. I am a snail and totally proud of it.

My sexy creature of a friend glared daggers at me, which meant if I was even a second later, she would have practically killed me. I tired ignoring her glare but gave up, and offered a big toothy smile, because without her I would have been more late. She smiled back, a fake smile of course, meaning she is pissed at me. I just turned away and stared at the sky for my safety not knowing what the flying cakes she was capable of.

The ride to the hellhole which people called high school was awful. Beth, was ignoring me, which pissed me off. Soon we reached our high school and Beth parked her Mini cooper near Alice's car. Alice was my second best friend, but the group that I hang out with is predictably weird: Alice and Beth are totally opposite and I am just in the middle and don't you start with the side chick.

Alice and I have known each other since childhood. We are like shampoo and conditioner, and we never leave each other's side ever. Alice is my lovely best friend as well as the top student in school and is aiming to get into Oxford. She is the most ambitious girl I have ever met, but you can't forget her stalking habits for her crushes when she has free time and also her non-stop gossiping. She is like a chatterbox robot, does that even exist?

I sometimes wonder, how the freaking hell does she have time for all this, with all the homework we get, I certainly don't. She stalks people but her analogy is that it's not called stalking but 'knowing everything about other people'. She likes to know everything about others, even if she doesn't personally know them. She is the bubbliest person I know. She always has a smile on her face and is the quietest of all, and they say the quietest are the deadliest is actually true in her case. Any guy would adore her innocence, but she has a crush already which she has stalked a million times, that I couldn't possible count.

Damn, she is totally falling for him. But she always keeps saying it's just a crush, which is surely a lie

Beth on the other hand joined our school recently. We clicked instantly because of our mutual hatred for math. Beth has this tough girl attitude and appearance but personally if you get to know her, she is totally a sweetheart from inside, like a coconut. She wears band tees and fishnet tights. She doesn't care about what others opinion is about her. She minds her business and carries the day like a Queen. She is practical and robust. I sometimes wonder how we even became best of friends in the first place. But here we are; I don't regret any moment of this mutual friendship, in fact I love it.

The three of us are practically invisible at school, besides a few teachers and Librarians; no one else notices us,not that it really matters to us as it keeps us out of the rumor mill and the center of attention which I personally hate.

"We need to meet some teachers before the first class so we'll see you later, Jenny!" My two best friends, who I love to death said ditching me, on my first day itself. I know they are angry but still you don't do that to your friend, Right? I guess I just need to put my girl pants up and start the day.

I ambled to my locker to collect my resources for my first period. Scanning around the room,it was full of different types of people. "Jocks the Jerks", which I named them," the cheerleader", "The nerds", who stuff their heads inside books and are always achieving their high grades, "the bad boy my ass", who harass juniors for their enjoyment, and then there's "my friends and I" who make up our own little group.

Ring...

The bell echoed inside my mind alerting me, I was going to get late if I did not get my ass moving.

Today luck is seriously not on my side.

Good going, Jenny. You're going to get detention and its only day one! Yay! Good for you!

Yeah, I know I'm exaggerating but the day had started off extremely bad for me.

I started to run towards my class hoping to get there at least before the teacher.

Thud!

I slammed into a wall from lack of paying attention, around the corner of the corridor. Damn! Who builds a wall at a turn? I stood there for the pain to come, shutting my eyes tightly, but I felt warm, muscular hand around my waist, and the arm was tightly wrapped around me, to hold my steady weight.

Gosh, last time I checked walls did not have hands.

Huh! Well, at least my bottom was saved!

I opened one eye slowly peaking, I was flabbergasted to see a tall buff figure, inches away from eyes, soon as I saw the person who'd caught me, my heart started to beat erratically. I was in the arms of the most gorgeous guy I'd ever laid my eyes on. I bet he noticed how fast my heart was beating, it felt like it was going to pound its way out of my chest. He had messy styled brown hair styled with the most mesmerizing, deep, blue eyes. They were the most angelic eyes I had ever seen. When I put the broken pieces of information together and registered the oddly familiar face in my mind I realized that I was in arms of the one and only, Austin Parker.

My eyes widened as it hit me. He was not only hot and stunning but a "bad boy my ass" of this school. He was also the star player of almost all the sports. He and his two friends almost never actually attended classes. They have permanent seats in the detention room with their names written with permanent marker. They are terrible flirts who use girls and then throw them away like tissues. They have been with most of the female population of the school. They are known for the trail of broken-hearts that they leave behind. I don't know if it's actually true or if it's all just a bunch of rumors, as I have never seen them with any girl even once but that's what people say about them. So it must be somewhat true.

They always get themselves into trouble, or rather create trouble everywhere they go. Each one of them has their own different vibe too.

Unwrapping his arms from my waist he rudely said, "Watch, where you're going, bitch!" bringing me back to my senses.

Then I realized that I was shamelessly staring at his face and felt my cheeks instantly heat up out of embarrassment. But then I registered that he had called me a bitch. No one is allowed to insult me like that. Not even the school's popular Guy.

"No need to be so harsh, jerk!" I snapped without thinking. My eyes widened with shock at what had come out of my mouth. I was not an ill-tempered kind of girl. I usually bottled all my anger inside, instead of letting it come out like that.

I don't know from where the sudden confidence came from but I further said "It was your fault, as Mr.-you-were-in-your-own-la-la-land-while-I-was-walking that caused me to bump into you. I was actually trying to get to class on time, not that you'd know anything about." I realized what I said and clamped my mouth shut.

Was I fed up enough with my life that I had to dig my own grave? What has gotten into me today?

Even his face was mix of shock, anger and many other expressions that I couldn't understand, and to just my luck the final bell went off at that moment.

Ring ...Ring.....

Gosh I have never been so thankful for the bell before.

Without giving the jerk a second glance I ran towards my class. To my surprise, Austin ran behind me to class as well, I did not know I had the same class as him.

"Ah! How lucky I must be that the both of you decided to attend my class!"Mr. Black said dramatically. Then he glared at us and with his deadly eyes he further said , "Meet me in detention today after schooland no sports for you anymore." He said looking towards Austin. Mr. Black's look was so intense that he could have kicked me then and there if I would have argued with him. I just nodded and made way to my seat quietly. Mr. Black was fuming with anger because of Austin's behavior; as he was ignoring him again.

The rest of the day was mostly normal except for the several pairs of amused eyes fixed on me. I hated the attention. Even my own friends were in bewilderment because of the little stunt I had pulled today.

The day wasn't even half over and I had landed myself in trouble already. Oh Dear God, please be on my side!

* * *

Chapter 2 - Detention

"Detention?"Alice screamed with disbelief plastered all over her face.

"What did you do now?" Beth said with same expressions.

"I was late to class." I said casually, not wanting to push the subject of the asshole Austin.

As if being late to class was an everyday thing for me.

"You're such a rebel." Beth teased,

I cursed Austin several times as I narrated the whole story of 'how I actually landed myself into detention' to them.

I have never been so angry with one person in my entire life.

"Could you feel his muscles?" Alice cried excitedly ignoring my curses.

She is a big fan of bad boys and has a huge crush on Recce Austin's best friends. Beth, however, hated them from bottom of her heart which was another similarity between her and me.

"Do you really think that she's crazy enough to feel up that self-obsessed jerk who had just called her a bitch?" Beth stated with anger.

Beth was right, he was a jerk, but I couldn't help but think about the arms that had caught me before I fell. They were really muscular and felt strong when they were wrapped around me and his body was just perfect. It was like the body of a Greek sex god but there is no way I was going to tell them that.

I was being all snobs to admit my own feelings for that bastard, let alone to my two best friends.

Austin's PoV

Damn!!

That weird silly girl ruined my entire day; as strange as it is for me to admit it, she was actually pretty cute. She was the girl who almost knocked me over in the hallway while running to class. I had seen her around in some of my classes; but I'd never had a chance to talk with her before.

She is probably one of the only girls who doesn't drool over me for my looks instead it seems like she hates me a lot for some unknown reason. She is the only girl, who's ever dared to talk to me like how she did in hallway and I was too flabbergasted to do anything about it. Her face was so innocent that it stopped me from unleashing my anger on her; that it made my heart warm up.

According to what I found from my sources, her name is Jennifer. She is cute, cheerful, and sweet and minds her own business. I've noticed her several times. She doesn't talk very often so her behavior in the hallway shocked me. I was totally surprised to see her like that.

When Mr. Black said "Both of you - detention" her face paled. If it were any other girl I would have been happy, but with her, things felt different. Even though I can't figure out why? But I seriously felt like doing something to Mr. Black, just to make her happy again. So to control my anger I acted like I didn't care.There was something about her that seemed attractive to me. Her angelic eyes; her soft, pink lips; and her innocence, was all so perfect.

God did I really just notice her lips while she was glaring daggers at me?

I've officially lost it. I never do that.

I know I am sounding all mushy right now but this girl can make anyone sound cheesy with her angelic beauty.

Why am I thinking about a girl who just totally insulted me?

❄ ❄ ❄

Chapter 3 - The project.

Jenny

Next was English class. Now, this is a class I actually have interest in. I mean, yeah, I get straight A's in all my classes even in math'. Strange isn't it? Even I am sometimes shocked myself as I would rather eat broccoli then solve a math problem. I hate math that much and try to avoid it like it's something repulsive.

But the luckiest part about English is - my best friends being in the same lesson as me. I hurried towards my locker and switched my books for my next period English, which I could not wait for and hurried inside the class.

"Rumors are going around that English teacher has an important announcement for us." Beth said with total excitement as Alice and I placed our books on the desk and slid into chair to be comfortable.

Alice raised an eyebrow at her statement.

"Really?" I asked with curious tone "What kind of announcement will spark a rumor in this school?"

"A surprise test" Alice guessed.

"Or there could be any project coming up." Beth replied with excitement. She just loves practicals than theory. We stopped our guesses as Mr. Jacob walked in.

"Good afternoon ladies and gentlemen." Mr. Jacob projected, turning around to face us. "Well, I bet you all must have heard the little rumors about the announcement." he stated, grabbing most of the student's attention as all of them sat straight in their seats.

"Any guesses on what the announcement could be?." He asked.

On this many students gave many childish answers which made the entire class laugh.

Stupid remarks invaded the room such as, 'A party at your house', 'you're resigning', ' you're giving straight A's to everyone', 'No more English Lectures'.

How immature can these people get? Mr. Jacob was totally stunned by these replies. Though I wonder how he can even expect something else from these students.

"Why don't you just tell us what this is about and end the conversation," A loud irritated voice from the back took everyone's attention. It was none other than Mr. Arrogant Austin. I guessed it without even looking back. Mr. Jacob gave his normal disapproving look and ignored his rude comment like always.

He continued saying "I must say, you all have extraordinary imagination skills but unfortunately, it's just a group project. In this project you will be preparing on the legend of Romeo and Juliet. This project will be very important for passing literature and the group whose project will be good will be chosen as Romeo and Juliet in our annual function drama."He informed".

I was very excited for the project. I looked towards the girls. And they knowingly smiled at my direction. "But your partners will be of my choice and I have already assigned your partners" My excitement level totally drained by listening to this.

Why do the professors have to be always so mean?

"When I call your names you should raise your hands so your partner will find it easy to locate you". He stated as he started calling out names. He was at the end of the list and only we three friends and the bad boys group was left. So it didn't require any scholar to guess that we were going to be paired with the bad boys.

Oh my god. Not with Austin. I was OK with the other two boys. I prayed silently.

"Alice you will be paired with Recce." I could literally feel Alice's happiness. I knew she was happy as her eyes turned to shade of dark blue, which happens only when she is extremelyhappy. She gave a big ear to ear grin as if Recce is some sort of God.

"Beth you will be paired with River, and Jennifer with Austin." As I heard this my mouth felt open wide literally touching the ground. Without thinking for a moment even I quickly shouted

"No."

To my utter surprise Austin yelled the same at the same time.

"How can I be paired with this girl, she is boring." Austin continued again rudely.

Dude if there was an award for being rude, he would surely win the first prize.

If it wasn't about project I would have totally fought with him but I ignored it all as I just wanted to get rid of him. But Mr. Jacob was not in the mood of listening .The guy even tried his famous puppy innocent face on which any girl would agree. But Mr. Jacob still didn't agree.

"Sir please try to understand we are like water and Fire we can Never get along "I said withpleading Eyes.

"It's your problem. Sort it among yourselves or else just Fail" Mr. Jacob Retorted.

"You may now sit with your partners to discuss about the project, its due in 3 weeks" these where the worst words from Mr. Jacob's mouth.

On listening to this, Austin sat beside me lazily not even bothering to bring his books in class. Typical Austin, instead he thought it would be fun to talk with the guy seated in front of us, and totally ignore me. From the corner of my eye I saw him looking towards me indirectly with a smirk on his face. That Idiot was ignoring me purposely. Gosh what's wrong with this guy?

When I couldn't take it anymore "You know we are sitting together for some purpose, right?" I said in a wrathful tone cutting their nonsense talks.

"I'm sorry, am I keeping you away from your studies?" He mocked. I heard some of the class laughing at his remark.

"Nothing to speak, huh?" He teased

He was really testing my patience.

"What the hell do you think of yourself?"I yelled at the top of my lungs.

Gosh what's happening to me? This boy was really capable of bringing anger out of me by annoying me to a large extent.

God even I didn't know I had so much anger inside me but it felt nice to see him in total shock. I mentally patted my back for such priceless expression from him.

He quickly regained his senses and leaned in so close that his mouth was only inches away from my lips. My body tensed up by his closeness and don't ask about my heart it went completely numb.

Oh my poor heart...

"So girl's got spunk huh. Interesting." he commented, lifting the side of his mouth in a smirk.

Till then the bell to the most irritating lecture rang and the class started to become vacant. I somewhat pushed Austin away from me.

But I missed his breath on my neck as soon as he backed off. What was happening to me?

"See you at detention nerd." He said with the smirk and my stomach started to give different feeling as I remembered about detention.

❄ ❄ ❄

Chapter 4 - The actual detention

I sucked in a shaky breath, feeling my throat constrict. Panic rose like bile in my body. My stomach was tying itself in knots. The thought of detention itself was making me nervous. Everyone was looking at me with so much disbelief, as if getting detention was a crime. Why people have to be so nosy these days? Can't they just stop poking their nose in other people's business for once?

I know the answer is 'no!' As I know they use other people's heart breaks and embarrassment as an amusement for their entertainment.

Though I was enjoying the little conversation with myself, I had to stop it to go to the 'Mini Hell' known as the detention hall. I hurriedly ambled towards the washroom, avoiding the strange glares I was receiving from literally everyone. I felt like a criminal walking towards the court.

I stood in front of the washroom mirror gazing at myself.

'Why am I even worrying? It isn't a big deal. Many students get detention every year. I tried to convince my mind.

But it was never by my side. Basically my mind always has to go against me.

'But, you have never gotten a detention in your life,' my inner voice taunted me. It never passes up a chance of harassing me.

'Now suck it up,' my inner voice spoke again.

I sometimes think that this inner voice of mine is my biggest enemy. I don't understand why it has to speak such negative words to me. There were only five minutes left. Then I had to go to the first detention I have ever earned. I bit my lower lip and took deep breaths through my nose, trying to suppress the feeling of nervousness.

'Should have thought about this before you opened your big mouth,' my Inner voice taunted again.

The moment I reached Detention Room, I blinked at the room before me. I was surprised to see so many students in the detention room. Austin and his friends were as expected, sitting on their usual seats. Austin was busy listening to songs on headphones totally ignoring professor in front of him. Gosh, if extreme Ego gave you a disease, he surely would have it by now.

As I was taking in the spooky scene of the detention room, someone cleared his throat harshly, making everyone's eyes focus on me.

"Are you waiting for some sort of invitation to come in, Miss Jenny?" I jumped in shock and looked up to see the angry face of Mr. Black. Instead of answering him I just nodded my head and ran towards an empty seat.

But even here, luck was unfortunately not on my side. There was only one seat, in front the ruthless jerk, Austin.

"Oh princess, you missed me so much that you followed me into the detentiontoo?" Austin said with a mischievous grin, which caused his friends to chuckle a little.

Ignoring him, I tried to concentrate on the sheet in front of me as my bloody punishment. I knew Austin was reading what I was writing from over my shoulder, but I decided to ignore him.

"So you are really one of the nerdy chicks, huh?" He asked, leaning closer to my ears. I felt a shiver and elbowed him away from me. This boy seriously doesn't know anything about personal space. I opened my mouth to reply to his cockiness, nothing but just air came out. If you guys haven't figured it out by now, than let me tell you, I am totally terrible at comebacks. I somehow end up making fun of myself, by just moving my mouth without any words coming out. He just laughed at my loss of words.

"So you are among one of those self-obsessed boys, huh?"

Thankfully I chirped back after my silly attempts at retaliation.

This was the fastest I have ever thought in such situations. He had the look of total amusement on his face by my comeback. He didn't expect me to speak.

Seriously speaking, neither did I, but then today many things are happening that I would have never thought of doing in my entire life. This guy was seriously helping me discover my rare hidden talents.

"Right." he said smiling more to himself.

"Are you always this disgusting**?" I asked leaning backward subconsciously. His smile widened.**

It was then that I realized what I actually did.

"It's all part of my charm, sweetheart." Austin said with a wink.

"This isn't charming." l told him confused.

"Everything I do is charming, sweetheart." He said widening the smirk on his face.

I turned my face away from him to hide my blush.A simple sweetheart from his mouth made my heart flutter in many ways. God, what's wrong with me?

"You forgot hot and good looking qualities of mine." He said smirking proudly.

"Are you sure you didn't mean your stupidity?" I asked with a smirk.

He leaned forward again, this time I felt nervous, he was too close. I took a deep breath to calm myself.

"Are you disputing my looks?" He asked.

"What if I am?" I said confidently which surprised me. All my hidden talents were coming out today. All thanks to this jerk in front of me who possesses the ability to annoy anyone.

"I would say you are dumber than I thought. Every girl would die to be with me. There's no one who would ever reject me. Even if you don't show, I know even you drool over my looks, sweetheart." His last words shocked me. My eyes popped at his response.

"In your wildest dreams, Parker"

He was surely good looking, heart fluttering, smart and whatever he said was true maybe even the last sentence but I am not going to state it in front of him. This will just increase his already large ego.

"I would rather say you are an Ass--"

I never got to complete my sentence as Mr. Black said, "Miss Winget and Mr. Parker is there something you want to share with the class?"

I was about to say no when over-talented Austin decided to speak for us.

"Jennifer here was asking me on a date, but I said no. She's just irritating me now, Sir." He lied with his most innocent face.

I don't understand. How can a Devil make such an innocent face? This had caught the whole class's attention. I was stunned in place.

"Sir, this Idiot is telling a fucking lie." I swore, unknowingly with all the anger.

"Language Winget, Don't force me to give you one more detention." Mr. Black warned me.

Then the bell signaling end of detention rang, so without waiting another second, I ran out of the room.

God! This guy seriously is an idiot. Why does he always have to embarrass me in front of everybody? Why?

❄ ❄ ❄

Chapter 5 - After school

Firstly due to being late to class, I got a pain in the ass detention and now I had to walk home alone. My house was pretty far from school. Cursing my luck again and again, I started walking. Austin had officially ruined my entire first day. If I ever get a chance I will totally take revenge for this.

The things which happened to me today were all nightmares to me. Colliding with the idiot, fighting, teasing, detention, scolding from the professor, project partner all these events were unwanted. Given a chance to change anything in my life I would surely change all happenings of this day. I would never wish for a day like this in my entire life. I was busy thinking of today, when a huge motorcycle stopped abruptly beside me. It instantly brought me out of my thoughts.

I felt like I had seen this motorcycle somewhere before, but was not able to recollect where, until the person on motorcycle removed his helmet and my eyes met his beautiful eyes.Oh my god, he looked like some Greek god with his well-known smirk and messy hair.

It was none other than Austin.

"Done with your staring?" He said wiggling his eyebrows. I realized then I was checking him out. God this is so embarrassing. To avoid eye contact, I suddenly fell in love with the road and looked down, not able to look at him.

With a slight grin he further said, "Come on princess, I will drop you home."

I know every girl in school would die for this opportunity, but I was amused. Why was he asking me out of all girls? I was surely still angry about him for ruining my day.

I will never forget the day; he ruined my reputation in front of everyone. I just decided to ignore him and started walking. Unfortunately, I couldn't walk faster than his motorcycle. He came again beside me.

"Are you seriously saying 'no' to me? Most girls in school would die for this opportunity." He said as if he had offered me a whole big, chocolate ice cream and I was ignoring it. I know I'm exaggerating but I totally get weak in the knees hearing ice cream.

"I'm not like 'most of the girls', I am not interested at all." I winked at him and walked away before he could answer, leaving him open mouthed.

God that felt good. After that he didn't follow me. I started walking peacefully, when god decided to make my awful day worst. It started raining so heavily that I was totally soaked in water by the time I got home.

'Perfect ending to the worst day of my life,' I thought to myself as I entered the house. I soon dried myself and changed into my comfortable frozen night ware. As usual my parents were on a business trip so again; I had the house all to myself. It's not like I am not used to it but for days like this, I seriously miss my mom. I was damn tired to do anything so I just put on songs on my headphone and went to another world of dreams.

AUSTIN'S POV

The boys were as usually around my house playing Xbox. It was our regular schedule after school we would hangout to discuss our day. But today I was totally out of my mind. I was continuously thinking about that nerd and her rejection. I was totally shocked by the rejection. Never in my life have I experienced rejection from any girl. I felt like someone has stabbed me.

I have never thought about any girl, not even about my past girlfriends for such a long time. I'm just not the type of guy who thinks so much. But this little nerdy girl had something different, which I was forced to think about.

"That girl seriously has some guts. Damn she must be the first girl who didn't fall for your charms. In fact she just rejected you." Recce said practically crying out of laughter. I just shot him a dirty look as I couldn't seem to fathom some words.

"Wow! Since when did Austin Parker start to have difficulty finding words?" My other silly friend, River spoke up. God they can't miss any chance of embarrassing me.

"She's hot though and different from other girls." Recce added. This literally boiled my blood with anger.

"She's not your type. She deserves a lot better than you." I said immediately without thinking.

"Is someone getting jealous?" River asked with a smirk. Seriously they act as if they are in kindergarten, but they are my closest friends. They know me in and out. We have been friends since childhood; they have always been by my side, in my happy as well as sad moments.

"Dude, you seriously have a thing for her, sort out your feelings before it's too late." River said. "You can't let your past relationships spoil your future life. You should move on and love the right chick."

I hate discussing or even mentioning my previous life. I ignored them and just went to my room.

But sleep was not by my side today. I just kept staring the ceiling. I know they were both right but trusting someone again and moving on was really difficult for me. I can't risk having heartbreak again.

World War Three was going on between my brain and heart about Jenny. It has not even been one day meeting this girl and she has already made my brain and mind go against each other. So to make peace between my mind and brain I decided to apologize to Jenny for my behavior.

* * *

Chapter 6 -Skipping school (Part1)

JENNY

The irritating sound of the alarm brought me back in my world. It was then I realized that I slept for a total of seventeen hours. Thinking about yesterday I Instantly frowned. But then maybe this is just the beginning of something worse as I still had a few more weeks to survive with that egotistic Austin. To make my day a little better I decided to ignore Austin totally, I mentally groaned and got ready for school. This is the most hectic part of my day.

As usual, I walked into school with my twoconflicting friends. They were fighting again which wasn't anything new but for once their topic of fight had changed from studies and parties to a much more stupid topic. Yeah you totally guessed it Right My friend, it was about Austin.

God seriously, I mean, why do they have to talk about him on the day I have decided to ignore him? More Importantly Why do they even have to talk about him?

I tried ignoring them but being in the middle of them, ignoring didn't help me at all. I was forced to listen to their stupid argument.

"Don't you dare ignore this guy, you do know a good love story starts from heated fight Right? You have a chance of having a great love story Jenny; Grab it tightly with your both hands" Alice over dramatically said.

"Are you nuts? He is not dating material stay away from him." Beth protested. They were fighting as if he has proposed to me. I had started enjoying their little useless fight.

"Speak of the Devil and the Devil is here." Beth spoke irritably. I didn't get for a minute about what she was speaking so I just stared at her with a blank face.

"Look there he is now." Alice gushed, as she nudged me with unnecessary force.

I turned around in time to watch the gorgeous Austin Parker stood Like an Angel beside my locker.

"What the hell is he doing at your locker?" Beth slapped my shoulder lightly.

I nonchalantly replied, "Firstly how would I know that, I am Right beside you guys. And secondly why will he be waiting by my locker? He probably doesn't even know it's my locker."

"Why wouldn't he? Bad boys always like good girls and you my dear you are the best good girl ever." Alice spoke dreamily.

I waved them goodbye and walked towards my locker. I forcibly tried to keep myself calm. All girls were literally glaring at me with jealously.

It's no big deal. He is just standing by my locker. It's not like he is on his knee proposing to me Idiots.

I walked swiftly towards my locker holding my books tight to my chest, hoping I don't trip over something, as I behave very weird when everyone's focusing on me. I literally sometimes even trip over air when this amount of people stare at me. So I tried being Extra careful.

"What are you doing here?" I asked more rudely than intended. My question brought his attention towards me.

Oh Jesus! He looked really awesome with his innocent baby blue eyes. Concentrate Jenny.

The next thing took me by utter surprise. He smirked and grabbed my hand, dragging me to the nearest exit.

"We are skipping today." He said excitedly taking me out of school as if I am his property.

Gosh is this Guy out of his mind?

"Mind to explain why I should skip school and that too with an idiot like you?" I said ripping my arms away from his grip and started walking in the opposite direction. To be honest, his touch was different and welcoming.

Next thing he did was even more surprising. He just pulled me over his shoulder. Gosh, this guy really doesn't know the meaning of rejection. I tried to hit and kick him. The keyword is 'tried', as he hardly even budged.

"Was that supposed to hurt, sweetheart?" He asked raising his eyebrow. "Because I must say that punch was pathetic."

I was tempted to slap him hard across the face, but I suppressed the feeling knowing he would not even feel my slap, so I decided to just stick by words."Put me down you fucking idiot. Everyone is watching." I yelled.

He totally ignored my instructions and continued walking.

"Oh, so our little nerd knows the good words, interesting." Austin said chuckling.

Oh so out of the whole sentence, he has just heard the cursing? Epic.

After walking for some more he stopped in front of something and finally placed me down.

"Has your brain finally crashed by being with all those nasty girls? I am never sitting on this thing." I protested as he put me down next to his motorcycle.

"Come on it's not death ride it's just a motorcycle princess." Austin said with a pout.

Oh my god. He again called me princess. I felt like I am on cloud nine. But again my silly inside voice decided to ruin my happy feeling.

'No Jenny he is just trying to play with your feeling. So you would sit on that motorcycle.' For the first time I agreed with my inner mind.

"Still I am not sitting on that motorcycle" I yelled again suppressing the silly blush.

"Stop calling it Motorcycle all the Time" He said again.

I cocked my eyebrow at him. If he was thinking that by telling me some stupid lie I would agree to sit on that then he was certainly mistaken.

"Then what is this, a magical chair?" I said sarcastically.

Ignoring my sarcastic tone, he said

"She is Cosset titanium series-...."

"Hold on, she?"I asked in disbelief. He smiled down at his motorcycle as if it's the most beautiful thing in world.

"Yes, she is Casey, my love." He said running his fingers tenderly down the motorcycle. Naming a motorcycle was such a childish thing, but I somewhat liked it.

"But I am still not getting on. She is scary and I don't know how many girls have been seated on this thing." I scrunched my nose in disgust.

"Actually you're the first one to ride on my baby, count yourself lucky princess."He said with a smirk.

He should totally stop calling me princess. It increases my heart rate to very unusual speeds. Which I suppose is not good? At last I agreed to sit on his baby because I had no other option. He sighed happily and handed me his helmet.

"If I am wearing this what will you wear?" I asked in curiosity, as there was only one helmet.

"I am going to wear an imaginary helmet out of thin air."He replied sarcastically. "Besides why do you care?" He said with a sly smirk.

I looked away from him feeling uneasy as he was staring directly into my eyes. Doesn't he know staring so intensely will kill me then and there by heart attack? Maybe he doesn't.

He tilted my head slightly to fasten my helmet. He checked if it is properly put. Oh God, this guy seriously cares for something. Defeated I took seat behind him. He climbed in front of me and all I could think was how sexy his back looks.

God this guy is seriously perverting my thinking.

I had no idea what to do with my two silly hands and I was worried if I would just let them flop by my side I would die of falling.

"If you don't want to die so soon princess, I suggest you put your arms around me." He said by reading my thoughts. I wrapped my arms around his waist tightly for my dear life.

"I hate you." I grumbled as his motorcycle roared to life.

"I know you love me, princess." he said with a light chuckle. As if it was damn obvious.

"In your dreams, jerk." I said rolling my eyes.

He laughed and shook his head in disbelief.

"Seriously, jerk is the only word you could think of?" he said in a fake sad tone. "I thought by now you would have written an entire new book on bad words for Austin."

The conversation died eventually as he concentrated on driving. I thought sitting behind Bad Boy who was driving as if there was no tomorrow would be scary but I was actually enjoying the ride. The ride was silent but millions of questions were going through my mind.

Where were we going? Why did he skip class with me of all people? Why is his back so hot? Why does he smell so good? I am seriously thinking a lot about him.

I was so engrossed in my thoughts that I didn't notice that motorcycle had stopped and Austin was standing in front of me laughing like a maniac until he spoke.

"Down to earth Jenny, I know you are mesmerized by my looks but don't stare at me like this in a public place. What will people think?" He said laughing. Laughing is an understatement, his eyes were literally watering by laughing and on this I felt my cheeks getting red again. Damn.

He obviously felt the need to comment on this.

"Wow. You blush so easily. Are you usually like this or am I an exception?" He said poking my cheek with his finger. I blushed harder if that was even possible and slapped his hand away.

"Quit that." I ordered looking at him annoyed. But stopping this laughing Idiot was a damn hard task.

❄ ❄ ❄

Chapter 7 - Skipping school (part 2)

We were in front of a little diner.The beauty of this place was indescribable. It had scenic beauty in abundance. I was totally wonderstruck to see the ravishing beauty in front of my eyes.Since, it was away from town it was very silent and relaxing. Everywhere there was greenery and the place was just beyond beautiful. I just stood there and stared and wished that this moment never ends. I wonder how Austin knows this beautiful place. God this guy is full of surprises.

"I promise; the food here is really good." He said confidently opening the door for me like a gentleman. I couldn't help but blush. A small middle-aged lady smiled and greeted us warmly, "Hey Austin, nice to see you again."

"Hey Clarissa!" He replied smiling back. He must have visited this place a lot of times as he knew everyone here very well.

"Come I will show you the table." She said grabbing two menu cards from the corner.

"You seem to be quite famous here; do you bring all your girlfriends here for a date?" I asked out of curiosity.

"Very eager to know about my girlfriends?" He said while raising his eyebrows. Oh so he sensed my curiosity.

God just kill me now.

"You are like an open book Jenny, anyone can read your mind from your eyes" He said again guessing my thoughts. Gosh Am I that easy to read?

Wait but why is it bothering me and why I am feeling jealous of him being with another girl?

'Because you like him idiot' Again my inner silly voice spoke up. I can't end up liking Mr. Bad boy it's like waiting for a boat on the airport. He will never love me back.

My chain of thinking stopped when he cleared his throat and continued, "The answer to your question is, you are just the second Girl to be here with me as I don't Date Girls anymore" I was astounded, astonished, bewildered, and all the other words that described Shock. That shock was totally plastered on my face as I was just staring at him in awe.

"Stop staring at me like this. I am speaking the truth"

"Then why all the rumors say the other way round?"I blurted.

"Oh so theserumors can beheard in libraries even, strange "Austin said with a smirk

"I do have alife outside Library even" I defended myself, though it was a lie.

"Oh Please don't even try to fool me. And about the rumors I have just spread them to be named as Heartless Guy of the College"

I was more shocked if that is even possible by this Information

"Why?"I asked again.

"Calm down Princess. You don't need to crack me in just one meeting"

"Then how do you know this place?"I spoke again.

I don't know when to shut my mouth. This has landed me in troubles much time but gosh I would never improve.

He just kept silent. I didn't know what to say. I felt guilty for pushing the topic more

I was about to say sorry when he spoke up all of a sudden ".Whenever I feel alone or angry I come here. It's like my thinking place. I feel loved and cared here. Actually this is my mother's diner. Even though she is no more, I have good relations with the staff members here. I feel her presence here."He spoke staring at nothing in particular.

He looked really sad. My heart cracked a little, looking at his sad face. I could tell from his eyes he was a mama's boy. I felt bad for asking him but deep down I felt good. Austin was opening up in front of me. Bad boy even had a soft side. Our orders came and we got something else to talk about.

"I really love the food here." He said with excitement evident in his eyes. His change in mood even made me happy. The food really was delicious. One question was still disturbing me all day.

"Why am I here?" I asked raising my eyebrow. He didn't respond to me for a while. He only opened his mouth to eat. I took this as a chance of staring at him. He looked quite as normal teenagers with emotions. Why does he portray an image of emotionless bad boy in school then? I don't understand.

After eating, "I" He started and then let out a breath "Don't know." He said by shrugging his shoulder.

"Are you fucking telling me that you forced me onto your stupid motorcycle, made me to skip school because you don't know?" I said in angry tone. I saw Austin's face he was absentmindedly staring at me. He was maybe in shock. But seriously how can he expect any other expression in this situation.

"Did the little nerd just swear again? I am really good at bringing this side of you, aren't I?" He said with a big grin on his face. This boy can never ever get serious. I ignored his comment and just decided to leave.

I felt a tight grip on my hand as I turned around "I just wanted to say sorry." He said nervously

"Gosh did you just say sorry?"He looked damn cute and innocent.

"One more confession like this Parker, and I might have to tell Everyone that you are a softy." I said smiling softly.

"Don't you even dare to speak about this to anyone" He warned.

"Now this is exactly the Austin I know" He smiled at me and shook his head.

After paying we left the little diner. I did enjoy his company so I said, "Thank you."

"It's my pleasure princess" He said with a huge grin.

He handed me his helmet and we set out again. As school was already half over I decided to just head home. When I was about to tell him my address I looked around and sensed similar road and in less time we were in front of my house.

"How do you know my address?" I asked surprised.

"I know every small detail about you princess, ever heard about sources."He said with a wink.

❄ ❄ ❄

Chapter 8 - Skipping school (part 3)

"Wait, why are you parking your bike here?" I sputtered. I know it was rude to ask him this after spending so much nice time with him but, me being me, words just came out of my mouth. I seriously need to control my tongue.

"Umm, let me think" He said dramatically tapping his finger on chin. I knew he was just pretending to think to prove my silliness. But then I know I am an idiot so I wasn't that embarrassed.

"As I don't have anything to do, genius" He said with a shrug.

"You are so annoying." I spoke.

"You will be stuck here with me for quite some time, Princess. So mind telling me something new?" He said smirking while walking to the door. I groaned internally and followed him.

As we walked inside the house, he did not mind intruding in my house at all as he placed himself on the couch in the living and started watching TV, without even asking. I just stomped towards my room to change into comfortable PJs.

When I returned to check on Austin, I saw the devil in the most silent mode. He had literally fallen asleep on the couch and the more interesting part was that, he had his arms securely placed around my Teddy. It was like a million-dollar scene. Seeing a bad boy sleeping like a baby with a teddy in his arms is like seeing stars in the morning. It was like treat to my Eyes. Even in his sleep he looked sexy as hell and a small smile on his face made him look a lot innocent. I wonder sometimes how he manages to be sexy all the time. At that very moment, I had an urge to kiss his soft lips. But my inner voice warned me not to. Focus Jenny you can't feel like this especially for a boy like Austin. He will seriously break your heart. My inner soul warned me again. I decided to go with my inner mind

I decided to capture this moment. So I removed my iPhone and silently clicked his pictures in all angles possible. This would be his most beautiful pictures. I thought with an evil smirk.

He must have heard a sound or something so he lazily opened his eyes.

If looks could kill I would have been six feet down by now. He looked like a lost innocent puppy. When he fully came back to his senses, he first felt totally embarrassed, which was expected, but when he realized what was actually happening his eyes turned to the size of soccer ball.

"Oh shit," he groaned. "Alright dear give me your cell," he said, taking a step forward.

"How about no, handsome," I said with a smirk.

"This is going to be posted on your dear friend, Facebook." I said running away from him as far as possible. He came closer so I started to run fast. I groaned as Austin shuffled all his weight on top of me. We were now on the floor with Austin on top of me. I could feel the silly blush coming again but I suppressed it.

"Get off me, you fat man!" I shouted on top of my lungs. The Devil just chuckled.

"Not until you delete the pictures, Princess."

I shook my head stubbornly. Using my entire strength, I curled over the cell, trying to protect it. Even then he was trying hard to get his cell. I was being literally molested by Austin. Some confused small part inside me was still sort of happy to feel him close to me.

You are seriously going crazy Jenny. You should really get your small head checked for damages.

"Please, get off me." This time I said with the most innocent puppy face I could make. As fighting against him was like a butterfly fighting against a fully grown tree.

"How about No" He said totally ignoring my puppy face

"I will give you ice cream please get off me." I offered.

"You know what I want princess." He threatened.

"What if I offer you one big chocolate ice cream bucket?" I said not wanting to delete the pictures.

"How about No Again" He said not even taking time to consider my offer. I frowned. I mean, who says no to chocolate ice cream?

"Well, then you are not getting the phone." I said stubbornly.

"Well I don't have any other choice then, do I?" He said raising his eyebrow.

What did that mean exactly? Before I could even think about what he was speaking his hands started tickling me. If you guys don't know then let me tell you I am extremely ticklish. I let out a high-pitched scream of laughter.

"Stop it please." I said between laughs.

"Are you going to give me my cell?" He said his hands hovering over me.

"Never" I said and he started tickling again. I bit my lip.

I wouldn't give up.

Oh no I'm giving up.

"OKAY." I yelled finally as his hand stopped.

"Was that a yes?" He asked with a wide grin.

I nodded. But my hands still weren't loosening its grip.

"That doesn't seem to be a yes." He said by pointing towards my tight grip.

"I might have been lying then."I admitted.

On that a smile graced his beautiful face. He looked different and more outstanding with his real attractive smile. The smile which even makes you smile, So I did.

"So you even know how to smile, strange?" He said with his original smirk.

"Of course, I'm not inhuman you know." I told him laughing. I was happy by the change of topic. But he being top of me was not helping me to calm.

Next thing he did was totally shocking for me. With a Serious Expression he leaned closer to me. I couldn't help but notice his flawless face. He leaned closer and now our faces were only inches apart. I ran my eyes over more subtle features on his face like small freckles, you could only see when you are really close, the cute dimples on his face.

I would have continued to stare at his beautiful face the whole day and list the small things that made him so attractive, but then I felt the mobile snatched out of my hand which brought me back to senses. Everything got clear. The idiot used his good looks to distract me and I totally fell for his trap.

My face was totally flushed by embarrassment, when I noticed how close we were. Our noses were actually touching.

With a victory smile he got off me and deleted all his pictures.

"Try something better next time princess." he said as he walked out of the house.

And my face was like a small baby when someone snatches his favorite chocolate from him.

❄ ❄ ❄

Chapter 9 - Project preparation (part 1)

School was normal today. Jocks and jerks in their place, as usual. Like a daily schedule, I entered the school with my two opposite friends. We exchanged books at our lockers and went different ways. Everything was the same. The only thing that was different today was that I walked to my math's class with a big smile plastered on my face. Shocked Right?

Want to know why?

Well it has a little something to do with the bad boy I was with yesterday.

Shocking again, isn't it?

YES, Austin Parker was the only reason behind my idiotic smile stuck on Face.

Few days back, if someone was to tell me that I would be happy because Austin or just that I would love the time spend with Austin, I would have laughed till my stomach hurt. But now that this was actually happening, I felt different, strangely a good kind of different. I was absentmindedly walking in my la la world when I felt huge hands pull me in into a dark empty classroom. I was going to kick that someone on the shin as always told by Beth, when suddenly I heard the familiar devilish laugh.

"Are you mad I would have died of heart attack, idiot" I shouted at the top of my lungs. Later I placed my hands on my heart to calm the rapid heartbeats; damn I was actually really scared.

I saw guilt on Austin's face.

"Oh, sorry princess I didn't mean to scare you this much. I just came here to say err... Hi" he said nervously scratching the back of his neck.

God he seemed so innocently cute because of nervousness. It should be officially declared illegal to look so cute all the time. It got my silly heartbeats to increase again. My whole anger instantly melted like ice on fire. He seemed to be actually sorry for scaring me. That was actually damn cute. At that moment itself I felt like kissing him. Silly teenage hormones I know.

"Well, Hi Austin..." I said giving him a real smile. He seemed relieved by my smile.

"Hello Jenny." He said again. My heart missed its heart beat when he said my name. It seemed sweeter than it actually was. I could feel the silly blush coming again.

"I see, I still have same effect on you, sweetheart." He whispered coming dangerously close me.

To avoid more harassment of my poor cheeks I pushed him little bit and ran to my class with the same idiotic smile. I heard him saying something behind my back but I didn't turn over. God I am seriously going crazy. But I actually loved this craziness. I hope it never fades away. The rest of the day till lunch was pretty good. I was really happy for no reason in particular. This is really an awesome feeling. When you are happy for a reason, you are in trouble, because then you have that constant fear of losing that reason which can take your happiness away at any time. But this was not the case with me today.

At lunch as usual I sat with my two friends in the corner as the middle tables are booked for popular kids. We were chatting normally when the trio of Austin, Recce, and River entered. I didn't even need to look at them to acknowledge their presence. The expression on students face speaks it all. Some girls take these to the next level. They immediately start acting like born sluts. Leaving Austin as the only predatory male in the lunchroom. He noticed the slutty behavior but seemed to be not interested at all. The most shocking thing was, of all the girls he looked straight at me with his baby blue eyes and gave me a real smile which literally brought my heart up to my mouth but I gulped it down. I felt all the tension dissipate within me. My silly blush again came on my cheeks. Such intense effect of his normal beautiful smile on me scared me. The glares turned to me which made me slightly uncomfortable so I decided to concentrate on our canteens floor.

You are the biggest idiot alive, Jenny. Of all the girls, he smiled at you, and you just ignored him. Oh gosh just bury me somewhere. Award for the silliest girl in the entire Universe will surely go to me.

"What the hell, did he just smile at you?" Beth asked shaking me to bring me back to reality.

"I knew there was some scene going on between you two!" Alice said in full excitement "Yesterday I saw you on his shoulder. You both looked adorable." Alice said with a wink.

"What!" Beth said obviously shocked. "Do I need to know something Jenny?" Beth said angrily.

I narrated the whole last day happening to my friends. About The diner, the home scene everything, leaving some parts out of course. When I finished, their faces were totally paled .Both my friends were in total state of dismay. Their reaction was like they were watching some ghost. I would have laughed till my stomach ached, if it was not such a serious situation.

To suppress my laugh, I decided to walk to class but Beth held my hand and turned me around.

"I am warning you Jenny, you should really stay away from that Austin guy. He is bad news"

On that, Alice protested "Every bad boy changes for good girl. Beth don't you read love stories. Maybe Austin likes her."

And in this way the great fight between my two friends started again on Austin's and my relation. They are sometimes too much too handle and literally overdramatic.

"Stop it guys," I said a little louder than intended, attracting most of the table's attention. Austin gave me a sympathetic look as if he was exactly aware of topic.

I lowered my tone. "Guys we are just friends or maybe not even exactly friends. He just wanted to say sorry for yesterday so I was with him. That's it. Please don't over think it." saying this I left for my class.

Next was literature lecture. As instructed, Austin sat beside me. Usually he used to ignore me but today was different. He greeted me with a genuine smile which in turn caused me to smile.

"Hey princess hope you enjoyed the little talk about me with your friends." He said with a smirk.

"How you know?" I asked curiously.

"I have sources sweetheart." His sources stuff was irritating me. So I concentrated on literature.

"Someone is in bad mood huh?"

"Didn't you get that from your sources?" I said sarcastically

"About the project" he said again. "Why don't you just do it and slap my name on it." He said leaning back at his chair smirking.

"How about, the other way round" I replied with same tone.

"Oh spunky, I like you already." He said just casually. With even this, my heartbeat increased.

God, when will my heart be able to differentiate between a fake and real feeling?

He again continued "So then princess, you are lucky enough to gain a study date with Austin." he said proudly. I laughed at his childishness.

"Meet me at the parking lot in the evening." He said with a wink and left the classroom.

What he meant by, was a date. Oh god was he actually asking me out on a date. My inner mind was literally dancing with happiness. I was really excited for spending more time with him. Ewww. From when did I started becoming so girly.

Chapter 10 - Project preparation (part 2)

I headed outside with my friends after the end of school. Austin was lazily standing in the parking lot luckily with a car this time. It is then I realized that I had to go with Austin which meant I had to tell my friends about this.

"Um Guys. I wanted to tell you something "I spoke with voice as small as possible. I just wished Beth didn't hear anything of this. But that was next to impossible as she was right beside me. They were just waiting for me to speak. Taking a deep breath I spoke "I am going with Austin today"

With this said I was instantly interrupted by Beth "What are you Insane?"

I tried to tell them the entire thing but was again cut by Alice "Woohoo second date huh Jenny. Have Fun"

I don't know when they will stop interrupting me in the middle. They didn't seem to stop anytime soon so I just blurted out "I am just going for project purpose" Luckily they did hear me.

"Just project work?"Alice said with a sad tone.

Gosh this girl seriously needs to stop making up stories in the mind. Before they could speak anything I waved my friends goodbye and headed to his car ignoring the death glares of Beth.

"Where are we going?" I asked.

"To my house, we need to crack this silly project. Remember?" He said kind of interested, which was kind of shocking. Don't get me wrong but I had never thought a guy like Austin would actually care about homework, or a project. That's just unbelievable.

The drive to his home was damn silent. As we both were silent but the whole volcanoes were boiling inside my body. The boy was driving as if there was no tomorrow. I tightly shut my eyes for my dear life. I don't understand why this Guy has to be always in so much hurry?

He must have noticed my fear as he slowed down a little. It felt good and I relaxed a bit.

"Sorry. I didn't mean to scare you by my drive." He said with a chuckle. After sometime he pulled in front of a beautiful house. House would not be proper word to describe sight in front of me. It was a fucking huge mansion.

The yard was beautiful with cleanly cut grass with blooming colorful flowers and amazing marble fountain in the middle. I turned at Austin and he was smiling at me. Yeah a genuine smile and not his signature smirk, the smile girls die for.

"So I see you like my house." He said molding his smile into smirk again.

"I wouldn't call it a house, it's a freaking mansion." He chuckled softly at my words.

"Come on, let's get you inside." Grabbing my hands he pulled me inside. His touch caused electricity to flow through my entire body. But he seemed to be not affected at all. Touching me is just normal for him but for me a whole bunch of butterflies start dancing in my stomach.

His house was beautiful in and out. We were walking on spiral staircase, when we heard a sobbing of small boy.

"Whoa, is my little champ crying?" Austin asked rubbing tears from the boy's eyes softly "What happened?"

"I broke my favorite action man." The boy said between his sobs.

I opened the door to see what was happening and I witnessed the school's douche mending his brother's action man. He seemed pretty cute with his brother. By the efforts he was putting to mend the toy, anyone could tell Austin loved his brother a lot which proved deep down inside a bad boy, there are feelings. I wonder why he likes to keep this bad boy image.

"Here's your action man totally ready for action again." Austin said kissing his brother. He was now literally grinning from ear to ear. You could say straight away he was related to Austin. He had same facial structure like him and was adorable.

"Are you Austin's new girlfriend?" He asked turning his gaze to me.

And also their behavior was same I must say.

"No, No. I am just his project partner." I said awkwardly.

"Does that mean we can go on date someday?" He said with naughty smile. My eyes shot open.

"She's too old for you, Tyler." Austin said laughing. We both headed to his room.

"Don't ever think of telling anything about this in school." He said

"Oh about you being a softy, huh?" I smirked.

"I'm not." he said embarrassed. I just laughed at his reaction.

We reached his room. I was shocked to see clean room in front of me. My theory of bad boy's room was proved totally wrong by Austin. I thought boys have messy rooms with clothes and books scattered here and there. But his room was even cleaner than mine.

There was a king sized bed in middle a flat screen TV with Xbox connected, a study table and couch. Walls were painted light blue and were decorated with many photos of Austin, his brother, family, and friends. I smiled looking at the pictures. Austin looked cuter in his childhood.

Austin turned to face me. "So sweetheart since we are in my room is there anything else you want to do other than that silly project?" he whispered coming dangerously closer to me. I could feel my cheeks already warming up.

Damn this boy exactly knows what to say to bring this reaction out of me.

Play it cool Jenny. He is just trying to distract you.

"Not so easy, Austin" I whispered in the same manner slightly pushing him away. I could see a small smile on his lips by my boldness.

"Let's just start the project."

"You are such a mood killer, I'm bored." he said by lazily sitting on bed. "How can you even think of a project with such a hot boy beside you?" I just rolled my eyes.

"Let's play twenty questions." he said suddenly rising from bed and coming closer to me. I was about to say 'no' but the innocent puppy face he made was irresistible.

"Okay."

"Let's start by easy questions as I don't want you to run away because of my talented questions." He asked "What are your hobbies?"

"Well I love singing, reading literature, gardening. And yours?"I asked curiously.

"Wow you are a total nerd." He said laughing on which I rolled my eyes.

"Well I love riding bikes, traveling, racing, playing guitar, reading to some extent and almost every sport."

"I am impressed. I hadn't exactly expected reading and playing guitar from a guy like you" I sincerely replied.

"I don't need to tell you my hobbies to impress you. As I know you are already impressed by my charms" he said with a playful glint in his voice. "But I'm surely not what you have heard about me." He added.

The twenty questions went swiftly. We discussed about every silly thing other than the project like favorite movies, favorite songs, dreams, ambitions etc. I never had thought in my nightmares even that I would be so comfortable with Austin but I was. Actually I was enjoying his company than anyone else. I don't remember laughing so much any time before. As much as this feeling was foreign to me, I wanted this time that we were spending together, to pause forever. I would love to forever stay like this with Austin. I feel carefree and myself with him.

Out of nowhere "Fancy a walk outside, you and me in the moonlight?" He said cheerfully.

I chuckled in response and agreed. Before I know he grabbed my hand leading me outside. It must be normal for him but damn it brings a whole zoo in my stomach so he should really stop holding my hands. His touch really gives happy sparks in my body.

I looked up towards the night sky. It was dark with moon and clouds. Just as I notice how Grey clouds are a fat drop fell on my forehead.

And soon it started raining. Rain makes me really happy. I yanked my rubber band off my hair and let my hair loose and then yanked off my jackets and boots.

"Hey what are you doing?" Austin asked with shock and surprised look.

"Stripping for you!" I joked. For a minute he actually believed me with his eyes glued on me and a grin on his face. Jerk. Just when he saw me doing nothing further he walked over to me removing his jacket.

"Jenny, its cold let's get out of here or else you're going to be sick tomorrow." He said with concern filling his eyes. It felt good to know that the bad boy actually cared about me. But I ignored him as it doesn't rain so nicely every day. I just started spinning around screaming at the top of my voice.

I know Austin would have totally declared me total idiot by now but who cares. OK I care but not when it's raining.

"Have you gone crazy Jenny?" He chuckled.

"No it just feels great in rain. Letting go of all the worries and just enjoying" He was listening so carefully as if I was giving him some sort of important lecture and at the end I could see a small smile coming on his lips which felt really great.

"Even though you are acting crazy, you look breath taking." He said surprisingly soft. I looked up at him and realized his eyes fixed on me, with a strange expression on his face. It looked like he was thinking about something very deeply. He stepped closer closing the distance between us

"You are making me insane, Jenny." He whispered coming closer "I feel good with you. You are my drug" He said coming dangerously closer to me.

The next thing totally shocked me. He kissed me lightly on forehead. Everything vanished. The whole world around me seemed different and most importantly beautiful. The place he kissed felt to most important part of the body. A sharp electric effect flowed through entire body. If I could stop time I would stop it here forever. Everything was perfect. A perfect kiss in the rain.

❄ ❄ ❄

Chapter 11 - Dinner out - part 1

Voices coming from downwards forced me to wake up. I tried opening my eyes but I was so tired that my mind wasn't ready to wake up. I blinked multiple times as a yawn escaped my mouth. I lazily walked to the mirror in the room. My eyes widened all of sudden with all the sleep in it long gone.

My hair was flying in every direction possible like doing a hip hop dance in the middle of a ballroom. I growled plastering my hands over my face and immediately turning around, as I could not handle the mess in front of me.

Yesterday's events struck in my head and involuntarily a broad smile stretched across my face. I had been smiling a lot lately I thought. All thanks to the egotistic Austin. Nowadays I always wake with my mind completely corrupted by Austin.

Suddenly his words before kissing my forehead crossed my mind. My eyebrows kitted in thought.

Was it the truth? Did he really mean that? If he liked me wouldn't he have kissed me on the lips? Would he ever consider a relationship with me? Kiss and Austin was all I could think of. Damn just a thought of it brighten my day. Is it crime to feel so this way? Because I felt extremely nice and happy just by thinking about him

Gosh I am turning crazy. I need to sort my feelings out. I growled once again. This Guy was just corrupting my head. He was like the virus, dangerous to my system but I still didn't want to get rid of it. I was finally awake because of him- not fully but still. He was probably the cause of it. I marched downstairs; there stood my parents in the kitchen.

I ran up hugging them tight."I missed you so much," I said happily emphasizes 'so'.

"We missed you too baby doll!" My dad said. His nickname always sends shivers of happiness down my spine, bringing an even bigger smile on my face.

Soon the aroma of delicious chocolate cookie filled the room. Let me tell you, my mom prepares the best cookies in the entire world and by saying this, I am not even over exaggerating. They are just that awesome. They are mouthwateringly yummy. Having an obsession of chocolate, I have been addicted to them since my childhood. I filled my mouth and hands with cookies as soon as mom entered and they both busted out laughing.

What's there in laughing in this? Can't I even express my love for chocolate cookies now?

My mom shook her head with slight laughter. "I actually want to talk with you about something." she said later

This got me shit scared. These words have power to scare any teenager, Right?

I wondered what she wanted to talk about. It's not like I have done something illegal. My test results were also super. It felt funny now as I was double checking everything. I was just trying hard to think of everything that could land me in trouble. But my poor mind wasn't able to think of anything.

"What do want to talk about?" I asked in wonder.

"Well we were just wondering do you have any plans tonight." Dad asked.

I left a sigh "I am totally free for this weekend." I replied still puzzled.

"Do you think you would be up for going out for dinner tonight at Mr. Parker's house?" My mom asked nervously considering my shyness.

I shrugged. Not caring where we had dinner. The only two things that were required were food and my parents. As they both were present, I instantly agreed for it.

"Sure but why exactly are we going to Mr. Parker's house for dinner?"

"Since our business dealing was perfect, our boss Mr. Parker wants to have family dinner with us." My dad said sounding proud of him.

I smiled and nodded. I'd liked that". My parents sighed happily as if their life depended on my agreement.

"That's great honey. We will be leaving in the evening. Don't go anywhere and dress nicely," mom said excitedly.

I nodded and walked towards my room. I had nothing to do; I sat in my room and opened the laptop. I had a Facebook account but I rarely used it. Most surprising thing is that I have eighty friends out of which half of them I don't even know but they claim to be in my class or to stay in my neighborhood. This proves that you would never be alone on Facebook

I logged onto Facebook and was stunned to see two notifications and four requests .This randomly happens with me. Three requests were from random guys whose names I couldn't even pronounce. So I rejected them instantly. I was extremely shocked by next request .It was from Austin. He had requested me to be friend. He rarely sends request to anyone according to what I have heard so this was shocking. He had even liked and commented 'beautiful' on my profile picture. I was beyond surprised by this but I still wondered where his ego subsided when he was liking my pictures and commenting on it?

I did a happy dance in my head. Butterflies filled my stomach assuming I was the 'only' girl he had commented for.

I immediately accepted the request. It would be crazy to deny the request right?

I clicked on his name to checkout his time line. Or you can say I was stalking his account.

So what if I'm stalking Austin. Nobody would know about it. Then who cares right?

His time line was freaking full with lots of pictures of his and his friends, some of his pictures were with girls maybe his past girlfriends. Just by watching them I felt a pint of jealousy.

This guy is really photogenic. On his every pictures he had 250, 350, 465 likes and some had even crossed 500. Even his comment box was flooded with comments.

Damn this guy is seriously popular. The little hopes which I had in my mind of getting in relation with him also vanished the moment I observed his account.

I clicked on his profile picture and chuckled. It was him shirtless taking a mirror picture with his remarkable smirk.

He looked stunning in all his pictures.

My heart skipped a beat when my laptop made a beeping sound. I had a new message. This rarely happens.

Austin: *Already stalking my account huh, princess.*

Oh My Gosh!! He messaged .The sun must have risen from the wrong side today. I tried to calm my nerves and typed

Jenny: *In your dreams Parker. I have many more important things to do than this.*

Austin: *Wow grumpy much. Huh?*

Jenny: *I'm not grumpy. Just wanted to know why are you bothering me?*

I asked a little rudely

Austin: *Can't I just message you without any reason?*

He said falsely sending sad faces. This brought a silly smile to my face. I ignored his over-dramatic comment when my screen made a beeping sound again.

Austin: *Besides, I thought for a change, it would be nice talking to the*

girl who 'drools' all over me.

Jenny: I*n your wildest dreams, got tired of chasing the girls that are behind you, huh?*

Austin: *For your information, princess, I never chase girls. Note that in your nerdy head.*

Jenny: *What's with the nicknames, asshole?*

Austin: *I know you love it, princess.*

My heart went totally numb at his comment. Gosh he can increase my heart beat even when he is miles away from me. I am in deep trouble, to hide my excitement I typed.

Jenny: *You are a pathetic flirt.*

Austin: *Oh baby now you are insulting me. My flirting skills are flawless. Until now no girl has turned me down.*

Along with it he forwarded a broken heart. God this guy is seriously so dramatic. This is kind of cute.

Jenny: *I'II be your first. There has to be a first for everything.*

Austin: *Playing hard to get, princess.*

Jenny: *Don't call me that!*

Austin: *Why so hostile? :(*

I realized then we have always ended our conversations with fights. For which I am the reason though. He had always tried to have a decent conversation with me. But I have always removed my wrath on him, maybe because of his 'bad boy' aura. I was about to reply back with a simple 'sorry' when my eyes pooped out their sockets.

Austin: *Lets be friends. Want to start over?*

Was this happening for real? I literally pinched myself to see that I wasn't dreaming...

Jenny: *Sounds good. But wouldn't it affect your reputation or something.*

I asked out of curiosity. Being friends with him was really something I would have never dreamed off.

Austin: *As if I care about that shit.*

He said it carelessly. On which I did happy dance in my mind. I wasn't expecting this reply.

'We just can't hang out in college ' or 'No one in college should know that we are friends.' Were the replies which I was expecting.

Austin: *I hope that smile is still on your face, princess. Catch you later.*

Austin's last message brought an awesome smile on my face. And I dreamt about him and fell asleep with a smile again.

Chapter 12 - Dinner out- part 2

"Jenny! You have not dressed yet." My mother screamed while shaking me to wake up. I finally opened my eyes, looking at her in my drowsy sleep confused then the events that occurred before came crashing down. Shit diner at Mr. Parker's house! I frantically jumped out of bed getting in the bathroom.

It was all Austin's fault again; he has now started to corrupt my dreams even. We are friends though. Just friends, I sighed choosing an outfit in my towel.

I picked out a black laced maxi dress, it was just above my knee. the top side was all laced including the sleeves and a line across the stomach was laced giving a glimpse of skin but nothing serious. It was perfect for a dinner out. I topped it with some red heels matching the rep lipstick that I applied on my lips. I was not a much of a dresser but it was my parent's boss house, I needed to put some effort in it. The drive was quite boring, as my parents were busy telling me how to behave. I know that this dinner was very important for them but who lectures 19 yrs old girl how to behave. I just ignored them, peeking outside the window.

I realized I was in the same lane were Austin's house was located. I had a weird feeling that there is some connection between this dinner and Austin. My heart started beating faster as my guess was proved right by the house in front of me. How foolish was I to not guess that Austin Parker is the son of worlds famous businessman 'The Parkers' since they are the only Parkers in the city.

As we reached the door my mom rang the door bell. I just stood the fidgeting. I hoped from the bottom of my heart that Austin is not at home. My hopes were shattered then and there as the door flew open. He stood right in front of me with his angelic smile on his face. His smile turned into remarkable smirk when he saw me. I would have died of nervousness. I avoided his stare. Mrs. Parker welcomed us with a bright smile. She seems too young and energetic. Mrs. Parker is Austin's step mom. I have heard it from my friends. But by the look she was giving him was very motherly.

"So this must me your daughter right." Mrs. Parker said "Well you are very beautiful, Jennifer " She said, engulfing me in a tight hug.

I said smiling slyly "Hmm thanks".

"Meet my son, Austin." Mr. Parker said addressing towards his son.

Austin gave his heart melting smile to my parents.

God, why does he have to be so cute? I was shamelessly staring at his perfect smile.

"And this is" My dad was interrupted in between by Austin "Jennifer" He said looking at me "we have actually met before".

"You have?" My mom asked astonished.

I nodded slowly "We go to the same school actually. Being in the same school and not knowing the school's bad boy is impossible." I said in my defense. Austin was stunned by my reply. His parents chuckled a little.

"So do you both talk at school?" My mom asked again. She can never leave any topic in middle. "We don't talk at all" I replied to stop the further questioning. But Austin being Austin can never keep his mouth shut.

"Don't lie Jenny. Strangers don't visit any ones house at night." He said with devilish smile on his face. Whipping my head in his direction, I expected him to explain the complete situation. He just didn't speak. I know he was purposely saying this but our parents surely didn't know so they were looking towards me with confused looks.

"Have you visited our house before?" Mrs. Parker asked. All were staring at me in a way; a police looks at thieves when he is expected to answer. I was speechless for some time. Austin was enjoying this situation. I made a mental note in my mind to take revenge of this.

I cleared my throat "We are project partners; I had come here for a project." I sighed. I was fed up of questions. But the luck was not by my side.

"Mrs. Winget" the devil spoke again. You must also know that Jenny and I sit together in literature class and are now best buddies" My mom's eyes literally bulged out at the last sentence. I was never a social person. My mom has always been forcing me to make new friends but had always failed. So she seemed more than happy to hear someone as my friend other than Beth and Alice.

"Isn't that right Jenny?" He asked with a smirk looking at my now irritated face. I was about to disagree everything. But my mom interrupted.

"That's great. I am happy to hear that my daughter is making new friends" She said in over excited tone. It seemed less of a 'business' discussion dinner and more of a 'Jenny's life' discussion dinner. I groaned inside.

"Mom he's lying. We barely talk about anything other than project."

"You are hurting my feelings, princess" Austin said making a sad face and placing his hands on his heart for a more dramatic effect.

"Oh honey. You don't have to lie" Mom said, smile gracing on her face.

Before I could embarrass more one servant came declaring 'the diner's ready'. I have never being so happy by hearing any words. I mentally thanked the servant .I could see a small frown on Austin's face. Servant directed us towards diner. Surely I have seen the house before but the food in front of me left my mouth open. All types of dishes one can think of were present on table with sweets and desserts. The aroma itself made my stomach growl a little but it was low, Austin being near to me must have heard it. I saw him laughing.

As I was busy eyeing the dishes all seats were filled. Only one beside Austin was empty. My parents really have evil minds. I sat beside him unwillingly.

When my plate was overflowing I picked up my fork and started to eat. I took one bite of chicken, I suppressed the urge of moaning as it sparked my taste buds .I was busy stuffing my face till I felt a kick on my right leg. I turned to glare at Austin to find him innocently acting as if he was eating food. I kicked him back and watched his face twisted in pain and surprise. I smirked satisfactorily.

But nothing can be peaceful in my life with this boy beside me. I again felt a hand on my naked knee. I let out a small gasp which turned everyone attention to me.

"Is something wrong dear?" Mrs. Parker asked concerned.

"Yeah tell us if anything is wrong, Jenny?" He said with a wink.

"No, Nothing" I said stammering.

Putting my fork down I slid out of my chair.

"Dinner was very delicious, Mrs. Parker." I praised her.

"Thanks dear. You and Austin can take a walk in the backyard while we talk." She said looking towards Austin.

Rolling his eyes Austin slid out of his chair.

"Well come on princess, we don't have entire day for you to just stand her." He said sarcastically.

As he opened the door, the view was awesome. The grass looked healthy. There was even a fire place and tea table in the backyard. The most beautiful part was the swimming pool the water was very clear.

Austin stood at the edge of swimming pool. I decided to take advantage of this. As soon as he turned to face me I pushed him inside. I could hear him speak some unusual words as water as well as climate was cold.

"Payback's a bitch." I teased him and ran towards our parents.

"You are so dead." He screamed getting out of pool but it was too late I was already in the safety of house.

"What happened to you?" My mom asked looking at Austin. I could tell everyone was trying to suppress their laughs. This pissed him off more

"Why don't you ask your daughter?" He asked pissed.

"I thought the trip in pool would help you keep calm." I said innocently.

"It's completely fine sweetie. Don't worry. Austin won't be angry on you."

Austin's mom said which brought smile on my face and a frown to his.

"Well Mr. Parker I think we should head home now. Thanks for the dinner." My dad spoke.

"No problem you are welcomed back anytime" Mr. Parker said with a smile.

The dinner with the jerk was finally over with the scores were equal.

* * *

Chapter 13 - Night Together

My eyes had turned red, make up was running a little, and hair was total mess when I returned home .My brain was ready to explode. One eye was falling asleep, yawning all the time. I was looking like a walking corpse.

I just madly wanted to hang out with my bed after such a long and tiring day I changed my clothes to comfortable PJ's as soon as I entered my room.

Before sleeping, like always, I checked the calendar for any submissions deadline. It was then I felt as if my brain short-circuited and needed to be rebooted. Damn the project on which me and Austin were working was due tomorrow which clearly meant today is only day of our project completion and we have not yet completed even half of it.

Why of all the boys I had to be partnered with Austin? Why God why it has to be always me?

I am so going to murder Austin tomorrow for being so careless.

It took all my might to ignore the calling of my bed and get the cell phone from study desk.

"Crap" I muttered to myself as I checked time on cell. It was past ten already. I sighed. As that Idiot was not concerned about the project at all I had to do it now all by myself.

God loves to torture me personally with different tricks and situations. After such a long day thinking of the project completion saddened me. I don't know what I was going to prepare for this bloody project but I had to do something. Sadly I did care about the grades at such an evil time of day.

I gathered all the little energy inside me and with heavy eyes sat on my desk and opened my laptop. I was very much engrossed in my project when I suddenly heard a tap on my window.

My hand unconsciously tightened around the pen in my hand.

The constant sound of a window tapping coming from behind me forced me to turn around, and my heart froze and my stomach turned icy as I saw a body outside the window. Fear clouded my mind and adrenaline pumped through my veins.

Oh my god is this a thief? What if he has a gun? What if he kills me? I don't want to get killed so early. My body started shaking.

Even though I was scared to death, I went closer to take a look at the window. I could hear my pulse beating in my ears. My teeth were chattering with fear. Just when the fear was about to overcome me I heard a tap again and someone calling my name.

Thief won't tap on window before robbing and he won't even know my nameright?

So there's no reason to panic I tried explaining my mind.

As I opened the window with shaky hands, I froze in my tracks by seeing a person in front of me. At 11'o clock at night Austin Parker had came to my room that to by the window.

God why does this guy have to be so difficult to understand? Only Austin can do this.

"Have I rendered you speechless again by my good looks and manly ways?" He said laughing. I frowned suddenly.

"No, I have been rendered speechless by your stupidity." I retorted with anger and fear quite Visible in my voice.

"Aren't you the stupid one to forget the project's due date?"Austin pointed out.

So he remembered about the project. Never in my dreams even I would have believed that jerk cared about studies and remembered about due dates more than me but actually he cared maybe way more than me, which was like another shocking thing for today.

"If this is your way of welcoming guests, I must say it's pretty cool." He said dramatically.

It then struck to me he is still outside standing on a pipe in cold so I invited him inside.

I know things strike me pretty fast.

"You remembered about the project?" I asked totally surprised.

"Just because I don't hide myself in a library forever like you people doesn't mean I don't care at all. For your kind information I get straight A's in all subjects." He said in a serious tone

This new piece of information made my mouth literally hit the floor. I couldn't think of any proper words in my defense as he was right I really spend my more than half the day in the library and freak out all the time for grades and he gets it so easily. Now I was really jealous about him.

"You are so clever." I stated in low tone.

"You sound so surprised" He said raising his eyebrow.

"I didn't really think you put much effort in the all this school stuff..." I said honestly.

"I don't." He shrugged "It's also a part of my charm you know it's like one of my inbuilt talent..." He said playfully.

"Good. So now we can complete this project early and I can have little bit of sleep at least" I spoke happily.

I was more than happy to see Austin here. At least now I didn't have to do the stupid project on my own

"You can sit over here so you can see the screen" I said ignoring his cockiness and pointing towards the stool.

"My masculinity feels insulted by this." he said eying towards the stool weirdly."Besides it looks weird"

"How can a stool be weird Austin?" I asked confused.

"I don't know, but I definitely don't want to use a stool"

"Well, then you can use bed or the best option, floor" I said

"I will take bed." He said as he practically dove into unmade sheets, and literally started playing with my bed.

"Your bed is so soft, same as mine. I love doing this all the time." He said practically jumping up and down.

A small chuckle escaped my mouth.

This boy is seriously childish. This is kind of cute. Focus Jenny he's here to complete the project.

"Stop lusting over my bed, we need to complete the project" I somewhat yelled which stopped him from doing childish activities.

Wow I didn't know I can be so dominating. I literally patted my back in my mind though for such rebellious work.

For the next few hours we seriously worked on our project which was really strange I never knew Austin could be so serious for such a long time. I was very impressed by Austin's creative ideas and infinite knowledge.

I have learned a lot about him by this project, which is why fortunately or unfortunately I am attracted to him.

After a few hours Austin was wrapped in my comforter which was of baby pink color. That sight made me laugh. It was awesome. If I could I would have framed his photo with comforter He looked damn innocent. I suppressed my laugh as I didn't want to break his serious mood.

After few more hours of hard work on project, the project was finally over. I bet, this project was the best project among all. This felt good since we had sacrificed our dear sleep for it. By now we both were half asleep. As I saved the project file Austin did a happy dance in front of me.

Oh my gosh my heart did a double flip. This guy never fails to amuse me. He always has something different in store.

I smiled whole heartedly at his soupiness.

* * *

Chapter 14 -Accepting The Feelings

I was amused to see Austin dancing like a crazy because of project completion. I never expected him to be so happy on such things. I was enjoying the scene, till then a soft pillow landed on my head.

Ouch from when did pillow started flying. I was confused .My confusion was cleared by looking at the guy in front of me with a mischievous glint in his eyes holding a pillow and about to hit me again. Oh my God. I grabbed a pillow near me and attacked him before he could attack .His eyes widened a little by my sudden attack.

Ha Ha No one can beat me in pillow fight. I have been playing this for ages. The next thing I remember we ended up playing a pillow fight for about an hour. We were both standing on my bed hitting each other like idiots.

God that was so fun. It felt so nice being with Austin so secure so carefree.

In very less time I have come very close to Austin. We have started being like we were always together. Thanks to the silly project we are doing.

In the middle of hate and fights I have started enjoying his foolishness and childishness. I know he is a total jerk and can't help it. But by spending quality time with him I have known it's all just a layer of who he is. There is another layer hidden beneath it, the layer, those who know him properly know it.

I am happy I got to know the real Austin hidden behind his 'carefree and bad ass' image.

Deep down he is sweet, loving, caring, sensitive guy who loves and cares for people wholeheartedly. He can be tortuously annoying when he aims to be, but he can be even amazing person without even trying. A goofy smile appeared on my face without realizing.

God I like him so much and being with him all the time isn't helping to control it. The feelings are getting stronger day by day.

OK So I am finally accepting I have feelings for Austin Parker, the guy totally out of my league. But it feels nice to at least not lie to myself all the time. I know we are total opposites and Austin will never think about me more than a friend. But this doesn't stop my feelings. It hurts when you love someone, but you know you can't tell the person because you can never be together. I wish someday he understands my feelings for him and loves me back. I know it's more than impossible. But being hopeful isn't bad. By this new discovery fresh in my mind I wish I wouldn't act more stupid in front of him.

In between fighting and thinking we fell asleep. After few, I mean really very few hours of sleeping, the irritating sound of the alarm brought me out my deep sleep. Groaning inwardly, I placed a pillow on my ears to block the noise of alarm. This is what I do always to ignore the alarm. I don't ever understand why I use an alarm even. They have never woken me.

Only Beth has the guts and power to wake me up, alarms are just useless.

"Shut the damn thing up" a very irritated male voice spoke up.

I sat on my bed faster than a Ninja, all the sleep in my eyes long gone. Gosh this is not a usual thing at all. A tall figure was comfortably sleeping on the sleeper sofa. I was about to scream on top of my lungs, when the guy on the sofa slowly turned over, that's when I saw the face of guy.

Oh my God what is Austin doing in my room? Oh freaking lord, what have I done?

I stressed my brain a little and all events from last night crossed my mind. A small smile crept on my face but that didn't last long. As the reality struck me the smile was instantly replaced by panic. My parents were in the house and Beth must be on her way. I had to wake up Austin before anyone sees him here.

With all the will power inside me I left the bed. Damn I still wanted to sleep.

"Wake up" I said shaking Austin to bring him out of sleep but the guy didn't even move.

"Wake up you sleepy head" I tried again but there was no success.

Waking up a sleepy person is really hard now I can understand Beth's struggles to wake me up. Poor girl.

What am I going to do now? Time was ticking faster and I had no other option. So without even giving a second shot I did what came to my mind. I just pushed Austin off the sofa on the floor

This was the worst decision ever I must say. The moment Austin landed on the floor he screamed on the top of his lungs, literally like a small guy.

Gosh what's wrong this Guy?

"Shh.. Stop shouting" I said placing hand on his mouth to stop him. He blinked multiple times to adjust his eyes to surrounding. Once he was fully awake his eyes turned open wide to the size of soccer ball. He was struggling through his shut mouth to speak so I had to remove the hand

"What the hell are you doing in my room?" He said with a shock expression.

"This is my house, Idiot"

"Oh shit what am I doing in your house?"

Though I was enjoying his uneasiness I had very less time to shoo him out of house so I cleared all the misunderstandings.

When he was satisfied with the answer he rose up from the floor.

"Why the hell you screamed earlier?"

"Falling down from the bed is not a daily thing for me, you know" Austin replied sarcastically

"Oh my god, you were scared, weren't you?""

"Oh please I am never scared, just a little shocked"

"Jenny, baby doll get up you don't want to be late to school, right?" My dad's knocking brought back my all senses.

Gosh my dad was waiting outside and I didn't know what to do. What do I do? I wasn't thinking of any reply.

"Will be out in a minute" I replied.

Dad was about to go but my destiny had other plans for me.

"Oh my baby doll." Austin said with a smirk on his face.

"Jenny is there anyone else in the room?"

Oh shit. I am going to kill this guy

"Yeah I even heard a scream before" My mom said joining my dad.

"Oh its your mom out there. Let me say hi to her. She is very fond of me "Austin whispered with a smirk.

"Just shut up and hide somewhere. I am opening the door" I whisper yelled.

Pushing Austin behind the door, I lazily opened the door.

With a fake yawn I said "What you talking about, dad ?"

"I just felt like I heard someone speaking"

"That must be some misunderstanding"

"Then what about the scream?" Mom acquired.

"Oh that girlish scream?" I said putting more effort on girlish part "That's my alarm tone, It helps me wake up".

"I must say kids these days have weird solution for everything"

"Whatever, come down soon. Breakfast's ready"

I can't believe my parents really bought this lie.

Hush thank God.

The moment I closed the door, Austin was standing in front of me.

"That wasn't a girlish scream" He retorted.

"Boys don't scream at all" I said in a same tone.

"Because they don't have cruel friends like you" Austin said rolling his eyes.

God how can he be so cool and relaxed in such situation. He must be having lot of experiences of sneaking into girl's rooms.

With huge soothing breath I said "Austin, you need to go home. I don't want my parents to think anything wrong. But with my parents down how can you go, God we should have woken up early..." I was going on blabbering when I heard him laughing.

Seriously laughing? I mean who laughs in such situation.

"Ha ha really sorry I didn't mean to laugh but you look so cute when you are panic. I couldn't control myself. You are so awesome Jenny." He said between his laughs trying very hardly to control laughing.

I felt a weird sensations in my stomach. I couldn't take my eyes off his flawless face.

"Don't worry princess. I know great sneaking out skills." He said walking towards the window. Next thing I saw he was safely near his car waving me goodbye.

Gosh this guy has some weird attractions with window I must say.

❄ ❄ ❄

Chapter 15 - Meeting The Bad Boys

"What no fucking way!" My both friends shouted at one instant.

I can't blame them though the new information I was giving them was really shocking. I had just finished telling them about Austin being my dad's boss's son and that I had dinner with his family. Their faces were as expected completely horrified. So I decided to omit the Austin's last night visit or else they will freak out more. I know keeping friends in darkness is not good but at this time this is good for them.

"Shh keep it down guys. I don't want entire college to know this" I said pulling them away from the crowd as they were attracting unwanted attention.

"How could you have not known that Austin's dad is your dad's boss? What have you been doing all your life?"" Beth asked annoyed.

I know they are shocked but hey it's not my mistake.

"Hey in my defense, this topic never came up till now." I pouted "What was I supposed to do? Go to my dad and be like "Hey what's your boss's last name and does he have any son that goes to my school? Who I sort of have a crush on?"" I blurt out everything.

I shut my mouth tightly with my hands as soon as I realized what I blurt out.

I just wish they didn't hear the last part but the staggered look they were giving me as if I have grown an extra pair of head doesn't require any genius to guess that they heard it.

God I am in so much trouble now. Can't my inner voice think a little before saying? I closed my eyes tightly shut and waited for them to come out of the shock.

Once they regained their senses, "What?" This was the second time they screamed together. If they continue this I will surely be deaf by the end of the day. The bell rang and saved me from the further torture. I was relieved a little. As Beth had a different class but Alice was still going to be with me which meant I was still in trouble.

Beth waved goodbye and walked away. I started walking towards class.

"Hey where are you going?"

"On Moon, to live the rest of my life there" I said sarcastically.

"Very funny, your moon can wait since I have to talk with you" She said pulling me away from class. I gave her confused look.

"You think, I will let you attend class after such a big confession..." Alice said grinning from ear to ear. I should have known that was coming.

"We are skipping Dumb..." Alice said with her eyes gleaming with joy as if she has just discovered a room full of ice creams for free. I tried to resist but damn it's so impossible to say 'no' to overjoyed Alice. She was literally jumping up and down so alas, I gave in.

We walked at the back of the school so no one could notice us bunking. There was a small cafeteria at the back especially for bunkers. We went there and ordered coffee.

"Oh so you and Austin huh? I knew there was something going on between you guys. The way you look at him is different ..blah blah .."

Alice was busy chattering. I chuckled lightly. She was assuming so much. I just kept on listening and suddenly she stopped speaking I looked at her.

"Oh my god. You are blushing Jenny." She said excitedly. At that time I noticed I was seriously blushing just on name of Austin. God this is so cheesy. What's happening to my brain? Is it losing its control?

I suppressed the blush to stop increasing more assumptions of Alice and slapped her hand away.

"I am not blushing Alice. You are thinking so much. I never said Austin and I are together. I just said I have teeny weeny crush on him. This will fade eventually." It seemed as if I was convincing more to myself then Alice.

I hope this fades eventually. I don't want my first heart break because of Austin. "Small crushes are the beginning of true love stories" Alice said proudly as if she had cracked something very hard. I just ignored her.

"So seriously why were you blushing?" She continued again.

"I am not blushing. You know it's quite warm here."

"Yeah, you are right in winter it's always warm." She said rolling her eyes.

I mentally slapped myself for such idiotic response who the hell feels warm in the middle of November. Jenny now it's officially declared. You are going mad.

" Just admit it Jenny, you can't lie to me you are not good at it" She said with quite an obvious tone.

"OK .I guess it's more than a crush." I said fighting the silly blush.

"Yes. I knew it. I just wanted to hear it from your mouth. Even if Austin was on other side of school I could feel the chemistry between you guys" she said dancing in the middle of the cafeteria. My best friend can sometimes act totally weird.

Was my feeling towards Austin that obvious?? Was I into him even before I knew?? A whole different set of questions had started in my head now.

"That's over-dramatic." I told to my now calm friend.

The rest of the time till lunch fled pretty fast. With Alice beside you, you have to be never worried of getting bored or getting out of topics. She can talk nonstop on any topic for hours and hours. You just have to nod your head at the proper time which I was good at doing. As lunch neared I felt little scared as I had to face the wrath of Beth. Beth can be really scary when she wants to be. I mentally encouraged myself into thinking positive.

I entered the lunch room with Alice. The place was still empty as the students were still getting out of their classrooms. I opened my lunch and unwrapped my chicken sandwich. I was damn hungry but my stomach was not in mood of accepting food. Even Alice was waiting eagerly for Beth.

After 5 minutes which seemed like hours, Beth arrived and sat quietly on table. I literally froze in my place. No one dared to speak anything. I could feel Beth glaring at me. After couple of seconds of her intense glaring Beth burst out laughing and even Alice accompanied her..

I mean they were actually laughing like idiots. What the hell. Have they gone crazy? Or did my confession kill some thinking cells in their heads??

They were laughing so hard all I could do was stare at them in bewilderment.

"Oh my god Jenny, look at your face you seem as if you have seen a ghost." Alice said between her laughs.

"You are not angry at me?" I asked looking toward Beth.

"Why would I be angry? You think we didn't know you liked Austin...?" Beth managed to say as she ceased the laughter. "We knew it much earlier. Basically you took very long time to realize your feelings but you know, I m happy. You at least realized it..." Beth said wiping the tears caused by laughing.

So they knew much earlier. Oh god from when have I been into Austin? I am the biggest idiot to not have noticed it.

"Then why did you go to the class without speaking a word?"

"Just to make a little fun of you" Now this was the voice of Alice which brought me to realization that I was being pranked by by my two best friends.

But when did they decide this? My question was answered by Alice

"We are 21st century girls. You know?" Alice said dramatically.

Oh my God they were WhatApping each other when I thought they were shocked and speechless. I knew this mastermind must be of Beth, her head is a house of devil."Oh jenny, your expressions were priceless you were damn scared." Words of Alice brought me back to reality.

"I wasn't scared why would I be scared?" I said defending myself.

They gave me a "you are kidding right." look and burst out laughing again. This time even I joined.

Wiping imaginary tears from eyes, my eyes met the gaze of Austin.

He had entered with his friends, he replied with a smirk. Shaking my head I took my eyes off him and focused on my lunch. It seems like my eyes have mind of its own as it quickly looked at the direction of Austin again. Austin and his two friends were heading towards our table. Austin with his remarkable smirk plastered on his face.

"Shit" I mumbled.

"Hey what's wrong?" Alice asked with concerned look.

When I didn't reply they wandered their eyes in lunch room to see the source of my cursing.

"Why the hell are they coming here?" Beth asked

"Maybe even he must have realized that he has feelings for Jenny and must be coming here to ask Jenny for a date??" Alice said drooling over Recce.

God even though they are doing project together this girl is still not over him, she's totally mad for him...

Seconds later, the guys had gathered near our table.

"I usually get reactions from girls but nothing that crazy." Austin said with a smirk.

Gathering little courage I had "What the hell are you doing here?" I said trying to sound little angry.

Not dropping his smirk at all "I just wanted to say 'hi' to my newest friend." He continued "I really enjoyed yesterday night." He said with a wink. My eyes turned the size of soccer ball and jaw went slack as my mouth opened wide with shock.

God has he taken oath to always mention half truth to embarrass me to a level of infinity? At this point I seriously wished mother earth could swallow me whole. More or less my friend's expressions were the same .When they gained senses.

"You guys were together yesterday night?" Alice asked with

stunned expression.

"By your friends expression I can guess you haven't told them about the night yet princess" He said increasing his smirk if that was even possible.

Even though we had just worked on project whole night, I could feel the silly blush coming.

God I seriously need to get my head checked. Suppressing the blush "We were together yesterday just to finish the silly project whose due is today" I said clarifying myself.

From corner of my eye I could see some relief on my friends faces.

"Wait a second." Recce said "So this is the girl you were talking about whole ride huh? Well things are going to be interesting then" He said confusing me slightly.

"Hey you are the girl that bumped into Austin right, I am hearing a lot about you from that day." River Austin's another friend said showing off his dimples.

"Actually he bumped into me." I told stubbornly.

"Okay okay" He said holding his hands in surrender.

"I don't think it is his mistake anyway. Your beauty is hypnotizing." Recce said with smirk, on which River smacked on his head.

Talking about both of them, River is sweet and seems to be more mature among them. Recce is more of a flirt then Austin.

"Anyways I am River." He said with a genuine smile.

"Jenny" I greeted offering a smile.

"Oh I know that." River said with a wink which turned my cheeks to the color of dark tomato.

"And these are my friends" I said pointing towards Alice and Beth.

They both waved together.

"And I am one and only Recce the hottest guy alive and unfortunately best friend of them." Recce said pointing towards Austin and River which caused him a punch from both.

Recce can never keep his mouth shut.

"Fuck that hurts please inform before hitting" Recce said sarcastically.

"Then keep you shitty mouth shut."

Everyone at the table laughed at their silly arguments. To my utter surprise they all sat down to have lunch with us. Never, I mean never in many years I have seen these boys with anyone else. They used to always sit away from other guys. So this was strange and shocking.

Every single person was glaring at our table as if a spaceship full of aliens had landed on our table. I know Austin sitting with us was as impossible as that but can't they mind their own business. I would not lie I felt happy to see them and most importantly Austin with us.

Alice and Beth were also shocked at first but then they started talking with their respective project partners leaving me and Austin in silence. I could feel Austin's glare towards me which brought a weird sensations in my stomach. I was acting all calm and relaxed outside but inside I was going all crazy. Common admit it, having lunch with a boy you have feelings for and avoiding him with full strength so that you wouldn't drool over his looks, is quite difficult and requires a lot of self control.

As the bell rang I quickly grabbed my things and tried to get out of the awkward situation.

"It was really nice time with you..." I said fake smiling "but I have to go to class." I stated hurriedly making my way towards the class. A sigh escaped my mouth which I didn't know I was holding.

"Jenny, you do realize that I sit right beside you in the next class, right...?" Austin said loud enough for me and rest of the canteen to hear.

I had actually forgotten about literature class.

Oh God one more extra hour with him.

❄ ❄ ❄

Chapter 16 - Drama Selection

"No part of me wants to go to class right now" I moaned grabbing my backpack.

Being close to Austin for one more hour and ignoring him was really like testing my non existing self patience.

"Come on Jenny. Literature will be fun." Alice said excitedly with a wink.

She is always excited to work with Recce. I hope they get together soon.

"Besides it's a final submission of project today. I hope my project doesn't get selected for drama. I can't bear that douche River anymore." Beth said with total hatred which concludes she had a bad project experience with River. I didn't hate River or something but he being Austin's friend is enough to know that he didn't pay more attention for completing the project. I was expecting such response even from Austin but his last night act totally confused me.

"Don't worry Beth; Jenny's project is going to be the best project. After all love birds have done it by sacrificing their dear sleep together" Alice said chuckling.

I never knew my friend's mind was so corrupted.

"Besides there are no other students in our class who share chemistry like them, Austin and Jenny's chemistry is perfect." Beth said tauntingly putting extra pressure on 'Chemistry'.

WOWW...Finally my two opposite best friends have selected a common topic to harass me...YIPEEE... Note the sarcasm.

We walked together in class. As instructed I sat besides Austin. Suddenly it hit me hard as rock, today is my last day to sit beside Austin... This is last time of getting jealous glares from girls.

Even though the glares were meaningless it used to feel so good. It felt as if I am more special to Austin than any other girl. Just thinking about this made my heart flutter.

Why does the heart have to interfere in all the things? Can't it just focus on doing its work of pumping blood...?

As strange as it sounds I felt really sad from inside. There was a day when I not even wanted to see his face and today I don't want to leave his side. Seriously time changes everything. I will really miss that ignoring attitude to friendly smile times.

I was shortly cut in my thoughts by Austin's million dollar smile. I did my best to not let him know how much his smile affects me but my silly butterflies don't understand. Thousands of butterflies erupted in my stomach.

God don't these butterflies have any other work. Why they have to always confuse and make me uncomfortable.

I just ignored him. Finally after what seemed like ages Mr. Black entered. Today he was going to grade our projects and select five pairs for drama. When he started checking the projects, I suddenly started feeling nervous. I don't want my project to be best or something but I even don't want any idiotic mistakes which will make entire class laugh.

It's a general fact that human being makes more mistakes when they're half asleep. Talking about Austin and I, we are far worse than normal human being.

Theamountofmistakeswedo,willevenmakethefoolproudofhimself. Mr. Black while checking was pointing out loudly. This was certainly not helping to calm my nerves.

Why can't he keep mistakes to himself..?? I was somewhat relieved to know that most of students have completed their project in last minute. It felt nice to know that I was not the only one in the crime.

In the meantime I felt Austin's hand on mine. My heart beat increased at unusual rate. I bet he could hear my heartbeats.

"Calm down Jenny, our project isn't that bad. Mr. Black will be surely happy." He said again flashing his million dollar smile. Suddenly all fears vanished and I felt really good. This boy has a killer effect on me.

Mr. Black gave a big satisfactory smile while checking our project. I left a sigh out of my mouth.

"Wow...it seems you have put lot of efforts in preparing project. I am happy to know this." He said looking at us. I returned the smile.

Austin being Austin can never leave the opportunity of getting appreciated.

"I knew it sir, as only a painter knows the worth of real painting, only you will understand the worth of our project. I have being waiting in library from last one week to complete this project..." Austin said proudly.

"I am impressed Austin..." Mr. Black said patting his back. I was in total state of Awe .How people believe each and every lie of his? Damn that puppy innocent face can make people believe anything.

I really felt like thanking Austin and laugh at the stupidity of Mr. Black. I mean seriously how he can believe on a guy who must have probably not even seen the library. Surprisingly we got an A+. I did a little happy dance in my head. God it feels so nice to get good results for our hard work.

My sacrifice of sleep was not vain. Just the thing was I was still feeling sleepy and was damn tired. After checking all the projects Mr. Black taunted some students for their shabby work and complimented other student's for their work.

"Now it's time for selecting five pairs for drama. You guys will perform in the school drama." Mr. Black continued "The first pair is of Alice and Recce. Their project is the best of all."

Everyone cheered for them. The first pair was confirmed since no one can compete with Alice in academics. The expression on Recce's face was priceless. He clearly knows he would have never been first if he was not in Alice's team. The shocking thing was he hugged Alice and thanked her. I guarantee Alice was in cloud nine, in her dreamland by then since she was smiling like an idiot for the longest time.

Mr. Black announced other two random pair names.

"The next two pairs I am selecting are totally unexpected pairs. I never thought in my dream that I would select these boys for anything like this." Mr. Black continued " These boys should be seriously thankful to their partners the name of pairs are- Beth-River and Jennifer -Austin." Entire class erupted in loud claps.

"Seriously it's really strange, the boys who rarely attends lectures getting selected among best project."

We all four had same shocked expression plastered on our mouth. Mine and Austin's mouth was literally touching grounds.

It's not like, I didn't want to be in the drama .Being in drama is full on fun. You can bunk lectures in the name of drama. But getting selected was totally unexpected. Alice, me and Beth had previously never being selected for annual functions. Heck we never even attended one but now we were part of it. It felt good, different. This is seriously going to be fun.

AUSTIN'S POV-1

After that deadly incident, I never felt like using Facebook again. Just random posts and upload. I had completely isolated myself from the outside world. I had limited my world to my two best friends and family, though I spent much of my time with my friends only. By my behavior others think that I show lot of attitude but it's just my way of keeping me away from getting close to anyone. Because when someone near and dear to you leaves you the pain is really unbearable. I know it's not best way to live life but it at least keeps you away from all the pain that comes up with being happy all the time. I was now really tired of ups and downs in my life. So I was living my life with no feelings. I used to never send friend requests to anyone back then and even now I don't. Of course for different reasons though. I never felt like talking to anyone after that incident. I was shown the real cruel face of world after that which wasn't really good but jenny is exceptional case. My inner mind spoke up

I don't know what was different about her but everything about her screamed just pure innocence which really attracts me towards her.

She seems to be flawless and pure. She seemed everything I crave for. I had never in my entire lifetime felt in such a way. This feeling was different but awesome. When she looked at me, I felt like I was lost in a sea. This girl was totally capturing my heart

so against my mind my heart decided to send her friend request.

I even liked her profile picture. Damn who wouldn't like such an innocent cute photo. This is totally not me. I never ever like anyone's profile picture. My 'like' resulted into a little dagger from some of my girl followers, why do they have to interfere so much in my life?

Basically that's a price for being popular. I could feel my nerves tingling like being tickled with a small feather after sending the request.

Gosh I have never being so nervous in such a long time.

What's happening to me? I had literally glued my eyes to screen waiting for notifications

somebody please kill me before I do something creepy

I heard the beeping sound of notification. I instantly Jumped at the sound of notification, I felt rejoiced to see the notification that had occurred on my laptop's screen. Jenny had accepted my friend request immediately which means she was on line.

It felt like my unexpected dream had come true. Gosh I sound so girly now.

I didn't want to sound desperate so I decided to harass her a little.

Eventually the chatting lightened so I decided to ask her what I wanted to ask her from quite some time.

"Can we start over by becoming friends??"

There was no reply from her .I knew it she never wanted to be my friend. Why would she? I have always just harassed her. I was about to logout when my screen made a beeping sound.

Jenny: - 'Sounds good.' God just that two words brighten my mood like anything, I was happy beyond the level of expression. To say I was shocked was an understatement .I was speechless, dumbfounded, overjoyed and all the adjective that represent surprise and happiness. I still couldn't believe that she would like to be my friend after our so many fights and Arguments.

Such an affect of Jenny on me was scaring me. She was trying to change the stone hearted Austin to soft hearted Austin that existed in the past. She was trying to bring out that Austin which is long time lost behind the shadows of past.

I always wanted to get over the past but the past was in no mood to leave me alone. I quickly logged off since I had silly dinner to attend. I got ready and went downstairs.

As the bell rang I went to open the door with a smile. I was shocked to see Jenny in front of me.

Gosh. She looked like real angel from heaven without wings in her dress. I wish I could take her in my arms and keep her with me forever. What was happening to me? Was I falling for her??

I vigorously shook my head to cleared my thoughts. But Me Being Me, I couldn't get enough of her

I was shamelessly drooling over her looks .To hide my expression I changed my smile to smirk. I could tell she was avoiding eye contact.The night was going to be full of fun.

To increase her awkwardness I embarrassed her a little in front of our parents. I know I am evil but how could anyone miss the blushing Jenny. My plan totally worked. She looked more red and prettier when embarrassed.

At dinner we had a little kicking fight. I was shocked when she kicked me back. .I never pegged Jenny to be mischievous kind of girl. The dinner was really funny. I was again being the playful, funny Austin.

After dinner, on mom insistence me on showing her house. I decided to show Jenny the backyard, the most pleasant place of our house.

I had many good and bad memories here which I was busy explaining her, when suddenly I heard a thud voice. I didn't understand what happened for sometime then I realized little Jenny had dared to push me in the water. Normally I would have turned to extreme red in anger but surprisingly I didn't feel angry in fact a small smile came on my lips.

Had water entered my brain or something? I was actually smiling like an idiot in the water.

Whole time I was expecting Jenny to speak about the project as today was the last day for completion but she had actually forget about it.

Can you believe Jenny our Miss Nerd had forget something as important as the project. I smiled inwardly because now I had reason to visit jenny's house in the night.

AUSTIN'S POV-2

I decided to go to Jenny's house because of the project. Who the hell cares about the project I just wanted to spend more time with her that's it. But I can't tell her this reason right. I know I am quite smart, right from childhood.

Jenny is actually addicting me to her; she is like my new found sweet drug. Surprisingly I never want to leave this drug.

I choose to take window rather than door to make my entry filmier.

You know right, girls are a great fan of clingy romantic movies maybe Jenny will get impressed by this. But the look on Jenny's face after seeing me was priceless .I would surely capture the moment if I had a camera with me. She was totally pale as if I was going to kill her. Considering she was scared would be an understatement.

I wanted to laugh catching my stomach but that wouldn't make a good impression right..?? So with full strength I suppressed my laughter...

After some time I got comfortable near her and we started discussing about the silly project. I don't know if it was the effect of Jenny's beautiful sleepy face or of the chilled wind, but I was coming out with pretty good ideas .Jenny seemed shocked and impressed.

First time ever I felt like patting my own's back. Good going Austin.

After some serious time of project completion, I was totally wrapped in her baby blue comforter I know it looked funny and she was laughing at me.

But who cares, it was really soft and comfy and smelled like her.

It brought me to realization that Jenny was girly like most of the girls. I mean who would have everything in their room literally of pink and blue color? Only girls.

As few more minutes passed the boring project was finally over. I can't even express how happy I was. I have never spent so much time on some silly project .God I have not even studied so much.

I wonder how nerds do this all the time and never get tired or bored of it.

I was seriously bored and tired to level of infinity even though I guarantee our project will be the best, but again who cares about that. My mission was accomplished.

I felt free from many things on my shoulder so I did a happy dance.

What's to laugh in this? Because a girl very next to me was laughing like hell.

I would be lying if I said she didn't look cute while smiling..

I threw a pillow at her to stop her hypnotizing smile but she attacked me instead and next thing I know, we ended up pillow fighting on her bed. I must say she was pretty good at this.

Damn .This girl always has something different to amuse me.

She is full of surprises. The kind of surprises I love. A smile tucked on my face. Our little pillow fight was actually lot fun even though I was losing shamelessly. My losing was surely worth it. The winning smile on her face was contagious .Even though I was losing I couldn't stop smiling.

I didn't want that angelic smile to fade even a by bit. So who cares if I am losing...?

I wish I could take her in my arms and be with her forever .This very thought saddened my mood .Maybe falling in love again is not in my destiny.

In between the pillow fights we fell asleep .I am not the early waking kind of a guy

Leaving the last part, the project, the dinner, the night with Jennifer was all memorable. They will never leave my brain even if I have a memory loss..

Can I ever let lose myself to love someone again with all the trust..???

❋ ❋ ❋

Chapter 17-Austin's Jealousy

Jenny's Pov

I made my way to Mr. Black's Office. He had called me to his office for God knows what reason. From last few days after project he seems pretty much impressed by me. The trip to office took only few minutes. I pushed opened the door to head inside.

"Ow" someone shouted as the door came to an abrupt stop. My eyes shot open in surprise and I immediately yanked door back to me, hoping the person is not much hurt.

I seriously need to get my brain checked. Nowadays it seems to wander more In Austin's dreams. That Idiot Austin is screwing my head

"I am so sorry. I was thinking about something different while opening the door. Are you fine..?" I asked concerned.

"I am fine .But please from next time never remove someone's anger on the poor door please." he said surprisingly calm.

"I will be careful from next time." I said little nervously scratching the back of my neck.

In my defense anyone would be nervous in front of a good looking tall slender figure Guy, and me being me I get damn more nervous .But who was he?

The male in front of me with messy brownish black hair had extremely pale skin. He was tall, skinny and looked smart .I was shamelessly staring into his beautiful perfect eyes. He was good looking and dangerously handsome.

'But not as good as Austin', my inner evil voice spoke up.

Oh my God from when did I started comparing other boy's looks with Austin's.

My thoughts were interrupted by a 'not so good voice' of Mr. Black's. "Oh Jenny you are here. Meet Mr. Harshal Warner. Your new drama professor .He will be guiding you guys in your play" By then I was totally dumbstruck.

How can such a young handsome good looking guy be a professor that too of Drama? It should be seriously claimed as illegal. It can be main point of distraction for many teenagers.

Mr. Harshal must have known my state as he just ruffled my hair and walked away without saying anything.

God he was even generous, the qualities Austin can never possess. Mr. Black told me to introduce Mr. Harshal to whole drama crew after school. I entered my homeroom and walked to where my seat was. The time till lunch flew pretty fast I suppose .As most of the time I was sleepy or in my dreamland with Austin. Don't judge me anyone would choose sleep over boring lectures.

I entered lunch room with my two best friends. In last few days our lunch table has loaded with boys and obviously that made our table center of attraction even though we sit in left corner end .Surprisingly from that day itself they started to sit with us daily and now there was no awkwardness .Actually we are now good friends. Our few day's lunch with them brought us to the conclusion that even Austin and his friends are pretty normal and friendly. At least his friends are normal.

"Jenny, I missed you so much." Recce exclaimed picking me up and spinning me around.

"Recce put me down I can't breathe." I tried saying this under his deadly grip.

"Oh extremely sorry but I missed your sweet innocent self face. And you even ditched me in the morning" Recce said with a cute pout.

Gosh Recce can sometimes act smaller than a small kid even. He has such inbuilt capabilities

"Awwwww. I missed you too Recce .Even though we just met yesterday." I said sarcastically.

Whole table including Austin erupted into laughter. It was like daily ritual of laughing on childishness of Recce. This guy was too sweet.

He was more childish than Austin. Rest you can imagine..

Frankly speaking I was enjoying their company. Our little table has like come to life by their presence. All thanks to the project. It was little awkward to talk with Austin with my messed up head but he has always been there for me whenever I needed help.

"You know what guys" Alice spoke up." I have heard we have new drama professor for teaching us and he is pretty young and handsome" Alice spoke up updating us with her daily dose of gossips. She is now able to talk confidently with Austin and River. In case of Recce nothing has changed pretty much.

"Male or female?" Beth asked excitedly.

"Male." She said excitedly "I don't know anything much about him though I have heard he's young and handsome and is even smart which most of boys lack in." She said tauntingly looking towards the boys.

All three boys were looking at Alice with daggers but she seems to notice nothing when she is gossiping. She just kept on blaberring.

"I wouldn't regret the decision of being in drama if whatever you are saying is true Alice." Beth said dreamily.

"Not only he is young but he also has a dashing personality. He is smart, generous, calm and has the most attractive voice in the world I must say and is surely handsome." I told them all the information I have known.

Everyone at the table stopped whatever they were doing and was now glaring at me with wide eyes. Austin literally stopped eating.

"How do you know so much about him...?" Surprisingly none other than Austin asked me speaking for first time today.

"I met him in Mr. Black's office." I told them casually.

"And someone's already having crush ha??" River said chuckling at my enthusiasm.

"Basically he is our teacher and for your kind information teacher student relation is illegal." Austin said more seriously. I could sense some jealousy in his tone.

Oh my God. Was Austin parker really jealous of some professor who had just arrived .This is gonna be Fun.

"Someone's jealous huh..?" Recce said poking Austin's cheeks.

"Don't be sad Austin it's just a tinnie minne crush, you still have a chance." Beth teased winking at Austin.

"I am not jealous and basically I don't want any chance with Jenny.

I can't get the only girl whom I don't want. Rest I can make any girl mine if I want." Austin said confidently glaring at Beth and Recce.

And by this the greatest egotistic guy in the world award goes to Austin parker. Were they really discussing about my chance with Austin.

Great when you have such great friends you don't need any outsiders to embarrass you. Austin continued "Besides, I guarantee I am more handsome and dashing than that guy so nothing to worry." Austin mentioned with a wink.

Wasn't this a little too much, I knew Austin was right. He was more handsome and dashing then Mr. Harshal. But I am surely not going to accept it. This will increase his ego to the size of universe.

The bell rang and every one hurried to their respective classes. It felt really nice to know Austin felt something for me, which he is not ready to accept. Or why would he be jealous?

❄ ❄ ❄

Chapter 18 - Arrival Of Drama Professor

The time flew pretty fast. Everyone was busy imagining cute new professor from their point of view. Like a guy with mustache or with a mole on cheek or with very big eyelashes some descriptions were funnier than this. Seriously girls nowadays have weird definition of cuteness.

Boys were cursing and girls adored the new professor, though no one had seen him yet properly. In just one day Mr. Harshal was on top of the gossip list. He should be proud of himself. In my seventeen years of student life I have never ever been on the top of the gossip list.

Even Beth and Alice were in their dreamy world, Entire Day. I could tell from their facial expression As soon as the bell for the last period rang they flew out of the class faster than air. I was left alone in the class.

Great Now I had to search Mr. Harshal by myself now. I mentally noted to myself to kill my oh-so-called best friends the very moment I meet them. With a sigh I started walking towards staffroom hoping I get Mr. Harshal there.

Seriously I was in no mood to search him everywhere.

"Boo." Austin came out of nowhere and scared the shit out of me. I closed my eyes and attempted to slow down the frantic breathing, ignoring the pit in my stomach. Gosh this guy must seriously try out for ghost appearance scenes.

He always appears without warning. Oh my pretty poor heart.

I was expecting to get an apology from Austin. But the boy in front of me laughing with watery eyes seamed in no mood of apologizing.

Bloody idiot. Remind me again why I felt in love with this guy? No one means No one can scare me to hell and be normal with me the next time. He counts in for a severe punishment. I gave him one last death glare and started walking away.

"Hey are you mad...?" He asked between his laughs.

"Why would I be angry? I love being scared by someone in hallway. It's really fun." I said sarcastically.

"I am sorry. I just like the reaction I get from you, you look damn cute being scared" He said pinching the tip of my nose giving me nothing I can do about that look. His mischievous look turned into an innocent puppy face expecting for forgiveness.

How can I ignore that innocent puppy face for more time? And in minutes my anger evaporated. So finally I gave up.

"It's ok just don't do this again next time." He agreed with a beautiful smile.

This is the reason you love him Jenny. My inner devil mind spoke up again but for the first time it was true. "Why are you out of drama class?" I asked him curiously.

"So are you. Where are you going?" He said raising his eyebrow.

"To search Mr. Harshal as Mr. Black has told me to show him to the drama room."

"And where is he?"

"In the staffroom, I guess." I said with finger crossed.

He didn't speak anything so I assumed it to be the end of our conversation and started walking.

"Hey wait. I have some work in staff room so I can bring Mr. Harshal if you don't mind?" Austin said stammering a little. I could tell that he was nervous as he bit his lip, and his eyes were dancing to every corner.

He had clenched fists to stop them from trembling. I have never ever seen Austin getting nervous while talking to somebody. His nervousness seemed adorable to me, as it depicted that I have some effect on him, which was good. I wanted to put him at ease but now it was not the Time for that.

"But Mr. Black has allotted this work to me." I said stubbornly.

Austin helping me without any of his evil motive is like a fish living without water, totally impossible. So I refused his offer. "You seem pretty excited to spend some extra time with Mr. Harshal?" Austin asked with total seriousness.

"Why the hell would I be excited?"

"Because you like him" He said giving me it is damn obvious look. "Why the hell you think so?" I asked a bit frustrated. I don't want anyone to think I like a professor when I actually don't. It's even illegal.

"I was just beside you in lunch room. I can hear as I have ears." He said in sarcastic tone.

Does he really think I can like someone in just one meet?

"That was just a damn joke Austin .I won't like anyone in just one day"."So you don't have crush on him?" He asked looking curious.

God did I use some other language before, he was seriously testing my patience now."No. I mean he is good looking, smart but certainly not of my type."You are my type dumb. I wish I could tell you someday. That feeling only saddened me a little.

"Excellent." He said hiding the glint of happiness.

He is happy just because I don't like him. Does that mean something? "Don't get me wrong. I just don't wanna get my friends in illegal relationships." he said walking towards the staffroom.These words broke my hopes and shattered those into pieces. I went towards the drama room.

"Hey Jenny, where were you?" Alice asked when all of my four friends circled me.

"I was busy searching for Mr. Harshal alone as my oh-so best friends decided to ditch me" I said faking sweetness.

"Where is Mr. Harshal then?" Beth said without even apologizing.

How rude. "Austin went to get him as he had some work in the staffroom." I replied little rudely. At this new piece of information both Recce and River looked surprised as if I have told them purely impossible thing.

"Wait, you mean Austin went to staffroom to bring Mr. Harshal?" Recce chirped in.

"Yeah, what's so surprising in this?" I said popping the word 'so'.

"You don't know Austin as we know him, otherwise you would have also been surprised." River informed.

"Something is really fishy. Austin never goes to staffroom. He avoids it like boys avoid studies." Recce said again.

This information was really shocking. It means he was really making some excuse so I wouldn't go to the staffroom, which means the last sentence he spoke was false. He was really concerned about my love life and me. How cute. This really lifted my mood.

But then why was he hiding his feelings.

"I think even he likes you." Beth said answering my unasked question coming closer to me.

"But why will he like me? I am not even near to cheerleaders when compared to them." I said half whispering so the boys couldn't hear.

"Not everyone likes cheerleaders idiot. You are beautiful in your own way..." Alice spoke from nowhere.

God this girl can even smell the gossip. The conversation was stopped in middle when Mr. Harshal entered. His entry was really different from every normal professor. Everyone welcomed with whistles and comments. Austin was beside him and my guess was not wrong. Austin was certainly smarter and hotter than Mr. Harshal or maybe that was just my thinking.

At least today I can have Austin for only myself to stare. Love is seriously crazy, even small things makes you happy as hell.

"You are hot" the head of the cheerleader commented "Like really hot."

Every single head in class glared at her. I know Mr. Harshal is hot and all but who would have guts to comment this in front of professor! My gaze then went to Mr. Harshal who was also damn shocked. He may be only few years older to us but even then, he was still our professor.

"Thank you...but please refrain from making such comments." He responded with slight blush.

Gosh Mr. Harshal was blushing, Epic moment.

"Why, it's the truth..."

"But I am your teacher..."

"A cute young teacher..." she said with a wink.

Mr. Harshal gave her an uncomfortable look. I figured it was just because he was standing in a professor's position or else I am sure he's ego would have increased to the size of Mexico.

Yeah. I believe all boys have ego as big as Mexico...

It wasn't a big thing that she found Mr. Harshal cute but it was surprising she said it so causally. As if it's a normal thing.

Mr. Harshal ignored the comments and shortly introduced himself.

It seems even though he was young, he had great knowledge of literature and he is a great fan of Shakespeare's plays. He even seemed pretty relaxed and easy to talk to type of a guy.

Next Mr. Harshal started explaining us about the play and the different roles. Everyone was listening silently. A bunch of teenagers listening to Romeo Juliet so seriously seemed funny. But Mr. Harshal had different addictive tone of explaining.

"Now as you have known the drama properly I want everyone to vote for Romeo Juliet among you people." Mr. Harshal declared.

The gossiping started again. Everyone started deciding whom to vote. It was quite clear that Austin was going to become Romeo so the role of Juliet was only the suspense. After fifteen minutes, results were declared.

Austin being selected for Romeo was not shocking. The shocking thing was that I was selected for Juliet. I would lie if I told I wasn't happy.

I was more than happy to work with Austin. Any other girl working with Austin would have seriously killed me from inside. A satisfied smile was plastered on Austin's and other's face, which didn't require a genius to guess that they had literally forced everyone to vote for me.

What can I say, I have the best of friends. And I am luckiest to have them. Mr. Harshal also seemed pretty happy by the selection.

"Jennifer, I personally wanted only you to be the Juliet. I am happy."

Mr. Harshal said excitedly. I could hear Austin snorted from behind.

I am so damn loving this jealously game. Mr. Harshal selected some other students for different roles and some for stages work. He handed everyone with scripts. Rehearsals were going to start after two days, which meant we had only two days to by heart the lines. The drama was in next month. That left us only three weeks to get the play just right, which was about a week shorter than usual.

❄ ❄ ❄

Chapter 19 -Night Turned Scary

To say I was surprised would be understatement. I was totally shocked and pretty all the adjectives that described shock. Not every day you hear Recce saying, "Guys let's take this play seriously and let's start its practice from today itself"

Shocker right? I know.

I was shocked too and everyone around me had somewhat same mutual expression.

Recce and seriousness are like total opposite of each other. I have never ever seen this guy serious.

Austin literally checked Recce's forehead and neck to confirm that he is not saying this due to fever.

I personally think his mom must have been constantly watching comedy shows when he was in her womb. It's my silly logic. Weird I know. But what can I say, I am born weird.

After class while heading to cars Recce said this. Everyone looked with suspicious eyes at Recce and when he didn't say, 'I was just joking' or 'Guys you seriously think I will say this' everyone agreed to meet and stay at Austin's house for drama practice.

"Yippee, let's go." Recce said in excitement.

"Yep" I said a little excitedly too. His happiness is that contagious.

Moreover, a night with the bad boys was really a new thing and I was seriously excited and a bit nervous for this. I really wanted to know how hanging out with bad boys actually felt. See I told you before I am weird.

Boys sat in Austin's car and girls sat in my car, expecting I knew the path of Austin's house. What they didn't know was that I was going to follow Austin's car .I am so damn weak in remembering roads.

Besides who would dare to open their eyes and keep a note of roads on Austin's death ride. I surely won't. We were finally outside Austin's house. And now it was time for Alice and Beth to get surprised. They didn't even hid the single bit of their surprise look. They were literally watching the scene in front of their eyes with huge wide eyes and jaw dropped.

"You are a fucking rich brat." Beth blurted out all of sudden.

'I have heard that before" Austin said with a snicker. His blue angelic eyes met mine and his smile turned into smirk that made me to blush easily. He must have recalled my same reaction with different words of course.

"Welcome guys." He said with a big smile as we entered the house. Recce and River must be daily visitors as they directly headed to the kitchen.

"Nice place." Alice commented.

"Thanks make yourself comfortable" Austin said politely heading towards kitchen probably to drag his two idiot friends out.

Our noble feeling of doing practice from first day itself was worn out instantly after reading the half of script itself. The words were really difficult and were going directly above our head. Totally out of our little collection of words,

Shakespeare must have taken really hard efforts to make this difficult play even more complicated Note the sarcasm....By the different pronunciations of words and by our way of preparation I guarantee the play is going to be unique but in different unwanted way. Oh poor Mr. Harshal he will literally bang his head with frustration or hang himself to death if he listens to our rehearsals. In very less time everyone's determination for the play had vanished and scripts and papers were replaced by snacks and cold drinks and in just few minutes, a serious night was turned into movie nights. Not that I mind. Even I couldn't take Shakespeare for some more time.

After a long fight on deadly topic of what to watch, as there was tie between chick flicks and action movies everyone settled on watching Horror movie. Ironic isn't it?

This is what seriously funny about group fights both group settle on some third thing itself that too after fighting for long time on different things. Austin had a separate room for entertainment. Not surprising at all for such a rich brat. We all headed to the entertainment room. Couches were neatly arranged and the room was pretty big. The couches had seats for only two.

Intentionally Alice sat beside Recce and Beth sat beside River and surprisingly none of them protested leaving place beside Austin.

I could literally feel evil laughs of my silly friends. Evil minds. As I had no other option, I sat beside Austin. Our closeness brought weird sensation in my stomach. I don't know if it was just my imagination or in reality he scooted closer to me. Our shoulders were touching now. I got jittery feeling in my belly, as a flutter of electricity ran through my body due to his mere touch .My heart literally skipped a beat. I tried to move bit away from him but I was frozen. Damn he smelt too awesome .His scent was driving me crazy. I literally clamped my hands tightly together to control myself. Even our knees were touching. That little touch carved me more for his touch. I tried to focus on movie selection so I could distract my mind from Austin's closeness. But damn it wasn't helping even a bit.

Why does this guy have to affect me so much when he isn't affected at all by my presence?

After again a fight on which horror movie to watch everyone (except me) decided to watch 'the exorcist'. Are they out of their Mind? I wanted to protest but I couldn't.

Now you must be thinking what's big deal with The Exorcist?

For your kind information let me tell you I am not that Good with horror movies and it scares me like hell. God please don't turn the night into worse. I prayed silently. I don't want to make fool of myself or scare Austin by my crazy nail attacks. To worsen the condition thunders struck in the background.

As if movie was going to be less scary. Everything was going pretty well, everyone was in their seats eating snacks and normal stuff. Accept me.

After only thirty minutes or so I was totally into Austin. His one arm was securely around me, that helped a little and I was literally digging my nails into his other arm.

Poor guy, he must be regretting the decision of sitting beside me.

On each terrible scene I used to just hold his hand more tightly and the poor guy used to just assure me 'it's just a movie.. Relax...' and surprisingly my veins used to relax automatically. How funny, I was hitting the arm of the guy who is helping me and whom I love the most. Horror movies really brings demons out of you. A thunder struck again, making me scream. Austin chuckled a little and pulled me more towards him.

God if I wasn't scared as shit I would have totally melted then and there in his arms.

But my heart didn't fail to do a little happy dance.

"It's raining." Beth words stopped my heart from dancing.

"Its indicating we should stop watching the movie." Alice said pretty much scared like me. Surprisingly River was All over Beth, totally scared. Damn I never expected River to be such a Guy. I had always thought of him as a fearless guy. But it seems that I was wrong. God he looked so childish. I wish I had camera with me. My unspoken wish was completed by Reece .He took the Picture of River. Lucky Reece River was so scared to acknowledge anything.

"I hate horror movies" I muttered

River sighed heavily "That's it. I am going to sleep" he said standing up. Everyone pulled him back to his position.

Poor guy he don't know his friends are more 'eviler ' if that word even exists."No you can't escape" Beth said holding his hands tightly.

He groaned and closed his eyes. A more suspenseful scene was coming everyone was silent. River was literally trying to sleep. Some evil spirit jumped on the actors and Alice and I screamed together.

I was holding Austin's hand so tightly I hope I don't mess with his blood circulation. Austin leaned towards my ears and spoke softly "Scared??"

Even this one word brought whole troop of wild butterflies in my head.

I somehow managed to nod my head.

"Get your head off the movie?"

"How?"

"Just think of sexiest man sitting beside you..." He said joyfully.

I couldn't help but blush infinitely at his remark.

"I knew it would work." he said poking my cheeks. I chuckled at his reaction.

Just when I was about to relax, the lights went out. Everyone freaked out. In just few seconds our couch got crowded with everyone.

How did we all manage to fit in a couch of two, was beyond imagination?

"Shit." I heard River cursing beside Austin.

"They are coming for us. We are going to die guys." Alice screamed scared.

My heart was about to come out of my heart. I was glued with Austin holding him tightly. To my pure luck he didn't leave my side or complained about anything. I should surely thank him tomorrow for this.

"Chill guys it's just a power cut" Beth exclaimed.

"Everything happens for a reason guys." River spoke.

"Guys don't freak out just be together nothing going to happen." Austin assured, still holding me tightly.

"What if Alice is right?" River said frightened.

I was too scared to even speak. Lightening struck again adding more fear to our bodies. Austin must have sensed my stiffness as he started making circles in my back with his fingers. God with his relaxing touch I can even face a ghost without a panic, just over-exaggerating.

He whispered in my ear" Don't worry Princess I am here right beside you." Those were the most relaxing words of my entire life. That very moment I wish I could kiss that so damn near face.

The thunders made the scene more terrific. As if repeating the scene from the movie. The trees were making scary shadows from glass.

"This is classic." River said "Tomorrows headlines going to be like 'Group of teens gathered to have fun get killed in a big alone dark house by an unknown force'" River said with a croaked voice.

"Hey my house is not haunted" Austin shouted at River pushing him off the couch.

We were no longer individuals we were mass of scared teenager, Except Austin and Beth of course.

After a long silence "We need to get off the couch" Beth said in painful manner. I bet she must have lost her sensations as she was poorly sandwiched between Alice and River.

Poor Beth, she had to face so much to be brave. "I am totally against your idea. You idiot" River said rejecting Beth's idea.

Beth was going to say something but was interrupted by a weird noise came from kitchen. I froze in my place.

"What was that?" I asked scared.

Can you imagine how scary it can be to hear someone's footsteps when you know there is no one present in the house?

Same was my condition. As some footsteps were coming towards us.

"Is there anyone else in the house?" Beth questioned.

Austin shook his head saying "No."

Oh My God! we were seriously going to die now without marrying. Fuck marriage I didn't even get to confess my love. This is not the right time for dying. Should I confess my feeling to Austin now? My inner Mind started battling. The sound was getting bigger and bigger.

"There may be a mouse inside the kitchen." Beth said getting up from the couch.

"And what is he doing? Playing hide and seek by making so much noise?" Alice retorted.

"Well to check that we need to go in the kitchen." Austin said rising up.

Now no courageous guy was left on couch so everyone rose up.

"Superman you go and do your investigation. I am good here." River spoke.

"Cowards die first." Beth reminded evilly.

"That was so mean. But I am still not coming." River said stubbornly.

"Guys" Rivers tone turned cold and serious " Don't panic" he said stammering" But there's someone standing behind us" He muttered freezing me on the spot.

Oh my Gawd there was really something extremely white with

black deadly eyes blinking at us. I, Alice and River were freaking like hell by now. Austin and Beth were calm but even they had quizzical look on their faces.

"Hey what do you want? Can we help you?" River said waving hand at the figure.

"As if he will tell you his intentions idiot" Austin said slapping his hands down.

"Why are you talking with it?" Alice asked tensed.

"I have no idea." he said innocently with low chuckle.

"It's just his panic speaking, chill." Beth retorted.

God she seemed mastered in all these stuff has she encountered anything like this before?

'Not a right time to think about this' my brain stated.

"Guys I think we should go ahead to check what it is?" Austin said without even slightest fear.

Is he Alien or something, Nah .He is devil himself in form of Human so he is not scared.

"Are you nuts .He must be having some super natural powers .He can kill you...blah blah...." Here it goes I started blab erring. I talk continuously only when I am damn scared.

To stop my unnecessary talk Austin placed a hand on it."Chill princess. Ghosts don't exist. By the way it felt nice to know that you care." he said with a wink.

In such a weird situation even how he can be so sweet.

The figure tilted his head and started walking towards us with angry expression.

Did we hurt his ego by neglecting his existence?

By now we all were cringing to Austin and Beth (our only hope for survival). My heart was beating so fast I thought anytime I could die of heart attack. Slowly the figure came near us and busted out laughing.

Laughing seriously? Was this laugh before darkness or something... I know I come out of worst phases but what I can say is that I am damn scared and can't even think straight forward. River was about to pass by panic attack when suddenly light came and Recce was in front of us with white bed sheets and torch in his hands.

He was laughing. Laughing will be an understatement he was literally clutching his stomach and laughing like an idiot. It was then that we all noticed that Recce was absent from long time ago. God! why this didn't strike us before. "Ohh my God your faces were priceless. I wanted to scare Austin and Beth. But I guess till then River would have long passed." He said laughing even more. Everyone was looking at him in beaming anger but that idiot didn't seem to care a bit. "You Jerk you fucking scared the hell out of me you idiot." River yelled throwing a whole bowl of popcorn on Recce's head.

In very next minute everyone was busy throwing snacks at Recce. I know throwing snacks at someone who loves food is vain but we didn't had anything else in our hands and we desperately wanted to remove our anger. At least we ruined his clothes. Yay But it didn't stopped evil from laughing at all. Poor Austin was trying to stop the mess we were creating in his entertainment room.

"Guys hit as much you want. No pains. No gains. I knew this was coming but your faces were mind blowing. I have some of your pictures captured in this." He said suppressing his laugh by removing the video shooting above us.

"Give that tape to me you fucking idiot you video shot this entire stuff." River said burning in anger.

"I never know you fear so much. Coward." Recce told River.

This was it. Even though River got scared before he still had ego and image to maintain. The next thing I remember River was running behind Recce with the aim of killing him. Now to tell Recce was scared was right .They ran inside the entire house in less than fifteen minutes. This was best revenge so we decided to spare Recce.

I must say they were great runners... By the time they came between us, River was beating the hell out of Recce and Recce was continuously trying to protect his face.. After long cursing and fighting and Recce's apologizing everyone calmed down.

By the end of all this drama it was actually 2 am in the morning. So everyone decided to spend rest of time in Austin's backyard as sleeping now was of no use. Another sleepless night.

Even though the night was scary and all I still got chance to be with Austin...So it was not bad time at all...

* * *

Chapter 20 - Is'nt Recee Acting a More Mature..??

Even after so much of running and hitting you can say Recce was not satisfied. He was the one who arranged the projector and white sheet in backyard so that we could see our scared faces and hit him more.

What idiot does this? Seriously, only Recce.

The blankets were already placed down with beautiful comfortable arrangement for us to settle down. It was not only the arrangement that stunned me I was more shocked by Austin's behavior. He pulled me to sit right beside him. I was out of my senses for some time. His smell brought me back to my senses and a blush crept on my cheeks.

"I don't want you to be scared again princess." He said exceptionally softly.

God, I so damn love this soft side of Austin. I wish I could have him forever...

Do you know the feeling being happiest as you laugh at yourself?

It was happening with us. The saying:

"You will be real happy when you laugh at yourself." was making full sense now.

Even though few minutes before we were scared as hell of ghosts now everyone, including River was laughing at the weird scary expressions. Obviously Austin and Beth were laughing at us. In that entire situation they were so calm as if watching a ghost is as normal as watching an ant.

This is the actual fun of being in a group of friends they turn the weirdest situations also in quite a remarkable memory. In between laughing and teasing everyone fell asleep. Even the ones saying 'let's be awake till morning' were in deep sleep.

Annoying sunrays shining on my poor face forced me to open my eyes. Evil rays. I would have loved sunrise even more if it had risen a few hours late. I hate waking up early but once I was fully awake I was thankful to sunrays. No one finds drool running from mouth attractive. On top of that I was resting my head on Austin's hand as if it was my own personal pillow. It's not like I would mind it. It was much comfortable and enjoyable then my pillow.

Err it was awkward. Gosh I was saved from big embarrassment.

I literally jumped to my feet to get away from that awkwardness. Everyone was sleeping like dead people. Gosh if there was award of sound sleepers we would have really won it.

I glanced over Austin's face. His face was more brightened by sun rays making his facial structure clearer. Damn he looked so sexy. I wish I could kiss those pink soft lips.

Focus Jenny.

Even Austin was struggling with sun rays on his face but the guy is so stubborn to wake and take blanket over himself.

I can't let my price charming struggle in this way. Can I.??

I placed a blanket on his face. A small happy smile tucked on his face. Awww that smile was so innocent. That smile alone made my day. I happily marched towards kitchen to make breakfast for sleeping idiots.

"You seem to love him a lot. Don't you?" The question as well as voice left me in total state of shock.

"What?" I semi yelled at the voice which even scared him a little.

What can I say. I was still half sleepy and never expected Recce to be an early riser.

I had actually expected all to wake up by nightmares and kill sleepy Recce for spoiling their sleeps. I know my imaginary skills are awesome.

No claps please. His early rising didn't actually explain how he knows about this. God did the girls blurt it out.

Oh my God did even Austin know about it. I was about to have a panic attack but I tried to act innocent. Doesn't every thief do this when they are caught?

"What are you talking about Recce. I would never like you even if you are the only guy left in entire universe and River is like my brother." I tried to change the topic jokingly but my attempt failed miserably.

"I know you are not that lucky Jenny. I am talking about Austin." Recce said with total seriousness.

I never knew until now that this guy can even be serious. I had seriously misunderstood this guy and this is really going to kill me. "Recce I think you should seriously get some more sleep you are talking total Non sense. Don't you know how much I hate him?" I tried to argue more even though deep down I knew he was right.

"Yeah, just because you hate him so much you placed a blanket on him right?" Recce said raising his eyebrow.

Why the hell is this guy here? He must be in court to screwing and torturing the thief's life... "I just helped him Recce, as sun rays were disturbing his sleep" I said defending myself.

"Even River needed blanket why didn't you notice him?" Recce asked again. Shit from when did this guy start observing everyone so much. I literally felt like I was in jail for a serious crime which Recce was investigating. "Err Recce why suddenly all these weird questions today?"

"Because today I have confirmed what I had been trying to find out from many days." Recce said proudly patting his back.

"And what is that?" I asked puzzled.

"That you are totally in love with Austin." He said confidently as if he is stating his feelings.

Even though it was true it felt a lot different to hear from somebody else's mouth. The silly idiotic blush still popped out. There seriously must be a book of how to stop the stupid blush from coming it can save many people from getting embarrassed. "Sorry to burst your little bubble of happiness but Recce you are coming to wrong conclusions." I protested.

Last thing I want is to everyone know about my feelings. It's quite embarrassing when everyone knows but the only one whom you love doesn't know.

"No Dear I know I am right. The way you were looking at him earlier, even an idiot will know you love him." Recce said confidently.

God! are my feelings written on my face or something? I was about to deny when he spoke up again "Don't even try to lie Jenny you are not good at it" So with a long sigh I spoke…

"Ok I agree I like him but if you dare to tell anyone about this, I will certainly cut you into thousand pieces and feed to the street dogs" I tried to warn him. But I doubt Recce must have heard anything other than I like him. The guy erupted out in weird happy dance as soon as I said that. It took me literally fifteen minutes to calm him down.

God how can this guy be this energized so in the early morning.

He can seriously get more excited than a girl who has lost some weight she was wishing for. "Shh calm down idiot I don't want anyone to know" I tried to calm him down more.

"Oh you are no fun at all" Recce said with a pout.

"I am sure Beth and Alice know about this and even River knows as we were investigating together. Then who else is left to be told?" Recce said pretending to think.

After little thinking he gave me the mischievous look, which I know what it meant.

"No are you crazy. I can't ask him out. I don't want to risk our friendship because of my silly crush. It will go away one day." I said seriously.

Even though I want to be more than friends I just don't want to risk our friendship.

"Sometimes you have to stop being scared of things and just go for it. Either it will work or it won't. It's life Jenny. Besides haven't you noticed any change in Austin's behavior when he is near you?"

"What do you mean?" I asked confused.

"Ok. So now its official you are a total idiot Jenny why the hell will he get jealous if he is not interested in you? He likes you Jenny." Recce tried putting some sense in me.

Oh My God am I really listening this in real or dreaming again? I literally even pinched myself to check whether I am dreaming or not.

"I have never seen Austin act like this in the past few years. He is scared to express his feelings again Jenny please don't give up on him so easily, please take some risk. I guarantee the fruit of this risk will be the sweetest." Recce said concerned.

By the new information a feeling of happiness overtook me. It felt so nice to know that the guy you like at least thinks about you in a good way. But one thing was running in my head, so I blurt it out.

"What had happened to Austin few years back?" I could sense the change in Recce's behavior. His eyes turned blank. "It's not my place to tell and you to listen from me...you should ask Austin."

He suddenly changed the topic and I didn't interrupt him as I could sense his discomfort.

"So when are you asking him out?" Recce said spinning me round excitedly.

"Who is asking whom out?" We snapped our heads in Alice's voice's direction.

By now everyone had entered in kitchen and Alice was looking at us with greedy eyes.

New gossip is like fuel to her system. "Our Little Jenny is finally going to ask someone out" Recce said happily.

"Who?" Austin asked rudely. I could sense impatience in his voice.

"It's a top secret between us, dude." Recce said with a smirk which caused Austin to frown.

Usually I hate people frowning but here we are talking about Austin, dude. Even his frown seemed cute like his dimpled smile. "Our little Jenny is growing finally" River said ruffling my hairs.

I noticed Austin walking away in little irritation

Oh my poor cutie pie. I wish I could tell him my feelings for him.

I wish I could tell him that 'You are my world, and that gravity always pulls me toward you.

AUSTINS POV

What the fuck. Jenny is asking someone else out. That very thought sent shivers through my entire body. I literally ran out to the backyard to clear my head. Recently because of change in her friend's behavior I had a feeling that Jenny likes someone. But I never assumed Jenny to man up and ask someone out kind of girl.

This means that she is damn serious about the guy. Why didn't she update me about her feelings then?

'Not a big deal, you are not her boyfriend or something.'

My inner mind tried to think positively .The act of kindness of my inner mind didn't help even a bit though. I was still feeling hurt. Even though jenny's decision of loving someone else was right, it didn't seem good. Why?

'Because you love her Idiot', My inner evil voice spoke up again. As if I didn't know it.

When I had met her for the first time, I wasn't planning to fall in love with her. I wasn't even looking for another friend, but Jenny changed all that. It all started with a small silly crush and slowly turned into something stronger. The attraction was electric and unexpected. She entered my life and literally turned it upside down. My mind tried to take control over my feelings but heart won over my mind and now I am hopelessly in love with her. Who wouldn't love such an innocent sweet girl..?

But she doesn't love me back. It was proven by now and this made my heart ache.

My blood boils at a fast rate even when River or Recce tried to flirt with her. I have never experienced such jealousy.

I know I am not good for her, still I get jealous thinking that someone else could make her happier than me. Someone else can hold her in his arms and not me.

During lunch, when everyone was talking about Mr. Harshal's so called beauty, the dreamy smile on Jenny's face left a glint of sadness in my heart. Even when River linked Jenny with Mr. Harshal I felt like punching River then and there. This feeling of jealousy and uneasiness was totally different.

It was totally going to kill me.

Even when Jenny was searching for Mr. Harshal, I felt like Mr.

Harshal will take Jenny away from me forever. I know I was thinking like a mad lover. But the feeling of losing her scared me to hell.

Even though there is nothing between us more than friendship, my concern towards her scares me like hell. I don't want to be a one side lover. Sadly I was becoming one. I looked for Mr. Harshal for her. I never ever visit the staffroom. Few professors were stunned at their place. I must say the look on their face was worth visiting the staffroom.

When Jenny informed me she didn't like Mr. Harshal in that way, I left a huge sigh of relief I didn't know I was holding. I felt like loads of weight being removed from my shoulder. When I was selected for Romeo, I forced everyone to vote for Jenny as Juliet. I didn't want any other boy to hold her in his arms. I can't risk someone else falling for her. She is damn innocent to choose a guy. I guarantee, she must have even chosen this guy without thinking much. But once I get to know that guy I am surely going to search for his history and geography.

Even when Mr. Harshal complimented Jenny I felt like ripping his head from his body even though his compliment was true.

Even during watching the movie, her scared face broke my heart into thousand pieces. I know it was just a horror movie but I felt like protecting her and making her feel safe in every condition. God I love this girl soo muchhhh.

But I can't tell her right. Not when my life is totally unorganized and screwed. I can't spoil her life for the sake of my happiness. She deserves a much better guy who is not haunted by his past and who can make her smile in every walks of her life by being beside her forever.

I want happiness for her which is certainly not in being with me.

Then now when she is taking the right step by asking someone else out, why I am acting so weird? I should be happy she doesn't like me. All the recent signs of her being attracted towards me were false. But here my heart is not ready to be happy. Even though it knows that Jenny had made right decision .Even though it knows I am not Good for her it still wants to be with her.

Why does heart have to intrude in personal lives. Why can't it just do its work of pumping blood?

I can't be selfish like my heart. I can't ruin Jenny's life. That incident has totally fucked my life and it haunts me 24×7.

❋ ❋ ❋

Chapter 21- Time For Some Drama and Action

After Austin's departure, it was fixed; whenever I get some alone time with Austin, I will confess my feelings. It's easy to be said than done.

From that day itself I started avoiding Austin like a drug and my silly idiotic friends tried every single trick to force me to be alone with Austin. They literally even tried to empty the classroom by fooling the students before home run but luckily Mr. Black arrived by then. Silly idiots.

Gosh! they can go to any extend to make me confess my feelings.

Lunch time was the most embarrassing moment. All the idiots had formed one team against me and were indirectly teasing me in front of Austin. I felt like ripping off their heads. But I had to act calm.

Only the one who have being humiliated in front of his crush will understand how embarrassing it is to be teased in front of your crush and still act cool. Let me tell you, staying calm in front of your crush is the most difficult thing to do in entire Universe. I was totally on the verge of exploding from inside but Austin's radiant smile glistened like a sunrise and melted my entire Anger.

Lucky jerks. In the meanwhile even rehearsals for the play had started. We had to rehearse in the classroom, because the playhouse wouldn't open their doors for us because of our mischievousness. We always ended up breaking things there.

The rumors were, that our principle didn't trust Austin and his group as even though they are bright students and sports champs of our college, they had damaged the college property a lot in the past. It's not that hard to believe on this rumor though. Some 'play lovers' were actually sad by this as our college has one of the finest play house. Frankly speaking I don't give a damn about all this. I am happy as long as Austin is around me.

Rehearsals were the only time we used to be together all day. That's the only reason why I loved rehearsals. Mr. Harshal was damn impressed by Austin and me. He kept on telling everyone that it is going to be the best play ever. He always complimented us saying "You both are great together."

Even though he was talking in reference to play it didn't fail to bring a weird sensation in my stomach.

The week quickly sped by. It had by now became my daily task to avoid Austin at any cost. It's not like I didn't want to ask him out, I was literally dying from inside to confess my feelings, but I was not ready to face his reaction or maybe my heart was just afraid of rejection. To avoid many further embarrassments during lunch I had started spending my most of the lunchtime in the libraries.

Yeah, boring I know, but at this moment I trusted libraries more than my friends. Rehearsals are the only time I get to spend with Austin.

Even though we used to rehearse more and talk less as Mr. Harshal used to be with us most of the time, Austin's mere presence brighten up my day. I know it would sound creepy, but this is the only time of the day I look forward to.

Even though physically I was avoiding Austin, mentally my mind used to wander in his dreams only. It even felt impossible to concentrate on lectures with him being in same class. All I could think about was his beautiful eyes and the way he used to say my name.

Gosh. I miss Austin so much.

I tried to listen to lectures carefully. I really did but every time I held pen in my hands, I found myself drooling his name with mine in a heart. Of course I'd roll my eyes at myself in disgust but I couldn't help it.

Maybe that's what everyone feels when they are in love. But God, I was seriously loving this feeling. You know you are in love when you're facing that person and everything around you seem to disappear. It's like nothing else matters anymore. The entire world becomes an accessory. You just feel complete and happy by just thinking about him. You feel like you need no one else to survive. This is the only way I can explain how I feel right now. I was in my own happy bubble and I don't want this bubble to burst anytime soon.

But as it is said, nothing lasts forever. My happy fairy tale was shattered to pieces by the scene in front of me. Austin parker kissing some random girl. I couldn't see the face of girl as her back was towards me.

Even though Austin didn't seem to enjoy it much, my heart dropped and it felt like it broke into ten million pieces. I quickly looked away hoping, if I don't see them together, the hurt would go but it didn't minimized even a bit. However I tried to hide the hurt very nicely. I kept my face blank of emotions and started walking away. I heard my name being called by deep voice of Austin's, but I ignored it. I kept walking straight out of school door into a small school garden .It was empty since classes were going on. I was about to walk out of the garden to the car parking lot when

Austin grabbed my forearm and turned me around to face him.

Damn this was really last thing I wanted to happen today.

"Jenny at least talk to me" He said with pleading eyes.

"Talk to you, about what?" I asked angrily.

"I know you saw the kiss. I want you to tell that I didn't kiss her willingly she suddenly crashed her lips on mine. I swear to God I didn't enjoyed it a bit. I was struggling to get out of her arms when you saw." He said with complete sincerity in his eyes.

God, that puppy face melted my entire anger. Why was I angry in the first place? It's not like he has betrayed me or something. Damn he doesn't even know that I like him, still he came to explain me the situation.

Awwwwww.....why he has to be so sweet...

God I had no idea what to say. Obviously words weren't going to come out at this moment so I decided to act.

Without thinking I reached up and placed my hands on either side of Austin's face. I leaned up and pressed my lips on his soft lips. Surprisingly he kissed back. Our lips began to sync together and fireworks bust behind my eyelids. God I should have done this before. Really, I should have because now that I have started it, I just don't want to stop. Call me a desperate or anything but if you have someone as awesome a kisser as Austin even you wouldn't be able to keep your hands to yourself. I pushed myself more towards him craving for more. Damn this feels so incredible.

The description of a kiss in novels and movies is nothing, and by nothing I mean absolutely nothing as compared to the feeling that you experience when it actually happens with someone you love. The novels on your bedside don't even cover half of what it actually feels like.

Austin moaned in my mouth and let me tell you it was the best sound I have ever heard.

❄ ❄ ❄

Chapter 22-Why love has to be so difficult..?

I could have spent the rest of my life glued to his face like that. However that couldn't happen as Austin jerked back after sometime. As if he has been recovered back to his senses after the worst shock. He glared in my eyes for more than usual time with shock and fear in his eyes. Later he shook his head slightly and took a step back and started walking away in opposite direction. Something about the look in his eyes -Sad, pleading, scared all at the same time made me to freeze on my spot for some moment.

When I regained my senses, anger took over me. I half ran towards him reaching out for his arm I turned him around with all the energy inside me.

Like any depressed and generally pissed teenage girl I yelled,

"You are fucking kidding me, Right?? You can't just walk away after I have confessed my love to you." I snapped at him.

I don't know what overtook me but I felt really angry and rejected.

His face softened for some time by my rage but then again turned rigid and emotionless as stone.

I stared at him waiting for some words that I always wanted to hear, but sadly they never came. Instead he spoke "I am sorry, Jenny..."

His words confused me. No one expects this reply as an answer for proposal.

"For What?" I asked little frustrated.

"For not loving you back, I think it's better to be just friends." He said coldly.

'Just Friends' is probably the worst words a person can hear from someone they are so in love with. Somewhere in my mind I could hear the voice of my heart breaking into million pieces. It felt as if somebody had just buried me alive when he said those words. His words seemed sharper yean knife. The knife had stroked in a perfect place. Tears started to form at the corner of my eyes. We were over even before we started. These words stabbed more in my heart like knife. Realization came down on me like bucket full of ice cubes that he left. He was gone. He was gone in just a blink of eye, without even looking back once. I had never been so confused in my entire life about my emotions before. I was happy seconds ago and now suddenly sadness was taking over me. I ran fingers through my hair trying to ease the pain but it didn't work. Sadly, I knew nothing was going to work.

Such a bittersweet memory.

I wanted to tell him so much that, I love him .I wanted to taste his lips forever. I wanted to tell him how much I loved him but he was long gone; leaving me behind with the tears.

Why did I have to fall in love with a heartless guy?

Do you know that feeling when you're just waiting, waiting to get home into your room, close the door, fall into bed, and just let everything out that you kept bottled in your mind all day? It was the same feeling I was having now, maybe even worse than that.

I rushed towards my house and locked myself inside my room.

Time like these, is when I am actually glad my parents travel a lot.

I don't want them to see me in such a mess. I landed myself onto the bed and just exploded. I cried with all the might. I cried until asleep.

Damn it was so hurting from within that I wished I could just turn numb forever.

The worst type of crying is the silent one, the one when no one is home, the one where you feel sadness in your throat and your eyes become blurry from the tears, the one where you just want to scream on the top of your lungs, the one where you can't breathe anymore. The one when you realize the person that meant the most to you, is gone and probably won't even return back, hurts the most.

God I have never cried so much ever but this was seriously hurting like hell.

I don't know from how much time I have been crying like that. The ringing of my cell woke me up. I snapped my head towards it.

I was not in mood to answer the call but what if it was Austin's?

Was he calling me to apologize for leaving me like that? That didn't sound something he would do, but my inner idiotic mind still hoped.

Grasping some courage I answered the call.

"Ugh Hello..?" I said gathering little left energy in my body.

"Jenny." Alice's voice exclaimed into my ears. Relief and disappointment filled me.

"Where the hell where you the entire day?" Her tone was demanding. I felt like a thief caught while robbery I swallowed a lump in my throat.

"I was..."

"Making out with my crush who ditched me after that" was not the reply she was expecting. So I needed to come up with a lie which would be believable. "I was." I trailed off again.

Think Jenny think.

"I was hanging out with my friends?" I replied uncertainly.

"Can I know where...?" She demanded again.

God demanding Alice is a lot scary.

"Shopping" I said stupidly.

You ruined it idiot. Why I have to be such an idiot?

"You hate shopping Jenny. Besides, you don't have any friends other than us so just spill up, what's wrong..."Alice said firmly.

By her demanding but caring tone I finally gave up. I started crying like a lost child in the park.

"Hey Jenny what's wrong. Stop crying I am coming there just hold on dear. Don't you dare do anything stupid." "Anything stupid like..?" I asked out of curiosity "Like killing yourself or throwing your favorite dress" I left a small chuckle as she hung up.

I got on my feet and washed my face to wash away the dry tears but it was of no use. I was literally looking worse than a zombie.

After sometime, I heard Alice's voice "Jenny..." And then a knock on a door, I opened the door. I could see worry plastered all over her face, Without hesitation I hugged her tightly.

"I ....I ....I..." I stammered burying my face in her neck.

"Shhhh. it's ok dear. I am here and everything will be fine" she said softly caressing my back.

She held my head and asked "What happened?"

"I ....I..." I tried to speak up again but my voice came cracking maybe because of crying.

She took me inside with her, in my room and vanished, even I had no idea where she disappeared.

Being alone with thoughts of Austin again haunted me, which made my heart cry out in pain. Oh my poor heart. I wish I just had a delete button so I could delete few memories away.

Alice returned with two cups of hot chocolate in her hands. This is why Alice is my best friend .She perfectly understands what has to be done when. I was seriously in need of some beverage to make my brain function properly again. And hot chocolate prepared by her is my favorite. It was like cherry on the cake.

Alice sat beside me. There was moment of silence. I knew she was waiting for me to speak up.

"Have you ever wondered what hurts the most? Saying something and wishing you had not said it or saying nothing and wishing you had." I said staring at nothing in particular.

"Jenny stop speaking indirectly, just tell me what happened"

"I told him today"

"You told whom what?" Alice asked confused.

"I told Austin that I like him-" I confessed .

"Whoa that's a very big step. And you are sad because?" Alice asked, extremely confused and shocked.

So with a long sigh I completed my sentence. "And he doesn't like me back." I spoke with gritted teeth to stop tears from coming but obviously it didn't help at all.

Speaking up to Alice actually felt nice. It's not like my pain vanished at all, but it seemed to fade a little.

"You are saying you confessed your feelings and Austin rejected you..?" Alice said shocked.

What was so surprising in this? I think I said last sentence loud as Alice immediately replied to it "Yeah it's damn shocking as even he loves you dumb ass. Haven't you seen the way he looks at you? He is totally madly in love with you. Now what will take that idiot realize his feelings?" Alice said irritably.

Here goes the rant. Alice is a nice listener and even a good adviser, but sometimes she thinks by her heart and not by mind which isn't always practical. Right?

I mean why would a guy reject a girl whom he loves a lot?

Silly Alice. Always thinks this is her La La world.

Maybe she must be saying this to cheer me up and show me some kind of hope.

I didn't want to let her down but thinking about it, why would Austin like me in first place. I am a shy and a nerd whereas he is totally opposite. He can get any girl he wants then why will he want me? Maybe I was expecting too much from our little friendship. I tried to push his thoughts away. Leave it to Alice to bring up the topic you always want to ignore.

"You even said he didn't pull off as soon as you kissed him so he must have definitely enjoyed the kiss which means he likes you Jenny. Just God needs to knock some sense into him" Alice said encouraging me. "You still have hope. Never stop believing in hopes, because miracles do happen every day."

Maybe just maybe here Alice could be right even though I hope Alice is right. What's wrong in hoping? A small hope cheered me up. God. I am so damn addicted to this guy. I must have stopped my feeling for him earlier.

I was busy in my train of thoughts when Alice excitedly squealed at me.

"You kissed him, how was it? How long did it last? Did he use his tongue?" "Whoa breath, woman." "Come on I want details now"

"It was awesome..." I said avoiding eye contact and blushing to myself. "It was the best kiss I must say" I closed my eyes visualizing the kiss. I suddenly missed his lips on mine. Smile crept on my face "There was so much love, desire in our kiss." My smile vanished when I remembered the next part "But then he left." I added sadly.

"Oh don't be sad dear .I know that idiot loves you. I guarantee he will ask you out soon. Mark my words. So for now cheer up" Alice said hugging me tightly.

I smiled a little and decided to forget it for a while. All thanks to Alice. That's what friends are for. They can make you laugh even in toughest situations.

Later to distract my mind Alice and I watched many movies. For the first time we both agreed on action movies. The situation lightened with movies and pop corns.

* * *

Chapter 23 - Time for some evil plan

Poke....

Poke....

Poke.....

I was abruptly dragged out of my dear sleep by incessant poking on my cheeks. I am seriously going to chop the head of the idiot who is doing this.

As my all senses were slowly waking up, I started hearing many different voices around me.

"Leave her alone." I think that's Alice who warned someone.

"No. I won't, she has been sleeping all day long." I guess its Recce who said, continuing the poke.

"Ugh stop poking me you idiot." I semi yelled forcibly opening my eyes.

"Yayy. Sleeping beauty is finally awake. How was the hibernation..?"

Recce joked grinning at me. I ignored him and slowly sat on my bed. I was shocked to see everyone in my room except Austin, obviously.

Everyone's eyes were stuck on me with immense worry plastered on their face. The other shocking thing was sun was about to set which means Recce wasn't lying, I literally slept all day long.

Oh my Gosh. All yesterday's happenings flashed in front of my eyes and I instantly felt sad. I am so sick of crying even then all I feel is like crying.

"I knew something has happened between you and Austin. Even he has locked himself up in his room since yesterday. He didn't even come out for dinner." River spoke for the first time.

This new piece of information stunned me. It was hard to digest. Why would anyone be sad after doing something purposely? I mean he was the one who broke my heart then why would he be sad?

Everyone was silent, deep in their thoughts, when Recce demanded.

"Spill..."

Gosh I never knew even Recce could be so demanding. Geez. Alice and Recce are going to make a great couple.

Any other time I would have teased Alice but this time it was sadly different. With a long sigh, for second time in 24 hours I narrated my entire life story to them. I saw sympathy on everyone face .This is what I hated much but there was nothing

I could do to change it. God I so hate this feeling of helplessness.

"I am just going to kick that idiot's ass. Who the hell he thinks my friend is?? How dare he break your innocent heart?" Beth roared with anger. I must say she was seriously angry, by her expression I guarantee if Austin would have been in front of her she would have surely reddened his ass. I had to literally catch her to calm her anger.

Even though he hurt me, I still want him to be alive and his ass to be safe.

"Don't stop her Jenny that guy seriously needs a hard kick on ass he has totally lost his thinking ability." River said with equal anger.

I am glad that Austin has locked himself up or else by now he would have surely be dead by these angry people.

"I am thankful to God. I at least have such awesome friends." I said happily trying to change the topic.

"We will always be there for you, always Jenny. That is what friends are for." Recce said side hugging me.

Even though talking with them felt better I just felt like an idiot for actually thinking Austin would love me back. I don't understand what was I actually thinking

"Seriously what are you going to do ahead Jenny?" Alice asked with serious concerned tone.

This question of Alice again brought the serious atmosphere back, which I was trying to forget. Bad luck. God what I am supposed to do now?

The guy with whom I have fully fallen in love with, has completely crushed my hopes by rejecting me.

"I have no Idea. I have never been so clue less in my life" I said the truth with a sad sigh.

My brain was continuously shouting to move on as if it was that easy.

"Why would Austin do this?" Recce sounded like questioning to himself.

"There must be some reason behind this. Gosh Jenny we have seen lots of love for you in his eyes all the time." River said.

"Reason my ass. Why cant you guys just accept the fact that he doesn't like me or else he wouldn't have left like that. Maybe it's entirely my fault, I was expecting too much. At some point you have to realize that some people can stay in your heart but not in your life" I said trying to put some sense in their heads.

"Maybe it will be better to move on? As Austin is never going to have feelings for me" Emotions started to leak through my voice as it started cracking in between.

"Yeah, even I think moving on is best idea." Recce said with slight smile.

"So what do you think about Chris, Jenny, the guy in your math class?" Recce continued wagging his eyebrows suggestively.

"Are you gone nuts? She is just thinking of moving on she has not yet decided to move on and you are already suggesting new guys...?" Beth asked little pissed.

"What's wrong in that? She is over Austin so she has full right to see other guys." River said supporting Recce.

What's wrong with both the boys? Few minutes before they were grieving over their friend's behavior and now they are finding different partner for me "So it's time to find new hot guys for Jenny. Isn't it Recce?"

River said with a smirk.

"Guys have lost your senses. I am not going to date anyone else." I said trying to stop their hopeless discussion. I mean how can I forget a guy I am already in love with??

"I need some time away from all this. I wish this were all a nightmare that I would just wake up from, but that's not true. My day was at an all time high by just dreaming about him and then my day just crashed and burnt right in front of me. I realized how much I actually love him, and the idea of being together, but now all I want to do is cry because I probably will never mean something to him ever" I spoke trying to explain them my situation.

"This is what I am trying to prove." Recce said joyfully again.

God isn't he acting weird. Should I call a doctor??

"Don't try to deny it, you really do love him Jenny, agree it" River said confidently.

Is it that clear that I am totally blindly in love with him?

"Ok. I agree I love him, but what's the use of it.?" I asked frustrated.

"Guys change the topic and stop harassing her now." Alice yelled little harshly trying to stop the topic.

"Changing topic will not change the fact Alice" Recce retorted.

"Guys we know Jenny still loves Austin and even he must be expecting the same thing. What if we do something Austin will never expect. He will be in utter shock...." Beth said excitedly after a long thinking.

"What you mean?" River asked puzzled.

"Just think guys tomorrow Austin will be expecting Jenny to be heartbroken we all know she is heartbroken but if she acts opposite of this tomorrow he will be confused and will be forced to think about Jenny and maybe in that time period he will realize his undying love for Jenny." Beth excitedly said this all in one breath itself.

Gosh how people manage to be so excited. Thinking about Beth's plan I still didn't understand anything so I patiently waited for more explanation.

Recce, River and Alice stared at Beth for some time. I thought we all are in same boat but later they all said together

"What an idea Beth."

"I never thought you would come out with such a great idea"

And many more sentences which proved only I didn't understand their so-called perfect plan.

"To surprise Austin, Jenny must date someone. I bet he will die of jealousy" Alice chirped in.

God what are these evil minds up to?

"Hmmm and for that we need a guy who is as good as Austin.."

River barked in.

Were they seriously discussing about my life by just ignoring me?

Oh what great friends I have...

Note the sarcasm.

"Guys I think Mr. Harshal and Jenny will make a great couple, as Austin already thinks Jenny has crush on him" Beth said intelligently.

"Bravo." Alice said patting Beth's back.

I officially declare my friends have literally lost their power of thinking properly.

"If you guys really think I will be ready for this stupid plan then I am sorry to crush your hopes." I said interrupting between their discussions.

"Jenny did anyone ask you anything?" Recce asked with devilish smirk.

"But Guys he is our professor." I protested.

"A hot young professor..." Beth corrected me.

"But"- I tried again.

"Shhhhhh" Everyone said in unison.

I knew there was no point in arguing so alas! I agreed to their so-called master plan.

"You hope this will work?" I asked with little hope.

"It will definitely work..." River and Recce said together.

"Isn't it a little risky?" I asked worried.

"We don't grow when things are easy Jenny, We grow when we face challenges" River explained.

"Besides seeing you flirting with Mr. Harshal will surely kill Austin a little from inside." Alice said happily.

❄ ❄ ❄

Chapter 24 - New day new begenning

Here's the thing about time: It doesn't give a shit about what you are, it doesn't care whether you are still shattered beyond repair or you have healed. It just keeps on ticking. Even if you want time to stand still, it doesn't care that you aren't ready to move on and face someone. All it does is 'MOVES AHEAD'

God I hate myself for thinking so much about that idiot, but my brain doesn't care about my liking sadly.

I was totally not in the mood to go to the hell called 'school' and face that heartless guy. But somehow I convinced my shattered heart. Such things happen in every teenager's life and life shouldn't stop because of such things.

Oh what great a line. I mentally patted myself for this.

What!? It works like this very rarely.

Loading myself with courage I got up from my best buddy (my bed) and after daily the chores, I decided to march towards the school.

Luckily Beth and Alice were always beside me in school discussing about the plan though, I will be lying if I said I am not curious about it.

My eyes were shamelessly searching for Austin as if it has mind of its own.

My entire world collapsed when I found Austin in canteen laughing with his friends.

Don't get me wrong his laugh was not devilish or something; actually it was his million dollar angelic smile because of which my heart melted again a little. But the smile on his face proved that he didn't feel anything about my heartbreak. That meant the guys had lied to me.

My whole courage disappeared and my legs started trembling the second I saw him. These are the days when I hate coming to school early. I sat on the other table to avoid his presence. Call me a coward, but I was not ready to face him yet. Even Beth and Alice joined me sensing my discomfort.

I was deeply engaged in my sad thoughts when a boy's voice interrupted my line of thinking, "You must be Jennifer right? Mr. Harshal is searching for you."

This confused me. Before discussing the plan Mr. Harshal had never called me. Something was really fishy

My all doubts were cleared by a smirk on Recce's face. So they have planed all this.

Gosh they are taking this plan really very seriously. From the corner of my eyes I saw Austin's smile fading.

Oh Gosh! this was actually affecting him!

With a big happy smile on my face I replied, "Thanks I will be there". To over exaggerate the situation I semi yelled at Alice,

"Can you please come with me to the washroom; I need to cheek my makeup"

"Sure", Alice said with a wink.

Austin's face was totally filled with different expressions. Damn he looked cute even when he was confused.

Beth was very hardly trying to suppress her laugh. So we three ran out of canteen before she started to burst out laughing.

When we were at safe distance away from the canteen and we started laughing out loud. I know every single person was weirdly staring at us for our sudden outburst but who cares!? They aren't aware of the reason so they are considering us mad but in reality we had very mind-blowing reason.

God his expression was so priceless.

"You must have seen his face man; he looked like a lost puppy."

Beth said trying to suppress her laugh.

"Yeah, Like a cute innocent puppy", I said unknowingly.

"Ahem Ahem...someone is drooling over the guy again..." Alice said elbowing me.

"Alice don't you think we should thank Austin for turning a robot into girl?" Beth said playfully.

Gosh, I must say, this girl has lots of guts.. I hit her arm with all the strength I had. And I must say it served the purpose.

"Stop attacking me." Beth said jerking with a little pain.

"Then stop being sarcastic" I said happily.

"Guys stop the violence you can continue it later we have to attend the lectures." Alice semi yelled at us, which made both of us quite. Alice can be damn dangerous sometimes.

Quitting the argument we marched towards our homeroom.

As usual I was about to sit in he front row, when suddenly Beth started dragging me behind.

God is she going to take revenge on me. Save me lord please.

By witnessing terror on my face Alice spoke up, "Calm down drama queen we are sitting on back benches today."

Confusion replaced my terror stricken expression. Alice choose the last bench of the last row, I had never been so confused ever, never in her entire life. Alice has left the first bench. I must say, It's like made for Alice only. Even forcing her to sit on 2nd or 3rd bench was impossible.

Every professor searches Alice on only first bench. So by now you must have known the reason of my confusion.

"Guys would you please enlighten me what is going on?" I asked being little irritated this time as they were totally ignoring me and constantly spying the door.

Gosh! Seriously why are they looking at the door like maniacs!? As if it's suddenly going to turn into something they have been searching for years.

"Shhhhhh Cant you stay silent and watch." Alice said without looking away from the door even for a second.

God I hate them so much for ignoring me all the time.

I was about to ask them again as I was damn bored to look at the empty door, when Beth spoke up "The victim is about to enter Alice keep an close eye."

Now what are they? Detectives!!? Ahaaa SHERLOCK HOLMES!!!!!!

Even I, focused on the door sharply. Whatever they were observing, I don't want to miss it.

Just like in the movies, Recce and River entered with Austin and my expectations shattered.

Don't get me wrong but they were waiting for the entry of the boys for such a long time, which we do see every day.

I was about to laugh at their stupidity but they were still staring at the boys like they were seeing them for the first time with a victory smile on their faces.

God! Am I imagining things or my friends are seriously going crazy.

Ignoring them I stared at Austin again. His face saddened a bit by seeing the front bench empty.

" Yayyyy....Plan successful." Alice said happily.

Gosh what is happening to everyone one today?! In a time of a nanosecond his eyes wandered through the entire classroom and undefined relief crossed his face when his eyes met mine.

I was still confused about the situation, when Beth thought it would be good to explain the plan to me.

Wow what great friends I have?

"Jenny, observing you I assume you didn't understand anything..."

Beth said sarcastically.

She continued, "Idiot...Austin's face fell when he didn't find you on the first bench and his face brightened when he saw you in the class. He was checking whether you are still with Mr. Harshal or not..."

Oh my God. This entire trap was set for this. And of all, he was searching for me all the time!

I literally jumped up and down full with happiness. I tightly hugged my both best friends caring less about my surroundings.

"You Guys are the best." I said being overjoyed. I hugged them even more tightly.

"Say something we don't know Jenny" Beth said faking seriousness.

Rest of the lecture went in a blur. I was busy staring at a sexy looking back.

Now even I find his back an awesome sight to stare, great. Jenny you are totally losing your control on your mind.

"You don't want to bore a hole in Austin's back, Right?" Alice said with a small chuckle interrupting my constant stare. My checks turned to light shade of red.

God why can't they ignore me at such times??

My checks turned to maximum shades of red if that's even possible, when Austin's eyes met mine for the smallest of nanoseconds.

The next lectures till lunch were pretty same. I wasn't paying attention to anything. Thanks to my nerdy image. No one disturbed me in my lack of interest.

Avoiding Austin, was rude and I couldn't do this all the time nor could I ignore my other friend's because of Austin. I gathered all the courage inside me and started walking towards our regular table. I was again stopped by same junior. He must be a friend of Recce or River as he seemed to know the plan. With a playful smirk he gave me a chit and walked away.

Now it was my turn to exaggerate the words of the blank chit. I could already feel Austin's hard stare in my direction. With calm and cheerful tone I turned towards the guys

"Sorry Guys, Mr. Harshal needs me AGAIN." I said putting more pressure on Again.

Before walking away, I heard Austin irritably speaking,"

"What's so important that he can't even wait for few hours." Yayyyy the plan is actually working. I did a happy dance in my head of course and Marched towards library.

I guess I have to eat lunch alone today because of this drama, but it's really worth it.

To make Austin more suspicious, Alice and Beth dragged me out of school forcing me to bunk all lectures after lunch so that Austin wouldn't see me till drama practice. I must say there is an evil mind behind their innocent faces. They had even dragged boys in this plan and their task was to keep Austin away from Mr. Harshal till the drama practice.

What can I say, I really have the best of friends. After spending time after the lunch break, doing nothing in particular we all three marched towards the drama practice classroom.

I don't know whether it was planed or my luck but Mr. Harshal arrived just few seconds after me and gave me one of his best smile. From the corner of my eye I saw Austin frowning.

For the first time even God was by my side, Yipppeee.

Even though the plan was working seeing Austin sad was breaking my heart. I felt really sad knowing I was the reason behind his sadness.

Why this boy has to be so stubborn in accepting his feelings?

During the entire rehearsal, Austin seemed out of space. He was trying very hard to hide his sadness. I wished I could tell him he was not succeeding in hiding it.

"Jenny, we all know you have feelings for Austin but staring at him like he is some tasty piece of meat, that too in public isn't good sweetheart.", Recce said with a wink.

"Recce you pervert! Keep your thoughts to yourself." I said feeling a little embarrassed.

He was about to say something, when Mr. Harshal's voice interrupted us,

"Jenny Can I talk with you for a minute?"

All our heads snapped at each other's direction mentally asking each other whether Mr. Harshal knows about the plan. No one answered positively which meant he didn't know anything, then why was he calling me?

* * *

Chapter 25 - The cabin party

"Jenny can you please come with me to my cabin ?" Mr. Harshal finally spoke.

Every single eye in the room directed towards me as if this was some kind of life changing question.

Teenagers these days are always in search of some kind of spicy story to ramble about. I mean chill guys this is just a normal question and not the last question of any quiz competition worth thousands of money involved.

Speaking about Austin; there was bitterness quite visible in his eyes. His facial expression worsened when I agreed to go to the cabin.

God I am so damn in love with him to make him jealous. Evil mind I know. His eyes met mine for a nanosecond and it seemed like he was silently pleading me to not go. Didn't he know that I would actually do the opposite of whatever he will say?

Ignoring his pleading glare, I walked behind Mr. Harshal. Feeling of rejection was all plastered on his face. He must know that this was what I felt that day.

Once in cabin Mr. Harshal finally spoke, "Sorry to call you like this in my cabin, but Jennifer I wanted to speak with you on this topic".

My heart beat increased drastically. God what did Mr. Harshal want to talk with me? Did he hear about our plan from somebody else? Is he going to be damn angry?

"I know jenny you have..."

"I am sorry sir, but seriously this wasn't my plan. We will stop this here only. I am really sorry. I promise even my entire group will apologize." I exploded cutting Mr. Harshal's sentence in between, feeling guilty.

"What do your friends have to do with your stage fear and why are you apologizing for that?" Mr. Harshal asked being utterly surprised.

Heck! Mr. Harshal was about to speak of stage fear and here I thought he knew about our plan.

Thanks to the heavenly Gods I didn't blurt out the whole plan.

"You have called me here to talk about my stage fear?" I asked being more confused.

"Yeah , what were you talking about earlier?" Mr. Harshal asked raising his brow.

I left a huge sigh of relief. To avoid Mr. Harshal's suspicious stare, I tried changing the topic.

I went blank, not knowing what to answer as nothing flashed my mind.

God why I had to act so idiotic all the time?

Thankfully Mr. Harshal decided to speak again "I Have noticed your performance. It seems you have stage fear. Look Jennifer, this play is very important to me, I don't want any mistakes in it and you must know the role of Juliet is the best part of the play. I want you to practice little more and overcome your fear."

I nodded obediently. He further continued, "But don't you worry about it, I will help you overcome your fear. I will help you with your dialogues. Just try a little more. I know you are perfect for this role."

I smiled lightly at this. Austin's matter had helped me forget about my stage fear a little. But I was a big coward when it comes to talking in front of strangers and I must say Mr. Harshal had noticed it properly.

"I wanted to tell you something more. I know this is your personal matter, but I really felt an urge to tell this to you, so can I.? "

God has Mr. Harshal planned to kill me today giving me heart attack?

I nodded a little giving him the signal to continue.

"I seriously feel that this Austin guy is totally into you, you must give him one chance"

I searched Mr. Harshal face for some sort of humor but he seemed serious. I went in utter shock by his words.

"Why do you think so?" I said pretending to be unaffected by his statement,

But inside I was mentally dancing with joy.

After all he was the first guy other than my group to confirm Austin's feelings towards me.

Why the hell that dumb doesn't understand this?

"Don't tell me you have no idea about this. The way that guy looks at other people besides you is like 'Come near my girl and you will be dead the second I see you out'. That's the reason I like wandering beside you .I do want to check this Guy's guts" Mr. Harshal said with a smirk.

Oh my God. Is this the reality or am I day dreaming??

He further continued, "Jokes apart he really adores you Jennifer, I have seen lots of love and care in those eyes of his for you."

It was really difficult to suppress my feelings. I excused myself and went to the washroom.

God I have never been so happy in my entire life. I was totally on cloud nine. I happily danced and sang to myself for five minutes enjoying the happiness I was feeling. I know it sounds crazy but I need to celebrate this in some way. After few minutes, I returned to Mr. Harshal's cabin calmly.

After few more do's and don'ts we both returned to our rehearsals.

Knowing it properly, Austin's eyes would be on the door itself I purposely laughed very happily on Mr. Harshal's words, which I didn't even bother to hear. Even Mr. Harshal gave me strange glance for laughing without any reason.

He must have officially declared me mad in his head by now. But who cares.

From the corner of my eye I saw Austin staring at Mr. Harshal so intensely that it would have cooked Mr. Harshal's brain instantly if Austin hadn't diverted his glare towards me.

I am not joking. His gaze was seriously that dangerous. This guy seems to have done some PhD in staring dangerously. I witnessed hurt and agony in his eyes. He seemed so hurt by my actions as if I had asked for both his kidneys.

Damn, I felt like a kidney mafia, who steals kidneys without letting the people know that their kidney is no more in their body!

Gosh this guy is so difficult. Even though he was rude and idiot I still couldn't bear agony in his eyes .I wish I could erase his pain and confront him in any way possible. But this guy seriously needs to know the taste of his own medicine. So by keeping a stone on my heart I walked past him towards the stage.

"Aha Jenny, the arrow has landed on correct place. I bet it won't take more time for wounded Austin to be at your feet", River said dramatically turning me around.

It was actually true, Austin was acting different and this was all because of this silly plan. I literally hugged Recce happily. I hope my Austin has not turned to ashes yet.

Waving them Goodbye, I followed Mr. Harshal. For next hour or so I concentrated on the play, obviously by stealing glances at Austin in between. I can't leave that guy so easily. Every time I glanced towards him, he used to be already staring at me, which meant he was watching me constantly.

Oh my freaking God! Austin Parker was staring at me.

I literally pinched myself to check if I was actually witnessing the reality or daydreaming.

What? Never in his entire life had Austin given me any attention. So this was something foreign for me.

Mr. Harshal's tactics were actually helping me to deal with stage phobia. I felt more confident than before. After rehearsing for some time we called it a day.

Everyone was busy packing their stuff when Mr. Harshal suddenly came to us.

"Jennifer you did pretty well. I know you would do better. And please think on what I said in the cabin" A small blush made its way on my cheeks remembering Mr. Harshal's words.

"Sure" I said to Mr. Harshal before he turned to talk with other students.

Just after Mr. Harshal went everyone asked in one rhythm,

"What the hell did Mr. Harshal tell you in the cabin, which made you blush so much..?"

God are they planning on destroying my eardrums?!

Austin was acting busy with his stuff but I knew his attention was towards us only, as the guy was packing everyone's belongings in his backpack.

Silly, I know.

"Guys Mr. Harshal wants to go on a date with me." I said faking cheerfulness in my tone.

Knowing the truth others eventually joined the flow.

"Whoa man, finally." Recce said spinning me around.

"The man really has guts to ask you out." River said.

"You must seriously go out with him Jenny. He isn't a coward like others." Beth said indirectly taunting Austin.

Austin was about to get away from us to ignore us like he always does when he has nothing to say but Recce's words suddenly stopped him in his tracks. Though the words were not for him but for Mr. Harshal.

"Mr. Harshal, party at my place today, will you join?"

Recce said with a wink in our direction, as if he knew this will stop Austin from going out.

I must say even devil will lose in front of their evil thinking.

"Why the hell are you keeping a party on working days?" Austin asked surprised even though the way of expressing surprise was different.

"The thing is we are pretty happy with the drama and the drama professor. So we just want to celebrate it." River said with a shrug.

"And as celebration is for the drama, Mr. Harshal has to come" Beth came out of nowhere begging Mr. Harshal to come.

"I am glad you guys like the drama and you want to celebrate your happiness, but professors are not allowed in student's party" Mr. Harshal said politely.

"Aren't rules meant to be broken?" Recce said with a smirk, which meant he isn't going to listen to anybody.

Finally with a sigh Mr. Harshal agreed to come to the party which was just planned five minutes before, which meant we had to do a lot of work now. After Mr. Harshal's departure Austin erupted again.

"Why is Mr. Harshal invited to a party about which I even don't know?"

"Because the party thing was planned just few minutes ago" River said patting Austin's back.

"Why does the party have to be conducted in such a hurry?" Austin asked in curiosity again.

God, why he is asking so much questions suddenly? Wasn't he going somewhere earlier?

"Try to understand my son, Jenny needs to answer to Mr. Harshal's proposal. We are just trying to make that required lovey dovey atmosphere."

Recce said overdramatically.

Austin's face suddenly felt as if something hit him strongly on his face.

God did I just see hurt on Austin's face?

"Do you think they will make a good couple?" Beth asked purposely to throw oil in fire, which was burning in Austin's heart.

With this Austin stared in my direction intensely. His stare was so sharp that I lowered my gaze to protect myself from his anger.

God why he has to be so angry!?

Without saying a single word Austin exited out of the room with total anger.

"Guys why are we rusting in this college, we should be match makers, we do it so well" Recce said playfully.

"Shut up jerk, it was our master mind. You boys are just helping us." Beth stated as if it was obvious. And then began the cat fight between Boys and Girls.

I couldn't control any longer and busted out laughing.

Oh my gosh! they were fighting like nursery kids.

"Yippee. Mission accomplished. You are really great Recce." Alice said vowing to Recce with a small blush.

What the hell is happening here!?

"Don't be confused Jenny, this was all Recce's idea to make you laugh" Beth explained.

Damn I am so lucky to have so awesome friends.

"Yeah, Jenny you look good this way, don't be sad because of that Dumbo's attitude. Everything will be fine." River assured me.

"Guys do you think he will attend this party, as he seemed a lot angry" Beth questioned.

"Austin has to come to the party or else our all efforts will go in vain." Alice said panicked.

"Chill guys, Austin will be the first to come to the party. Note my words. He won't leave Jenny to spend alone time with Mr. Harshal" Recce said confidently.

"Yeah, Recce is Right. Austin will surely come. We now just have to arrange the party in few hours" River said making a few calls to make some arrangements.

Next hour or so was totally wasted in arranging a party. Throwing a party is seriously a hard thing. Inviting everyone, decorating hall, Arranging food and drinks, Gathering proper music, hush its lots of work to do. Thankfully boys had many sources which made our work somewhat easy. And finally, the party was totally arranged.

God I hope the night really goes swiftly and as planned.

* * *

Chapter 26 - Party preparation

I was peacefully sleeping in my room when the two devils entered my room and decided to ruin my sleep. Sleeping beauty consider yourself lucky, you have got to take the longest nap without interruptions. How can that even be considered as a curse? It's a damn awesome boon.

I wish I had a curse like that.

"Idiots why are you waking me up so evilly." I lazily tried to say something like that, rubbing my eyes.

God why am I not allowed to even sleep after such a long tiring day!??

"Human mode Jenny, we don't understand alien language." Guessing by the voice it must be Beth who said this. I was still half asleep.

Gosh by waking me up evilly in middle of my sleep if she is expecting me to be normal, then I must say, she doesn't know me at all.

I was about to fall in my dreams again when Beth mercilessly shook me so damn hardly that all traces of my sleep was long gone and I was wide awake.

Can anyone be any more evil?

I don't think there is any such word like that, but if it is, then it's certainly made for her.

"What?" I asked being slightly pissed.

Gosh, no one has any right to come between my dear sleep and me. But sadly no one understands this.

"The party starts in an hour and here you are sleeping like a pig, so go get ready now." Beth said raising her voice totally ignoring my little anger. I should get used to being ignored by now.

I nodded in her direction and started walking towards the bathroom. I saw Alice beside my closet .She seemed to be thinking about something deeply as she was focused on finding me a perfect outfit. Gosh she looked more troubled than a guy who had bought wrong chits during his exam.

I don't fully blame her.. As finding a perfect outfit for a party in my closet is like finding water in Sahara Desert. I am not a party person and I don't wear much dress. I ignored her and walked towards the bathroom. I quickly showered and cleaned myself.

"Hey Guys," I said peeking my head out of the bathroom door.

"How do you think I should do my makeup?"

"Make it pretty." Beth said sarcastically not even looking back at me.

"Wow!" I stated completely amazed at how unhelpful someone can actually be. So I just kept the makeup reserved for later.

"Let's see what I am going to wear today?" I said trying to be excited .My whole excitement shrunk the moment I saw an outfit laid on bed for me.

God have their minds totally crushed or they are planning to torture me?

No offense to the dress. The dress was actually a pretty good dress. But it was little too small for my liking. It was the dress my Aunt had gifted me on my last birthday. I have never touched it ever since.

Damn why did I have to talk about this dress with Alice. Fuck my silly sharing qualities.

Both Beth and Alice were looking at the dress with full admiration as if it had just fallen from heaven into my closet.

"This is perfect dress for tonight." Alice said jumping happily.

"Certainly" Beth nodded in agreement.

"Whoa I am not going to wear that." I said breaking their dreamy bubble.

"Did anyone ask your opinion?" Alice asked raising her eyebrow.

Gosh why I am not taken into account in anything that totally involves me. This is purely evil.

"Why can't I wear my comfy jeans and a tee like Beth?" I tried reasoning.

"Because the party is specially thrown for you and we don't want Austin to reject you again. So stop blabbering and go change." Alice ordered.

"You have to wear this dress at any cost. The choice is yours; you have to go for easy way or our way." Beth said with a smirk.

I knew their way would be worse, so I silently went to the bathroom to change. Beth did my makeup her way, going for having eyeliner and eye shadow. Alice curled my hair slightly at the ends.

Gosh...I felt like a hooker.

When they finally allowed me to look at myself I was in total shock. The girl staring back at me didn't look like me. For the first time ever, I looked different and surprisingly good. I wouldn't tell them this obviously. This would certainly boost their ego to infinity.

I liked the way I was being tweaked; certain kind of confidence automatically came with this look. Confidence is what I needed badly today. I whole heartedly thanked both of them.

"Austin is surely going to get a heart attack by your killer looks." Alice said with a wink.

"He definitely will not be prepared for what is about to hit him." Beth said with smug grin.

I don't want Austin's topic to start again. It's not like I don't like it or something, but his topic makes me blush a lot and I seriously don't want this happening now So I tried changing topic.

"Guys has any one realized, we still don't know where Recce stays?" I questioned both of them.

I hope in excitement for the party, they didn't forget such important issue.

"Don't worry about that dear. I have called Recce and he is coming to pick us" Alice replied with a shrug. As if calling Recce is quite normal thing for her.

Gosh only for few days I have been out of my mind and it seems like years have been passed since then.

"Seems like I have missed something, huh?" I said elbowing Alice.

"Oh shoot, you don't know about that day right?" Beth chirped excitedly in our conversation. Alice tried shutting Beth's mouth but I must say it was a lame move as Beth easily took Alice's hand away.

"Recce had given ride to our little Alice after school as she said her car was not working. I totally didn't buy this shit though." Beth informed me.

"My car seriously wasn't working" Alice argued.

"And you couldn't call me, right?"

"I was about to call you, when Recce came and offered me ride." Alice tried reasoning again.

"That is not the point. The point is Recce asked Alice's number that day and our little princess gave it. And from that day these both idiots are acting really weird." Beth said explaining her point.

Alice didn't argue further as her cheeks were turning to an extreme color of crimson red.

Oh my Gosh! Alice was blushing which proves everything is damn true.

God I am so happy finally their story is progressing.

Beth was about to continue but the noise of the bell saved Alice from further embarrassment.

Lucky. Such things never happen with me.

As soon as I opened the door, Recce's happy face came in front of me. He looked awesome and fresh as always.

God how can anyone be so fresh after such a long tiring day?

From the moment he entered the house his eyes were fixed on Alice. It seemed like they were communicating through their eyes.

Why didn't I notice their mind-blowing chemistry before?

'Because you were busy with your own life drama', my inner mind reasoned. As if I didn't know that. I felt guilty for being selfish. Their little staring contest was finally disturbed by Beth, clearing her throat purposely.

I saw embarrassment on their face.

How sweet. Gosh I am seriously going to unite them one day.

After regaining his normal jolly composure, "Whoa do you intend to aim and kill my friend giving him a heart attack today?" Recce said playfully shuffling my hairs which caused him death glares from both the girls.

Oh poor boy, didn't he knew that touching girls hair in front of their friends, who practically took lots of efforts on the girl's hair, is a big crime.

He apologized to the girls, which saved him from further wrath.

We were about to leave when Beth's next words surprised both Recce and Alice.

❄ ❄ ❄

Chapter 27-Jealously overflow

We were about to leave when Beth's next sudden words surprised both Recce and Alice.

"Recce, what exactly is going on between you and our little Alice?" Oh my freaking God Recce's facial expression was hilarious.

"Beth, we should get going or else we will be late for the party."

Alice said trying to avoid the uncomfortable situation Beth tried to create to make them confess. Taking advantage of their little conversation Recce fled out of house to his car.

We drove to Recce's house. His house was pretty awesome, just like a dream house. A big house with a garden ahead and security. Man these Guys are pretty Rich.

"Your house is pretty big. How many people will be here? " I asked being little nervous.

"Plenty enough to occupy the entire house" "Recce replied with a shrug getting out of the car.

Many cars were lined up in driveway. Drunken people were stumbling all over the place and loud music was in full swing, typical teenager's party.

God how did they even invite so many guests in such a less time.

"Whoa I must say you guys took this Austin's jealousy plan and party thing damn seriously. But I like it." Beth said patting Recce's back.

Beth seemed pretty happy by this. Parties and late night outs are the things that described her perfectly. We had attended few parties just for Beth's sake.

"Anything for Jenny" Recce said with a wink.

Gosh!! How I did I get so lucky all of sudden? I felt special.

"You guys think Austin will turn up in this party?" Alice asked being worried which caused me to worry even a little on the inside.

"Chill guys. I bet Austin will be already inside eagerly waiting for Jenny's arrival. " Recce said confidently.

We entered into the house. It was bigger from inside and more beautiful, a huge chandelier at the top and rich furniture decorated with suitable artifacts and not to forget the crowd. By the amount of people crammed into this house I wouldn't find Austin even if he was present.

Even then my eyes were shamelessly roaming in the entire party as if it had a mind of its own just for his one glimpse.

Damn!! I was acting like total deseperate.

"Your search for prince charming is over princess. Here I am, in front of you." River said hugging me happily.

Even River looked perfectly awesome. He wore a simple blue buttoned up shirt with perfectly disheveled hair, poking in every single direction and black jeans and sneakers to keep the look up to the mark.

I tried focusing myself on the discussion which was going on between us, but my eyes being the most stubborn part of my body, were still wandering in search of him. River must have noticed my stupid --eyes-searching - Austin -- behavior.

"He is sitting at the bar with a drink in his hand and greedily staring at you from the moment you entered." River said with small crooked smile.

Everyone chuckled at that statement.

But my eyes instantly turned in the direction of the bar. I bet my eyeballs moved even faster than sound.

Gosh he was seriously staring. He didn't even stop staring when I glared towards him. I couldn't express the happiness of that moment in words. I was even above cloud nine.

Cloud infinity?

I hope nothing turns bad now.

Suddenly I felt happier. This happiness certainly needed to be celebrated. I dragged the girls to the dance floor. We danced for half an hour or so on wild songs. We laughed, moved our hips pretending to be seductive but ended up laughing at each other. People rolled their eyes in our direction. But who fucking cared? I was damn happy. Man this was real fun. In the middle, even Recce and River joined us. We were crazily dancing over the best songs. I have never enjoyed so much at a party before.

From the corner of my eyes I could see Austin enjoying our craziness with a smile. We danced wildly until our legs finally gave up. God I seriously owe my friends a lot for such an awesome day.

"Someone seems very happy today, Huh? " Alice asked playfully poking me.

"Isn't it because someone who is not able to keep his eyes away from your beautiful face?" Recce asked with a smirk, which caused my cheeks to heat up instantly.

Man this bloody blush. Why it has to come all the time?

In middle of our creepy conversation Mr. Harshal joined us. By his appearance no one could have told that he is a professor in some school.

Man he looked damn hot and sexy in that grey blazer and his

simple breathtaking smile that gave a heart attack to many girls. No doubt Mr. Harshal's followers are going to be crazy looking at him.

Austin, who was all the time near the bar drinking and just staring at us, decided to join us at that moment, with his drink itself. It than clicked to me, that Austin had been drinking a lot seen evening.

Oh no! Don't drink!

Austin joining us basically proved Recce's assumption right. Austin was just here to know what was happening in between Mr. Harshal and me.

I can't let Austin's expectations fail, how can I?

"Want to Dance??" I asked Mr. Harshal directly interrupting whatever they were talking about, with a big smile. I think the small amount of alcohol I had earlier was finally kicking in. It was good though.

Austin looked up staring into my eyes. Hurt and confusion was clearly visible in his eyes. I felt guilty for acting in such a way ignoring him .My heart cranked a little by his expressions. I wish I could tell him it's always him with whom I want to dance with. But I shook off the feeling knowing that was not possible at least not at that moment.

"Umm...Uhhh" Mr. Harshal stammered.

"If you don't want to dance, you can just ignore the offer." Finally Austin spoke breaking the silence.

Who the hell he thing he is to speak between us?

I don't know from where I gathered up courage exactly but I literally grabbed Mr. Harshal's hand and dragged him to the Dance floor. "Come on. One dance wouldn't harm"

"Fine one dance." Mr. Harshal gave up and followed me to the dance floor.

Oh poor Mr. Harshal. He must have totally declared me officially-mentally- retarded by now in his mind though.

Mr. Harshal placed his hands on my hips and we started to move our body on the rhythm. I was surprised by Mr. Harshal's dancing skills.

From the corner of my eye, I saw Austin angrily throwing daggers towards us and drinking like a maniac.

God why he is drinking so much?

By now I bet he is totally drunk and he would definitely get a bad hangover tomorrow when he wakes up. His bad.

I tried ignoring him and concentrated on the dance.

"You don't want me to live a long life, do you?" Mr. Harshal's words confused me.

He must have sensed my confusion as he continued, "Didn't you see Austin's death glares. I am probably going to die by the time this party ends." Mr. Harshal said dramatically.

I tried acting cool from outside. But from inside my heartfelt lot warmer by his words.

Pretty soon I lost in world of my own, which only has Austin in it. Thoughts of Mr. Harshal Dancing with me were long gone.

I think I had lost my senses and the capability to recognize what I was doing as the little alcohol I had was rushing in my veins and every brain cell I had, was being destroyed.

People were dancing all around us; mostly teenage girls and boys, I hardly recognized anybody. The dance floor seemed to be on fire with the loud blasting music were there was not enough space to dance freely, so it was common to be pushed a little then and now.

Only you knew there were people who were purposely pushing, Pervert Bastards.

Suddenly, someone pushed me hard from behind and the moment I realized it, it was too late. I was in the arms of Mr. Harshal with his one hand around my waist and we were down on the dance floor our faces just inches apart.

Oh my God! Mr. Harshal looked damn attractive from this close view and I was literally drowning in his sexy cologne. Shit Jenny, control yourself.

The people around us stopped suddenly to get a clear view.

Thank god, these idiots have at least this much sense to stop dancing otherwise we would have become fresh human squash, crushed by the other drunkard humans.

Mr. Harshal helped me to get up and asked, "Are you ok Jenny?"

"Uhh mmm ...yeah." I murmured looking at floor.

But the thud sound, I heard the next moment forced me to look up.

Someone got slapped. Who?

My vision was blurry due to the consumption of the little alcohol.

All I saw next was Austin in front of me, with Mr. Harshal having his cheek covered with his hand; eyes almost popped out. The skin near his cheekbone was red with slight finger marks.

Ohh no Mr. Harshal got slapped! Am I too drunk to imagine things or Austin really just slapped Mr. Harshal.

Rubbing my eyes, I opened my them again to get a clear view. I diverted my face to see angry Austin's faces.

Oh god, this little alcohol is a really bad thing, now I can see two Austins.

"How dare you?" Austin literally spitted those rage, on Mr. Harshal's face and he continued again.

"How dare you to even touch her? You are taking advantage of just because she's drunk and dancing with you? You bloody pervert, don't you understand a teacher-student relationship?? Don't you dare to go near her again or I will rip you apart."

Oh my god, the Austin in front of me was a total different Austin. In other cases I would have even liked this Austin. But in case of Mr. Harshal, this was wrong.

With the corner of my eye, I saw Recce, River, Beth and Alice grinning widely and at the same time they were little shocked with Austin's behavior.

I gave them stern look saying, 'you arrogant jerks!' I know this was going to end bad. I shouldn't have approved of the Making-Austin-Jealous-Plan.

But as usual they ignored me and concentrated on drama ahead.

Mr. Harshal was going to speak something, until Austin hit him again in the face, a loud punch. I was able to see slight blood coming through his nostrils.

Oh my God my friends are seriously going to pay for this.

And Austin spoke again,

"Don't justify yourself, don't dare to speak." I was going to interrupt him, as there was a jolt of anger upcoming from inside of me. He overacted. He shouldn't have punched him. He should have at least let him speak his side. He's our teacher, Idiot Austin. Don't you have any respect?

He's getting jealous to a dangerous extent. What if he kills someone due to this jealousy? Oh no!

But my interruption was not taken into consideration, the next moment I saw Austin taking hold of my wrist and dragging me out of the dance floor and we were out of the Recce' house.

Damn...this is really bad...

❄ ❄ ❄

Chapter 28 -Drunken confession

I don't think I have ever seen Austin move so fast, walking us both out of party.

I caught the worried glances of my friends and gave them assuring smile. No matter how much drunken Austin is; he doesn't scare me at all.

In fact I feel the safest when I am with him in any condition.

Palpable excitement bubbled through my chest. The effect that alcohol had on me was long gone

Gosh Austin Parker is more intoxicating than alcohol.

Austin kept shooting glances back at me; as if I am going to vanish at any second. I smiled at him reassuring him that I am not going anywhere.

It's funny how my feelings for Austin are always all over the place. I can go from hating him extremely to loving him the most in just few seconds. That's what scares me a lot.

Once out, Austin pushed me against the wall of an empty corridor.

He leaned forward and pressed his forehead against mine. I know people around were watching us. I could feel their weighty glances but at this point I don't care about it at all.

"You make me crazy", Austin said coming dangerously close.

I know it was alcohol that was speaking and not Austin, but these were the most honest words I had heard from Austin in a long time and I didn't want to lose the moment.

"I love the dress" Austin whispered in my ear and I gasped as his teeth lightly scraped against the skin of my throat.

"But so did every guy present here". He continued driving me crazy with his genetic ministrations,

"I want to kill them all".

"You are feeling murderous today ", He said. I felt his sexy smile against the crook.

Gosh that was the best feeling in the world. I wish I would stop the time forever. Drunken Austin is a lot better than a sober Austin.

"It's your entire fault; apparently you like the idea of me in prison", Austin said nuzzling his nose against me.

I lost train of my thoughts that could blame me for this?

Somewhere between all this I'd been totally lost in Austin's world. Austin ran towards a guy shouting "I am going to knock out your teeth,

Bastard."

Luckily Recce and River along with the girls came out at the right time and stopped Austin from fighting.

Lucky guy I must say.

After stopping Austin from hitting the guy the boys handled the other guys. In that blink of a second, Austin was nowhere to be seen. Now where the hell in this big party can this stupid be?

Everyone went in different directions to find him. After walking in the sweaty crowd again I finally spotted him and man the sight was beyond hilarious!

Austin was on dining table dancing like maniac, swinging his hips from side to side.

People surrounding him specially girls, they were busy cheering him; literally feeding his Texas's size ego and taking his pictures.

God how can this guy turn from totally angry young man to totally happy teenager in just few seconds.

It must be the alcohol. Only Alcohol can do this.

Wiping my phone out I decided to record his miserable dance but then I realized I should probably stop him and prevent his further embarrassment. I made my way towards Austin pushing people aside and pulled him down. Luckily, he came down easily but the idiot was still dancing. I texted everyone about Austin and dragged him all the way out, where everyone else were waiting. I knew Austin was heavy; but didn't expected him to be so damn heavy. Once I reached safely out I removed Austin's hand and left him there on ground, hopefully he could manage to get up on his own as even the last ounce of my energy was totally used up by now.

Luckily Recce helped him get up and sit on table we all turned our attention to drunken Austin who was in his whole world smiling to himself. Pure Devil.

Few minutes later everyone started asking him silly question's as though being so drunk he would seriously answer them all.

I know I have bunch of idiot friends.

I chuckled mentally at their stupidity.

"Oh shut up guys, let's just take him away from party before he goes inside again" I said imagining the horror if he went inside again.

On this everyone started looking at each other's face. As if I just asked them for their kidneys.

I mean was this question so unusual?? I don't think so.

"NO...We can't take Austin home in this condition, his mom will bury us both alive." River and Recce shouted in unison.

After lot n lots of argument it was finally decided that Austin will stay for night at my place.

Oh my poor luck, how I am supposed to handle this drunken Idiot for one whole fucking night.

Luckily Alice sensed the tension on my face and said, "We won't leave until he is asleep".

A little relief crossed across my face.

It took them about five minutes to get Austin inside the car because of Austin, Recce fell three times and even River stumbled few times; trying to make Austin sit inside the car.

Damn that Idiot, he kept trying coming out of car by the window.

Hell, I totally scratch my earlier statement. Drunken Austin is lot more trouble.

Recce took the driver seat and Alice on front. I was well adjusted beside Austin. On our entire way to my home Austin was busy saying ABCD in reverse order and playing drums on River's head.

Seriously I mean who says such childish things when he is drunk, probably only Austin.

The boys had to literally pick him up to get him inside the house.

For about 20 minutes we were busy forcing Austin to drink lots of water so he can pee and finally come to his senses. Finally after lots of water and several pees Austin uttered the three magical words for which we all were eagerly waiting for.

"I Am Sleepy."

Damn these words sounded sweeter than I love you at this moment.

Everybody hurriedly took him to bed fearing Austin would change his mind at any moment. After assuring Austin isn't going to wake up until morning River stood up,

"Sorry Jenny. We have to leave now, as we need to end the party or else by tomorrow that house will be on fire."

"And also we need to clean the house before my parents come." Recce added.

"Even we should get going. Sorry sweetie but it's too late now. Now we won't get any taxi or something. So we need to leave with boys." Alice said

"My house is on opposite. River you leave me and then go to the party. Recce you leave Alice. Enjoy alone time you both." Beth said with wink towards Alice and Recce. I am not sure if I am imagining it, but I could swear I saw a light blush spreading rapidly across Recce's cheeks. He clears his throat seemingly eager to ignore the topic at this point; he rapidly went out of the house.

Oh Jesus, seriously she won't leave any chance to harass them.

With this everyone left the house leaving me alone with drunken Austin. I just hope he doesn't wake up.

Feeling extremely exhausted I directly went to my room. I expected myself to fall asleep in no minute but when I turned the light off and tried to sleep I only ended up tossing and turning in my bed just trying to sleep.

I tried to keep my eyes shut telling myself not to move much until my system finally shuts down. I don't know for how long I just lied down on bed for sleep to come and get me. But sleep was far away from my reach.

Finally as I got tired of trying to sleep I decided to watch some random movie, as sleep was miles away from my eyes. I got out of my room and fumbled in dark for lights trying not to make any noise as Austin was finally asleep after creating lots of trouble. So when I heard some voice say hey the moment I entered living room I couldn't help but throw remote towards the sofa and shriek.

Who won't be scared if at middle of the night they hear some random noises out of blue especially when everyone at home is asleep?

"Oh my God, Jesus .You broke my head "the voice said again. I turned on the light and whirled around to see Austin giving me expression of disbelief.

"You fucking Idiot .You scared the crap out of me." I said with all the anger inside me.

Gosh when the hell is this guy going to greet me like normal people?

"What? I just said hey." He said innocently as if I am going to buy that shit.

"I thought you were asleep Idiot."

"Oh so you thought I am a Ghost huh?" Austin asked with a smirk.

"Not a Ghost, just a burglar" I said with uncertain tone.

"Oh so you decided to use your remote bomb on him?" Austin said with a laug "Jenny what will a thief do on a sofa? Wait for you to wake up?"Austin asked amused.

Though he was right, I didn't want to accept it.

"I wasn't thinking straight" Was all I could speak of.

Ignoring his smartness I spoke, "Why aren't you asleep?"

"Because I couldn't sleep" Austin said with a smile.

"Why are you awake anyways?" He said lifting his eyebrow.

"I am not sleepy either." I admitted.

This is where our conversation ended. I wanted to talk more but he seemed engrossed in deep thinking. From the look on his face he looked little sober. He seemed even sad. I have never seen Austin so sad before. The sad look on his face broke something inside me several times. I desperately wanted to know about what he was thinking but by the look on his face I couldn't gather enough guts to ask him. So I decided to leave him alone.

I was about to leave when he finally held my hand and spoke up "I drank after total three years today"

I don't know why this was disturbing him but by his expression I guessed there was a story behind this. So I sat beside Austin and waited patiently for him to continue. "You know Jenny, once you are hurt, you get scared to get attached with anyone again, because you start thinking that everyone one you love will always end up hurting you. I tried moving away from my past really hard Jenny but I couldn't." His words cut me like a blade. I stared at him and was paralyzed by the coldness in his eyes. He was finally opening me about his past, which I always wanted to know.

Was he rejecting me because of someone in his past?

I wanted the answer for my question.

"I tried to erase her from my mind, but parts of her memories remained, like pencil marks on soft paper that cannot be rubbed away completely. And if you try to rub too hard, it tends to tear the paper apart.

But I was not a piece of paper that could tear apart. Instead, every conscious effort to forget her only made me tear up." He said.

Though he was trying his best to detach himself from words I knew it wasn't that easy for him to talk about his past.

I opened my mouth and the first thing that came out was "Tell me more."

"Three years back I had finally become popular by now, and had gained the attention of the entire school. I was loved by every girl. Most importantly I had started enjoying the popularity like any normal teenager.

Taking advantage of my popularity, I didn't give fuck about anything and everything. Being the most stupid horny teenager, I used to attend every party to find new girls. At one such party I saw Bella. I instantly fell in love with her boldness and happy nature. There was something different in her than other girls. She was just like you totally different or at least she was showing off to be different." He said with a sad sigh.

Placing both his hands on his eyes to avoid eye contact he further continued" I started chasing her from then and came to know from my friends that we were in same school. Soon we started going out. I never had such strong feelings for any girl back then. This was my first time.

I was going through different phase of my life. Late night calls, Bunking class to be with her, early waking up to take her to breakfast, Remembering each and every special day to celebrate just with her had became my new routine. Surprisingly I was in love with this new life changes. The time I spent with her were the best time of my life. It was my first and was going to be my last love. I was ready to commit my entire life.

We were together for one whole year. On our first anniversary I had given a big surprise party. Everyone was invited as I was going to propose her to be mine forever. I was a lot happy as she was with me. But it seems destiny had some other plans for me then." He said fake laughing a little at himself.

"That night, my entire world turned upside down in front of my eyes and I couldn't do anything. I saw Bella kissing someone in front of my eyes and I just stood there watching. My heart shattered into thousands of pieces. Anger filled my entire head. To clear my head I instantly went out of the party. Sadly she never came behind me. I cried a lot that day. But No one listened." He said moving hands harshly over his head.

Fuck I never knew Austin has gone through so much pain.

He continued with cranky voice. "Though I knew I was cheated, my heart was not at all ready to accept it. I was still not ready to forget her.

I decided to meet her again face to face to clear the misunderstandings if there were any. My brain knew there weren't any misunderstandings between us but I wished my heart was right and my brain wrong.

But the moment she entered the hotel where we had decided to meet she came with the boy she had kissed last night. It was confirmed then and there my brain was right. She introduced him as her boyfriend.

The next words that she uttered were more shocking. She said that, "We are together from last three years."

I completely lost interest in love when she said that she had interest in someone after a complete year of our relationship.

My entire world collapsed at that very moment.

I was being fooled for total one year. She used me to become popular and I thought she loved me. All promises which I was wishing to fulfill were all based on lies." After a long pause he said again

"You think I don't get it." He said his fixed on some distant object

"But I do. I know how it feels like when you have given your everything to that person" He paused mid sentence not at all looking at me "Everything you do, everything you say is only for her happiness. In your head you see dreams of growing up with her and living forever."

His tone was even but his words tumbled like he couldn't control them. "You believe that it's her and will only be her"

His words struck me so unexpectedly that there was nothing I could do but stare at him. He was exactly narrating my entire present story.

"And suddenly other person rejects you." I muttered silently.

"And suddenly it's over." He repeated.

I bit my lower lips and avoided looking at him. I couldn't handle seeing the miserable way his shoulder has sagged. I couldn't handle seeing him look like he had just gotten out of the terrible storm that has taken away his will to live.

I could hear struggle in his voice as he continued speaking "From that day I started drinking day and night. I started remaining unconscious all the time to forget all the pain I was feeling. My friends, family tried to sober me and help me to get over it. But all was in vain. I know my entire family was sad and suffering because of me but I couldn't do anything.

I was helpless. I broke all the contact with outside world even with my family."

Tears formed at the corner of his eyes. It made my heart burn a thousands time. I almost wanted to make him stop talking. As it felt like I was ripping apart bandages that covered his deep wounds. But sooner or later he need to open up. He can't keep everything bottled inside him for long time. I crossed the space between us. Wiping the tears I placed my hand on his hand. Surprisingly he placed his head on my shoulder and continued "My mom died because of breast cancer." This was another shocking thing I had heard. I knew Austin's was mom is no more but never knew the reason behind it.

"She was diagnosed in hospital in her last stage. She was in the hospital for three weeks. Even doctors had frankly said there's no chance of her survival. The worst part is that I got to know about her cancer when there was only one week left with her. I am the worst son any mother can have. I was not with my mom when she needed me the most. She used to ask about me daily. But I was damn engrossed in my bloody heartbreak.

Recce and River had tried to tell me several times but I had always ignored them. I wouldn't have even known about my mom's condition if one day I hadn't got call from hospital saying that my mom has only max one week left with her."

He paused for a long time. I tried rubbing his back softly to calm him down, to prevent him from one more breakdown.

"I only got last one week to spend with my mom because of my stupidity which I thought was love I wasn't able to see real sufferings my family was going through. My mom died in front of my eyes. Before dying she asked just one last wish from me 'To quit drinking.'

Today I even broke my mom's last wish. I am a very bad son Jenny.

I am trying very hard to bring my life back on track. But I am totally fucked up. My life has totally messed up beyond repair now." Saying this, most unexpected thing happened. Austin started crying like a baby.

This is not the reaction I had expected from him. For a second I was so startled that I couldn't manage to form any coherent sentence.

Oh my God this was total different Austin in front of me. He was so broken from inside. It was like Austin is not at all the kind of person he tries to show in front of world. There is a little, soft hearted guy who has failed in love who wants to be loved but is scared to fall in love again.

For some time I didn't know what do. I just managed to saying "One day someone is going to hug you so tightly that all your broken pieces will stick back together"

'I just hope that someone is me...' I silently spoke to myself.

I didn't try to stop Austin. I let him cry in my arms. He desperately needs to remove every bad thing about his past from his system.

After a long time he felt asleep again in my arms. This time, a more sound sleep..

AUSTIN'S POV

The moment I opened my eyes, I felt like I was in heaven. Damn I was in room of the most beautiful girl, she was sleeping peacefully on her bed. A small smile crept onto my face. I would have kept staring at her all my Life but the question of how I landed on this sleep sofa was troubling me a lot.

Suddenly all of last night's events came back to me.

Oh man, what the hell was I thinking last night? I shouldn't have given in so easily.

Basically I wasn't thinking at all last night but that's not the point the point is that now Jenny knows everything about my past, which was the last thing that I wanted.

Damn, it had taken me one long year to open up to my friends & in only one freaking night I blabbered my entire history to her, why?

I groaned inwardly, and then I came to my senses when I realized that I just kind of, had mental conversation with myself. That fact is definitely a topic of concern but the more pressing area of concern was my feelings.

Am I really starting to feel something for Jenny? Oh Jesus what's happening to me?

Have you destroyed all your thinking cells Austin? How the hell can you think like this again? You can't just fall in love again. Not after everything that has happened. Your past experiences, with love screwing you up before, you can't fuck up your life anymore. My inner self tried explaining, actually it was trying to prevent me from making the mistakes that I've made before.

The damage that past experiences have made is beyond repair and I don't want any more damage to be done. I can't handle any more pain. So I wrote a note to Jenny instead.

"I am extremely sorry Jenny for everything that's happened in the past. I know that I have harassed you a lot and even broken your heart. I'm sorry. Please believe me; none of it was planned or intentional.

The relationship we had was amazing but I can't give you anything more than this. My life is already fucked up. I don't want to fuck your life up too. So let's just be strangers again. Strangers with good memories"

Last sentence crept a small smile on my face. The time spend with her were really among the best memories of my life. But this had to end before destiny decides to end by his cruel way.

I placed it on the table under the remote. I know that it's going to hurt her a little, but this is the right decision for both of us. I hope she will understand it, and forgive me.

I sighed internally.

Why does my life have to suck so much??

I sighed again and walked outside the house. Luckily, River had kept his car for me outside. I sat inside the car. I took deep rapid fire breaths to clam myself down but unfortunately they had no soothing effect on me.

My head started to hurt slightly. Drinking yesterday was not a good idea at all. My hands started shaking a bit & hot tears started to well up in my eyes threatening to run down my face.

Seriously why am I on the verge of crying? What is wrong with me? I angrily twisted the car keys in the ignition and the engine roared to life. I immediately started driving. By the time I was half way home my car speed was double the speed limit. Lucky for me there weren't many cars on the road nor was there a cop in sight. So the chances of me landing in jail were next to nothing.

I made it home earlier than normal. Luckily my parents and even the little devil weren't home. I used the spare key to enter the house. I took a long, hot shower, with loud music blasting in the background. This was all to keep my mind from wandering to places where it shouldn't.

Thinking about Jenny was the last thing I wanted to do right now. Just for a few minutes I wanted to rest and not think like I used to. But it wasn't successful for very long. My mind was not at all ready to leave the topic of Jenny at all.

Throughout the last few months my life had completely changed.

Gosh why I cant I live a stable and peaceful life?

To shut my mind up for some time, I took a sleeping pill and drifted off to sleep.

The moment I opened my eyes I heard two familiar voices coming from down the hall. I marched towards them to give them my final decision.

Actually one sleeping pill didn't have any effect on me. I was still wide awake after sometime. Jenny had floated into my mind again and again; I couldn't seem to forget about her, so I made my decision about it, and I was about to share it with my friends now.

"I am leaving." I said instantly without even greeting them.

I know that sounded rude but I desperately wanted to tell someone what I had finally decided.

"Missing Jenny already, huh?" Recce said with a wink. Gosh this guy can never think straight.

"Guys I am talking about leaving town and not coming back. As soon as the play ends I'll pack up and get out." I said it all in one breath. My heart started to pound furiously in my chest the moment I finished talking. Phew.. That was harder than I thought it would be.

"Are you still drunk or something? Maybe talking in your sleep?" Recce said while touching my forehead to check for a fever.

Now what's with that? Can't I talk about leaving town in a sober and steady condition?

I didn't say anything. Sensing my silence they understood how serious I was.

"Can we know what's going in that fucking head of yours?" Recce said angrily grabbing ahold of the front of my shirt.

Luckily River, the calm guy of our group, saved me from choking to death by stopping Recce.

"Austin what's the matter, why are you just leaving town out of blue, did something happen?" River asked the same question, he just asked it in a calmer manner.

Damn, why didn't I think of this before? Of course they'd want to know why I am leaving. I can't tell them the truth. What should I say now?

"I am bored of this town. I wanna see the rest of the world, and I can't do that if I'm stuck here."

Seriously Austin?

Are you Dora the fucking explorer now? Let's explore the world now! Why can't I come up with one good reason? Why my mind has to ditch me everytime I need it?

Though this was the most childish reason any one could think of, I was still hoping that they'd buy into it.

"Do you honestly think that we are stupid enough to buy the load of shit you just fed us?" Recce exploded.

"Wait a second. This is because of Jenny, isn't it?" My eyes widened. I looked away from them in order to hide my expression.

"No way guys, of course it's not because of her. It's just that I am fed up with the complications in my life." At least that was a decent answer for once!

"And what exactly are the complications in your life right now?" Recce asked raising his eyebrows expectantly.

I couldn't find a suitable answer to give, so I decided to keep quiet rather than saying something stupid again.

"You fucking Idiot! Why can't you just accept your feelings for Jenny...?"

"Shut up Recce. I don't have any feelings for Jenny." I said raising my voice this time.

I wish shouting it out loud would change the truth. I knew I was lying.

"Stop lying to yourself dude." River said interrupting our heated conversation.

"I am not lying. I seriously don't love her at all. Love doesn't exist at all. It's all just attraction and that lasts for a very short time. After the attraction fades it's just the hurt that's left." I said with all the energy I had.

"Austin you can't live in your past forever. You need to move on. I know Dude sometimes its very hard to move on,,but once you have moved on trust me, you will realize that it was best decision you have ever made. You must know dude all girls are not the same." River tried putting some sense into me.

"Please guys, stop trying to put feelings in me that aren't there. I am heartless. I don't have anything left to lose now and I can't bear the pain again. Please just spare me. I can't move on."

"But Austin...."I cut Recce off in the middle of his sentence.

" If you truly consider me your friend then, promise me that you guys won't tell anyone about my leaving." After saying this I left the room to avoid further conversation.

Jenny's Pov

My eyes widened as I read the note Austin had written to me before leaving. My vision blurred with tears and they started to drip down my face. But I didn't cared. I just sat there and cried my heart out.

Why the hell did I have to fall in love with a guy who wasn't in love with me at all??

If I hadn't fallen in love with him then I wouldn't have been hurt like I am now. Why does destiny always have to play cruel games with me?

I don't understand why I agreed to their silly plan after a massive heartbreak. I was a fool to think that maybe, just maybe, Austin would like me back this time. But I was wrong. He just doesn't have a heart. His past has just made him heartless. But there is nothing I can do about it. I can't just put feeling into his stone cold heart. It's better to just move on now before I develop stronger feelings for him. I closed my eyes took a deep breath. "I will not wait for Austin anymore. I accept the fact that we aren't made for each other."

The rest of the day was a blur. Facing Austin again after everything that had happened wasn't as hard as I thought it would be. He went back to ignoring me. This time the feelings were mutual though. We were both doing everything possible to avoid each other.

Luckily it was him who decided to ditch the lunch table this time.

So at least I had my friends with me. After the party incident Austin had even stopped rehearsing with us. He had started distancing himself from everyone.

I knew why he was ignoring me but I couldn't understand the reason behind his sadness.

He had achieved what he wanted. We were strangers again. Shouldn't he be happy now?

But he wasn't. Anyone could tell just by looking at him that he was miserable. His eyes held a deep sadness. It seemed like he was in a war with himself and he was failing miserably. The fact that he was failing seemed to sadden him even more. Whenever I saw him, he would be in his own little world. He was always concentrating and thinking about something very intently. I knew he was making some important decision about his life, but I didn't know what specific decisions that he was making. Only that he was making them alone. Out of curiosity I talked to Recce, "Do you have any idea what Austin is actually planning. ?" His entire body stiffened for a nanosecond before he relaxed and regained his normal composure again.

"What are you talking about? He must just be rehearsing his lines for the play or something. Leave it alone, lets go to the canteen, I am starving." He said trying to change the topic.

I decided to ask one more time.

"Recce I know you are lying. We are just coming out of the lunch room you can't be hungry again so soon. Please tell me the truth. I'm worried."

Thinking for sometime to himself he finally gave in.

"Jenny, Austin is planning to leave town..."

My entire world shattered the moment I heard him. He was still talking but my mind wasn't able to process his words. It was stuck on the fact that Austin was leaving. I should've been happy knowing that Austin was leaving forever; maybe it would help me forget him faster. But just the thought of him leaving made my legs wobble. From now on there wouldn't be anyone to call me sweet nicknames, no one to send me silly Facebook messages, no one to force me onto his crazy motorcycle, no one to do idiotic projects with me in the middle of the night, no one to have pillow fights with, and no one to make me skip school.

Just the thought of losing him completely made my eyes fill with tears and I felt like holding him tightly and never letting go.

Recce tried to console me but I wasn't in the mood to calm down or understand. I ran away from him and ditched the after lunch lectures.

I ran blindly in the direction that my feet were taking me. The moment I stopped I found myself in the school garden, the place where I gave my first kiss away.

I sat on one of the benches to clear my head trying to grasp the current situation but it was no use. I'd never get used to the thought of Austin leaving.

I cried like a baby while sitting there. Luckily no one interrupted in the garden. I got ready to go rehearsal, as I didn't want my friends to suspect that anything was wrong.

"Good morning class today we will not be having regular rehearsals." Mr. Harshal said entering the playroom. Each and every student had a confused expression on their faces. Their confusion was cleared up when Mr. Harshal continued.

"Today my friend and expert play writter Mr. Malik is going to join us. He has done lots of studying on Shakespears plays and with my begging and pleading with him," the class laughed at this part, "he is here to explain you guys the beauty of Shakespeare' s play today."

A tall handsome guy entered the class as soon as Mr. Harshal finished introducing him. His entery was literally like that of a Hollywood actor, Girls cheering and whistling, the boys stunned and jealous by the personality.

Damn. Mr. Harshal's friends are even hotter than him!

Shut up Jenny. He is still a professor. Though I had controlled my mind many girls were shamelessly staring at him with mouths wide open. I couldn't blame them though. He is seriously worth staring at.

Mr. Harshal later introduced him to us and all the classmates to him. Pointing towards Austin and I Mr. Harshal said to Mr. Malik "Those two are the leads, Austin as Romeo and Jennifer as Juliet."

Ignoring Austin completely Mr. Malik directly said "Damn Harshal. I must say you have chosen a very lovely Juliet. Your play is going to be amazing just by her presence alone. I am telling you."

My knees turned wobbly. I couldn't believe what I was hearing. Those words made me happy to be honest, I wanted to hear those words from Austin.

"Jennifer, you are a very beautiful young lady though." Mr. Malik said.

"Thank you." I blushed. I wasn't really used to those kinds of compliments.

He took my hand to his lips and tenderly gave it a peck. If it was even possible my face turned redder than it was before.

Woah. He was like a typical old fasioned gentleman! Hot and classy!

I tried keeping my eyes away from Austin but they just kept coming back to his eyes. To my complete surprise, I swear I saw his lips twitch into a crooked smile.

Ha! I caught him! He was just pretending to be unaffected. Gosh why does this guy have to be so different and unpredictable?

It's not like I know many guys to compare him to, but I can tell he's different.

Silencing the class Mr. Malik started speaking about the idiotic play. It's not like I don't like this play or anything, but today after a long time, Austin and I were going to rehearse together, but now I can see that it's not going to happen, me and my blasted luck.

"Guys Romeo and Juliet is a beautiful play. It's especially beautiful for teenagers. In this play, Shakespeare is trying to show how young people tend to confuse appreciating something that is beautiful for love. This happens due to the fact that love and beauty are very closely connected."

He further explained, "Confusing appreciation of beauty for love isn't good, and can even be deadly. Romeo seems to have a habit of falling in "love" with beautiful women, and he dies in the end, because of this "love". Beauty can be a difficult concept. It changes over time and people have different opinions of what is beautiful and what is not. In Shakespearean times, a woman was considered beautiful if she had pale skin, light hair, bright eyes, and red lips and cheeks.Women went to extreme measures to achieve these ideal characteristics, plastering their faces with white cream and covering their cheeks in rouge. A fully made-up woman in Shakespearean times would look rather ridiculous today, and even Shakespeare criticizes "ideal" beauty in one of his sonnets. Shakespeare's sonnet is similar to Romeo and Juliet because Shakespeare is showing that beauty is not needed for love, and Romeo and Juliet ends in tragedy for Romeo." Later he started explaining meaning of each an every dialogue. It was then that I totally spaced out. I don't know what I was thinking about exactly but I was definitely not concentrating at all.

I came out of my intense thinking because someone was vigorously shaking me.

It was then I realized that I was unknowingly looking at Mr. Malik because of which he thought I was shamelessly staring at him. Gosh what's happening to me? How can I space out so often?

Coming towards me "it's improper to stare at someone in public." Mr Malik said with a wink.

"Staring at Mr Malik, huh?" Alice said nudging me.

"Stop it guys. I wasn't starting at him! I just spaced out and now he thinks I was staring at him." I hissed at them. "Only you could do something like that, Jenny only you." Beth said suppressing her laughter.

"By the way is his explanation finally over?" I asked changing the topic.

"No dear he's only halfway through. He's given us a fifteen minute break." Alice replied.

"God just help me survive his lecture. No offence to anyone but who the hell explains entire Romeo and Juliet in one fucking day?" Beth said with rising irritation in her voice.

"By the way, where are all the boys? Are they going to skip the last half?" Alice asked.

As if I would know the answer to that question. After the fifteen minutes yes we're counting, Mr. Malik entered followed by the boys. Reece and River entered first and then Austin entered after some time with a smile on his face. I couldn't stop staring at him. God, I miss this Austin so much.

Back off Jenny strangers don't stare at each other so much.

After few minutes without informing anyone Mr. Malik just ran out of the hall like a maniac and never returned. Poor Mr. Harshal went after him to figure out what was going on. Later we came to know that Mr Malik was found in the washroom irritated and sleepy. The principal even had to call the doctor to treat him. God knows what happened to Mr Malik but fortunately it saved us from further torture. From Austin's facial expression I think that Austin is the one behind all of this.

❋ ❋ ❋

Chapter 29 - Time for some real confessions

Austins POV

Seeing Mr Malik leaving the stage and running like manic made me lot happy. I knew he wasn't going to return anytime soon. So I just left classroom with a huge satisfied smile on my face. Damn doing something Idiotic like this after a long time felt really good.

"So you don't like Jenny right?" Recce's demanding voice from behind startled me.

Damn what's the matter with them, now they even started scaring people, great.

By the way why are they again starting Jenny's topics, that too in the school premises?? Did they know anything?? I just hope no.

"Guys why are we discussing about Jenny again, haven't I already made it clear yesterday that I don't like her?" I said annoyed.

"Yeah yeah. We know you don't like her at all. Probably you even hate her. People nowadays just put lunesta (sleeping pills) and Detrol LA (loose motion pills) in someone random's drink for fun Right?" Recce said sarcastically.

Oh shoot! How did they know about this?

"We followed you Austin" River retorted reading my facial expressions.

Damn I should have known they would never leave me alone.

What should I say now? Should I say It wasn't me, maybe my twin. Shut up dude. Think of something practical for once. Jesus why did my brain have to always leave my side whenever I needed it.

"If you don't love her then why are you jealous of Mr Malik flirting with Jenny. Damn he wasn't even flirting he was just trying to be nice." Recce asked again.

I just stayed silent staring at floor. Why can't this Idiot understand I don't have anything to explain.

"Austin we are asking you something. Why did you put that medicines in Mr .Malik's drink?" This time this wasn't Recce demanding.

This time it was River demanding with lots of anger in his voice. River doesn't get angry easily. Which meant I am in deep shit now.

Gosh why of all sudden my two best friends have to turn detective and investigate my love life?

Because it didn't existed before. My inner mind reminded me.

"You know Idiot. Mr Malik was found on toilet seat sleeping."

Epic. Man I wish I could see Mr Malik in that state. This is exactly what I wanted. I couldn't control my laugh so I gave in and finally laughed like there's no tomorrow.

"What the fuck Austin. Stop acting like Idiots and think for once like a grown up. What would you have done if it had turned out in something serious?" River shouted again.

"Chill guys. First of all I knew it wouldn't do any serious effect on him and secondly he deserved it. I can't just let any one flirt with my friends."

Hush finally some sensible words came out of my mouth.

"Friends or just Jenny huh?"

Gosh not again this topic.

"Stop it Guys. Not again"

"Shutting our mouths wouldn't change your feelings dude. Man up and go ask her out."

"Guys I am telling you this for hundredth time. I don't like her. Why can't you just understand?"

"Because your actions aren't proving your words wrong dude" Recce spoke.

Recce had a point. I never knew Recce would come up with something like this. Genius. Is this really the Recce I know?

Like always to avoid the topic I started walking away from them, when Recce spoke "Jenny knows about your leaving, Austin." I froze on my spot.

I didn't want her to know about me leaving as I didn't know how she will take it. Now that she knows I am leaving, was the sadness on her face before because of this? Will my absence affect her so much? Was I really taking the right decision? My mind got occupied with many questions.

That night, the rehearsal was finally at the Playhouse. Principle had finally trusted us by seeing our rehearsals. He was actually happy with our play. It was the last one before the show opened, and we had a lot to do. Right after school, the boys in drama class had to take all the props from the classroom to the Auditorium. Recce and River being angry with me, I had to pair with Samuel, the nerd of our class. The only problem with Samuel is that he's not exactly the most coordinated individual. We'd be walking through a doorway, carrying one of the heavier items, and his body would work against him. At every critical moment when I really needed his help to balance the load, he'd stumble over some dust or an invisible object, and the weight of the prop would come crashing down on my fingers, or on my leg. The worst was when the entire table had came crashing on my pinky toe. God, that literally killed me. With lots of patience I stifled all the cursing rising in my throat and just changed the partner.

Moving the props had taken three hours, and we didn't finish setting them up until a few minutes before everyone else had to arrive.

Soon people started to fill the Auditorium. There was different excitement in the air, everyone was practicing their last minute lines and enjoying this moment. But with everything else that was happening in past days, I was in a pretty awful mood.

In our last rehearsals, Jenny and I ran through our lines without even thinking about them, and Mr Harshal didn't say the word 'marvelous' at all. Actually we didn't present it well at all, but we had our own personal reasons behind it, we weren't in mood of performing at all.

He had concerned look in his eyes afterwards. This play was very important to him and he had given his hundred percent to it. Making this play successful was his dream; I had seen that passion and love in his eyes while Rehearsing.

The night of the play was cool and crisp, we had to arrive an hour early, and I had been feeling pretty bad all day about the way Jenny was behaving. She was sad because of me. I could see a lot of hurt and feeling of rejection in her eyes. She'd never been anything but nice to me, and I knew that I had been always a jerk.

I saw her in the hallways between classes, and I wanted to go up to her and apologize to her for everything in the past, but I didn't have enough guts to do that. My past was constantly poking me.

When I arrived she was already in the Auditorium backstage faking happiness. She was trying very hardly to show everyone that she was fine, she was happy. But I know she wasn't. I wouldn't ever forgive myself for this.

She hadn't put on her costume yet- as I know she was supposed to wear a white, flowing dress to give that angelic appearance. After that, we went our separate ways to get ready. I headed toward the men's dressing room. My costume was already in the dressing room. Earlier in the rehearsals we had our measurements taken so that they could be altered.

"Ladies and Gentleman Riverbank High School welcomes you all!! Today the students of our school are going to perform on Shakespeare's famous play ROMEO AND JULLIET."

I slightly jumped at the voice of Mr Harshal as play was about to start and I was still getting ready. Luckily I am not there in the first few scenes. As soon as I got ready, I came out. The students managing plays along with characters of first act gathered up backstage. Jenny was still in her dressing room when the curtains finally opened. The auditorium was absolutely packed, as Mr Harshal had predicted, they had to set up two extra rows of seats all the way across the back.

Normally the place sat four hundred, but with those seats, there were at least another fifty people sitting down. In addition, people were standing against the walls, packed like sardines. The amount of crowd increased my nervousness. I had never thought this much people will turn out to watch the play but I was wrong.

The play started. Mike and Eddie the characters of the 1st scene entered.

(These are few scenes from Romeo and Julliet)

Act I Scene I

Enter SAMPSON and GREGORY of the house of Capulet, with swords and bucklers SAMPSON and GREGORY, servants of the Capulet family, enter carrying swords and small shields.

SAMPSON (Eddie):

Gregory, on my word, we'll not carry coals.

GREGORY (Mike. The random guy from school.):

No, for then we should be colliers.

SAMPSON (Eddie):

I mean, an we be in choler, we'll draw.

GREGORY (Mike):

Ay, while you live, draw your neck out of collar.

SAMPSON (Eddie):

I strike quickly, being moved.

GREGORY(Mike):

But thou art not quickly moved to strike.

SAMPSON(Eddie):

A dog of the house of Montague moves me.

GREGORY(Mike):

To move is to stir, and to be valiant is to stand. Therefore if thou art moved thou runn'st away.

SAMPSON (Eddie):

A dog of that house shall move me to stand. I will take the wall of any man or maid of Montague's.

At this point I was supposed to make entry. As soon as I stepped on stage, everyone was absolutely quiet. The crowd, I noticed, was mainly old ladies of the blue-haired type, the kinds that play bingo and drink Bloody

Maries at Sunday brunch in short high standard play lover type of people. Though I could see some friends near the back row and few teenagers even, I could even see parents of few play actors. Surprisingly even mine. It was high time now, if you know what I mean, to be standing in front of them while everyone waited for me to say something. So I did the best I could to put it out of my mind as I did the first few scenes in the play, which were without Juliet aka Jenny.

ROMEO (Austin):

What, shall this speech be spoke for our excuse? Or shall we on without apology?

BENVOLIO (Recce):

The date is out of such prolixity. We'll have no Cupid hoodwinked with a scarf, Bearing a Tartar's painted bow of lath, Scaring the ladies like a crowkeeper, Nor no without-book prologue, faintly spoke. After the prompter for our entrance. But let them measure us by what they will. We'll measure them a measure and be gone.

Act I scene 4

ROMEO(Austin):

Give me a torch. I am not for this ambling.Being but heavy, I will bear the light.

MERCUTIO(River):

Nay, gentle Romeo, we must have you dance.

ROMEO(Austin):

Not I, believe me. You have dancing shoes. With nimble soles. I have a soul of lead so stakes me to the ground I cannot move.

MERCUTIO(River):

You are a lover. Borrow Cupid's wings And soar with them above a common bound.

ROMEO(Austin):

I am too sore enpiercèd with his shaft To soar with his light feathers, and so bound, I cannot bound a pitch above dull woe. Under love's heavy burden do I sink.

And the play continued Further. Neither of us blew our lines, though we weren't spectacular or anything. When we closed the curtains for next act, we had to quickly reset the stage. I still hadn't seen Jenny-I guess she was kept away from the stage because her costume was made of light material and would rip if she caught it on one of those nails-but I didn't have much time to think about her because of rearranging the set.

The play was going perfectly fine. The scenes that were without Juliet (Jenny) were not exactly perfect but people liked it at least. The claps were saying it all.

Next was my scene with Jenny. The moment Jenny came on stage for the balcony scene I froze on my tracks. My heart did three sixty degree flip the moment my eye fell on her. My brain was constantly telling me to look away but this time my heart wasn't at all in mood of listening.

My eyes were just struck on the girl who had my heart wrapped around her finger.

Don't even ask me how it happened, because I still can't explain it. One second I was standing there in front of her, staring at her, and in the next second I wasn't. Instead of speaking my actual lines, I took a step closer to her and found myself reaching for her hand. She was shocked by my out-of-the-play act but didn't respond. I took it as signal of acceptance, I took her hand in mine and looked right at her, moving just a little closer. She didn't exactly step back, but her eyes widened just a little, and for a tiny, flickering moment I thought if I am doing a right thing or not and debate about going any further. I paused and smiled, sort of tilting my head to the side, and the next thing I saw was that she'd closed her eyes and was tilting her head, too, and that our faces were moving closer together. And we kissed. Yeah you heard me right. We finally kissed. I have kissed lots of girls in past but this kiss was different and wonderful in its own way, and all I can remember about the moment is that when our lips first touched, I knew the memory would last forever.

It felt so perfect. I felt so perfect. I didn't want to stop ever. The kiss was making my breathing ragged. My heart was drumming against my chest. Kissing anyone, even Bella hadn't affected me so much before. And I am so sure this kiss affect me so much because I am finally in love with her.

I looked in her eyes, smiling with all the feeling I could muster, knowing that I couldn't keep the words inside me any longer. "I love you, Jenny," I finally said to her. "You're the best thing that has ever happened to me. You came into my life when all was dark, and you gave me light to live my Life again. I cant keep this feelings to myself anymore. They say people in love can be foolish, I don't mind being fool for you forever .Please just give me one chance"

❄ ❄ ❄

Chapter 30 - Love in the Air

Jenny's Pov

"I Love You Jenny." My breath literally knocked out of my lungs as I realized what he just said. I rubbed my eyes again and again to make sure I was not imagining things again. Gosh is this really happening or I am just dreaming again? Is this even possible? Did Austin really just kiss me? Damn this seems so unbelievably good to be true.

I was totally confused and in a state of Awe

My poor brain was trying to analyze the data at the speed of 1000 mb/s but still was incapable was encountering what actually the truth was.

I pinched Austin to check weather I am dreaming or not. I pinched him really hard I guess

"Oww!! That hurts" Austin said rubbing the spot.

Oh my fucking Goodness it's real. Damn I still can't believe my luck. I did very weird happy dance in my head. I felt like literally flying in the air I felt so light and happy

Gosh I can't believe this. Austin Parker the difficult and weird guy is actually confessing his love for me. Damn he even kissed me. Wait this being reality means Austin's still waiting for my answer. My heartbeat increased at an uncontrollable speed.

I just hope he doesn't hear it. Damn I should really stop talking so much with myself.

I closed my eyes and replayed everything in my head slowly relishing every moment. I didn't dare to utter even a single word. I was still afraid I would trigger the moment and everything would just vanish like a dream and we would go back to being strangers. I seriously don't want that now.

After gathering enough strength I finally opened my eyes and stared in Austin's eyes. I was still scared that he would start laughing any moment and say 'Jenny I was just joking. You are not my type. Just look at your face. You get serious so easily.' But luckily that never happened.

Instead immediately his eyes flashed my way, they were mesmerizing. My breath was stuck in my throat. I just kept glaring in the endless pool of his deep eyes. His eyes depicted immense sincerity and lots of other emotions which I couldn't encounter. His eyes never left mine even for a second. "Please" he said trying to pour all his emotions.

"I know I have hurt you a lot in the past. But all I am asking is for just one chance to prove that I am totally in love with you and I won't hurt you again. Am I too late for even that one chance?"

I knew he was saying the truth. As his eyes were burning with millions of different emotions.

Oh My God Oh My God…I wish I just don't faint by this over happiness. Finally I decided to respond to his words.

I can't keep him waiting for a long time, right? I just nodded in agreement knowing my voice would just crack if I tried to say something. My heart flustered when Austin smiled. It was his real smile. His signature million dollar smile, it reached his eyes fully.

Damn of all the things I had missed his smile so much. If possible his smile just brightened my day even more. Gosh this is probably the best day of my entire life.

It was like living a dream with open eyes. I wanted to ignore the terrible need arising in me to lean forward and kiss him. But I so wanted to kiss his lips. And before I knew, I involuntarily smashed my lips to his. The flavor of his tongue inside my lips literally made me see stars in daytime. After recovering from the shock of me kissing him he pulled me closer. I could feel his strong abs against my body. The smell of his cologne was making me dizzy. We both were lost in each other. The intensity the passion of our kiss was making my heart beat violent against my chest. I don't know for how long we kissed but this kiss was the different. I don't know if it was really different or it just seemed different because he had just confessed. But it was one of the memorable kisses. We both didn't have any intentions to leave each other's lips but the loud applause of crowd forced us to separate.

Damn it was then I realized that I was in auditorium in front of five hundred peoples kissing Austin.

Hell even my parents saw this stunt of mine. I didn't have courage to face the audience so I just stared at ground intensely. The silly smirk on Austin's face was clearly telling that he was enjoying my discomfort.

Jerk.

By the claps and whistles I can say, the crowd enjoyed our drama even more than Romeo and Juliet.

Though our performance was the best, we didn't win the prize as we didn't performed actual Romeo and Juliet. But who cares. I got the best present I could ever imagine. Better than that trophy and that is Austin, and I never want to lose him again.

Austin's POV

Jenny and I parted just after my confession. I still can't believe, I finally confessed. Man this felt so good. Why didn't I confess to her before? Life would have been a lot simpler.

We went in respective changing rooms to change. Once I entered the changing room I danced and jumped around like a total idiot. I knew there were people outside. I was just very happy to care about anything. I wouldn't be any happier than this ever. I had finally confessed my love to Jenny and she had been so good to forgive me and accept me.

"Woah" finally Recce said giving me tight hug.

Man I missed this Recce so much.

"We are so happy for you dude" River said giving me a manly hug.

"We knew you had feeling for Jenny. But we never knew you could be so romantic" Recce said proudly patting my back.

"Yeah dude that was so damn Romantic and well planned I must say" Recce said happily.

"Why didn't you tell us about the plan before? We could have helped you in this rather than being angry, though this couldn't have been any better." Recce said hitting me on my head.

Do they really think I had planned all this before?

Was I that good?

"Guys nothing was planned before hand. At first even I was confused by my actions. It was my instant reaction after seeing Jenny in that beautiful attire and I am really happy for this." I confessed.

"Really?" Recce asked shocked.

"Man, Than I must say that kiss was awesome" Recce said with a smirk.

"So how did you feel when you kissed her? Man, how do you feel finally after confessing?" River said nudging me with Elbow.

There were no suitable words to describe how I felt. To put these beautiful feelings into words would be like to define them, to quantify them, which means to limit them. There would be a beginning and an end. There is no definition, nor any limit, nor beginning or end to her beauty, or to how exactly I felt after this precious moment. But still I tried explaining them.

"I would be lying to you guys if I told you it wasn't the best moment of my life. I don't know how it happened and from when. But I really love her. I just do." I said honestly.

"We know that Idiot. Weren't we the one telling you this before? "

"After that incident, I had started believing that dreams never come true and that love doesn't exist. What exists is just an attraction, but this quickly changed after seeing Jenny today. The moment I saw her, I felt something happening inside me and then I felt sad for breaking her heart, this proved that it was not just a attraction and that I was actually in love with her. Seriously Guys I am feeling like the king of the world with all my wishes fulfilled. Why didn't I listen to you guys before?" I said happily.

"Because you are a mentally retarded person" Recce stated as if it was a matter of fact.

"You could have just said idiot Recce." I spoke

"Nah that would be like insult of all Idiots, even they understand things faster than you." River said with a smirk.

I just stared at both of them for a good time waiting for them to take their words back. "Dude stare at us for how long you want but that would not change the truth." I heard both of them giggling

"Jokes apart, Austin are you really sure you want to do this?" River asked with a concerned face.

"What you mean?" I asked puzzled.

"What I am trying to ask is, are you really ready to be in relationship with Jenny? Sorry to say this man but if you hurt her one time more. We will smash you" River said in serious tone. You do not want to mess with River. Not at least physically, River the pacemaker of our group boxes. When I say boxes I mean he boxes in national competition of boxing championship.

Yes this dude is fierce.

I took a deep breath and though for few second. What I don't want to be killed by my own friend. So I thought again. Finalizing my answer in my head I spoke "Yeah. I am more than ready for this. Damn I am finally moving on. Aren't you guys happy for me?" I tried blackmailing them emotionally which actually worked in distracting them.

Both River and Recce stared at me a moment longer then they exchanged glances among themselves. They communicated through their eyes for some times and then turned back to face.

"Congratulations dude. You are no longer single." They said hugging me again.

Man they were all acting all girly today.

"So when are you planning to take her out huh lover boy?" Recce said poking me.

"Woah. Slow down guys. Aren't you guys little too excited." I said trying to calm them down. They were literally acting like teenage girls discussing about their first crush.

"Shut up dude. And just answer whatever asked." River said.

This was strange as usually he is not interested in all such stuff.

"What should I exactly do, Shut up? Or speak? Because your sentence didn't make any sense" I replied smartly.

"You know what he means now just speak up idiot." Recce said irritably.

They both wanted to know it so desperately as if their entire life was depended on my answer.

They both continued staring at me with their hungry for gossip eyes. So I finally gave in and spoke up. "Actually I am thinking of asking Jenny out today itself." I said scratching the back of my neck nervously.

"Man I must say you are going faster than metro train." River said with a smile.

"Wait you can't go anywhere. Your parents are waiting outside to meet you" Recce said holding me back.

Oh shoot. I knew mom would never let go of this. She was happier than me when I kissed Jenny. She was extremely ecstatic that I found a girl like Jenny. There was different spark in her eyes, which told that she knew this was going to happen.

"Tell them I have gone for a run" I said instantly.

They looked at me with crooked eyebrows and puzzled expression on their faces as if they were searching for a word worse than mentally retarded. It was then I realized it was a totally idiotic excuse.

"At five thirty? Dude it is not even evening yet." River raised his right eyebrow even more when he spoke.

"That to after such a big confession and show, Are you nuts?" River said without even trying to suppress his laughter.

"Yeah. I need to get in shape." I replied dumbfounded, that was only excuse I could conjure up in such less time.

"You know what you are seriously losing your thinking abilities. But don't worry we will come up some good excuse. You just don't fuck up the things with Jenny again." Recce said patting my back.

Jenny's pov

I returned home after the drama. My parents had to go out for some work which meant I am home alone again. Today I don't regret being home alone at all. It is better to be alone rather than being surrounded by thousands of questions.I decided to take a nap to clear my head. I wouldn't sleep though. Damn how could I even feel sleepy after so much? Thousands of questions where running through my head. I was dying to meet Austin again to check whether it's still not a dream.

With my mind corrupted by many questions I walked towards the door. Thankfully I made it to kitchen safely without crashing into anything I walked over cabinets that held glasses.

"Haven't you heard about the locking the doors when you are home alone?" Voice came from behind me and I instantly drop my glass in sin making a loud clattery noise my eyes widened.

I simply stared in horror at the kitchen tiles before me on the walls not daring to turn around & face the source of voice. If he is a burglar, he may not have weapon with him but if he does that what will I do. I am going to need one weapon to take this guy on.

Where the hell do all the weapons go when you need one? But do burglars even come in the evening? I really don't know. Oh crap I am going to die on the best day of my life itself.

"Jenny calm down it's just me" voice said from my back again

Who is me, and how does he knows my name and address even? Oh my Gosh was he following me for few days to know me.

My breath rate increased at unusual rate."Jenny just turn around now" the voice demanded. I did exactly as he said, afraid for my dear life.

Of all the days I surely don't want to die today at least. The moment I turned around, I saw none other than Austin with his signature smirk.

"Oh my God Austin. You scared the hell out of me." I said placing hands on my chest to decrease the adrenaline rush in my body.

Damn this guy exactly knows how to shock me by being a burglar or by just confessing that he loves me.

Automatically I blushed at the previous memory. At that particular moment I felt extremely infinitely lucky. All the sadness stress anger of being rejected was pushed to back of my head.

God I still can't believe. Austin Parker not only kissed me but also admitted that he loves me that to in front of hundreds of people.

"Who do you think I was?" Austin asked widening his smirk

That really lovely cute smirk of his brought me to my senses.

" I thought you were some sort of burglar" I replied honestly.

"You and your burglar stories" saying this he chuckled softly at my idiocy coming closer towards me like the weird and useless person that I am l just stood there extremely still. I could have even walked towards him, but no, I just had to turn into a statue. With a gentle tugging of his finger he pushed me back against the edge of Kitchen Island then as if I am not already having a heart attack because of his simple touch he stepped more forward and closed distance between us. My lower back was now pressed against the counter stop & Austin held both sides of my waist with care & delicacy. Without warning, my breath glitches when I gazed up at him.

The mesmerizing handsome guy in front of me took a deep breath as his beautiful eyes closed & opend to pierce mine with an emotion of pureness and truth. He opens his mouth to say something but there's nothing but silence for few moment.

"I" he starts never fail to keep perfect eye contact.

"Austin what?"

"Look, in the auditorium, I mean don't say 'you like me' back if you don't mean it" he said it all in one breath.

"Well I meant it Austin and you knew that I was going to say it" My heart beat increased due to sudden built up of nervousness.

Austin eyes were now only focused on mine. His breathing was heavy & mingling like mine.

God I have been waiting for this moment for a long time. But I couldn't form correct words. I was simply frozen and immobile.

With lots of guts I stared straight in to Austin eyes.

"I love you too Austin".

And next few moments of my life were probably the best .Why? Because Austin smiled at me. His real amazing breathtaking smile with his eyes showing happiness that I had never seen on his face before.Hell if Austin wasn't in front of me, I would have been jumping up and down doing cartwheel all over the place Damn how I get so lucky all of the sudden?

* * *

Chapter 31-Sudden Date

"So will you um mm come on a date with me?" Austin said looking down at a floor shyly scratching the back of his neck. When the words left his mouth I gasped instantly. I could feel my nerves tingling like being tickled with a small feather.

Gosh was this happening for real? Damn I have never seen this guy so uneasy before. He was so nervous that I had a feeling he would start biting his nails like a little girl anytime now. It was my turn to smile now.

"ls Mr. Romeo nervous huh?" I teased.

Austin scoffed.

"No. Not all" He said confidently, but I could still sense the nervousness in his hazel eyes. "And I prefer Mr. jerk ass more" He added further.

"Well Mr. jerk Ass, unfortunately for you..." I started purposely with negative sentence and I could see disappointment filling in his eyes slowly. Damn seeing my words affect on him made me happy internally.

Evil I know.

But now I can at least say we both are sailing in same boat, which felt good though. "I would love to go out with you, Austin." I finished the sentence grinning ear to ear at him.

His eyes immediately brighten up like 440 volt bulb. He smiled with happiness and amazement.

"I am feeling like the happiest guy on planet." He said pecking my lips softly. Gosh it was so damn good.

I literally craved more for his lips on mine the moment he left my lips. I know I am getting a lot needy. But no one I bet, No one can resist this awesome Guy in front of me, I bet.

"Now don't get all mushy on me." I teased.

"Oh princess, I' am far away from being mushy and soft and you know that." Austin said winking at me, causing me to blush crimson.

Damn why I have to blush at everything he says?

I seriously need to get used to this before I die of over happiness.

"But where to go?" I asked curiously changing the topic to prevent myself from further torture. "A secret place you would certainly love" Austin said confidently opening the passenger side door for me. I just stood there in awe. He had never I mean never in his entire life opened door for anyone according to what I have heard. And this was surprisingly second time for me.

Gosh I feel so special already.

He smiled at me sweetly, as I slid into car.

Weird again but certainly good type of weird, I wish this smile never fades.

It was strange, as this Guy usually doesn't smile ever. Just has 'I don't fucking care about anything' expression stuck on his face all the time.

This day is going like a dangerous but interesting roller coaster ride I must say.

After the car started Austin grabbed my hand in his and hold it as he drove. This was the sweetest act I had ever witnessed. His mere touch made thousands of butterflies erupt in my stomach. He had never been so sweet to me in the last few days at least. So everything was fucking killing me like hell from inside though I was trying to act a lot calm from outside.

"We are here" Austin said excitedly like a child outside the fair. We got out of car and I must say I was totally awestruck by the scene in front of me.

We were on the top of the big cliff away from the actual noisy world. It was surrounded by lots of trees and below us was beautiful ocean and above us was never ending sky which looked damn close as if it was just one touch away .

God I was literally having the heaven experience. It looked so beautiful like a dream destination

"Beautiful isn't it?" Austin asked softly coming dangerously close to me.

"Yeah." l said in a breathless manner.

The sight in front of me was something you will find in pictures and paintings and movies l never thought l would ever see something so beautiful like this in my real life. "Like a dream." I added

"I know" Austin said looking directly at me "It's just like a dream" he said and smiled happily.

The sincerity in his eyes made me to forget the beauty in front of me. For a second I was just lost in his mesmerizing eyes.

I so damn wish this is not a dream. I don't ever want to lose something so beautiful as this.

Breaking the eye contact he slid onto the hood of his car and sat. I followed after him and sat next to him gazing out to the beautiful sight in front of me. In the middle of enjoying the nature involuntarily I placed my head on his shoulder. He wrapped his hand around my waist and pulled me closer to him.Gosh this was picture perfect moment, just Austin and I under the never ending blue sky.

Both of us stayed silent enjoying the scenario. It was a comfortable silence. Only the sound of Austin's rhythmic heartbeat was audible to me.

The sun was slowly going down the horizon. As it went down, the burning light of the sun got dull and it looked like a huge disc of orange and yellow. The sun's orange was mingling with the light blue color of the sky and it produced a vast contrast of different colors.

It was like watching a large screen slowly and beautifully changing its colors. The scene was truly breathtaking. The dull light of the sun somehow illuminated everything in a way I had never seen them before.

Everything was almost still and the effect of the light made the scene looked like a painting. The sun was gradually going down and by the time it almost disappeared. The sky had patterns of different colors, from light purple to a dull blue. The scene looked mesmerizing.

The birds were also chirping and flying away to their homes, which completed the scene of a perfect sunset I had always read about in books. This was so damn beautiful. I was totally lost in the beauty of nature.

Without looking at me, Austin dragged me further into himself and softly placed a kiss on my forehead, which made me melt a little on the inside. "I had developed some feelings for you from the day you hurriedly crashed into me in the hallway of school itself, but l was too idiot to realize its love then." He said all of sudden which drew my attention to him.

"You crashed into me." l said interrupting him in middle.

I know it was a lame comeback. But what can I say I like to ruin everything that's going perfectly fine

It's just my official work.

"Will you let me finish at least?" Austin said slightly annoyed that I interrupted him.

I smiled sheepishly at him. "Sorry, continue"

Austin rolled his eyes at me but continued anyways. "Well since that day you have been on my mind like a virus, 24×7. You were slowly destroying my system. I couldn't sleep that entire night just because of you. It was starting to irritate me that l couldn't stop thinking about you. You had literally made my heart and mind against each other.

Something about you had made me curious, maybe it's the way that you didn't care about who I was, or maybe it was because of the confidence you had shown that day, or maybe because of all our fights and your idiotic comebacks" He said smiling to himself which even brought a smile on my face.

"I don't know what but there was something about you that was making me insanely crazy about you. I am still crazy about you. I have seriously never thought about anyone so much." Austin was fully engrossed in thinking by now.

The fact that Austin used to notice me even back then, widened the smile on my face .I wanted to tease him but I didn't dared to interrupt again as I wanted him to continue. Don't get me wrong but this guy takes very long time open up. "I started carving for your company from then.

The time I spend with you started becoming the best time of my day. So I always tried spending more time with you. I felt like I needed to be around you more for my dear life, if l didn't see you l felt almost incomplete. By being with you I started feeling alive, happy and young again. I started living my life again.

Then that project we had where we had to work together brought me even closer to you. I found myself thinking about you more constantly. In my entire life I had never given priority to completion of any sort of project but just because I would get to spend some extra hours with you, I came to your house sacrificing my dear sleep and let me tell you, I don't regret it at all." He said with a large smirk, which lasted for just few seconds though.

"The dinner with our families showed me a different side of you. I thought messing up with you in front of our parents would scare you away but you didn't get scared instead you stunned me by your next move and that pulled me towards you more. I started comparing you to all girls of our school and surprisingly you always came up to be much better than any of them all. I started falling for you more and more. Consider yourself lucky" He said with a smile on his face.

Gosh his each word was literally accelerating my heartbeats. I was literally flying in the sky by now. Gosh I have never been and I bet never would be so happy like this, ever. I was literally living the best days of my Life. The last sentence was extremely true; I do consider myself really lucky.

"Entry of Mr. Harshal further cleared my feelings for you. His constant flirting, your interest in him literally boiled my blood from inside."

This was new information for me, I couldn't control myself anymore and I finally gave in "Oh Wait. Who told you I was interested in Mr. Harshal?" I asked confused. "Your actions towards him was enough to make me think that you like Mr. Harshal. And then I heard you were going to propose him. Just the thought of you being with someone else made me uncomfortable."

Oh so our plan was actually working I mentally noted to myself to thank the guys later.

Austin further continued "I used to always think why I get so uneasy seeing you with somebody else when you are not even mine?

My question was answered when you kissed me in the Garden of school.

Damn that was one of the best kiss of my entire life. That kiss changed everything. I would always remember that moment, as at that moment my all doubts were cleared. I became hundred percent sure of my feelings for you.

"Then why do you reject me?" I asked curiously returning my attention to Austin.

"Firstly, I was a lot happy to know that you feel the same for me. All the feelings that I had bottled up inside my heart started emerging out again. I started feeling like you are the one for me. But I didn't have the guts to accept my feelings. I was scared to fall in love again, as it is damn easy to find someone who makes you so happy. You start giving them all your attention because they make you forget everything bad in your life.

They are the first person you want to talk to in the morning and the last before you sleep. It all sounds great to be with that someone, but it is scary to think about how easily they could just leave you and take that happiness away too when Ever they want. I didn't want to give the control of my heart to anyone again. Time heals all wounds, they say, but heartbreak is a wound deeper than most. Emotions can range from profound sadness to intense anger to utter emptiness in the course of a single day, which is exhausting. Having to face the person you loved at school or elsewhere can be excruciating and draining. Crying yourself to sleep might even become part of your daily routine. Most of the time, it seems impossible to find the strength to just let go and move on. I didn't want to experience this all again.

It literally crushes your heart to a thousands pieces and its damn painful, trust me. I thought acting like you didn't exist would help, but it absolutely didn't help at all. Although I was ignoring you all the time, my mind was constantly busy thinking about you. I used to always keep a watch on you from far. I didn't want to break your heart after knowing my feelings for you but I felt I was not right for you. So I started maintaining distance.

That was the worst period of my life. I was dying from inside every day. The thought that this rejection isn't affecting you at all just broke my heart.

Then I saw you and Mr. Harshal close to each other during the party and I felt a piece of my heart fall to the pit of my stomach.

His flirting and talking with you used to kill me every day. So at the party I finally gave in and punched him. I know, I shouldn't have done that. Even I realized that later but till than it was too late. The harm was already done. Though you were not my girl then I still couldn't see you with anyone else. At the party I came to my senses and understood I am in love with you a lot and can't live without you." He said glancing at me straight in the eyes. I bet my cheeks were a shade of dark crimson when he looked at me.

"But I thought it was too late by then. I had realized my mistake later. I know I should have said a yes then itself. But I just couldn't. By seeing you always happy with Mr. Harshal used to make me sad. I didn't want to make our lives complicated again and wanted you to be happy always. And me being the jerk I thought you couldn't ever be happy with me so I decided to leave the town forever and go away from you after the play.

That was the hardest and most foolish decision of my life." He added sadly.

Seeing him sad broke my heart.

Though I knew about it, hearing it from Austin's mouth made it seem more real. A small tear involuntarily rolled down my cheek. At that moment I realized how dull my life would have been without Austin. I mentally thanked God for his change of mind. I really wanted to know the reason behind his change of mind.

"What caused you to change your mind?" I asked with low shaky voice.

"Don't ask me that, because till now even I am confused about it. Before the play I had completely set up my mind to just leave for good as soon as the play ends. But the moment I saw you on stage I completely froze. I couldn't think of anything else but you. By now my subconscious mind had fully taken over the control and then I kissed you. Even my brain realized then that you weren't just a friend but very much more than friend.

You were the person that broke down my hard exterior and saw the real me, you were the person that didn't care about my past, and you were the person who l trusted more than River and Recce. You were and still are the person I love. And this was the last chance for me to express my feelings. So I let my subconscious mind take the next steps. I am so glad that my subconscious mind took over or else I am a hundred percent sure I couldn't have done anything like this. I really love you a lot Jenny. I know sometimes I mess up and do things that make it seem like I don't care but trust me you are my entire world."

By now tears had started freely falling from my eyes. Gosh who wouldn't cry at this? Staring straight into my eyes, wiping the tears Austin said "I Love you a lot Jenny, really I do"

"I Love you too Austin. Without you my life would have been completely dull and meaningless. You fill bright colors in my life" I finished off looking at him with a smile.

It felt really nice to finally speak up my feelings in front of Austin. Today was really a big day. By now it was almost dark.

"One of the best kisses you ever had huh?" l asked as the smirk on my lips stretched trying to lighten the mood after so many confessions. I can't let my Boy be sad. And it actually helped.

I saw a faint blush creep up onto Austin's cheek. Gosh this boy seriously looks awesome with his cute small blush, even more awesome than a blushing bride. "Did l say that? I mean.. Uh, urn." l giggled softly at how flustered he looked. He rubbed the back of his neck nervously. "Fucking hell, yes, I agree that was literally the best kiss l have ever had, Happy."

I patted his hand "It's okay. I know I'm a good kisser. I have heard it from many Guys." I teased.

Austin's eyes turned into a size of Soccer ball. "Who else have you kissed?" Austin said it all in one breath itself.

It was hard not to laugh at his expression.

God he was so damn curious to know. But l kept a straight face. "Sweetheart, you know you are not the first guy I am kissing right?" I said, mocking him with a smirk on my lips.

Austin grunted and muttered something under his breath that I couldn't quiet catch. "Can we leave now?" He asked. "Or are you going to continue talking about all the guys you kissed in the past." He growled out. "Is that jealously I detect? Oh My Gosh is Mr. Jerk ass jealous?" I fake gasped. It fun messing with him. Hey he's been doing it to me ever since we met! It was time for my revenge and boy this is real fun.

"Me and jealous, whatever..." He said straight forward but I could tell he was jealous.

"You so are jealous of all the other guys l kissed. Let me tell you they were all awesome kissers, especially my first kiss with guy that I had met in eight grade was mouthwatering." I played on as l pretend to try and remember.

"Will you shut up as I am not at all interested in your crap?" He bit out.

"Well if you are not interested then why do grunt on my mentioning of first kiss?" I retorted smirking widely.

"I was surprised!" He tried defending himself.

"By what?" I asked with a raised eyebrow.

"By the guts of the guy who dared to kiss a nerd like you" Austin said with a smirk. This guy will never improve. You don't even want him to improve my inner voice said which was actually true for the first time.

I smacked his chest lightly which was of no use, as he didn't even feel it. All of sudden Austin got off the hood of car and I literally gasped again for second time today when he knelled down beside me, taking out a small black box from his back pocket.

"Austin." I whisper as my jaw dropped in utter surprise.

"Shush Please don't say anything and just let me talk. I have not done this in a long time and we can go slow because l don't want to rush you into anything." Saying this Austin opens the small box and I gasped again as a stunning silver ring with a heart saying, 'A promise' comes into view.

"Now l know you are little surprised to see this ring. But l just want to promise you that l will change for the better. I will move on from my past and never look in my past again. I will totally change. No spreading rumors. No running away from situations. Nothing because as cheesy and cliché as this may sound, l need you in my future and l really want us to happen so will you do me the honor of being my girlfriend?"

With a hand over my mouth, a silent tear slides down my cheek and l stay frozen in my seat. "Austin." l breathed against my hand, not knowing what to say. This was the best moment of my life. I didn't know if it would work or not, but I wanted to take risk.

In my entire life I had never thought I would fall in love with someone so different and so stupid and indeed he will love me back. It was like unexpected dream coming true.

"I would love to be your girlfriend." I said sliding down the hood of car.

Jumping up from his knelt position spun me around happily.

"You said yes! You actually said yes. Damn this is so unbelievable. I promise I would never let your expectations break. I would always be with you forever and ever. Damn I will even change for you."

He said happily.

"I don't want you to change for me Austin. I love you and it means that I accept you for the person that you are, and that I do not wish to change you into someone else. I love you for who you are and I accept you as you are.

I will love you and stand by you even through the worst of times I know your deepest secrets and do not judge you for them, asking in return that you do not judge me for mine. I love you enough to not to let go." I spoke proudly.

He smiled widely before leaning down and crashing his lips against mine. The kiss was sweet and filled with passion. When we both pulled away we were breathless. Austin took my left hand out, removed the ring from its cushions and put it on my ring finger as he stared into my eyes with a wide smile.

"Is this actually happening? My heart is beating faster than l have ever felt it before." I told him and he smiled widely "It's actually happening, dear." He said kissing my forehead.

Surprisingly later he took out another box from his other pocket. "Now what?" I asked,

"This is for me. It connects with your ring." He said opening the box and I smiled as box had bracelet that said, 'I will be here forever'.

"Want to see?" He asked and I nodded my head."Give me your hand."

Holding out my hand in front of him, he flipped it and connected the heart with the bracelet, completing the statement. "I'll be here forever, I promise." Austin whispered and a happy tear slides down my cheek before I throw my arms around his neck and kissed him with all I had.

"Oh and about the guys I kissed." I saw Austin's jaw clench again. One part of me still wanted to continue the game. But I gave up finally "They don't really exist, you were my first kiss." I said giving his hand a small squeeze.

❄ ❄ ❄

Chapter 32-Morning full of Revenge and Embarrassment

"Good morning sleeping beauty" I heard a pleasant male voice and felt warm kiss on my forehead. Since I am the only person in the house, I thought I was dreaming about Austin again. "Stop haunting me in my dreams all the time Austin" I said with a groan & tried sleeping again. Turning around the opposite side. But I heard the voice again saying, "Wake up lazy bones."

What's with the names? Can't he at least say my name in my dream?

It clicked me then that maybe it's not a dream. So I lifted a pillow and thrown in the direction of source of voice in hope that it will shut up. But I was wrong it spoke again.

"Please leave me alone Will you" I said or at least I tried saying something like that. The voice remained silent for some time & then I heard strong muscular voice shouting in my ear. Oh My God! I sat up instantly faster than Ninja, my hair sticking in all direction possible.

I reached for the source of voice who gave my poor ear heart attack so damn early in the morning. But the source was nowhere near me instead I witnessed Austin lying on the floor laughing with all energy he had. His guffaw echoed in the large room.

"You?" I said with all anger boiling in me.But he wasn't scared of it at all.

"You must have seen your face. Man it was damn hilarious" He said between in laughs.

"You will pay for this. Mark my words" I said with same anger which made him to stop laughing.

I thought he finally noticed my anger. I was about to pat my back proudly but by then he again started laughing. This time more intensely.

"Jenny you don't know how to be angry so stop making fun of yourself"

I just kept staring blankly on his laughing figure.

What is seriously the matter with this guy the amount of energy & freshness he contained, even after sleeping literally in the morning was astounding.

Gosh! How can this Guy be so fresh & energetic all the time. I always feel is like I haven't slept for months or even years even though I sleep all the time?

Coming to my senses, I lazily started making my way to washroom. Before my poor mind could encounter what was actually going I was pinned to bed with Austin on top of me.

Dang! Does he want me to die today of heart attack?

How can he even do this? For one moment he was on the floor laughing till literally tears coming out and the next moment he is on top of me just inches apart totally serious with lots of love in his eyes.

Gosh this is why I love this guy. No matter how much he irritates me at the end of the day he would still do something that would melt my anger completely.

Utterly aware of our close proximity my heart beat increased rapidly. I guess he heard it as I saw a small smirk on his perfect soft lips.

Just to irritate or tease me more he leaned little further just inches apart from my lips directly staring into my eyes our noses were literally touching. I desperately wanted one of his addictive kisses. But he was acting mean, just playing with my urge.

MEANY

Not able to control my urge of kissing him anymore I finally gave in and kissed him like there is no tomorrow. God what happening to me I never was so greedy for kisses what will he think of me, pushing all thoughts aside I started enjoying kiss after little shock he finally started kissing back.

Damn the kiss just made my day brighter. Even if I kiss this guy 1000s of time I still wouldn't get use to it. It always brings whole idiotic troops of butterflies in my stomach.

I sometimes wonder when butterflies fall in love do they feel humans in their stomach? I know I am weird. But that's my second name.

"Needy much huh ?" Austin said with a smirk "If you just wanted a kiss so badly you could have just asked, no need to be so aggressive" Austin said innocently coming near me again. My cheeks were already in color of bright red. Austin was fully enjoying my discomfort I could see amusement in his eyes.

"Calm down dear, I am just kidding. Damn you blush so easily"

Luckily he dosen't embarrass me further and started kissing again, this time with lots of passion and love. As if he was trying to show me his love thorough kisses.

I pushed Austin away and stood up all of a sudden remembering about morning breaths. Eww I must be smelling worst. I witnessed confusion in his eyes poor guy.

"Still angry about me waking you up early Huh?" Austin said with irritably.

"And even though you are, you just cant live me in middle of kissing. I want to complete that kiss. " Austin said stubbornly coming close to me again.

Darn he looked so cute and innocent. It took my all will power to not to kiss him again.

"I surely am angry but I will take revenge of that next time."

"Then what happened to you now?" Austin asked confused.

"Hmm I haven't brushed yet" I said nervously "And I must we smiling real yuck" I admitted.

"Oh so that weird smell is coming from you. Damn you seriously stink like shit" Austin said dramatically placing hand on his nose. I just stuck my tongue out and ran in washroom.

I heard him shouting from behind "Calm down Jenny I was just joking."

Shutting the door behind me a small smile tucked on my face. No morning in my entire life have been so special.

How did I seriously get so lucky to find a soul that perfectly grooves with me.

Today officially is the first day of me being Austin parker's girlfriend. God I was on cloud nine.

All yesterday's memories flashed in front of my eyes and my smile turned into a wider ear-to-ear happy smile. Gosh I had never being so happy in my life. I just wish the happiness stays forever. Austin stays with me forever.

The mere thought of him was enough for driving me crazy. I brushed my teeth and took a quick bath to clean myself hurriedly to meet Austin soon but when I came out I was met by silence.

Austin was no where in sight I searched him in the entire room. I thought he must have left. When I didn't find him I dressed putting more effort to look a little better as today I was in total mood of dressing up.

I started walking towards kitchen for breakfast. When I reached; I was shocked seeing Austin in kitchen preparing cup cakes for me. The smell of cupcakes itself was mouthwatering.

Aww how sweet.

He had gathered all the ingredients around him and was preparing some more.

Dang is he preparing cup cakes for the whole country.

I know I am probably over exaggerating but they were really in ample amount. I was about to interrupt his baking when morning incident flashed before my eyes. No one can wake me up absurdly & breath peacefully ever after.

I needed revenge and this was golden opportunity to take my revenge. With an evil smirk I grabbed the nearest ingredient I can lay my arm on, it was flour luckily. I poured it all overs Austin's head. Austin froze on his place as flour slide on his body. I almost choked from laughing. Damn his face was so shocked. I wish I could take his picture. It was so damn awesome.

I was so busy in laughing that I didn't noticed Austin had a whole gallon of milk in his hand before I could even encounter what was happening, I was totally wet with milk. My laughter came to an immediate halt.

"Did you just ruin my hair?" I yelled.

"Sorry to break your imaginary bubble but I just did princess" Austin said with smirk.

I picked up the jug of ice cold water instantly from the table & poured the entire content over his head "Oops" I said smirking "slipped. Sorry".

"Oh I bet you did it on purpose" Austin shouted shoving hands in cupcake batter & launched it on my face. It's when the hell broke loose we were running in entire kitchen throwing whatever came in our hands at each other and laughing like retarded people. At one point Austin got a can of whipped cream & squirted it on top of me for that I threw broken eggs on him with a satisfied grin.

In between laughing & running around the house like idiots, we had totally forgotten about the time

"Woah! did Earthquake personally visited your house?" Beth's shocked voice brought us back to the real world. All the guys were behind Beth with somewhat same shocked expression as that of Beth except Recce. He had a smirk on his face as if he knew what exactly happened.

"Having fun love birds?" River inquired grinning at us flashing his shiny white teeth after recovering from shock."Damn it Guys, if we wouldn't have interrupted them right now they would have been kissing like there's no tomorrow" Recce said with dramatic sad sigh. It was then I became aware of our awkward position. I was standing literally glued to wall and Austin was dangerously close to me. Though we were not at all about to kiss but it surely did seem like it.

"You can still witness it now" Austin said with a smile. His words confused me. I didn't know what he exactly meant. I was about to ask him when he was suddenly kissed on my lips in front of everyone.

I heard woos from everyone. Way to makes it more awkward I just hid my face in Austin warm chest to avoid the embarrassment. But Austin was not affected at all he must be used to this kind of teasing "Is anyone among you really gonna tell what exactly happened here??"

Alice's curious question luckily attracted everyone's attention but It wasn't for long time. Eventually everyone's attention turned back to us.

I kept my head down to avoid eyes contact from the corner of my eye I observed Austin. His hair was wet due to water and he had turned to ghost white color like due to the flour. He was totally drenched in multi color ingredients. If I hadn't been covered in food myself then I would have laughed wholeheartedly.It seems like even all were observing us for few time as suddenly the room was filled with laughter of four idiots standing in front of us. "You guys look damn funny" Recce said in between his laugh not even trying to suppress it.

"This is entire your fault." I accused glaring at Austin.

"My fault?" Austin replied shocked.

"Weren't you the first who flicked flour on my body?"

"That" I said "was because you woke me early in the morning, jerk" I shouted getting something of my shoulder & ready to throw back at him.

"Woah, Seriously?" River butted in "We don't need another room to clean up Guys."

Damn he has to be always right.

My thoughts was cut short as I suddenly heard snapping sound from some where.

"What are you doing? " I asked cautiously watching a voice fidgeting with her phone.

"Taking pictures, Dumbo" Beth retorted.

"Of?" I asked suspiciously.

"The cutest couple ever" Alice said dreamily.

The blush instantly crept on my face. As if this whole situation wasn't embarrassing enough.

To avoid further embarrassment, I huffed and spun around walking back to my room. Austin obviously not taking me seriously, laughed and jogged after me.

I took a bath and washed my hair to remove the oiliness, for second time in one hour. I walked back to the kitchen. I was shocked to see Austin already changed. I was just going to ignore all the demons in my kitchen laughing at our rebellious work but the grumbling of my stomach reminded me of delicious cupcakes.

Who the hell would say 'No' to cupcakes? Surely I won't.

I entered the kitchen searching for the cupcakes. I heard Beth saying "Damn Austin you prepare world's best cupcakes." I felt my mouth instantly watering. My urge to eat cupcakes increased more. Alice's next words just broke my heart. "I wish there were some more."

What the hell did she mean by this?

Didn't they keep even one cupcake for me? No this cant happen. I still kept searching.

"Sorry Jenny, but if you are looking for cupcake, then it's of no use this is the last bite of the last cupcake" Recce said shoving the last bite of Cake with extra chocolate in his mouth. I helplessly watched my last cupcake go into Recce's wide stomach.

What did just happen? Weren't they prepared for just me at the first place? I just stupidly stared at everyone's face. They just actually ate all the cupcakes without me? I glared at Austin for long time expecting some reply from him but he just sat there with amusement plastered on his face. God can this day get any worst?

I just angrily grabbed the apple from fridge and went to my room leaving all mess in kitchen as it is. When I don't get anything to eat, why should I even clean the mess right? Apparently it turned out, no one cares about me so after spending little time in my room waiting for someone to come and apologize, swallowing my self pride I shamelessly went down myself to check out if anyone's even there or not. Luckily the kitchen was clean & everyone was gathered around Recce; who was reading a book.

A book Seriously they chose a book over me? How special the book must be. I never even knew boys have interest in reading a book. I went closer to see the name of the book & froze on my spot. The idiots were reading my personal diary.

God why I had to keep my diary on the dining table yesterday? Snatching diary from Recce's hand I shouted "Don't you guys have any manners? How can you touch someone's personal diary?" As usual ignoring my angry Alice spoke "I never knew you wrote a diary" with a dramatically sad sigh she continued "how can you hide such an important thing from me?"

"Alice it's called personal for a reason right?" I asked raising my eyebrow.

Austin interrupted the topic.

"I never knew you had crush on our chemistry professor that

to in 3rd grade." He said making a weird face as if having a crush was a biggest crime. Though it was many years before, my cheek still couldn't stop blushing. Seriously what the problem with me I want to be angry but I am blushing like an idiot. The Assault just didn't stop here.

God how much they must have read?

"We never knew you loved Austin from so before. Damn you were totally crazy for him Jenny"

As if I didn't know that, Genius!

I got the answer to my question instantly by their question. They had read it all. Gosh Kill me.What have I done so bad to get embarrassed all day today.I just wished Mother Earth to open up and swallow me whole.

But No I had to be still alive for further embarrassment.

"Waiting for a ship on airport huh??"How deep Recce said sarcastically. "I must say love have made you a philosopher, my child." Beth said patting my back trying to not to laugh. My face immediately reddened.

Now it's official, today God is taking personal interest in embarrassing me. Ha what Fun. Note the sarcasm.

"GuysGuys"Austinsaideventuallyattractingalltheattentiontowards him, thankfully. But I never knew worst was about to happen now. "Diary told us about her past. But the present breaking, news: Jenny Dreams about me every single day. Today when I was waking her up I heard her saying this."

It was then when I seriously felt like digging a hole and burying myself hundred feet below the ground and never to come back again.

"And she was desperate to kiss me this morning. So you can imagine what she was dreaming, Right?" Austin said suggestively. Make the hole 200 feet deep. What a hilarious day I must say.

God I just hope this all is a dream.

* * *

Chapter 33 - Halloween craze I

After being embarrassed and being laughed at for a really long time, Austin at last pitied me. And he actually changed the topic

"What's the reason behind everyone visiting Jenny house so early in the morning?" Austin asked.

"Yesterday being the big day for you both of you, we just wanted to hear all the juicy gossips. So we decided to surprise Jenny" Alice said excitedly.

I somehow knew Alice would be the first one to ask all the details out of me. Heck I was just expecting the call from her at night itself considering her greed for gossips.

"But instead we got surprised as we entered the house." Beth said with a smirk.

Damn this girl won't leave even a slightest chance of embarrassing people. That's why I like to call her Pure Evil.

Satisfied with the girl's reply Austin turned towards the guys.

"And why the hell you people are visiting Jenny So early in the morning?" Austin asked curiously.

"What? Can only girls crave for gossips? Even we were curious to know." River said with a shrug. I never knew even guys like River were sucker of gossips. This was total new information.

"Guys you do realize that you could have even come to my house for that?" Austin said raising his eyebrow.

"Yeah we could have if you were at home idiot." River said with the Duh tone.

In all this conversation Recce was damn silent and there was confusion plastered all over his face.

Damn why this guy has to be confuse all the time.

I wonder why he is confused now.

"Wait wait. We were looking for Austin to ask him about his yesterdays Date with Jenny?" Recce asked scratching his head innocently.

"Yeah. We wouldn't go at Austin's house for lunch in the morning. You do realize that Recce, Right?" River said irritably.

"Damn did I just sacrifice my sleep for this? I thought we were going to Austin's house to discuss about the party." Recce spoke innocently.

Everyone's attention turned towards Recce instantly.

"Dude you throwing party? " Beth said excitedly.

"No I am talking about school party" Recce clarified.

"Since when did the principle start throwing parties for play's success?" River asked confused. "You guys seriously don't remember todays date or are you just acting dumb?" Recce said Annoyed. "As per my information our play was on 30th October which means today is 31st October. What's with the date?" Alice asked this time. "Oh fucking shit.

Today is Halloween party at our school. How can I forget this. God I had been waiting for this day since ages" Beth said dramatically.

Satisfied by Beth's reply the scowl on Recce face turned into huge grin and hugged her tightly" You are the best of all" Recce said happily.

"Are you seriously this excited for todays Halloween party?" I asked with a frown.No offense to the party. The Halloween party at our school is actually pretty awesome. It's the only party of school in which alcohol is allowed not officially though. Seniors arrange everything in the party. And watching the students in different costumes and that to totally wasted is fun.

But damn how can be anyone so excited for this. "Yeah I am excited for party even. But I am more eagerly waiting for trick or treat." Recce said with grin never leaving his stupid face."I am Eighteen now and I am Not going for trick or treating." I said firmly giving him are you crazy look. Disagreeing with me Recce said "You are never old for trick or treating, Jenny".

Woah that was deep. Does Recce really think so deeply about anything?

"I am. And basically even you are. Besides, I haven't gone for trick or treating from last three years." I stated.

"What a waste." He cried offended expression crossing his face.

"You have already missed three whole bags of candies. How could you Jenny?" Recce said childishly. "I don't like candies anyways." I tried lying to avoid going for trick or treat.

"Says the girl who is crazy for anything that contains chocolate." I turned to face Austin who was smirking widely.

"Don't tell me you are going for trick or treating?" I asked staring at him with wide eyes. "Yes he is going." Recce said chirping in our conversation "We haven't missed any trick or treat ever."

This was really surprising. I never thought this boy would be so into trick or treating. Damn I don't know little about them, Shame on you Jenny.

"Yeah. Because we are always been dragged into trick or treat forcefully." River stated.

"Whatever. Thats not the point. The point is we go every year and we are going this year too." Recce said stubbornly.

"We are not going Recce. Not after what happened last year." River said trying to suppress the smile.

"What exactly happened last Year?" Alice asked

Her Eyes were curiously focused on River for knowing new information about Recce.

"Recce was so high on sugar that he was acting weirder than children. From every single house he had snatched handful of candies.

It took us literally one whole hour to stop Recce from trick or treat and take him to the party. And the party was more hilarious." River said giving in and laughing like an idiot. Austin continued further "Our drunken friend had gone on terrace last year and was screaming on top of his lungs gathering all the public outside the building. Drinks plus sugar takes Recce to a totally different world."

The very next moment we all burst out laughing. It was not cute smile at all but a real tear jerker laugh. Recce stayed silent for sometime with his face crimson red from rage and embarrassment.

"Done with laughing? That's the actual fun of Halloween. You can act as silly as you want. Guys we cant let such awesome moment pass. It comes only once in a year." Recce said with a pout.

"Recce stop using this dialogue all the time." River said.

"Guys I think Recce is right. We should go for trick or treat. This is our first Halloween together. We should make this special." Beth said.

Woah! What's with Beth. Why today everyone is acting so out of their character. Beth was never like a girl who would talk so cheesy.

"Right. I am in." Austin Informed "And even you are coming" Austin said pointing towards me. His eyes showing lots of excitement for trick or treat.

"I am in too" Alice Chirped happily. "Gosh I am going to dress for Halloween after so many years"

"But Guys" River tried Interrupting.

Gosh at least he was in my team. But sadly we weren't in the majority.

" Shh. No buts" Recce interjected "We are going trick or treating. Either you come willingly or I will kick you two Idiots out of the house myself"

This Guy has turned totally crazy. Doesn't he know we all are legal adults? One is definitely not suppose to go on trick or treating after turning eighteen, at least according to me. Its like snatching candies from the poor children, who actually deserves them.

"This argument maybe new for you guys but this is our every Halloween ritual. River just can't say No to Recce, that too for Halloween. He is surely going to come." Austin said as if stating a fact.

"Ok Ok .I am in. There has to be someone to record Halloween embarrassing moment right, Dude? " River said with a smirk.

"Yeah Yeah Whatever. So its fixed we all are going for trick or treat in the evening. Damn this is going to be so much fun."

And in this way, Ladies and Gentlemen my presence was totally ignored again and I was forced to do what I didn't want to do let me add *Again*.

"So what's everyone going to wear" Recce asked excitedly totally sounding like Girl.

Gosh he was happier than small boys in the candy store.

"I'm gonna be a witch" Beth said with same excitement.

She always wanted to be dressed like a Witch for Halloween. As she thinks it's a perfect Halloween dress. Crazy I know. But my friends are full of craziness. And they think this is quite normal.

"Suits You" River said with a smirk.

Beth just stuck her tongue out in response.

My only companion who was on my side had so gracefully left my side and was enjoying the talk that it seemed like he was never against it.

"I would dress like Rapunzel. No Cinderella looks better than me. God I am so Confused." Alice Grumbled.

"You look much prettier than both." Recce said to Alice, which caused her to turn into darkest shade of red.

Recce's trying again Aww.

Why the Hell does this boy not understand that Alice is already in love with him. He just has to muster some courage and ask her out rather than throwing clingy cheesy lines.

Is this so hard for him?

"I don't have anything to wear" I said frustrated. I was never good at choosing costumes. My mom used to do that for me.

Damn I miss my mom now.

"Don't worry Princess. Recce has solutions for all." Recce said taking out some black gown with ugly face drawn on it

"Ihavemadeitmyself.Iknowit'snotthatgood.GodwhoamIkidding?"

"It's perfect." Recce said grinning proudly.

I raised an eyebrow "And what is this exactly?"

"Dementor, Idiot"

"And who is he?" I asked confused.

Austin and River mumbled something under their breaths, which seemed like cursing, as if by asking Recce this question I have committed some biggest mistake of my life whereas Recce looked shocked totally shocked.

"Don't tell me you don't know Dementor from Harry Potter? Are you kidding?" He said as if knowing characters from Harry potter is like our fourth basic need.

"Just tell me you were just kidding" River prompted in my ears.

"I don't know. I have just seen the first part of Harry Potter .I don't remember characters" I said honestly totally i.gnoring River's warnings

From the corner of my eye I saw River banging his head on Austin's shoulders dramatically.

Gosh what's the matter? Recce looked like he'd been slapped by someone on face very hardly "You have only seen first part of Harry potter? What's wrong with you Jenny? Tomorrow itself we are watching all the parts of Harry Potter. Even the first"

With an amused smile on my face I told Recce" I never thought a guy like you would like movies like Harry potter."

His offensive look grew. "Please enlighten me which type of people watch Harry Potter"

"The nerdy type of people who don't have anything better to do in their spare time. But last time I checked you, your life was much happening"

"My life still is." He snapped at me with anger." What's the problem with you Jenny? We are taking about Harry potter here. How can anyone not like this movie? Every people who have little bit of brain like this movie" Recce said shaking me.

Gosh this guy is seriously addicted with the Harry Potter series. I wanted to say something but the moment I opened my mouth only air came out. Damn I was again at loss of words.

It was then I realized why Austin and River groaned simultaneously.

Luckily my Knight in the Shining Armor rescued me for the second time today. "Just ignore him Jenny. He gets too emotional when it comes to Harry Potter" Austin said with a sigh.

"Hey I am not Emotional. You guys just don't have good choice of movies." Recce said stubbornly.

He was about to start his blabbering about Harry potter Again when suddenly River spoke up causing Recce to shut up. I bet everyone would thank River later for his interruption.

Jenny note to your self: never in your entire life talk to Recce about

Harry Potter.

"We can discuss about this later. Now can we just focus on Halloween"

Finally it was 4 o'clock. After leaving my house later everyone had decided to meet at my house again at 6 o'clock so we could go for trick and treat before the party. I was still confused about what to wear.

Luckily the girls were coming at 4 o'clock so we could get ready together. The doorbell rang signally their arrival. I just hope they have some good idea for my costume.

"Jenny I swear to God if you still haven't decided what you are going to wear, I will cut you into pieces and feed you to street dogs" Beth said the moment I opened the door.

What a way to enter someone's house. Ironic. Beth doesn't like me blabbering about dress, and talking about Halloween Parties. she always wanted to attend high school's Halloween Party but she couldn't attend because of me and Alice's lack of interest. Now that she was finally getting the chance to attend the Halloween party she wanted to grab the opportunities with her both hands tightly and enjoy it fully without any obstacles. And she seemed lot excited for this.

Her excitement was not good for me though.

She was looking at me for answer. If I am going to die today I better die soon, thinking of this I stood in front of Beth with my eyes tightly shut I spoke "Sorry for disappointing you. But I haven't decided yet what I am going to wear. I am so damn confused" I said it all in one breath.

I don't know what made them both laugh, the terror on my face or my uselessness in deciding the simple costumes but the next moment both Beth and Alice were laughing with laughter tears in their eyes.

"Oh Jenny I was not serious about to kill you" Beth tried saying between her laughter "Dear I was just kidding. Man just look at your face" Beth said, still laughing.

I left a sigh of relief I didn't know I was holding for long, on this their laugh doubled.

I just stood their with neutral face waiting for their laughter to end which didn't seemed to end soon. So I just left them at the door and started walking towards my room.

"Chill Jenny. We have lots of ideas for you costume." Alice said excitedly. And from that moment itself the hunt for perfect costume began.

* * *

Chapter 34 - Halloween craze

After thinking about all the costumes available, the girls finally came to senses and realized that now we don't have enough time for costume shopping. So finally it was decided that I would wear a simple dress and do little extra makeup so I would look a little different at least. So we finally started dressing hurriedly as it was already 5.30 which meant we had only half hour to get dressed. We got dressed as hurriedly as possible.

Alice had finally settled with Cinderella's outfit that consisted frilly, sleeveless, pink and white dress with pink ribbons. She pulled up her hair in beautiful french twist and did her makeup light. She looked like a real princess with her face fair and clear, her lips pink and her eyes blue.

Damn Recce is going to go crazy looking at Alice.

Whereas, on other hand Beth totally looked like a real witch. She looked really monstrous with dark makeup that had made her lips look bloodless. With a witch hat and a broom she totally looked like one. At the last moment they decided to dress me also like a princess as Alice had brought an extra dress with her. So here I was dressed like Alice the only difference was that I was wearing baby blue color dress with light makeup and they insisted, more over forced me to keep my hair open with light curls. I knew none of my say was going to be considered so I just kept mute.

Because of the door bell they stopped doing extra make up on me (lucky me) and got down. As soon as I opened the door I was met by dementor and two more weird character, I was about to ask them who they are actually but maybe Recce guessed my confusion and said, "Don't tell me you don't know even these characters. They are from part one of Harry Potter"

I didn't know the character names but I seriously didn't want to hear Harry Potter lecture again so I tried changing the topic saying "I know their names I was just shocked to see River and Austin in these characters."

"As if we had any choice" River said "We were forced into wearing this" River said faking sadness.

Though the costumes were weird they all looked good.

After a long conversation over each other's costumes, Recce excitedly said "Let's get started for the best Halloween ever"

Gaggles of children and teenagers were already out by the time we started walking down in my street. I had thought that we would be the only teenagers for trick and treat and children would be throwing daggers at us for stealing their share of candies. This was the main reason why I had forced all to wear masks over their costumes. At least children won't know whom to curse exactly. Right.

But the picture before me was totally different many groups of teenagers were happily wandering in groups with pillowcases in their hands for collecting candies.

Gosh! I so damn missed this happy feeling.

I am glad I accepted to come. I was already feeling like a child again. I decided to let loose myself and have little fun.

"Lets attack our first house guys "Beth said getting into the character. I bet she is going to scare half the people. We all followed behind.

Austin never left my hand. His presence beside me itself made my heart go la la. This feeling was totally new but I was loving this feeling.

God I will never get used to this feeling.

"Damn you look so awesome today. More beautiful than a princess" Austin whispered in my ear and the whole troop of butterflies erupted in my stomach. I thanked the girls mentally for forcing me to wear this.

I don't know; was it their every years tradition or just excitement but Recce and River stared pressing door bell continuously.

"Guys" Alice scolded swaying Recce's hand away.

"What?" He complained, as if pressing someone doorbell fifty times isn't weird at all.

"That's rude." She said pointing at the doorbell.

"No it isn't rude on Halloween. It just shows how excited people are for candies" River said with a full grin.

"You weren't so exited before. What made you to fall in love with candies so suddenly? " Beth pointed out.

"Excitement is in the air sweetheart." River said with a wink & started pressing the doorbell again.

Crazy weird people.

I just hope now that instead of candies the lady doesn't come out with a gun.

"No one must be at home." Austin said observing the house "or else they would have been out long back."

Recce's shoulder sagged with disappointment. Much to Recce's relief the door opened. Immediately all of us shouted in sync trick or treat.

The little old man who opened the door brightly smiled at us.

"Ah group of teenagers I see. You all look so cute. "Glancing at

Beth and Recce he further continued "and dangerous."

The old man seemed pretty generous as he was offering us king sized candies. Recce & Alice picked up the Kit Kat bar quickly. River & Austin went for Dairy Milk, Beth picked up the Hershey's bar. I was still shocked at the generosity of the strange man. Finally I managed to come back to my senses after being kicked by Recce. I grabbed Hershey bar quickly.

"Thank you" we all said in Rhythm and started hunting for our next house.

"Woah we earned a jackpot at the first house itself" Recce said cheerfully. His cheerfulness brought smile on my face.

"You really don't act like a guy of your age" Beth said.

"Well in that case would you believe me, if I said Recce is actually older than us" Austin said point between him and River

"Nope." Alice and Beth said immediately as if this is most impossible thing on earth .

"Well he is." River admitted, "by few months not a big deal though, as he sometimes acts worst than Austin's younger brother."

Recce smacked River's head "Dude shut up. I can be more mature than you both. I just don't want to be."

"Think whatever makes you happy. We all know the truth" Austin said with a smirk.

A warm smile settled on my face. My life had seriously changed a lot after being friends with these boys. Though they all seem tough and rude from outside they are soft and very sweet from inside. Because of them in my life, my life had become little extra brighter. Being together boys always acted immature and stress free more like them self, which was a refreshing view. I wish this innocence never breaks and they always remain together.

The next few houses were the fun sized kind of houses, much to Recce's dismay. To me, it didn't really matter, since there were only a few types of candy I liked. For the next hour, we migrated from house to house, taking goodies from my good neighbors.

After the awesome trick and treat I was looking forward to the party.

I must say every single moment with my friends is full of fun. Maybe that's the pros of having friends. I have missed this fun all my life. But now that I have opportunity to have fun I won't leave it.

The moment we entered the party I was awestruck. Our school hall was so changed, I couldn't recognize it for a moment. It seemed like it came straight out of a cheesy horror movie. There was horror movie attraction from a theme park, with electronic skeletons mulling about everywhere.

Shrieks of terror and moans of pain came from hidden speakers. The whole thing screamed danger.

Austin did notice my shock. “Close you mouth dear before flies go in it.” Austin whispered in ears.

“Damn this is so awesome. We should have attended all the earlier Halloween parties.” Beth said hopping up and down.

Her excitement was fully expected though. Even I felt bad for not attending the last parties.

This party in front of me was no normal party. Every arrangement was made to look it like a Halloween party. Halloween punch with a floating, frozen hands were made for the Halloween effect. The food table was covered with a black and orange tablecloth, and on that there were scary plastic spiders, worms, and cobwebs. Hay bales, fake small mummies and lots of dry pumpkins were used for party landscape.

While we were busy looking at the party, River was intensely staring at someone in a funny manner.

“Boo!” The person in front of him suddenly cried, sending River flying backward, with an incredibly girly shriek escaping his mouth just before he fell flat on his back.

This sent Recce over the edge.

“Ha ha ha dude! Nice scream. And you guys tell me I am not mature enough?”

The vampire guy by whom River got scared of, was also laughing loudly. I tried to suppress my smile, but I couldn’t. So I finally gave in and joined everyone in laughing. Even though mask covered River’s face, I figured he was blushing. “Y-you scared the hell out of me. Damn you are real. I thought you are artificial” he said to the Vampire getting up from the ground.

“Don’t worry, you’re not the only one,” it responded in an amused tone.

“Thanks. That made me feel better.” River said sarcastically.

“Guys, “ River said sharply as we started walking away “We will never speak of that again.”

“Sure,” all agreed simultaneously trying to control their laugh.

“That would be good for you guys” With that everyone stopped laughing.

“I am going to play the games before I get too drunk.” Recce said. “Are there games too? I thought there’s only drinks drinks and drinks.” I said excitedly.

"Yeah there are. And they are just awesome games. We being the members of the student council choose them ourselves." With this said, we all went to check out games and let me tell you the games were pretty awesome.

I must say, the seniors and the student's council members had to put lots of efforts in arranging the Halloween party. The first game was called as Halloween feel box. There were boxes full of items like spaghetti noodles, peeled grapes crashed Oreo and little smokies and many more things and the contestant has to use their hands to guess what the items are with their eyes closed.

The other game was Halloween Guess Who Game.

In this game a piece of paper was taped on the back of contestant with a Halloween character written on it. The contestant had to guess whose name is on their back by asking the other guests for clues.

There were many more games. But Guess who Game was the funniest. The contestant's weird guesses and the student's acting in front of contestants was lot fun. This fun doubled when the boys decided to have little fun.

It was officially proved now, that the boys couldn't have fun without harassing anyone.

They decided to harass Blake Millers who was the contestant of Guess Who and was going to people for help.

River called him where we were and then the real fun started. 'Minions' was written on his back.

The guys enacted every character apart from Minion. After many trials and failures, Blake irritably withdrew his name from the competition and removed the piece of paper from his back himself. The moment he came to know that he was tricked the expression on his face was priceless.

Unable to control our laughter any longer we finally gave in and started laughing like maniacs. Surprisingly even Blake joined us. That moment was hilarious, I must say.

Later we tried many games and surprisingly we did win in a few games. The night was getting better. After enjoying almost all the games and wandering here and there, all decided to finally drink. Drinking was never my thing so I decided to go for cold drink. Besides, there has to be someone sober to handle the drunken idiots.

Everyone went to have drinks and I went in search of cold drinks. After getting what I was looking for, I headed back to where everyone was previously sitting. But many teenagers shouting Recce's name and some random guy's name surrounded our table of six.

What the hell was actually happening?

With lots of efforts I made way through the crowd and reached front. The scene in front of me cleared why everyone was shouting. There was a drinking competition going between Recce and some random guy I think he was a senior, as I had never seen him in my class.

To confirm my thoughts "What is happening here?" I asked Austin.

"They are having a drinking competition. The one who will drink five beers first will win." Austin explained.

Damn this was crazy.

By the number of empty bottles beside Recce, it was quite clear that he was going to win against the other guy who was just wasting his time. Recce had already emptied three beer bottles and was having his fourth whereas the other guy, was still having his second. As expected, Recce did win but at the end of fifth beer he was totally drunk. And we all were in serious trouble now.

******

After an hour or so, as expected, our star tonight Recce was missing. And me being the only one totally sober, to keep an eye on everyone was my duty according to Alice.

So here I was, searching for Recce in the entire hall. I even checked a few classrooms. From the window of the classroom, I saw Recce near the Principal's statue in the garden with a big pumpkin in his hands.

"What are you doing here Recce? Where did you find this pumpkin?" I said hurried coming out of our building near Recce.

"Jenny, my sweetheart. You solved my big problem" Recce said trying to hug me but because of the big pumpkin in his hands he couldn't.

"Ugh. Leave it I will just thank you after the task is done."

"What are you exactly talking about?" I asked confused.

"From last ten minutes I was busy thinking how would I put this on his head alone but now that you are here my problem is solved" I was shocked for a moment.

Does this boy want to get expelled?

"You know this is the statue of our principle, Right?" I asked Recce to check how much drunk he was.

"Oh really. That would be more fun then". My guess was Right. Recce was totally drunk.

"Oh no. No! You can't do that".

"Yes. I can do that" Recce said trying to rhyme the sentence. "How do you even come up with ideas like this?"

"It's a gift. I am born intelligent" Recce said and tried patting his back proudly which he couldn't.

God what should I do now?

"You are not going to put this up there!" I said again this time. I tried to sound sterner.

"Why Not?" Recce asked innocently.

"Recce, you will get in big trouble." I tried explaining him though I knew it was of no use.

"Try to enjoy life a little Jenny. You know even you would want do. Nobody's here to watch us, it's the perfect opportunity. The right time, the right place - the stars are aligned! It's our destiny" Recce tried to convince me. He could be such a drama queen when he is drunk.

"It would be too big for principal's head" I tried reasoning.

"Yuppie. You're in," he exclaimed happily.

"Don't worry, I'll do the climbing Jenny"

In what kind of universe does 'it won't fit' translate into 'great idea, count me in'?

"Give me some credit. I know the way you're thinking. If you really were against it, you would have stuck to saying no."

Dammit! This guy could even think when he is drunk and you can't even think properly when you are fully sober, shame on you Jenny.

Actually his idea was kind of brilliant. And he was saying the truth too. I had never done anything like this in my entire life and really wanted to do some thing bad ass. But I would never give him the satisfaction of admitting that out loud.

"Here, hold this for me for a minute," Recce addressed me and handed over, the pumpkin, almost crushing my nose and started climbing the statue. Idiot Recce and his silly Excitement.

"What the hell are you doing here with a pumpkin? Weren't you supposed to look for Recce?" Austin's sudden voice from behind scared me for a moment.

When he came near me I just pointed towards the Recce climbing the statue and he understood everything.

"And you seriously are helping him in do this stupid prank?"

"Not willingly." I lied." He isn't ready to come anywhere without doing this. So I am helping him so that this could finish fast before anyone comes here. I just don't want Recce to get in trouble." I said all in one breath.

The second part was true though.

"Give this silly thing to me" Austin said pointing at pumpkin. I did as he said and was expecting Austin to yell at Recce for his idiocy.

"Good idea champ. Why didn't we think of this before. This would be so much fun. I would like to see principal's face tomorrow first in the morning..I am in" Austin said excitedly.

My jaw struck to ground the moment Austin changed his words. God what's with these guys. They all are acting so weird and different today.

And surprisingly I am loving it. Seriously the excitement is in the air.

"I know brother" Recce said happily.

"Isn't this a stupid prank?"

"Who said that?" Austin asked acting surprised.

"You" I said pointing towards him.

"Woah girl don't blame me. I just said you are stupid to not call us."

Ending the topic there itself, we watched Recce as he heaved himself onto the principal's statue.

The guy being drunk had more balance than me.

I would have stumbled thousand times but Recce was climbing as if he does this everyday.

This made me think how many pranks they must have played before.

I mentally noted to ask Austin about this later.

"Okay, I'm good. You can give it to me," Recce said. He was holding onto the statue with his left hand, reaching for the pumpkin with his right, his knees bent slightly. He grabbed the pumpkin and placed it on top of the statue, covering the head of the principal.

Recce smiled at me smugly. "See? It fits perfectly"

"It's tilted." I said after observing the statue. I must say, the statue with a pumpkin head looked really weird. Tomorrow entire school's going to be on fire.

"That's alright," he said and jumped down bringing me out of my thoughts, standing right next to me to admire his handiwork. "This statue doesn't need to win a beauty contest Jenny" Austin said with a chuckle.He was right. Then he grabbed his cell phone out of his pocket and gave it to me. "Here, take our picture with our beloved principal" Guys said with a huge grin.

I slapped him. "Are you out of your mind? I'm not going to take a picture of you! That's evidence which could be used against you! Gosh, promise me you never consider a criminal career."

"Aw, always looking out for me. I'm touched." Austin grinned at me and kissed me on my forehead.

This is what I love about Austin. He can be so sweet without even trying to act sweet.

"Get a room guys or at least go in one of the classrooms" Recce said pulling us apart.

It was then I realized we should run before anyone notices us.

We were now safe away from statue in front of our school. River, Beth and Alice were waiting at the entrance for us.

"Where the hell were you people from the past half an hour? We were waiting for you like idiots here!" Beth yelled.

Before I could explain anything "Austin and Jenny were making out in the backyard. So I was waiting for the show to get over." Recce spoke up innocently.

"Shut up dude. You didn't even give us to kiss each other" Austin said smacking Recce's head.

Gosh why did they have to always discuss about our non-existent romance.

I just shushed both of them and narrated the entire story to them. It was then all the three broke out laughing. They were laughing so hard, that even we started laughing.

"Nice work dude." Beth said patting Recce's back.

"From where did you got the pumpkin?" Alice asked all of sudden.

It was then that it struck me, that Recce didn't answer to this question before. So I eagerly waited for his answer.

"I just saw it in front of boy's washroom." Recce said with a shrug. Listening to this River started laughing like a crazy again.

What was so funny in this?

Everyone stared at River with confused expression.

"Dude did you hit your head to the ground when you experienced a fall before?" Recce said amused by River's laugh.

"Shut up man." River said trying to control his laughter.

"Then what's with the laughing?" Beth asked.

"Recce has picked up Mr. Black's Pumpkin."

"Are you out of your mind River? Professors don't attend this party. You know that, right?" Austin asked raising his eyebrow.

"I know that dude. I saw him in the washroom and came to know that he was curious about how Halloween parties of our school actually are. So he had come. He had used that pumpkin to hide his face. But once we came outside, the pumpkin was not there. I had to search for this

Pumpkin in entire school. At last Mr. Black went home without seeing the party."

"Ha Ha. Poor dude."

With this we all laughed again. After many years I had laughed so much in a day. I don't even remember when I had laughed so much with friends.

I was seriously lucky to have them in my life.

"Guys I need a drink. I am going inside." Drunken Recce said. With this Austin and River picked Recce and placed him inside the car.

That was so much fun. With this, the best day of my life came to end. I hope there would be no more complexities as Recce was falling asleep.

"You are looking very beautiful today Alice. I love you" Recce said before finally falling asleep. Woah! that was big confession.

The blush and happiness on Alice's face made it crystal clear that she had same feelings. I could smell a good love here.

I hope Recce mans up tomorrow and asks Alice out. Or else what are friends for ??????????

❄ ❄ ❄

Chapter 35 - Match Makers

We had decided to gather near my locker a bit early on monday morning. And that was where we were heading, making our way through the hallway.

The guys were there already waiting for us.

"Morning." Austin greeted me with a kiss.

Gosh this erupted a whole troop of butterflies in my stomach. Damn I am never going to get used to this feeling. I couldn't stop blushing. This is what Austin actually enjoyed though.

"Hey girls," Recce greeted me with a big grin "Let me guess why Alice just did a one-eighty turn down there. She forgot something in the car right?"

I nodded. "Book."

He shook his head in disapproval.

"Aren't you paying a little more attention to Alice these days Recce?" Beth asked with a smirk.

Gosh the blush on Recce's face was hilarious. I could see he was trying to hide the blush very hard but sadly it was of no use. He was still blushing like a girl.

"I read all about what you guys did yesterday" River said in an amused tone which immediately changed the topic. Lucky Recce. Such things never happen with me.

"I really must say-"

"You read about it?" Recce interrupted him.

"Yeah. Haven't you guys seen it? It's on our notice board."

"It is?" I asked again to confirm.

River nodded.

"Wow," Recce couldn't hide his excitement about the fact that our little mission has been publicized; he had a huge smile on his face.

"Was there a picture, too?" Austin asked suddenly.

River sighed. "Yeah there is. I must say, that pumpkin looked hilarious on the principal's head." He said with a stern look at Austin and me. Obviously angry for not involving him in the prank or maybe high fives between Recce and Austin were simply bothering him. "They declared it to be a case of vandalism."

"Woah Awesome...!!River man, you really missed out friday night,"

Austin stated and I could tell that he was ready to jump into a detailed retelling of everything again.

"I missed it because my friends were too drunk to call me" River said faking anger.

"Do you really think we should talk about it here, Guys? We can talk about it later" I said, looking around us. There were quite a number of students lingering in the hallway and we really didn't want anyone to know that we were the ones to responsible for the act of vandalism committed on Friday night.

"Hey Jenny do you know why everyone is staring in our direction?"

"No, why?"

"Something's up. They keep staring at us for some reason. What if they know about our little secret?" Recce said tensed.

I worriedly looked at the hall and realized that no one was watching in our direction. The jerks were making fun of me.

"You worry too much, Jenny" he simply replied.

"Hey!" I slapped him.

"Don't deny it, you know it's true."

"So how did you do it? Did you both...," Beth trailed off, pointing upwards to the ceiling. Ah, she was asking if they both climbed on the statue.

Here goes the topic again.

"Nah, only Recce was on the top. And he was the one who put it on. You know. It was his idea, actually," Austin answered his question, trying best to avoid mentioning the statue, just in case one of the students passing by catches a tidbit of our conversation. Better safe than sorry.

At least he is being careful.

"Well, first Jenny and then Austin helped me to get it up there," our fellow criminal admitted.

"True." I stated.

"Jenny thought it wouldn't fit, but it did." Recce grinned at me. "I told you so."

"Yeah, yeah. But it was crooked," I felt the need to mention once again.

"Who cares? It doesn't need to win a beauty pageant, right?"

"I still can't believe you guys did that. I mean, it was pretty much illegal," Beth said, leaning against the locker.

"Oh, we did it, believe us. I wanted to take pictures, too, but Jenny wouldn't let me." Austin said with a pout, his cute drool worthy pout.

"Damn right. Really, he should be glad that I stopped him from doing something so foolish!"

"We could have shown them to our grand children one day. They would have been so proud of us," Austin pouted a little more.

"Hey Guys I need to go to library. I will meet you guys at the lunch." Saying this Recce hurriedly ran away.

This was most shocking thing. First of all, Recce never leaves the conversations midway and secondly he never never visits library. Even if he is being told to go to library by any of the teacher he wouldn't go. So this was strange.

"What happened to this guy?"

"Why did he run away all of a sudden?" Beth and I bombarded questions towards the boys simultaneously.

Maybe she must have found this strange even.

"Because Alice is coming" Austin said pointing towards the hallways.

"So what?" I asked confused.

"We told him what he said yesterday before falling asleep"

"That somewhat explains the situation. Oh my God is Recce is avoiding Alice then" Beth asked excitedly.

"Yes Genius."

"Does that mean Recce likes Alice?" I asked happily.

The Guys were about to say something. When suddenly Alice spoke up.

"What did I miss?"

"Nothing. We were just discussing about you." Austin said.

"About me?" Alice asked confused.

"Yeah we were thinking about yesterday. Why would have Recce said 'I love you' before falling asleep?" River said placing his finger on his chin to show that he was in deep thoughts.

As soon as the words left River's mouth a huge blush crept on Alice's face. Which was enough evident to show that the feelings were mutual.

God I am so happy for them. After trying very hard to manage her blush "I think it doesn't meant anything to him. According to me they were just drunken words." Alice tried speaking up. But I knew she didn't want that to be true.

"Actually you are Right. Even Recce think that. When we asked him he said it was just a drunken mistake"

The moment words left out of Austin's mouth .I saw immense hurt in Alice's eyes. She hide it immediately though.

"I knew that" Alice said. She was very hardly trying to act like these words didn't affect her at all. But I knew she was shattered from inside. Her heart was breaking from inside.

At that very moment my blood boiled with anger. I never had thought in my weirdest dream even that Recce wouldn't like Alice back. By the way Recce used to look at Alice, by his change in behavior around Alice I always felt like he had feelings for her.

But now that he has confessed to his friends that he has no feelings for Alice, I felt like ripping his head apart. How dare he play with my friend's feelings?

"Guys I am going to class. Will see you all later." Alice said with a crooked smile.

There was still time for bell to ring but I knew that Alice wasn't in mood to stop. So I let her go.

"Where the fucking hell that player Recce is now?" I shouted with anger.

"Even I want to meet him. I am going to crush him into pieces for playing with my friends feelings" Beth said with same wrath.

We were attracting many attentions I knew. But at that moment I didn't care. I was really angry at Recce and sad for Alice .

We were expecting some serious response from the boys but all we got was a laugh. It can't be counted as a normal laugh even. It was pure devil laugh. They were laughing so loudly that happy tears had started to come from their eyes.

Have they gone nuts? How can they even feel like laughing in such a situations?

"What's the matter with you guys?" I semi yelled for them to listen. But the evils didn't hear me at all. They were still busy laughing like idiots.

"Stop laughing now. Or else I will bury you Guys here Alive." Beth's threatening voice caused them to stop instantly.

I must say Beth's words threatened them pretty well. They didn't dare to smile even.

"Would you guys please enlighten us about what actually the matter is?"

"We lied to you guys earlier" River finally spoke up.

"We were trying to fool Alice. But by the looks on your face we think you guys got fooled too" Austin said.

With this, the idiots started laughing again. This time more severely.

"Sorry Beth but we can't control our laugh seriously." Austin said while laughing.

"Damn the look on your faces where hilarious. I wish I had a camera with me to capture your faces." River said while wiping his happy tears.

"I would have seriously framed your picture and gifted it Alice and Recce."

Austin said between the bits of laughing.

This guys were going crazy.

We were getting more and more curious by the weird behavior of the boys. But we didn't have any other option but wait.

After sometime the idiots finally sobered up "OK OK. We lied to you that Recce doesn't likes Alice" Austin spoke up.

"Yeah actually the truth is that Recce is madly in love with Alice. Damn he even speaks about Alice in his sleep" River confessed.

River's shocking confession calmed my anger. I felt like dancing madly with happiness. At last it was finally clear that Alice and Recce both liked each other.

But I couldn't understand the reason behind why the boys lied earlier?

It seems like today Beth and I were thinking at same frequency. As she asked the same question.

"Why did you guys lie earlier then?" Beth asked puzzled.

"We lied because we wanted to know about Alice's feelings for Recce" River stated.

"You could have even asked directly."

"No one accepts their feelings so easily babes. Or else we would have been together months ago." Austin said with a wink.

He had a point there. I never knew boys could even think so wisely. But again River and Austin proved me wrong.

"Now that we know how they feel about each other, what should we do next?" Beth asked happily.

"We should make them an official couple" Austin replied with a shrug. As if it was the easiest thing.

"I know that dude. But how?" Beth asked again.

"According to me we should do something that will force Recce to ask Alice" River stated. "From what I know about Recce, I guarantee he would never man up to ask Recce out on his own."

But as the bell rang, we had to head to our classes, so we decided to come up with something during the break.

As expected, neither Alice nor Recce were at the lunch table. Both were hiding from each other, which was good for us though. We could now plan for something better now.

After thinking for sometime and rejecting thousands of ideas, we finally made a plan. Surprisingly the mastermind behind the plan was Beth. Gosh! I must say, that today many unexpected things were happening.

We all ditched rest of our lectures, and went to collect the things required to execute the plan.

Actually the plan was to decorate our guest room very nicely and then call both of them and lock them in my room. I know this was an evil plan.

But what else could anyone expect from Beth? Her mind was just full of evil ideas.

I hoped this plan would work and Recce would ask Alice out.

Firstly, we went to the supermarket to get red balloons, roses, candles and teddies. Once everything was collected, we marched towards my house.

Damn I was so excited.

We were assigned to prepare Alice and Recce's favorite food whereas boys took the responsibility of decorating room romantically.

Let's just hope they would decorate the room as per Alice's standard and not just keep anything anywhere and call it decoration.

After preparing some dishes, we went to check the room. Our chins literally hit the ground the moment we saw the room in front of us. They had completely made a makeover of a room in good way. I never knew even boys could think so out of the box.

There was a little table decorated with candles with awesome fragrance and around the table, a big heart was drawn with rose petals on the bed and was written I LOVE YOU in a big capital letters with the help of rose petals. Rest, teddies and balloons were kept in the perfect places, which made room more presentable.

We were at loss of words. I was sure now that Recce would ask Alice out.

The room was so beautifully decorated, and its vibes was so romantic, that even the people who hated each other would propose to each other here.

"Some compliments on our work wouldn't kill you two" River said staring towards us.

"What can we say, we are at loss of words" I admitted sincerely.

"You guys really decorated this by yourselves?" Beth asked puzzled.

"What a great compliment" River said sarcastically.

"It's beautiful" Beth finally admitted.

A big grin plastered on both Austin's and River's face.

"We know we are the best" Austin said proudly.

"If you guys have finished appreciating each other, can we discuss further?" Beth asked irritably

"You are mean" River retorted.

"I know" Beth said.

"Guys instead of surprising both, why don't we tell Recce about our plan? This way it will be easier." I suggested.

"Brilliant idea. Alice will be happier to know that all this was planed by Recce and not by us" Beth added.

Approving out idea, Austin called Recce. It was very strange to know that Recce was still in the library hiding away from Alice.

This boy was an idiot, seriously.

Since Recce had nothing to do at all he agreed to come without asking any questions.

The moment Recce entered the house, the boys attacked him and blindfolded him.

I didn't understand why they had blindfolded him, as now it was not a surprise for Recce.

But damn the fear and confusion on Recce's face when the two attacked him, was hilarious.

I must say, these three act like total fools when they are together.

The boys took Recce in the guest room. We went behind them.

Recce was totally surprised to see the room in front of him. For a moment he just kept staring at the room, then at River and then at Austin and then the room again.

"Guys I appreciate your efforts but I am not gay. Austin you even have a girlfriend now. How can this even be possible?" Recce said after recovering from the state of shock.

The boys removed their hands from Recce's shoulder in a blink of an eye as if their hands were on fire.

At that very moment Beth and I burst out laughing. Damn this was such an out-of-the-blue response.

"We are not proposing to you idiot."

River said smacking Recce's head upside down.

"I have a girlfriend way much better than you." Austin said looking straight in my eyes. I instantly felt blood rushing to my cheeks.

Bloody blush.

"Then are you expecting somebody else?"

Recce asked scratching the back of his neck.

"No" River said with a shrug.

"Then why all this preparation?" Recce asked more confused this time.

"For you" Austin replied.

"But I am not Gay"

"Idiot will you just shut your mouth and let us speak" River spoke this time.

"This entire preparation is for you. You have to propose to Alice today. She will be here in few minutes." Austin explained.

At this Recce pinched his arms and yelped in pain.

What the hell this guy is doing now.

"What was that?" Beth asked curiously.

"I was just checking"

"What? Are you still alive or dead?" River asked raising his eyebrow.

"No Idiot. I am checking whether I am dreaming or not." Recce spoke innocently.

"You are not dreaming Recce. We all know you like Alice. Just man up a little." I finally spoke up.

"Who told you this?" Recce asked suspiciously looking at Austin.

"Even we where there in the car yesterday" Beth informed Recce.

"Shit. Even Alice must have heard this than.

What should I do now?" Recce asked panicking.

"Just say again what you said yesterday."

"I can't"

"Why?"

"Because yesterday I was drunk today I am not."

"So what you want to drink now?" Austin asked with a smirk.

"Anything that can serve the purpose" Recce replied with same tone.

Boys will be boys. They can never be serious.

"Shut up Guys. Recce, are you so weak that you need help of alcohol to express your feelings?"

Recce just shook his head.

"Speak up Recce "

"Didn't you just tell me to shut up. You are too confuse Jenny."

"Can you be just serious for one moment."

"Recce be brave now or else don't come crying to us when Alice starts loving someone else." Beth said in stern voice.

"You guys think she likes me?"

"Are you crazy? Can't you see? She is totally into you. She had a huge crush on you even when we were not friends”

Beth’s new information caused everyone to turn in her direction.

“Are you serious?” Recce said with a big grin. He was not even trying to hide his happiness.

Aw...that was so sweet.

“So are going to propose to her now or just let her slip out of your hands?” Austin asked seriously this time.

“Look who is talking about manning up and accepting their feelings.”

“I do have the girl who I wanted, so that doesn’t makes any sense now.”

“Recce, I am calling Alice here now. You just get ready.”

“Wait what will you tell her?”

“That Austin broke up with me.”

“Woah that’s a brilliant idea again” Beth said patting my back.

“Wait why is that a good idea?” Austin interrupted.

“By this, Alice will be here faster” Beth explained.

She was right. I had messaged Alice the same and had received reply way faster than expected

“I will be there in a minute with a Ice cream .Dont do anything silly till then”Was Alice’s Reply

“Awww she is so caring”Recce said which lead severe teasing from others.

ALICE POV

Today’s day was going to be evilly bad. I knew Recce didn’t have feelings for me, but listening from other’s mouth made it seem more real and heartbreaking. I never wanted this to be true. But now that it was true, I felt like throwing up. I had a headache. The pit of my stomach whirled with pain. Tears were starting to form at the corner of my eyes. I sucked my tears and took a deep breath. I didn’t want to cry in front of my friends. So I made an excuse of going to class. I didn’t feel like going to the class. I wanted to ignore everyone. So instead, I went to a park near my house. When I reached the garden, I finally broke down. Tears started freely falling and I didn’t make any effort to even stop them. I was feeling lot of pain and it was the only way of taking pain out. I was dwelling in my sorrow whole day when suddenly in the evening I received message from Jenny.

“Austin broke up with me”

Was all the text read.

I didn’t wanted Jenny to be alone. I knew how hard heartbreaks are. And how harder it is to deal with it alone. I wiped my dry tears and got ready to go to Jenny's place. I took ice cream on my way. Maybe this will help us both get out of our sorrow.

Jenny had later messaged me to meet her in her guest room which was strange. The door to Jenny's house was open. Which was even stranger as jenny never leaves her door open when she is home alone.

I hurriedly rushed to the guest room getting more worried.

The moment I entered the room I was met by total darkness.

What was going on here? I thought to myself.

"Woah so you are here finally" A male voice spoke all of sudden. The voice seemed similar. But I wasn't expecting a male voice so without thinking about anything, I just screamed on the top of my lungs. The figure in front of me had to literally put hand on my mouth to shut me up.

"Shh.. It's me Recce." The voice whispered.

When he was sure that I wouldn't shout again, he slowly removed hands from my mouth.

"Damn that's a lot of noise for a girl like you" Recce said with a sigh.

"I am sorry I wasn't expecting you, so I got scared." I said embarrassed.

"Why are you here? Jenny even called you?" I asked again curiously.

"By the way where is she? Is she OK? Is she crying a lot? I swear I am going to kill your friend-" I started blabbering again when I realized why I was here.

Damn I didn't even give him a chance to answer.

He was just waiting for his chance to come. Poor Recce.

He looked so cute and innocent thinking about the answers. Focus Alice, he doesn't likes you back. My mind reminded me. My heartbeat literally stopped the moment when the lights of the room were turned on. The view of the room made me miss countless heartbeats. It was decorated with red and white heart shaped balloons. Rose petals were scattered everywhere. On table my favorite black forest cake in heart shaped was placed over which Recce and my name was scribbled. On the bed were the most amazing words I thought I would never hear from a guy in front of me.

Hell yeah I LOVE YOU was written on bed with rose petals. Damn! All this was more beautiful than my dreams. Another unexpected and the best thing was, by now Recce was on his knees.

Oh My Gosh..!! I was feeling like flying across the blue sky. I was seriously on the top of the world.

Today my best dream was going to come true. I eagerly waited for Recce to speak.

"Alice I love you, so much, more than my life and I would do anything for you. I want to be with you everyday. Hear your voice everyday. Though its loud sometimes" He continued with a chuckle "I want us to be together in an unbreakable bond. Would you make me the happiest and luckiest man on earth and be by girlfriend?" He asked pulling a blue box out of his jacket pocket and opening it. Nestled inside the silk lining of the box was the most beautiful ring.

In the center was a diamond that reflected the sunlight, sending sparkles around me, and smaller diamonds were surrounding the bigger diamond on both the sides. The ring was just perfect.

My throat caught and my eyes watered but I pushed all of it aside to give my answer to the guy of my dream.

Although my heart was beating faster now, yet I tried my best to look calm.

"Recce" I tried saying further but I couldn't speak anything more. My words flattered. Tears brimmed in my eyes. I knew I wouldn't be able to speak anything now so I just nodded, my head indicating a yes.

He flashed his pearly white smile which makes my heart goes crazy and swiftly placed the ring on my finger.

Gosh this is the best moment of my life. I just hugged Recce tightly cherishing every minute.

In a very less time entire room erupted into 'whoas' and claps. All my friends had by now gathered in the room.

"So it was all planned huh?" I asked.

"Yeah. But we didn't know you even had a ring dude" Austin asked puzzled.

"I have been thinking of asking her out for a long time. So I had starting keeping the ring with me all the time. But this wouldn't have been so special without you guys" Recce said hugging both Austin and River.

"Even we helped you Recce" Beth interrupted.

"So, liked it?" Jenny asked me.

"Liked? I just loved it" I shouted with excitement.

"So how you feeling now?"

"I am not only happy but also shocked, jovial , surprised , hurt, excited everything it's like some dish you prepared and every freaking spice is added to it. Yes that's how exactly I am feeling right now "I said Everyone openly laughed at my description.

"But why did you guys lie to me before? " I asked all of a sudden.

"Because we wanted to see you with so much mixed feelings" River said with a chuckle.

"What did you lie to her about?" Recce asked confused.

"That you don't like her at all" Beth said with shrug.

"Why did you guys say that? You knew that I liked her, Right?"

"We wanted to know about Alice's feeling so we lied." Austin explained.

"Woah! You did all this for me?" Recce asked happily.

"You are the star of our group buddy. Anything for you." River said patting Recce's back.

"Now can we cut the cake? I am actually very hungry" Recce said pointing towards his stomach.

Damn this boy can never change. But do I even want him to change? Never, this innocence is what makes him more unique.

We both cut the cake and fed each other and our friends. Recce put some cake on my nose. I rubbed my cream coated hands on his cheeks.

With all smiles and giggles the best day of my life ended. Or I must say my new life started.

❄ ❄ ❄

Chapter 36 - Girls Night out

Now that even Recce and Alice were couple, love was totally in the air. Life had become much better and everyone was happy. Everything was perfect except Beth and River's life. Poor Beth and River had to be always with us lovely dovies.

As usual, the guys picked up Austin and me from my house to went to the school. You must be confused by my last words. Let me clear the confusion. Yes now we all six go to high school together. Last few months have helped us to strengthen our bonds stronger. And we are damn close now.

Gosh! I had never thought my life would change so much in such a less time. I had real friends or let me say, a whole gang of friends now.

Another big revelation, Austin comes to my house at night when my parents are out. He says he don't want me to be alone in my big house.

Aw isn't that sweet.

According to him, spending night with your partner doesn't always mean you are crossing your limits. Sometimes it simply means cuddling with your partner. Sometimes it means, just keeping your head on his shoulders. Sometimes it means, just sharing a bed or just simply sharing a warm feeling.

His words had touched my heart.

He had once asked me "You know what real love is..?"

When I had shamelessly said "No"

He had said staring in my eyes "It's waking up in the middle of the night, for no reason, shifting under the blanket and feeling the heat of person next to you. You turn around to see them in their most peaceful, innocent and vulnerable state. You kiss their face in the most gentle manner, so as not to wake them up. You turn back and there is a sweet priceless smile on your face. You feel an arm wrapping around your waist, and you know it doesn't get any better than this.

You can't make your relationship strengthen with spending more time in Bed; you have to the keep promises, which you've made. You have to just not say those magical words, but also prove it every day - every night. Treating your girl right is much more important than kissing her.

Understanding her secret wishes is much more important. Joining her pieces of broken heart is much more important. Leaving her with beautiful memories is much better than leaving her in bed."

This had made me fall for him even more.

Damn now I was totally head on heal in love with this guy. I never knew Austin would turn out to be so sweet and understanding.

"Just long, deep, hard kisses doesn't make a way for any relationship. But few roses, magical words, and true promises makes a beautiful relationship. - Without any doubt." He had explained me further. I was totally lost in my wonderland when my thinking was abruptly interrupted by overly excited voice

"We are coming to your house today Jenny" I knew it was Alice's voice without even glancing at source of voice. She has become more cheerful and happy after being with Recce.

This guy is seriously having a lot effect on Alice. I am glad the effect is good.

"Cool so are you guys joining us for dinner or something?"

Austin spoke up trying to match excitement level of Alice.

"Sorry pretty boy, but by 'we' Alice meant just Alice and me. We are thinking of having Girls Night out today" Beth cleared.

"Woah that's not fair" Recce chirped in.

"Yeah Recce is absolutely right this is rude. You guys are stealing a little us time from me" Austin said childishly pointing between him and me.

"Aren't you Guys like always together?" Beth asked raising her eyebrow.

"But tomorrow is a weekend" Austin tried reasoning though this reason was silly.

"What's the connection between weekend and our Girls Night out?" Alice asked this time.

"I don't know" Austin said with a shrug.

"Dude, didn't you just say they couldn't have girls night out because tomorrow is a weekend? " River asked confused.

"Yeah I said that because I was out of reasons OK" Austin said it innocently.

With this everyone erupted in laughter. This was our daily routine. Even lunch time had become more enjoyable because of these silly guy's fight and arguments.

"I think girls night out would be a great idea. We haven't had our girl time in a long time" I said breaking the argument.

"But I wanted to come tonight." Austin said with a pout. The voice of bell signaled the end of our conversation.

Rest of the day went in a blur. I had none of the classes with Austin, but few classes with the girls. Time just flew after lunch.

I was walking towards my locker, when I was suddenly pulled by very strong hands into an attic room and was immediately met by soft lips.

Few days before I would have panicked in a situation like this but now even this has been part of our daily routine. This was like our sneaking out place.

I let him overtake me as usual. I kissed him back though. With his hands still on my waist, he lifted me up as I held onto his face. He pulled me closer to him. It felt so good to have his lips on mine. As I melted by his kiss, all I could think about was how I could kiss him for a lifetime and beyond. We made out for a while before both of us pulled away for a breath. Our foreheads were still against each other as we were both breathing heavily with our eyes closed.

"I will miss you a lot today" Austin finally spoke up.

"Can't you just cancel it by saying you have some other plans or something?"

"Austin they are my friends they know me well. They understand when I am lying. Besides I haven't spent quality time with them in last few weeks. I miss them" I tried explaining.

Austin nodded with a pout. Gosh he looked damn cute. I couldn't resist his charms anymore and I kissed him again. He didn't mind it at all, instead he immediately kissed me back. Constant sound of horn brought us out of our dreamland. We knew it was River he does this everyday to gather everyone near his car.

"Damn from tomorrow I am going to bring my own car. "Austin said irritated.

We left the attic room hurriedly. After finishing my work at the locker we marched towards the car.

Though River saw us, he was still honking which confused us. When we went near the car we found out the reason behind his still honking. Alice and Recce were still missing.

"Sorry sorry Guys I had some work in the staff room" Alice said running in our direction followed by Recce.

"Yeah we can tell that by your heavy panting and happiness on Recce's face" Beth said with a wink I could see blood rushing in her cheeks though Alice was trying to hide her blush very hard.

"So boys night out it is" Recce said excitedly changing the topic by now all were settled in the car

Lucky Alice. Damn this boy always saves her.

"Recce it's girls night out not boys night out" Alice classified.

"What you mean by that? You think you guys can have night outs and all the fun, and we can't?" River Said happily.

"When was this decided" Austin asked confused.

"When you were day dreaming in the history class" Recce pointed out.

"Whatever." Austin said trying to not drag his day dreaming moment.

"So now it's fixed, we will leave the girls at Jenny's house and rush to my house. Damn I am so excited" Recce said bouncing up & down purely showing his excitement.

"Recce before going to your house we can stay for little time at Jenny house, what say?" Austin asked.

"Yeah that would be a great idea" I added.

"We could watch movie together "Alice spoke up happily.

"Yeah we haven't done even this, in a long time" Beth agreed.

"Yeah you are right .We could have stayed, but we have plans" Recce said with a fake smile

"Yeah he is right" River added with his signature smirk.

It was clear from their way of speaking that they didn't have any plans they were just ignoring us just like we did in the morning.

"What plans do you actually have?" Beth asked raising her eyebrow

"Sorry it's a boy thing" Rivers said shutting Beth's mouth. Without further argument the boys left us at my house and went away.

"Do you really think they have plans?" Alice asked.

"No it was damn clear from their way of speaking that they were lying" I pointed out.

"Girls let's not affect our mood by this and let's just have a rocking day" Beth spoke.

We all changed into our PJ's and prepared bowl full of pop corn with lot of chips and junk food and sat in front of the idiot box.

The biggest question in front of us was 'who was going chose the movie'?

As usual, Alice was in mood of romance and Beth in mood of action. For a change I was in mood of some horror.

We decided to watch horror movie first as we all are scared to watch horror movies at night.

Isn't every girl scared to watch horror movie at night?

We decided to watch conjuring.

"Don't go there don't go there you are going to get killed bitch."

Alice shouted.

"Chill Alice it's just a movie" Beth said irritated.

This is our daily ritual whenever we watch horror movies.

Alice gets too much involved in the movie. After the horror movie we watched 'A walk to remember' our all time favorite movie which always helps us to forget about ghosts. After watching movies with lots of yelling and crying, we all were finally hungry.

"Guys what do you want to eat?" I asked in a very unladylike voice that came from my stomach.

"Pizza" both of them shouted simultaneously. Pizza is our usual menu.

I jumped up from the couch and began rummaging through the cabinets and fridge to see what I can find to make Pizza. No one was in the house to cook so that meant, it was up to me to fend for myself and for my friends and well, I'm not the best cook.

If it doesn't come frozen it doesn't get made. My eyes lit up when I spotted the ready to cook pizza on the second shelf of the freezer. It's meaty, goodness! was calling out to me and I couldn't resist. The smell of the pizza quickly began to feel my nostrils and I took in its heavenly smell. Nothing is better on a cold day other than pizza and a movie.

"Damn this smells so good when the bloody hell is it going to be ready?" Beth asked being most impatient when it came to pizza.

"According to the box, we have to wait for more five minutes. So what do we do now?" I asked.

"What must the boys be doing now?" Alice chirped from nowhere.

"Damn I miss Austin" I said.

"Even I miss Recce" Alice said instantly.

"Did I say that loud?" I asked placing hand on my mouth.

"Yeah. You girls are becoming love sick" Beth stated. The ring of oven saved us from further lecture.

"Let stalk your boyfriends on Facebook" Beth said all of the sudden with a grin on her face.

Without wasting any time we took pizza out and logged on to my Facebook account.

It seems like the boys are really having fun as they were posting many photos on Austin's time line today. Maybe they somehow knew that we would get bored and stalk their profiles.

We didn't want to prove their guess right, so we just surfed down without liking any of the pictures.

After seeing many photos of Austin and me mentally drooling over

Austin and his perfect body features, there came one picture that caught our attention.

"Who's she?" Alice asked.

These girl was standing beside Austin with Austin's arm around her shoulder and they both seemed pretty happy and in their own world.

"She must be Bella. Austin's ex girlfriend" I told them.

At that particular time I fell very jealous of her. She was really gorgeous with angelic eyes. She was tall tan and flawless. I can see why Austin went for her. She was totally perfect.

"Are you okay? "Alice asked placing hands on my shoulder.

"Yeah I am fine".

"Don't worry Jenny. What they had was long time ago. Now Austin has you. And we all know he loves you a lot" Alice assured me.

They were right. Austin loves me now and that's what really matters.

"Lets do something else. I am getting bored." Beth said closing the laptop.

"Yeah we are here to have fun and not to stalk our boyfriends" Alice added.

With this Beth went to the kitchen to look for something.

After eating so much, is this girl seriously still hungry?

"Who wants to have little fun?" Beth asked with a huge grin plastered on her face.

Before we could respond, Beth pulled out a big bottle of alcohol from behind her.

"Oh No. We can't drink this. Its my Dad's "

"Oh come on Jenny. It's not a crime to relax a little once in your lifetime. Besides, your dad won't even know that there is a bottle missing. There are so many bottles there." Beth reasoned.

"Yeah it would be damn fun" Alice said excitedly.

Beth and I, both stared at Alice in shock. Alice never agrees for something illegal in a go.

Alice is seriously changing a lot. For good though.

"Don't worry we will keep lime with us. It reduces alcohol's effect" Beth spoke up, sensing my tension.

Just a little wont hurt. Besides, if not today, I won't be able to taste it again anytime soon. So I gave in.

"Alright" I said "Lets have the fun today" I said excitedly.

"Great" Beth squealed happily.

"Glasses?" she asked further.

"Cabinet above the sink." I pointed.

After taking our glasses, Beth poured Alcohol in it. We raised our glasses above our head for "Cheers".

After this, Beth began gulping down the liquid followed by Alice. They seemed to enjoy the taste.

It's when the real night started.

I turned up my glass and took a long sip until my brain froze.

Oh wow! that hurts.

I grabbed my head to hold it.until the pain passed and then again made an attempt to finish my drink. Wow this is good. Although

I think I can still taste the alcohol, I'd definitely drink it again.

******

Two things were moving constantly through my mind as soon as I opened my eyes.

One, when did earthquake come in my room to make it so untidy? And two, why was Austin standing next to me with an amused expression on his face along with a bottle of Advil and water bottle?

I tried to ignore the intense thumping in my head and the nauseous feeling in my stomach to ask him what he was doing here but every time I opened my mouth I felt like I was going to hurl. Mental Note, never drink again.

I honestly don't know how people handle this on a daily basis.

"Here take these and rest for ten minutes." He said with a smirk.

Without saying a word, I held out my hand to take the pills from him and tried my best to sit up in my bed. The keyword is 'tried'. Damn I couldn't sit up on my own bed even.

After enjoying my situation for a little more time, Austin helped me to sit and toss the pills into my mouth. I laid back down taking the cover over my head.

"Or maybe thirty minutes." He joked after hearing my moaning from underneath the blankets.

My head was pounding like hell. What did I do last night, ran into a brick wall or constantly bang my head on a stone? All I did was drink little alcohol. Maybe a little too much. Actually, after two glasses I had lost the count.

But how can something that taste so good make you feel so bad?

As the pain started to ease away, I felt like it is finally safe to talk. But what do I speak?

"Where is everyone?" I asked and finally spoke.

"You mean your back up dancers?"

Recce said appearing from nowhere.

"They are sitting down in the kitchen having breakfast and complaining about their head aches." Recce said with a laugh.

"That's the reason we are here. Can we borrow the Advil if you are done with it?" River said with a smirk.

Gosh this was damn embarrassing. This was the very first time I had drunk in my entire life. Why did I have to be so drunk?

I just nodded. Taking the Advil, they left the room.

Well that's good. At least they all are safe.

My mind was stuck at the word 'back up dancers'.

Oh My Gosh! What exactly happened last night?

Well whatever it was, I have a feeling the embarrassment hasn't even started yet. And I was not in the mood to get more embarrassment but I wanted to know what happened last night.

"When did you get here?" I said with my head still buried under the heavy blankets.

"We have been here since 4 A.M. looking after you people. And don't feel bad about it. We enjoyed every bit of it" Austin said with a chuckle.

"Do I even want to know?" I cringed just imagining what must have happened.

"Yeah, you should know it. Damn you were totally different and a new girl yesterday." Austin admitted

Oh lord. It must have been very bad.

"How about you tell me about this, never" I said after resurfacing from the cover.

He gives me a sideways grin. He looks good even when laughing at me.

Wow my boyfriend is so hot.

"Well. That would have been OK, but I want to tell you" He starts settling himself in on the bottom of my bed.

"It all started after I received a very weird voice mail from you asking actually not asking singing-You were singing on the top your voice one direction song- Baby you light up my world like nobody else. Heck it was so fun. I never knew I rock your world so much" Austin said with a wink.

"Oh no. Please tell me you are lying" I say while burring my face into the palm of my hands.

"Why would I lie? And that's not all."

"Of course it isn't."

"Then you proceeded to tell me how much you love me. Which

was very nice to hear from you. Though it seemed like you were comparing yourself with someone else."

Suddenly the memory of us checking Austin's account crossed my mind. I must be comparing myself with Bella. Did I say that loud to him? I hope not.

"Did I say with whom I was comparing myself to?" I force myself to ask.

"No you were about to say someone's name but then line got cut" He answered with a chuckle.

I mentally noted to thank my friends for snatching the phone from my hands.

"I am so sorry." I apologize.

Well this is it. He will probably dump me for a far less crazy person. Great job Jenny.

"Chill Jenny, there is more to come." He laughs.

"Believe me, I have seen drunken people but I never seen and heard any thing worse than what you did last night."

"Did?" I panicked. "What did I do?" I got a feeling that I was going to regret asking that question.

"After that, I called you back and you didn't answer. I became a little curious about your further confessions and decided to come to your house and even the boys joined me"

"I personally think your dance on the dining table on all kinds of freaking songs was the best part of the night."

"What?" I shouted awestruck. "We were dancing on the table?"

"Yup. You guys are lucky we didn't think of taking your videos." Austin said with a smirk.

This explains the word back up dancers. God what I was thinking of yesterday. Probably I wasn't thinking at all.

I bet the rest of the house was as wreaked as my room was.

"How bad is it? The house I mean."

"Not too bad considering we spent most of the morning cleaning it up. You're lucky you have friends like Recce and River and a boyfriend like Austin" Austin said proudly.

Oh thank goodness.

"Well thanks for taking care of me last night. And believe me I have learnt my lesson about drinking. I will never ever drink any sort of alcohol in my entire life."

"Well I wouldn't go as far as to say never, just not without me. Next time I don't want to miss even half of the fun" Austin said with a smirk.

"Oh and just for your information, I will never be able to listen to that songs again without thinking about that dance you did for us." He adds. "Hell! you guys were on fire." If that didn't send the blood rushing to my cheeks then nothing would.

That was just the icing on the cake.

Don't make eyes contact, don't make eye contact, I chanted inside my head.

"When you are done, come down. Everyone is having breakfast. I will be waiting for you downstairs. I will prepare coffee for you by then. This will help you with the hangover"

Well that's going to be one awkward moment, a cup of coffee.

Once I was ready for further embarrassment, I cleaned myself and went down for breakfast.

Everyone was busy discussing about something, but the moment they felt my presence behind them, they just erupted out laughing.

Woah! this was weird. One moment they were serious as hell, and the other moment they just started laughing out of blue.

Something was fishy.

"What's so funny" I asked.

"Come on Jenny, join the talk. Recce was just telling us what we did yesterday"

I was embarrassed enough for a day so I just took coffee from Austin's hand and went to watch TV.

There was a Christmas party invitation card lying on the table that reminded me about Christmas.

Damn how could I forget that Christmas is coming in two days.

Which means I will get to see my parents and have lots of Fun, Christmas is the best day of the year for me. Santa, Christmas tree, Gifts, Parties, Decorations and Family dinner is what I like the most about Christmas.

I excitedly went in the Kitchen again.

"Guys get up. We need to go shopping. Christmas is coming. We need Christmas tree, Bells, Tinsels, Candles, cute Santa and much much more" .I said hopping up and down

"Woah chill dear. I have never seen you so excited before." Austin said side hugging me.

"Jenny loves Christmas a lot" Alice added.

"Yup I love it a lot. I get to have dinner with my family. Party with my best friends, snow and lots of gifts. Christmas is full of fun. This time it will be more fun as even you guys will be there" I said jumping up and down again.

I don't know what was exactly happening to me but I was feeling very happy. It was going to be my first Christmas with Austin and his friends.

"Sorry to break your bubble of excitement Jenny but your parents had called to inform that they couldn't come for Christmas this year as there is lot of work load" Beth said in a sad voice.

I felt like my entire world was falling apart. My parents had never canceled our family dinner before in my entire life. Tears started to fall down from the corner of my eyes unknowingly.

Austin hugged me tightly whispering in my ears "Its OK sweetheart."

"Oh sorry it's just that I have never celebrated my Christmas without my parents" I said wiping my tears. "But I guess there is first time for everything. At least I have you guys; we will have fun on Christmas" I spoke trying to cheer myself up.

Austin loosened his grip around me and my all friends stayed silent. It's when I sensed there was something wrong.

"What?" I asked expectantly but no one replied.

"Guys we will be spending Christmas together, right?"

No one spoke again. There was pin drop silence. My heart was beating rapidly. I had the feeling that I was going to hear something worse.

Recce was the first to break the silence.

"Jenny I always spend my Christmas with my family. Sorry I can't come" He said sadly.

"Me too" River added.

I looked with expectant eyes towards Austin. But avoiding eye contact, he said "We always go to my grand parent's house for Christmas celebrations"

I felt my heart crushing for the second time. I thought the girls would say they would be there for me like always but their silence spoke lots of words.

"You guys also have other plans, right?" I said looking at their direction.

They just nodded their heads.

"Look Jenny" Beth started speaking. But I didn't have enough strength to listen to their reasons. So I just headed out of house. I don't know where I was going, but I just kept on going away from everyone. I heard few voices calling my name but I just ignored them. I was not angry at them I was just sad.

Now though I had so many people in my life, I was still going to celebrate Christmas on my own. Alone. Even my parents were going to ditch me.

I felt so alone and hopeless. I felt like crying. But I had no ones shoulder to cry on.

I just kept going. I found myself near the ice cream corner. Exactly what I needed. Ice cream always tends to make my mood good.

I must have eaten half the ice cream shop but today my mood didn't changed by a bit even.

I still felt sad and hopeless. Eating half the ice cream parlor didn't changed the condition at all. I was still alone for Christmas.

❄ ❄ ❄

Chapter 37- The Night of Unexpected Events

The moment I reached home I was expecting everyone to be still home waiting for me for apologizing to me but I was wrong. I was met by empty house and utter silence. At that very moment I had checked my cell for calls or messages. I was expecting at least a miss call or a message from Austin but I was met by disappointment again.

I felt sad and angry, and lots of other feelings at that very moment. I didn't know what to do exactly to subside this feeling so I just decided to sleep until this uneasy feelings went. Basically the sleep helped a little.

I slept till I felt grumbling of my stomach. That is basically by night.

Woah! I must say, I am seriously damn stressed about this Christmas thing as I had literally slept for eight long hours.

But the sad part was that the uneasy feeling hadn't passed completely yet. I was still expecting somebody's message or call.

I still wasn't able to settle on the idea of me celebrating Christmas alone or not celebrating it at all.

24th December was the worst day of my life. I had nothing to do yet and I didn't want to sit ideal. I had literally done homework of the entire week, cleaned house twice, done grocery, read all the novel I had. Yet I had lots of time to waste.

Poor me. I finally was out of activities and I still had an entire night to waste.

What could I do now? I thought to myself.

But I couldn't think of anything. So I decided to do the same thing I did yesterday.

Yeah Right. I decided to sleep.

I tried closing my eyes and falling asleep by listening to silent songs. But even this didn't helped.

I was still awake like an owl and was absent mindedly staring at the ceiling above.

At sharp 12'o clock my cell rang. You must be thinking how I knew its 12'o clock. I had checked the time before picking up the phone.

I know, silly me.

But 12'o clock in watch made me excited. I excitedly picked it up hoping it to be my parent's call. But I was wrong.

The call was neither from my parents nor from Austin.

It was from some unknown number.

"Where is my son?" A Female voice that seemed to be stressed, asked.

Though she was stressed it still didn't explain why I must know about her son's whereabout.

"Sorry I don't know what you are talking about" I asked confused.

"Aren't you Austins friend?" The voice spoke up again.

I was shocked for a moment by so much information, but when I came to my senses finally and I replied. "Yeah".

"Can I know whom I am actually speaking to?" I managed to ask further.

"You are talking to Mrs. Parker. Austin's mom and he is not picking up his phone. So I thought he must be with you." His mom said it all in one breath.

"Oh my God. Where must have he gone at this time?" I said getting panicked.

"Oh dear I am so sorry to put you through tension too. Why don't you just come here so you will be updated about his whereabouts" Rather than staying at home and thinking like maniac about Austin, I found the offer of going at his home better.

So I just took my dad's car's keys and sped off to Austin's house. I just hoped Austin was safe wherever he was.

I saw Mrs Parker outside the house waiting for me.

"So any news about Austin?" I asked instantly as I came out of the car.

"No dear but calm down. We will find him soon. Don't worry. You come inside."

I was expecting chaos inside the house. But the moment I stepped inside the house I was met by silence and darkness.

Mrs. Parker took me in the middle of the hall and all of the sudden Rose petals were being showered on me and lights were turned on simultaneously.

Then later everyone started emerging from the rooms shouting "Surprise!"

For a moment I couldn't understand what was actually going on. But when my poor brain finally came to know about the situation, it started dancing madly inside my head.

I know I am over exaggerating. But Damn! this was most unexpected and the best thing happening to me ever.

My friends and family was all together with the Santa Claus and beautiful Christmas decoration was everywhere.

I have never been so surprised in my entire life.

"How can you even think that we won't come to meet you for Christmas, princess?" My dad said breaking the silence and hugging me tightly.

Damn this was the best moment of my life.

My family and friends had teamed together to surprise me on the night I love the most- Yeah Christmas night.

Gosh the surprise was awesome. No kidding.

The entire hall was decorated to give a Christmas feeling. The hall was decorated with the traditional colors of Christmas like pine green, snow white, and heart red. Blue and white all were used to represent winter.

With a Christmas tree at a center decorated with images of Baby Jesus, Father Christmas, Santa Claus and the star of Bethlehem and typical winter symbols like snow flakes, penguins and polar bears. This was the cutest decorated Christmas tree I had ever seen. The entire hall was decorated with different colour ornaments, wreaths, garlands and Santa was standing right besides it with lots and lots of gifts and many more decorations this surely is going to be one of my best Christmas.

"Woah Christmas party." I said hopping up and down.

Damn! I was feeling a lot excited.

"Guys you could have told me before. My day wouldn't have sucked so much at least."

"But then you wouldn't have been this surprised even." Austin said coming closer to me.

He had a point there.

He wrapped an arm around my waist and in slow motion he spoke "Merry Christmas princess" with a kiss on my lips.

Damn at that very moment my day was not at all bad anymore. Everything around me disappeared and I was lost in world of pure happiness.

The "Ahem Ahem" noise of Mr. Parker brought me back to reality. It was then I realized that I was shamelessly making out in front of our parents.

God just kill me or bury me alive seven feet below earth.

"Don't be embarrassed dear we already know about your relationship" My mom said with excitement.

"We even know that Austin comes to stay at our house at night" My dad spoke up.

I was totally shocked by this new piece of information. Its not like my parents were strict or something but staying at night at someone's house is like taking the relationship to a next level which my parents disagree to mostly.

"And you are OK with it?" River chirped in our conversation.

"Yeah. I was little angry when Mr. Parker had told me but..."

"Damn! Even Austin's parents know it?" Recce spoke up cutting my dads words in middle.

"Woah you are the coolest parents in the world" Beth said. That was actually what I wanted to say.

"What do you guys think, just because we aren't home all the time we don't know what our children do?" Mrs. Parker spoke this time.

"Then why didn't you stop Austin from coming to your house?" Beth asked confused.

"Because I trust both of them completely and by the way Austin looks at Jenny, I can surely tell that he wouldn't ever even think of cheating on my girl." My dad explained.

"And we are happy to know that Austin loves our sweetheart more than us." My mom completed.

"Now that you all trust me so much, I believe you wouldn't be mad at my next decision?" Austin said all of sudden.

"Is there something more?" Recce asked confused.

"Yeah there is one more surprise" My mom spoke up with excitement.

"And Jenny's Mom knows about it?" River asked with stern look.

"Chill River, I just wanted to take suggestions from the elders for this, so I approached her" Austin spoke sincerely.

"Why didn't you tell us this before?" Austin's dad asked him this time.

"Because I wanted to surprise you all" He said with a shrug.

Gosh what's going on in the head of this guy?

"What are you talking about dear?" Mrs. Parker said.

"Yeah we thought it's just the surprise party." River said this time.

"Please tell us fast. I am excited to know about the surprise." Alice asked bouncing up and down.

Damn this girl was always excited for new gossips.

"Gosh I can't believe there is still something more" Recce chirped in.

"Be patient guys. You will know about the surprise very soon." Austin said nervously.

And then he just whistled. On the sound of his one whistle Santa clauses emerged from the other room with a huge beautiful cake.

That's not surprising at all. The more surprising thing was actually the words written on the cake.

I couldn't believe on my eyes at all. I rubbed my eyes again and again but the words didn't changed.

God can this day get any better

"Will you marry me Jenny?" Were the words written on the cake.

To confirm that it was real I looked over Austin He was already on his knees with a ring.

" I love you with all my heart and soul. And I promise this will never change. You are the love that I had always hoped for, The dream I had chased for so long. You are the wish that I had always had in my heart, you are the wish I thought would never come true, but now when I have found you, my dream has become reality and my wish has come true. I will make sure that we never move apart. Even if the whole universe goes against us, I promise to you from my heart that my love for you will never fade away. And I will love you more and more with each passing day. I love you jenny I love you a Lot...Will you please marry me?"

Gosh this was the sweetest proposal ever.

No idiot will dare to reject this proposal. And I am not that idiot. For a moment I just looked at his handsome face with unshed tears burning in my eyes.

I don't know what that idiot actually thought but his next words made me feel guilty

"Well it's okay if you don't want to marry me now!" Austin replied with total sad face.

Since I was not replying he suddenly got even more nervous. I felt really bad for making him sad

"I love you idiot!" I yelled, crying and laughing at the same time. I unwarily threw myself at him. We kissed once again and this time it was a deeper with knee weakening, chocolate melting hot kiss.

"Yes..Yes I will marry you" I said happily with all the strength inside me. Happy tears started to fall from my eyes and I didn't even tried to stop it. I knew they weren't going to stop today.

Austin slid the ring in my hand and damn! the way he looked at me with all the love in eyes made me fall for him even more, if that is even possible. Getting a guy who looks at you like you are his entire world is the luckiest thing for any girl. Actually, I was the lucky girl in this case. I didn't know how to express my happiness. I couldn't control my feelings anymore and I just kissed Austin hard again pouring all my emotions and love in it.

The happiness on the face of my family and friends was the proof of my correct decision.

Gosh! I still can't believe I am going to be The Austin Parker's wife. I was surely on top of the world.

This made Christmas more memorable and special for me. This is what Christmas teaches us, Isn't it?

To believe and trust on Jesus whole heartedly and to hope for miracles and then they would surely happen.

******

"Mom Dad, why are guys packing? Are you guys leaving today itself?" I asked confused and bit sad.

"No dear. We all are leaving today" My mom replied pointing her fingers at me, dad and herself.

"What do you mean?" I asked getting more confused than before.

"Sweety, did you forget again that today we had to go to your aunt's house, like we do for every New Year?"

"Oh my god. How could I forget something this important?" I said.

"Its OK dear. With so much happening in your life you are bound to forget things. Just pack your bags soon. We are leaving in the evening."

"We are going for how many days this time? "

"For a week sweetheart" My dad replied this time.

I wanted to meet Austin for a few hours before I left. So I quickly messaged him to meet me in the garden nearby after lunch and went to pack my bags.

Now, let me tell you, packing is the thing I hate the most because I am never able to decide what clothes to wear on what occasions. I am a total disaster when it comes to packing. I always require mom by my side when I am packing. I was about to shout for mom's name but my mom was already at my door with a knowing smile on her face.

"Dear I know you would need my help. Lets see what we are taking then?" With this, it took us total one hour for packing.

After packing and having lunch I hurriedly went out to go the Park.

"Awwww missing me already princess?"

A voice said hugging me tightly from behind.

Damn I really missed him and was going to miss him a lot in coming week.

I wish I could take him with me.

"Hello day dreamer. The boy of your dreams is in front of you." Austin said waving his hands in front of me.

Though it was true I didn't want to increase his already large ego."Shut up. Who said I was dreaming about you?

I was just staring the guy behind you. Damn he is so-" I never get to complete my sentence as I was interrupted by the words of egoistic idiot.

"I can prove you that you were actually dreaming about me and not staring at that guy" He said smugly, as if stating the obvious.

"You can't say what I was doing; I was actually staring at that cute guy." I replied lamely making commas in air with my fingers to emphasize the word cute.

"You sure?" He said as he started approaching me in slow strides.

"Yes." I stated, trying to be calm. So this is the time when the boy approaches the girl while the stupid girl takes steps backwards and ends up locked in the boy's arms

He reached me and touched my cheeks, which made me feel like my cheeks were on fire. A shiver ran down my spine, but I covered it efficiently.

He removed one of my curly strands from my forehead and leaned forward, making my legs wobble.

He kissed the space between my eyes and, coming close to my right ear, he rubbed his lips on the place beneath it and Whispered in his husky voice.

"Are you still sure you find that guy more attractive than me?"

I still tried to reply sternly 'yes'. The keyword is tried. As only a 'hmm' came out of my mouth.

He came closer to me and the animals that live in my freaking stomach decide to do the Harlem Shake.

"Seriously Darling, your heavy breathing pretty much confirms my belief. You want me. Just admit it sweetheart" He winked at me while giving me a lopsided grin.

"Whatever makes you happy at night dear" I said teasing him.

"Why you have to be so stubborn. Why can't you just admit that I am more attractive than that stupid guy?" Austin said with a pout, Gosh that awesome heartwarming pout.

"Someone is feeling jealous." I literally sang it in high pitched voice. Damn! this boy is driving me insane.

"So you have called me here to make me jealous huh?" Austin said with a fake hurt expression.

"Awww sweetheart you are thousand times better than that guy. And if this makes you feel any better there is no guy behind you I was just drooling over your looks"

"Really?" Austin said childishly flashing me his 540 volts bright smile.

Gosh! How I suddenly got so lucky to have this handsome guy as my boyfriend and now my future husband?

I just kept on staring at him again. Can't help the guy is total drool worthy.

"Earth to Jenny. What's matter with you today? Aren't you dreaming a lot today"

"I am going to miss you a lot next week" I spoke up without thinking.

"What?" He asked confused. "Are you going somewhere next week?"

"Yeah. I am going to my aunt's house for next entire week." I told him. His facial expression fell all of the sudden.

"And you are telling me now?"

"Actually even I came to know about this today morning" I cleared.

"Can't I come with you?"

"No Austin. I am sorry. Its just not family get together, we are going to my aunts house because tomorrow is the fourth death anniversary of my cousin. She had died because of some tragedy." I spoke up. Tears had already started to form in my eyes.

Luckily Austin didn't poke into the topic about my cousin more, or else I would have surely cried. He must have known that by my facial expression. We talked in the garden for some time and later as promised to my parents, Austin left me at the airport and went away but not without a long kiss.

Damn I am so going miss this a lot.

As I had no time to meet friends all had came to the airport to meet me.

Gosh! I felt so special. After hugs and final goodbyes we were all set for this family get together.

Third Person's POV

Today while returning home from boarding school after a long time of four years, I coincidentally saw Austin. Surprisingly, he was not alone but with a girl again. She seemed extremely happy with him.

God! why he has to every time get all the cute girls. By the expression on his face, it was damn clear that even Austin loved this girl maybe even more than Bella.

With incidents that had happened with him in the last few years, I had thought he would never ever fall in love again. But dang! I was wrong.

How come I wasn't told about such an important news?

But I wont let him be happy ever again. Not after what he has done to me. It was only because of him that I had rot to in that boarding school of idiots for four long years without seeing my friends and family. And here he is enjoying his life fully again. Because of him I had to waste four precious years of my life doing nothing. I will make sure that his entire life turns to hell. Be ready for a storm in your life Austin.

Without wasting any time in going home and meeting my parents, who even don't care about my whereabouts and me, I marched directly to the High school to gain information about this girl with whom Austin was roaming.

After a few hello and hi's from I don't even know whom, I finally started searching for a girl who could actually help me.

I went to my only Admirer and equal partner in crime, Ashley Carter the known queen bee of this high school who had kissed Austin because I had told her to do so.

Actually Ashley is madly in love with Austin. But Austin hates her from the bottom of his heart. This situation is what I take full advantage of.

Ashley can do anything and everything to break Austin's relations. Her motto in life is, 'if he isn't with me he can't be with anyone else.'

I was shocked how come she hasn't done anything by now. Let me tell you, she is pure evil. Cruelty is in her blood.

It was her who used to keep me updated about even a little thing happening in Austin's life for years when I was in boarding school..

How come I wasn't updated about this is what I wanted to know now. Though one more question was constantly revolving in my mind

Who that girl is? As her face seemed to be little bit similar.

From Ashley I came to know about Austin's life, about his girlfriend and to be wife Jennifer.

I couldn't believe my ears for a second. Austin was going to be happily married and I still wasn't updated about this.

"You Idiot .Why haven't you ever mentioned about the girl Austin is roaming with?"I asked with anger in my voice.

"I had told you about this. She is the girl in front of whom I had kissed Austin to make her feel bad." She informed me. The scene she had described, then came in front of my eyes.

"But by what I had seen today I can tell that, that act hasn't done any harm to their relationship." I said with gritted teeth to control my anger.

"You are right. Austin had cleared the misunderstanding and

accepted his feelings during the play day and from that day itself they are happily together." She informed me.

I felt my blood boiling inside my body. I felt like punching her but I couldn't as she is the only source of my information.

"Why hadn't you informed me about this before?" I said punching at the wall nearby removing all my anger in the punch.

"I didn't want to bother you then as you were going to return in few months so I had thought I would tell you when you returned."

"Who the hell told you to use your own brains Idiot? If you had brains, Austin would not have been in relationship with any other girl before" I said stating a matter of fact.

"Don't you dare question me about my brains. I have this very strong information which would surely break their relationship." Ashley said guaranteed.

"And what's that?" I asked curiously this time.

"Jennifer Winget, Austin's girlfriend is the cousin of Diana Summers. I hope you still remember her." Ashley said with a smirk.

For the second time I couldn't believe on my ears. I was shocked to know that Jeniffer Winget was the cousin of Diana Summers whose death mystery hasn't been solved yet. The situation is going to be very interesting.

Time to have some surprise Austin. Be ready for the ups and downs in your life.

******

Jenny's Pov

The moment I reached my Aunt's house, the nostalgia hit me. Diana's absence was heavy in the house, though she had died in some restaurant.

Its been four long years after the death of my cousin Diana Summer.

But I still sometimes wonder what must have happened to her. She was a very cheerful and a bright person. She was full of life and always positive. And the main thing was that she was totally against suicide. So the court's final words were unbelievable.

They had closed the case saying, "She had committed suicide because of depression"

But her death is still a mystery to me. I still believe she did not suicide and its a murder case. I wish one day I find her murderer. I desperately wanted to know why someone had killed my sister. I want to know reason behind her death. I cant let her death to be a mystery forever. I wanted her to get justice. As Diana had no enemies, damn! she used to be friendly with everyone even with her haters, always trying to make everyone smile.

I still remember the night when I found her in her eternal sleep. She was found dead in some hotel's room, just after her birthday. I tried to wake her up as I began to weep. But she could not hear any of my pleas. She was already gone. I still sometimes find it so very hard to believe that she has gone .

I miss all the little ways in which she used to show that she actually cares, there are so many good moments we shared; Looking back on my life's assorted scenes, I sometimes realize that she had taught me what love truly means; she was my trusted confidante and best friend. On whose loving support I used to always depend. Gosh! I miss her so much.

When I used to look at her smiling face in all my photos, memories used to flood in my mind as I touch the mementos from the happy times we had together. But now that I am watching her photos, it bring tears and make me sad. As the time we spent together went by in a wink, life was not as long as I had like to think. Sometimes memories bring comfort and make me smile, but there are times when grief takes over for a while.

A tear slid down from the corner of my eye the moment I entered her room. Her room was scattered with relics: the bed she had slept in for so many years, her clothes hanging like shadows in the closets, a handful of videos and books. There were lots memories pinned to each corner of the room.

This happens nearly every year. I try to control my tears every year when I enter her room as she was totally against crying but I couldn't. The more I think about her, the more I cry. It's a cliché, I know and I am sure you must have heard it before, but you never get over losing someone you love. It's not like a wound that heals ever. It's more like losing a limb. You learn to live without the limb, but it never grows back, and you never, ever forget that its gone. Strangely though, the nature of my grief has changed over time. It's been four years now, and the bodily tension I feel whenever I think or speak about her is starting to dissipate.

I try being strong for her parents whenever I come here. They have lost their only child. It is the only time in the year when I see little happiness on their faces because of everyone's gathering at their place. They say they see Diana in me. So I try to become like her, strong and joyful only for them. I don't want to ruin their only happy moment. Though I know her parents, would never be the same. Their pain was almost visible, as if a piece of their bodies had been cut out. They had lost themselves too, or at least the little version of them an happy version. Right from that day I have never seen my uncle and Aunt have a real smile, they were just forcing a fake smile in front of entire world. I will always wish she was still here. I will always wonder what she would look like and what she'd be doing if she were still alive.

So I wiped my tears and hopped down to spread happiness.

"So what's special today?" I said hugging my aunt Sophie from behind.

"Everything that my Jenny loves" She said with a huge grin.

"Even plain rice tastes good when it's made by you" I said hugging her more tightly.

"Stop buttering me. I know that you want chicken. Its all ready." Aunt said.

She knows I love chicken specially prepared by her. But I never tell her to cook it by myself as it was even Diana's favorite dish. But I was lucky as Aunt prepares it every year without my telling her to.

"You are the worlds best Aunt" I said happily spinning her around.

It was our every year tradition. My family used to come few days earlier at Aunt Sophie's house while my other aunt Lily used to come direct on the day of Diana's death anniversary.

After dinner together, with lots of talks of happy and sad moments, we finally decided to call it a day. We haven't told them about my engagement as according to my parents we should wait for a perfect time and then surprise them when everyone is present. I agreed with them as there was nothing to disagree.

I headed to my aka, Diana's room. I was about to explore the room again to cherish the old memories but I was disturbed by noise of my cellphone indicating I have a new message.

I reached for my cell. Seeing Austin's name on it increased my excitement level.

Damn! I already miss this guy and it hasn't even been one full day.

Austin: Hey beautiful I know we haven't spoken all day after you left but just know you haven't stopped running in my mind from the moment you have gone. I am just thinking about you. I already miss you sweetheart.

Reading the message a whole troop of butterflies erupted in my stomach.

Me: I miss you too.Austin: Aw. I am happy to know that. Can't you come back soon then?

Me: I wish I could. But the death anniversary of my cousin is day after tomorrow and after that we are declaring about our engagement to all so schedule is tight.

I tried to explain. Though I wanted to go back too.

Austin: Then why did you go there few days earlier?

Me: Because tomorrow is my cousin's birthday. I don't want my uncle and Aunt to be alone on this day. Tomorrow is my sister's birthday. She would have been 21, except of course she will be forever frozen at 17.

The night of her birthday flashed in front of my eyes.

We had celebrated her birthday as usual; Just normal wishes and a little party. I wish I could have known then that this was her last birthday. We could have at least made it memorable.

Me: Hey what happened?

I asked Austin as he didn't replied for long time.

My screen flashed again. Telling me that I have a new message.

Austin: Just remembered someone whose story was same as your cousin.

Austin's reply made me curious. I wanted to know more about this. But his next message clearly showed that he wasn't in mood to talk anymore.

Austin: Hey It's too late now. You must sleep. Good night and take care of you princess. Love you.

Me: Love you too. Good night.

I replied and locked the phone screen to sleep. But I couldn't. I don't know why but I felt the connection between my cousin and someone who Austin remembered. I tried sleeping but I couldn't sleep .I remembered about the message Austin had sent. For a very long time I was thinking about the connection between Diana and the girl Austin mentioned but I couldn't find any connection as Diana was neither in our High school nor did she live anywhere near us. I finally gave up on thinking and slept as tomorrow was going to be long day.

Next morning I woke up early in the morning and started preparing the cake. Chocolate cake to be more precise. As it was Diana's favorite. Uncle Jason, Aunt Sophie and my mom dad were not home. I knew they had gone to visit Diana's grave. They do this every year. I don't like to visit her grave on her birthday. It helps me to think that nothing's changed and she is still between us. I always text 'happy birthday' to her old number. In return I always get a thanks, it's not my birthday but thanks in advance, or most randomly, who are you, for the first time I had got 'message failed' because her old number is as dead as she is. It feels nice to do so, though the nice feeling doesn't last for long, but the idea, the idea of contact is great. Though for little time but it feels like she is with me.

This was going to be her 21st birthday. We had decided to make her 21st birthday special. And even though she is not with us I will still make her 21st birthday memorable. I hope she is watching me from somewhere.

To my utter surprise my other Aunt, Aunt Lily with her family was at the doorstep with a bright smile on her face.

"Woah! How you guys are here early?" I asked with surprise quite clear in my voice.

"Can't we come early like you? And we have a surprise for you" My uncle John spoke up.

Uncle John is the eldest and the coolest uncle. He is the one who always keeps our family happy and bound together.

"We are here to celebrate Diana's 21st birthday sweetheart" Aunt Lily spoke up this time.

"I bet you must have already planned something. So what's the plan huh?" Alec my cousin spoke up with glint of sadness in his voice.

"So here's your surprise!" Uncle John said pointing excitedly towards Alec my cousin.

He is like an elder brother to Diana and me. Having an elder brother and his advice at hand can help you avoid a lot of relationship heartaches. Or, at least, get through them. He taught us how to understand boys and men alike. You don't have to worry about any creepy men coming around with your older brother in the picture. Having an older brother can be a gateway to learning so much about the world. Damn! we have learnt so much together.

Everyone used to fear our trio with me being little silent and Diana and Alec being a lot mischievous we used take the entire house on our heads. This is what our parents have told us. He was closer to Diana than me because Alec and Diana have been together literally since childhood as they live in same locality. Alec and Diana have been in same school and high school. They shared a very strong bond. Sometime even I used to feel awkward with them.

I was totally shocked to see Alec at my Aunt's house as after the death of Diana, Alec had become completely devoid of emotion. Worse, he had became guarded, defensive, almost hostile. He didn't want to visit her grave and didn't want to meet with any of her friends that would make him remember her. I'm sure the psychological explanation is that he was trying to protect himself from the overwhelming emotions. But I was scared as I didn't want to lose my brother too.

Remembering all the old days, I hugged Alec as tightly as I could. He hugged me back with the same warmth. We have shared many memories together.

After holding back my emotions I finally spoke "Though there is nothing special planned yet, now that you are here, I am sure we will make this day huge" I said happily.

"I am proud of you sweety for planning her birthday every year. I think it's a great way for the family to all get together and remember her. I know It's not really like we are "celebrating" her birthday as we used to do before, but its like we are remembering and honoring her. Spending time with family is a great way to do this. Also the memories of her never go away, so it is emotionally soothing to be surrounded with people who also love and miss her. If she is seeing us from above, she would be definitely happy with you Jenny" Aunt Lily said kissing me on my forehead. "Besides we are even going to get a chocolate cake to eat" Uncle John said trying to cheer us up. This always works.

As I was explaining the plan to Alec and others, my mom dad along with Aunt and uncle came. The smile and happiness on everyone's face was unexplainable. No amount of money in the world could buy the happiness that I was seeing on my Uncle and Aunt's faces. The sense of fulfillment I saw on their faces has no substitute. It was expected though as they had seen Alec after total four years, Alec is like their son they never had.

"Alec, I am so glad to see you here" Uncle Jason said hugging Alec. Happiness clearly evident in their voice.

"He had to come. How could he even dare miss Diana's 21st birthday?" Aunt Sophie said with same happiness.

"Yeah you are right. I was an Idiot to miss all the earlier birthdays and stay away from all the things that reminded me of Diana. I have learned now that, a person is never really dead until they are forgotten. I feel so guilty now. But today I am here to correct my mistake from now onwards. I will cherish every memory I have spent with Diana. I will live and enjoy that life again. I will never ever forget her and will keep her alive in my heart forever. And all this is because of someone who is been constantly inviting me to this birthday party from last four years." Alec said hugging Aunt Sophie tightly.

Aunt Sophie has been constantly inviting Alec every year. Though we all had lost our hopes, she was always confident that one day Alec would come to Diana's party. Today my Aunt's wish was fulfilled.

After prayers in the church and after taking the blessings of father that we do every year for peace of Diana's soul, we all marched to orphanage. Diana always wanted to celebrate her at least one birthday with orphan kids but she never got chance to do so. We all planned to go to orphanage to fulfill her wish. We went room to room of the facility, spending quality time with the children who readily offered big warm hugs and loving smiles. We gifted something or other to all the children at the orphanage. We offered food to them and even celebrated the birthday by cutting cake.

The smiles on their faces were priceless. Gosh! I was never ever going to forget this day. We captured each and every moment by clicking pictures and make those moments priceless and our greatest treasure.

Looking into the hopeful eyes of these children, listening to them and sharing a moment with them made me more inspired than ever about my future. We all have our crosses to bear with our parents besides us in all our ups and downs, but these children are fighting against almost unimaginable odds without anyone, and yet they have all the hope in the world in their hearts and brightest smiles on their lips. This was the best day of my life. I personally think everyone should visit orphanage not to help the orphans but to learn from them that how to be happy in all the situations.

By a heart to heart conversation, the smiles we bring on their face were the greatest return gifts ever. We decided to visit the orphans on her birthday again. This was literally her best birthday ever.

It was almost mid night when I returned back from orphanage. I quickly checked my phone which I had forgot in the drawer while leaving to church. I was shocked to see twenty messages and ten calls, all from Austin. Few messages were about him missing me and few were totally filled with concern. Gosh I felt so lucky and wanted. Without wasting any time I quickly started typing.

"I know you must be sleeping by now, but still I am messaging you as I know I wont fall asleep without expressing my feelings now. Sorry I was out whole day and forget to take my cell with me so I couldn't message you earlier. But I want to tell you that lIcan't seem to get you off my mind.

I hope you know that you are an amazing guy and l feel so lucky to have you in my life. You make me happy in ways that no one else can. The small things you do for me, the way you care about me, truly makes me feel like a princess and I can only hope I do the same for you. Anyway I hope you slept well and I hope you wake up to this and it puts a smile on your face. That adorable smile of yours. And I hope you have a great day, babe."

After typing such a big message which I hope will put smile on Austin's face I finally called it a day. I was so tired that I directly went to bed and fell asleep. As I had to wake up early tomorrow.

The moment I opened my eyes I checked my cell instantly. But sadly, Austin was still asleep maybe as I had no new messages. I left a quick text to him saying "I will be busy today too, so I'll talk to you later. Love

You Miss You" Clicking a send button I marched downwards.

Today is very special day. Today is death anniversary of my beloved cousin Diana.

We don't waste our day in crying rather we spend the entire day remembering Diana. As according to my Uncle - Death Anniversaries that mark the day our loved one's passed away can be tough days, but with a little bit of forethought, it can also be a sweet-tender day. So we try making this day memorable. Like every year we took flowers to her grave and said our prayers first. We lit candles in honor of our loved one Diana. Then we all settled in the garden beside the graveyard.

Looking at old photos and home videos of Diana, we tried to recreate old days by telling each other those great-funny stories. We laughed and we enjoy remembering but no one cried as we all remembered what Diana used to always say. There is a time to mourn, to ache, but there is no time to rebuild our lives.

It's important to celebrate every chance we get.

Life is hard enough. Death comes and taps each of us on the shoulder.

Everyone's been touched by cancer, heart disease, car accidents, Alzheimer's -do you know anyone who has not experienced at least one or more of these?

Life comes in packages-life-death, babies-old age. We cannot open our arms to one and reject the other. We must somehow, learn to embrace both.

We have now learnt to smile in our sorrows too.This is all because of Diana. Gosh I miss her so much.

We hosted a lunch party and gathered the family members those who were closed to Diana.

After a peaceful lunch and enjoyable evening where we made lots of new memories and recreated old ones, I finally bid my Goodbye to Diana's grave. After saying my goodbyes to all the relatives and family members, I visited to a place where I feel closer to Diana. I went to a garden nearby where we three used spend most of our time whenever I used to come visit them. Whenever I come here, I feel like I am with Diana. Visiting this garden after a tiring day makes me feel like I am at home. I come here every year just to refresh old memories. While I was sitting on a bench thinking of happy old days, a young boy came to me with two envelopes saying that he has been told by someone to give this to me. I scanned entire park with my eyes to see whether I know anyone from whom I can get this envelopes but everyone was a stranger.

Without thinking any further I opened one envelope. It had a letter in it.

I have been seeing and observing you from last few years .You seem to be very close to your cousin Diana. And from your efforts I can guess that you are even eager to know the killer Diana. So I am here to help you. I am sending you few clues that will help you to catch the killer.

You don't know me so don't try to even search for me. But Diana used to know me very well. So just for her sake I am helping you. You can consider me a well wisher of Diana.

After reading the letter I opened the other envelope. I was shocked to see the evidence in it.

❄ ❄ ❄

Chapter 38 - The Night of Terror

The moment I saw the pictures in front of me, that were evidence of Diana's death I was totally shocked and devastated. My entire world turned upside down. My brain became numb. I couldn't understand what to do in situations like this.

Who wouldn't be shocked in the situation like this where you see the picture of your future husband as the killer of your cousin?

The pictures and the evidences clearly revealed that Austin was in the hotel room of Diana on the day before she died. Which meant he was the last person to meet Diana before her death.

By their facials expressions anyone could tell they were having a huge fight on some issue.

I felt like I was riding a roller coaster of emotions. I was sad, shock, angry and also in disbelief and lots of many other emotions.

My mind was not at all ready to accept that Austin must be killer of Diana but my brain was screaming with anger. Austin is the killer.

I just wished my mind is wrong but at this very moment I was with my brain. I felt blood boiling inside me. My body was totally shaking I didn't know what to do next. So I did the first thing that struck my mind.

I instantly messaged Austin telling. "Our relation is over. I am not going to marry you anymore"

Just after the message was delivered my phone over flooded with Austin's messages and calls. But I was in no mood to explain anything so I just switched of the cell phone to cut all the contacts from outside world. I just sat there silently staring at the shining stars.

I missed Diana a lot today. If she was here she would have told me what should I do in such situations. But she wasn't here. I was just alone sitting at our usual hangout place with just memories. I don't know when I started crying actually but the next moment I remembered I was crying loudly trying to remove out all the pain I had bottled inside me.

I don't know for how long I cried but a tight warm hug sobered me. "Jenny darling, what's the matter dear?"

Hearing my mom's voice I gave up again. All the feelings that were bottled up inside me came out. I started crying again this time more severely.

I don't know why I was actually crying for Diana death or for

Austin's lies but I was totally feeling hopeless and vulnerable.

"I miss her mom. I miss Diana a lot today." I spoke between my tears.

"I know sweetheart. Even we all do miss her. But you do remember that she hates crying, right?" My mom said wiping my tears.

It was when I realized my mom was not alone she was with dad and Alec. I saw same expression on his face as on mine. I felt my heart break inside me. I knew he had feelings for Diana but his feelings were so intense and true that I came to know today. At that very moment I decided to punish Austin or whoever who has killed Diana for Alec.

I can't bring Diana back for him but least I can give justice to Diana.

"I broke up the engagement mom" I blurred out all of sudden.

"We are aware of that. Austin called." It was my dad who spoke out this time.

"Wait Jenny is going to get married?" Alec spoke all of sudden with glint of excitement in eyes.

"Sorry Alec but I was going marry. Now I am not marrying anyone." I explained.

"Jenny you can't break an engagement over something. I don't know what happened between you guys but Jenny fights do take place in all relations that doesn't mean you have to break the marriage" My mom explained.

Agreeing to my mom's words "Your mom's right Jenny. Marriage is the beginning-the beginning of the family-and is a life-long commitment. You can't just break it over silly fight.

We can solve the problem by talking dear." My dad further said. "No dad, this problem can't be solved by talking. Mom Austin has- " I was about to say but was cut in middle by my overly protective brother.

"Cheated on you? How dare that bastard cheat on my sister. I am going to kill him. Jenny give me his address." Alec said with gritted teeth. Deep deep down I felt little good as old Alec was back but the pain was so much that I couldn't express my happiness.

"What? Austin cheated on you? How dare he?" This time it wasn't my parents or Alec's voice but it was Beth's voice.

"And Recce is calling and messaging me to know what's the matter is? How could he?" This was Alice this time.

I was shocked to see Beth and Alice there. It was what I really needed though. My girlfriends.

"Guys what are you doing here?" I asked puzzled.

"We heard about your engagement breaking so we tried calling you. But as you weren't picking any of our calls we decided to come here" Alice explained hugging me tightly.

"Are you OK?" She asked again with concerned filled eyes. I was about to nod my head when suddenly,

"Are you gone nuts. How can she be OK after a failing engagement and a cheating fiancé.?" Beth interrupted.

"I am going to kill that idiot" Beth continued with anger clear in her voice.

"Go ahead. I am with you girl" Alec said with same anger.

"Guys guys. Stop it Austin didn't cheat on me."

"See I knew it he wouldn't cheat on Jenny. He is a good guy" My mom said happily.

"Then why you canceled the engagement?" Alec asked.

"Urgghh..It's complicated." Were just words I could speak this time. For which I was getting different glares from everyone.

"Lets go home. We can discuss on this topic later." My dad said breaking the tension.

"Actually we want to talk with Jenny for a while urgently so you guys proceed we will see you at home" Alice said addressing everyone.

Surprisingly everyone agreed. Now there were just three of us. They were giving me those intense glare which they give me when they know I am hiding something from them.

"Jenny we are not here to play staring game. We need valid explanation." Beth said finally frustrated.

"Guys I don't know how to tell you this"

"Obviously by your mouth Jenny." Alice replied in 'duh' tone.

"I mean, I don't know from where to start?"

"How about starting from very beginning. " Beth spoke up.

"Guys what's up with these silly answers"

"Damn why are you asking silly questions then" They both spoke simultaneously.

"Enough with the silliness guys. Jenny just tell what's the matter." Alice spoke this time.

"I guess these pictures will tell you what the matter is" I said handing them the pictures I had got from the stranger.

By the expression on their faces I thought they had got what I am thinking. But I was wrong.

"Woah! Austin was in relation with Diana even?"

Alice said with surprise plastered on her entire face.

"Are you really breaking this marriage because of this?" Beth asked joining Alice's league.

Gosh what's the matter with these two idiots today?

"Guys I am trying to tell you that I think maybe Austin is the one who has killed Diana" I said it all in one breath.

"No" They both shouted in unison.

"Are you out of our mind Jenny?" Beth said further.

"Austin would never kill anyone." Alice said.

"Even I had thought so. But this evidence tell different story." I said staring at the pictures.

"What you mean?" Alice asked.

"Look at the room in which they are standing guys. Its the same room in which Diana had been found dead. Which means Austin is the person whom Diana had met last. Guys there has to be some connection." I tried explaining them.

"Whoa is this really that room?" Alice asked again.

"Yeah" I said nodding my head.

"Gosh I can't believe this" Alice said.

Tears had again started to form in the corner of my eyes.

"Aww Jenny don't cry. Just this picture can't conclude that Austin has killed her. We will need some more valid proofs." Beth said wiping my tears.

"What more proofs do you need Beth?" Alice spoke up.

"I still don't believe Austin would kill anyone."

"I hope you are right Beth. I really love Austin a lot. But I just can't be in a relation with the murderer of my cousin."

"So that's the reason behind breaking the engagement?"Beth asked this time.

"You did absolutely right Jenny" Alice consoled.

"Guys we can't just put Austin in fault without knowing his side" Beth spoke up.

"I am not able to decide what I should do now?" I said putting my face in my hands.

"You should file a complaint against Austin" Alice spoke up.

"Woah woah. Guys calm down don't you think we should talk about this with the elders first?"

Beth was right. So we decided to listen to her, as she is the one who always thought practically.

As expected, everyone was sitting in the hall waiting for me. Alec's parents were not there. I guess they must have returned home. As I entered the house, Aunt hugged me tightly.

"I know Jenny you miss Diana a lot so do we but you shouldn't put your life at halt because of her" Aunt spoke up.

"Mom, dad I know you guys are waiting for reason behind me canceling the engagement."

"So why don't you tell us?" My mom spoke up.

"Should we go inside is there anything personal that we shouldn't know about?" My uncle spoke up.

"Yeah Jenny we can totally understand." Aunt added.

"No. It's actually something related with you guys." I replied in low voice. My reply confused everyone.

Without wasting any time I spoke up. "I have found the guy who must have killed Diana."

"What? But reports had said that she had died of suicide" My Aunt spoke up surprised.

"You really believe that shit?" I asked?

"Who the hell is that guy?" Alec spoke up breaking the silence.

"Austin" I said staring directly at my parents to see their reactions. I can say they had frozen in their spots for seconds.

"Add lots of shock, crying, regret and anger to your expression for many hours and you will know how I felt for the first time" I said staring at them.

"Jenny do you even understand what are you actually talking about?" My mom said shaking me slightly.

"Mom I have evidences."

"What are you talking Jenny. Austin can never kill anyone." My dad said joining the conversation.

"What evidences do you have?" My Uncle spoke. I saw a little hope in his eyes for the first time.

"Trust me we know this Austin guy personally. Jenny, I guarantee there is some kind of misunderstanding here." Dad spoke up.

"No dad there is no misunderstanding. Once you will see what I saw, you will truly believe me"

"Oh My God! My daughter was killed and all these years I had been thinking her death was my mistake as I haven't brought her up well" My Aunt spoke up. Tears were already wailing up in her eyes.

"No Aunt you were the best mom and Diana was best child among us. Don't ever doubt yourself" Alec said hugging Aunt tightly.

"Yeah Aunty. Alec is right. Diana died because of some Idiot. Don't worry I will find out the culprit behind it and give Diana the deserved justice"

"No Jenny, I am going to kill Austin. How dare he kill our Diana" Alec spoke all set to kill someone.

"Stop you guys, we can't take law in our hand. We will file a case against him if the evidences are powerful." Uncle spoke up.

"Jenny show us the evidence" Dad demanded.

I showed them the photographs.

"Jenny what are these photographs about?" My mom asked surprised

"Mom this is evidence. By this photograph it is damn clear that Austin had met Diana in that hotel room in fact Austin must have been the last person Diana had actually met"

"Jenny I still can't believe this. Austin is a nice guy." Mom said.

"Mom sometimes situations force people to do certain things. I am not telling Austin has killed Diana. I am just suggesting that Austin must have killed Diana. What's the harm in checking it out?"

"I think Jenny is right. We will go to Austin's house tomorrow with police. They will look into the matter" Alec said.

With this said, every body went to their respective rooms. I bet no one would sleep, everyone was just waiting for morning.

God! I just hope my doubt is wrong.

Austin's POV

I was desperately waiting for night as Jenny was going to message me at night. But her message

"Our engagement is over" in the evening shocked me. I felt a sharp sort of ache in my belly my brain literally stopped functioning. I tried calling and messaging her lots of time but she didn't pick up any of the call or replied to any of the message.

So I got fed up of trying to contact with Jenny. I then tried calling Jenny's mom dad. Luckily Jenny's dad picked up the phone second time.

"Is everything alright there?" I asked them all of sudden.

"Yes son. Everything is totally fine. What's the matter Austin? You seemed to be extremely tensed" Her dad spoke up.

"Then why did Jenny break the engagement?"I asked again without answering their question.

I was expecting for some kind of reason from them but I was just greeted by same shocked and confused words.

"What? Jenny broke up with you? When?"

"She messaged me about this earlier." I told the truth.

"Don't worry son I will talk to Jenny immediately and call you soon" Her dad said disconnecting the line.

Now I had no other chance than waiting for their calls. So I conference called Recce and River and explained them all the situation. I am lucky enough to have friends like them. As they reached my house in just fifteen minutes.

"You are joking with us right?" Recce asked.

"Does my face look like I am joking?"

"No. It's means you serious. Jenny really broke the marriage?" River asked.

"I am really not getting what's going on. I called her parents but even they didn't know anything about this." I explained.

"Let me call Alice and ask her" Recce said removing his mobile out.

He tried calling Alice after but the surprisingly shocking thing happened. Alice didn't pick up the call.

"Damn she rejected my call. She never does this" Recce said frustrated.

Recce was saying the truth Alice never ever rejects Recce's call even if she is in any sort of emergency.

"I think something very bad is going to happen." I spoke up my feelings.

"Shut up dude. She must be busy somewhere." River said.

"It's just not about Alice dude. Many weird and unbelievable things are happening which are forcing me to think in this manner"

"Just chill dude. Every thing will be fine. Jenny's dad has told he will call later lets wait for his call" River informed.

River was right, we didn't have any other chance other than waiting for his call. That wait for few hours literally seemed like long endless years. We were all literally sitting in the hall with all the cellphones in front of us. Yeah we were so desperate.

Finally after few hours, my phone rang. The name on the screen told that its from Jenny's dad though I was waiting for this call desperately, I suddenly felt my nerves tingling like being tickled with a small feather, my palms became all sweaty, my heart started racing. I was extremely scared to know what was about to happen. I knew I had to pick up the phone but I didn't have enough courage to pick up the phone. Luckily Recce picked up the call for me. Gathering up all the energy in me I spoke up "Hello".

I put the phone on speaker so that I wouldn't have tell my friends everything later.

"Hey son. I know you are worried about Jenny and waiting for the reason about why she has canceled the marriage all of sudden. I would have told you the reason but she has strictly warned me to not to tell you the reason."

"Is it something very bad?" I asked. My palms got really sweaty again.

Damn! I was so scared and nervous.

"I cant tell you the intensity of the reason I can only tell you that she will be at your house in the morning and you will know the reason then". I was about to ask further questions but I it was of no use as Jenny's dad had already kept the phone. I just stood frozen with my phone in my hand staring at nothing in particular. I had no other option rather than waiting for morning. I had to just wait for my life to be ruined further.

"Austin just relax dude. I guarantee there must be some sort of misunderstanding which would be surely solved in the morning"

"I don't think so dude I seriously feel like something very bad is about to happen".

I was trying to think what the matter could have been, but my poor brain wasn't able to recollect anything that must have gone wrong. I tried to convince myself that, when I meet her tomorrow we will talk things out and she would accept me again. Maybe I have wronged her in something that I would correct myself and everything would be back to normal. I would ask for just one chance and maybe then everything will be back on track.

It was then I realized that I was back at the place again where I was few years' earlier. Scared and heartbroken and madly in love. I felt hopeless, despondent, desperate. It was the worst emotional pain I have been through in my life, by far. I felt anger boiling inside me for breaking the promise that I had made with myself. I felt awful for falling in love again.

Life is maze, Love is a riddle!

I never saw this end of my marriage thing coming, and was so naive about this that I never even entertained the thought that this relationship would ever end. It just wasn't an option.

That whole night was like a terror night. I was literally scared like a student who is scared before his exam results. All I knew was few hours later my life would not be the same. I couldn't even blink properly for entire night sleep was totally out of question.

Luckily River and Recce were always beside me encouraging me and supporting me. I won't ever forget them. Finally the night of terror faded and a new day started.

At somewhat 8 ‘o clock I heard a doorbell ring, I knew it was Jenny now. I felt my pulse quicken and heartbeat beginning to speed. I went up to slowly door and opened it. I sucked in a shaky breath, feeling my throat constrict. Panic rose like bile in my body. I suddenly didn’t know how to speak. I just stood blankly, staring up at the terror before me. My palms were clammy, and it was all I could do not to knot my fingers together.

“Hello.” I managed, the word rolling out of my mouth like tumbleweed.

❄ ❄ ❄

Chapter 39 -Search for Criminal

Austin's PoV

"Arrest him officer he has killed my little innocent daughter" Said an unknown lady pointing her finger at me with anger clearly boiling up in her voice.

Seeing police officers early in the morning at my door steps with two unknown persons imposing murder case on me made me to froze on my place. Damn I couldn't even form suitable words. Luckily, "Who the hell are you Lady?" Recce questioned coming beside me. "You must have come to some wrong place officers as we don't even know these people." River further explained officers. Totally my words. I mentally thanked my friends for staying overnight.

"They are lying officers" said new voice. The voice seemed more familiar though.

When the person behind the voice came into picture my entire universe shattered. It was none other than Jenny.

"Jenny what are you doing here? Who are they?" I said or at least I tried to say.

"They are the parents of a girl who you had killed mercilessly, Austin" Jenny said with lot of anger and hatred in her eyes .

Gosh what the hell is happening here?

"Is this any kind of prank or something? Let me tell you I am totally not in mood of any type of prank now" I said involuntarily as the events that were happening with me from yesterday were total unexpected events.

"Do you think we are mad to wake up so early in the morning to fool you. We do have many cases to handle." One of the officers spoke up.

He had a point. Which meant this is real. Oh God why can't I once live my life with peace?

"Jenny are you out of your mind?" Recce spat with anger.

"I have evidences Recce" Jenny spoke with equal anger.

I have never seen Jenny so overwhelmed with anger. Oh God Save me.

Recce was about to say something but was cut by River "Stop it Recce this conversation isn't going anywhere. Let Jenny explain what the actual matter is?"

It was when we all stayed silent for Jenny to speak.

But instead of speaking she removed some photographs from her purse and placed it front of me.

"So you are telling me that you don't know this girl?" She interrogated.

"I know her. She is Diana Summers. She was my good friend" I spoke up instantly scared of Jenny's anger.

Call me a coward, chicken Heart or whatever you want but the girl in front of me was fuming with anger which no one could withstand. Damn I haven't seen anyone so angry.

"We are her parents." Said the Man who was with police officers other than Jenny and unknown Lady Maybe Diana's Mom.

"Woah Woah Woah are you Guys trying to tell that you think Austin has killed Diana Summers?" Recce spoke up again.

It was when the entire picture became crystal clear to me. The cousin about whom Jenny was talking about was Diana Summers .

"But why do you think that I have killed her?"I asked Jenny baffled.

"Because according to the photographs you had met her on the day of her death that too in the hotel room where she was found dead." Jenny clarified.

Damn she has done lot of study on photographs I must say. I tried to speak but only think I could feel coming out of my mouth was Air.

Gosh where's my voice hidden again?

Why it has to always play hide and seek when I really need it.

"That doesn't proves he has killed her" Fortunately River spoke up in my defense.

"You have no right to decide that. We will decide that. We have little proofs on basis of which we have to take Mr. Austin to police custody" Said one of the officer.

"Trust me officer Diana was my best friend. Why would I kill her?" I finally spoke up.

"By your facial expressions in the photographs it is clear that you guys were not in good terms." Jenny spoke up again.

Damn was she doing PhD on photographs last night?

"We were having a little discussion" I clarified to shut Jenny's mouth.

Damn what's with this Girl.

"We can't trust you Mr. Austin without any proofs. Every criminal speaks in same way to save himself" The Officer spoke up.

"Mind your language officer." River howled.

"Anyway we would have to arrest you, Mr. Austin"

The officer said again removing handcuffs from his pocket.

"You can't arrest anyone without strong proofs" Recce protested.

"I know. But we will still have to arrest him as they have filed complaint against him." Officer said pointing towards Diana's parents.

"Jenny believe me. Austin won't kill anyone I have known him since childhood" Recce tried convincing her.

"Recce I hope you are right but please try to understand me. I am just trying to give justice to my dead sister. I just have just this evidences so I have to take action on this"

"Recce let her do whatever she wants to do. She don't trust me, what's the point in explaining anything. Lets go officer" Saying this we marched towards police station.

I wasn't sad for being dragged into some case I wasn't even aware of but I was sad, because Jenny didn't trust me, rather she trusted on some unknown person she doesn't even know.

Jenny's Pov

"Jenny I still think you have filed a case against the wrong person" My mom spoke up the moment I entered the house.

"Mom there is the police officers to decide that so you please don't start again" Saying this I ran direct to my room.

"Jenny switch on the television fast." Beth and Alice said storming into my room totally out of their breaths.

"What's the matter?" I asked worried.

"They are telecasting about Austin on all news channels."

They both said in unison, they were saying truth. All news channels were literally inside the police station torturing Austin with their useless questions. He looked so pale, livid and dejected. Luckily Recce and River were there to keep him away from the media. I felt guilty for putting Austin in this situation.

Damn I am such a terrible girlfriend. Tears started falling from my eyes.

"What's the matter Jenny?" Alice said hugging me tightly.

"I can't see Austin in so much misery."

"You can still withdraw your case against him you know that right." Beth stated.

"I can't do that. After many years I have finally found one evidence, I cant let it go."

"Close your eyes and ask you heart Jenny, do you really think

Austin can do something like this?"

Beth was right deep deep down my heart knew Austin wouldn't ever do anything like this. But what if my heart was wrong? I know I was just being selfish. But I just wanted to find the killer of Diana by any way possible.

"Beth please, stop. I don't want to get weak. I know I am terrible girlfriend but I want to be a good sister for the sake of Diana and Alec" Saying this I switched off the TV. I tried closing my eyes for few minutes to stop thinking about all this but sleep was miles away from me. I just lay on my bed staring at the ceiling.

In the afternoon, at somewhat three, I was called to the police station. I was shocked to see many people there-Uncle, Aunt, Alec, Austin, Recce, River and a Lawyer were all gathered and more shocking thing was Austin was outside the jail signing some papers.

"Did you withdraw the case?" I asked my Uncle walking beside Austin. Our eyes met for nanosecond. The hurt and agony in his eyes and his tired posture broke my heart into pieces. I wanted to go there and hug him tightly tell him "Everything will be Alright" but I couldn't as I was the main reason for his trouble.

"No dear. Austin has just got bail" Alec spoke.

Austin was still staring in my direction, but I couldn't muster up even courage to look at him. Damn I miss him so much I miss his touch, his kisses.

'Focus Jenny focus' I tried telling myself.

"So this case is over now great." I said with sarcasm quite clear in my voice.

"Jenny they can't keep Austin in jail for long time without powerful proofs." Alec tried to explain again.

"But they have to take some action besides there are little evidences" I opposed.

"Miss Jenny. I know you are concerned about your sister but you just can't blame my client on basis of this proof" Austin's Lawyer spoke up.

"Besides we aren't declaring him innocent we have just released him to gather more proofs against the case to prove that he is innocent." Police officer said.

"What do you mean?" I asked confused.

"Austin is given time of one month to find the criminal who have killed Diana or else he will be taken into police custody again." Officer said again clarifying his statement.

Though I didn't kneow there was something like this in book of law but I felt happy from inside to know that Austin is going to be out of jail for now at least. God! I just hope Austin isn't the one who has killed Diana.

This would bring my entire life to a halt and I seriously don't want that.

The sadness, disbelief, anger and all other mixed feelings on his face broke my heart in thousands of small pieces. Though I saw it coming, it still hurt a lot to see Austin in pain and misery. It was damn clear from his expressions that he wasn't expecting this from me.

Even I had never thought that life will bring us on such difficult paths.

But what can I say, life is a bitch.

It likes to mess up with people's lives by surprising them with weird situations. It's like one day you are perfectly fine than suddenly the next day you feel like you are ten feet below the earth's surface with all the pressure. That's life. It's totally unpredictable. I believe life is not always fair, and everyone needs to accept it and move on with their lives. I am just trying to do that.

I couldn't withstand fierce and sore looks of the boys so I sped away from them.

Austin's POV

"Thank God you are finally out of jail." River said the moment we reached home.

"What's the use everybody already knows about it." Recce said.

"They are already showing news about you on all the channels" Recce added.

Though he was right, I don't care. The only person from whom I would have liked to hide this scene was the main creator of the scene what the point in hiding from anyone else. After going through so much, I still missed her. The hurt an worry on her face was making this more miserable.

I felt totally helpless again; this is what I was afraid of.

Whenever I am happy, life somehow finds the way to destroy it.

"I don't care about that. Do mom dad knows about this?" I asked to stop Recce from blabbering.

"Yeah they are coming back home by the next possible flight." River informed me.

"Damn it. What's happening with me?" I said punching the nearest thing to remove my wrath on it.

"It's not the time for getting angry dude. It's time to think and act wisely" River said holding me back.

"Yeah he is right. I thought Diana had died of suicide but by what they are showing in news now I think somebody must have murdered her." Recce pointed out.

"He has a point there. Somebody must have done this to take revenge from you." River stated.

"Who could have done something like this?" I asked puzzled.

"Bella" Both of them said in unison.

"Are you guys out of your mind?" I said with disbelief.

"I know she cheated on me but I think she would never kill anyone." I said sincerely.

"Austin, this can be Bella as her friend was the one who had informed us that Diana has committed suicide. Remember? And she had even told us that we should not go to her funeral in such a situation" Recce Muttered.

"She must have done this to show that you were not present to her funeral as you were trying to hide from everyone. And after few days her friend and Bella both had vanished all of the sudden" River added.

"But why the hell would she want to take revenge from me" I retorted.

"That's the point to think." River mumbled.

"After three long years why all of the sudden this case must have been reopened" Recce said absentmindedly.

"We have to find this soon Guys." Recce added.

"For that we need to find Bella first." River answered.

"Yeah you are right. By the way why had you gone to meet Diana on that day? Wasn't it your first anniversary on that day?" River questioned.

God I was so fed up of questions by now but I knew staying silent wouldn't help.

"I had gone to meet Diana as she had messaged me on Facebook to meet her for the last time in her hotel room as it was her birthday on that day." I retorted sincerely.

"Damn she was a crazy bitch" Recce said freaking out.

"Chill Recce, she just loved Austin" River tried to calm Recce.

"What Diana loved Austin?" My mom's tensed voice was heard before we could even see her.

Damn!

"Who the hell was Diana? Austin is there something you hiding from us.?" My dad inquired.

"Dads there's nothing to hide in this. Diana and Bella were best friends so I got to know about her from Bella"

"And so?" My dad asked signaling me to continue.

"So we started partying together and we became pretty close friends. I don't know what made her fall in love with me. But that changed everything." I narrated everything.

"What changed?" Mom asked rapidly.

"From that day she started doing everything to ruin Austin and Bella's relation. They started fighting everyday just because of her." This was Recce who spoke up this time.

"Getting fed up of her behavior Austin once" Recce was cut in middle by mom.

"What did he do?"

"Mom I didn't do anything I just warned her to stay away from us" I tried explaining.

God what's happening with my life? I don't want to go back in my past again but it seems like my past is not in mood to leave me alone.

"What were your exact words?" My dad asked seriously.

"Dad why does that matter?" I asked confused.

"Every single word matters in a serious case like this"

"Stay away from us or else you won't be alive to see your future" I said after thinking for some time,

"What?" My dad asked in amazement.

"Dad, that were my exact words to Diana" I told dad.

"I got that."

"Then why you seemed confused?"

"I am not confused I am shocked. You had threatened that girl to kill her?" Dad asked worriedly.

"I had said that in frustration that doesn't means I killed her Dad." I stated.

"I trust you because I know you. But if police officers or court find witness who would tell them about what you said that day, they will certainly put you behind the bars."

"They have got the clip" A new voice spoke up.

It was none other than Beth. I was shocked to see Beth here. "Beth what are you doing here?" I asked puzzled.

"I don't know why but my heart is saying that you are innocent so I am here to help you in any way possible."

Her words of trust brought me happiness.

I wished instead of Beth it would have been Jenny.

No worries Austin, one day even she would trust on you again. My inner mind spoke up sensible words for the first time.

"What do you meant by 'they have a clip'?" Recce asked.

"I don't know what clip they have. But Jenny has received one more letter saying that you will get your another evidence in our High schools CCTV footage. The unknown person has even mentioned some date." Beth disclosed.

"Was the date 20th December?" Recce inquired.

"Yeah exactly it was 20th December 2012 or 13 something" Beth confirmed.

"Damn it's the clip about that day" River spoke in frustration.

"What day?" Beth asked.

"On 20th December Austin had threatened Diana to kill her in the hall way." Dad explained.

"Damn shit." Beth cursed.

"We are in big trouble now" River muttered.

"We need to think something on this case soon" Dad warned after a long long silence.

"Guys Guys do you Guys Notice one thing?" Recce spoke.

"What?" Everyone asked in unison.

"There is someone who is sending Jenny evidences to prove that Austin has Killed Diana. That means the sender is the one who must have actually killed her. And he/she is just trying to fool Jenny by involving Austin into it." Recce explained.

"He has a point here. Besides the sender knows many things about Austin's past which means the sender is someone you know and she/he is trying to take revenge from you" River added.

"The only person I can currently think of is Bella." They both said in unison.

"But why would she do so after so many years?" I demanded.

"Because she doesn't wants to see you happy" Recce stated.

"Now how can you say that?" I asked puzzled.

"Just think when you were sad and alone that is without Jenny when your life sucked." River spoke.

"Yeah you were a total rude stone hearted guy with no emotions and feelings." Beth added.

"I got it when he said sucked. No need of exaggerating it. What's its connection with this tell that" I asked

"Huh back to the point when your life was meaningless there was not even a little hint of Diana's case but now that you are happy she is trying to get you involve in this case because she doesn't want to see you happy." River completed.

"Exactly my point." Recce stated.

"Austin, I think your friends are right. These case will be crystal clear when we will meet Bella"

It was when the search for Bella started again.

Jenny's POV

The moment I reached home from police station, I saw Beth and Alice sitting in my room again. They seemed tensed.

"What's the matter?"

"Jenny there is another letter for you" Alice spoke softly.

"From your so called well wisher. If he/she really is your well wisher why she/he don't directly comes and meet you." Beth demanded.

"Yeah Jenny I think someone is trying to fool you." My mother spoke up coming near me.

"Mom these evidences can't fool anyone.

And I am not a kid to get fooled" I stated.

Saying this I grabbed the letter from Beth's hands.

It read,

"I know the police officers have left Austin on bail to find some evidences to prove that he is innocent but trust me he is not innocent." The fact that this so called well wisher is keeping track of our each move made me suspicious. What if someone is really trying to fool me. There was one more letter inside .I readily opened it shaking all the other thoughts away.

It read

"You will find your second evidence in your high school itself. Just check the CCTV footage of 20th December and the case will be solved."

This was strange. By now I had thousand of questions running in my mind.

Who actually this so called Well Wisher is? Why is she/he helping me? How does he/she knows so about Austin and Diana? Why all of sudden after so many years he/she is giving me evidence?

Damn my head was literally jammed by all these questions. I was confused about my next step.

As today I had a second thought on whether to trust this unknown person or not I decided to take the help of officers. Instead of going to high school first, I went to police station and narrated them everything in details. Right from the beginning, the officers decided to come with me to the high school. I called Alec too so that I don't feel alone. He was right outside the building waiting for us. I felt my heartbeat rise the moment we entered the control room of the high school. I really wish Austin to be innocent. I had no guts to lose one more important person from my life. As the clip of 20th December started I held the hand of Alec tightly. Surely I was not ready for the big evidence.

At somewhat in the afternoon the incident in hallway shocked me.

There were many people gathered in the hallway and the center of attraction was none other than Austin Bella and Diana.

"Would you please stay away from my boy friend Diana? Enough is Enough" Bella shouted."Why? Are you scared of me snatching your boyfriend from you?" Diana said with a smirk."Why would I be scared?" Beth asked."Because I have widened the options for your boyfriend to choose. And even you know that I love your boyfriend more than you" Diana shouted back.

I was stunned to hear the words that left Diana's mouth. Even Alec had same expression of aghast on his face.

Diana Summers, my soul mate, my cousin and my better half was madly in love with Austin Parker and I never knew of that. What a bad sister I was?

And all these years I thought I knew my sister in and out. But I was wrong actually I knew nothing I concentrated on the next conversation between them.

"Both of you stop it. Diana I don't know what made you fall in love with me but let me tell you one thing, I love Bella a lot so stay away from us or else you wont be alive to see your future" Austin warned Diana

"I am going to kill that asshole. How dare he speak in this manner with Diana?" Alec said getting furious. Luckily police officers stopped him.

Where was I when my sister was going through such a torture? I must be rusting in the Library like always.

I felt guilty for leaving my sister alone in situation like this By now tears were freely falling from the corner of Diana's eyes. She was heartbroken and I didn't even know that. I felt guilty. Maybe she was really under depression and I couldn't just guess it like she used to do.

My trains of thoughts were cutoff by a very loud noise voice of an officer.

"Jennifer this is really strong evidence against Austin. We can use this against him in court."

"Before that I need to go to Austin's house. I want to know everything in details." I told the officers.

"Are you mad to go there now?" Alec spat with anger.

"I want to ask him something"

"Jenny he is damn killer" Alec shouted.

I know he was shocked with so much information so I didn't argue with him. I told him to go home as I have some other work. Luckily he did buy my lie. We all went on our separate paths.

I reached Austin's house few minutes later. With all the guts I rang the doorbell.

The door was opened by none other then Beth. This was totally out of blue incident I had never thought I could find Beth here.

Heck what is she doing here?

"What are you doing here?" Beth questioned

"Exactly My question. Why are you here Beth?" I asked stunned.

"To help him"

"Now tell me why you are here?" She asked again.

"I want to talk to Austin" I replied.

She told me to come in. Surprisingly everyone even Austin's parents were present in the hall. All the faces shared only one expression of astonishment and shock. No one dared to even utter a single word for a long time.

Luckily Beth spoke up "They know about the clip Jenny."

"I am glad you told them about this as I am here to know about this" I said addressing everyone.

"What do you want to know Jenny?" Austin said ruthlessly.

His cold voice sent shivers in my entire body. I froze on my place. My brain suddenly became numb. I was totally out of questions for few minutes.

Gosh what do I do now?

After taking a long breath I finally asked in a weak voice "How did you know Diana?"

After a long pause Austin started speaking. Austin narrated everything in details to me. From the very beginning from how he met Diana till the incident in the hallway.

Their story hit like a strong slap to me as Diana had never ever talked or even mentioned about being friends with Bella or Austin before. That made me wonder why was Diana hiding so much from me. "What happened after that day?" I asked again looking for the first time in his angelic eyes.

Gosh I miss him so much. When you are in a habit to be with someone daily, just a day without them feels like a very long boring year.

Focus Jenny my mind warned me.

"After that day Diana never talked or even smiled at me again. She was moving on which was a good thing for us. But few days before her birthday she had messaged me on Facebook that she wanted to meet me and she had even said that not say refuse because its her birthday. She had even promised me that she would never meet me after that" Austin revealed.

He further continued, "So on that day as in the evening I had planned surprise party for Bella I went to Diana hotel room in the morning. Guess the photographs are of that time." Austin said with a sigh.

After lot of thinking I spoke up. "Do you still have that Facebook message?"

"Yeah. Why?" Austin asked confused.

"Can you remember the date when she had messaged you?" I asked again.

"Not exactly but it was few days after the fight so maybe 24th or 25th of December" He replied.

"How can this be possible?"

"What you mean by this. I am not lying trust me" Austin said honestly.

"I mean how could Diana send you Message on day of Christmas?"

"Why can't she? It isn't illegal to send message to someone on day of Christmas".Austin said sarcastically.

Damn this Guy won't stop being sarcastic ever.

'But that's what you love about him' My inner mind spoke.

It was actually true

"Hello Jenny you there?" Bella shook me to bring me out of my thoughts.

It was then it hit me that I was intensely staring at his angelic blue eyes. Gosh what's the matter with me. Can't I just control my feelings for once?

"Hmm Yeah, I know that its not illegal. I am just trying to say that Diana couldn't send you message on 25th December because on somewhat 23rd December her Facebook account was hacked."

"What?" Everyone shouted in unison

* * *

Chapter 40 - Meeting with Bella

Austin's Pov

"What?" I asked in total distress.

"Did I say in Aliens language or something for you to not understand?" Jenny spoke sarcastically.

"I understood what you said stupid. I wanted to say or rather ask that how could you disclose such an important piece of shit after so long time?" I asked in disbelief.

"Well I didn't know it had something to do with a case. I am not a genius to know everything." Jenny said in a duh tone.

"Haven't I mentioned it before?" I asked getting annoyed.

"No" She replied instantly which shut my mouth for few seconds. "What happened? Did cat get your tongue?" Jenny spoke.

"Though I am enjoying this silly fight of yours very much we still have case to crack. Remember Guys?" Beth Asked amused.

"And to crack this case we need to find Bella Asap" Recce spoke up.

"Guys we will go search for Bella from tomorrow" I said to Recce and River.

"Even I am coming with you Guys" Jenny spoke up again.

"No we can do it be ourselves" I replied instantly.

"Excuse me? I am not asking you I am ordering you. I am one who have filed complaint against you so I do have rights to investigate in the case." Jenny demanded.

"You go and search for Bella by yourself then." I said agitatedly

"Why? Do you want to bribe her to change her words?" She asked with a raised eyebrow.

"Do you seriously think I will do that?" I asked frustrated. I never knew Jenny thought so low about me.

"No. But I just sensed that this would get me to come with you" She said with a big grin.

Gosh what's the matter with this girl. At one moment she is all rough and tough and at next moment itself she gives a million dollar smile which is the only key to unlock my heart.

Gosh I miss her so much.

"What's with the fights huh?" My dad said interrupting our conversation.

"Sorry dad she started arguing first" I said pointing towards Jenny.

"As if you didn't say anything at all." Jenny instantly replied back.

The anger and hatred that was in her eyes yesterday seemed to have faded today after the conversation which was a good thing.

"Enough" My dad shouted getting fed up of our fighting.

"Oh I am sorry Mr. Parker" Jenny said calmly.

"Austin and Jenny you both will go and search for Bella together." Dad ordered.

"But..."

"Dad.." We both tried interrupting at a same time.

"No Arguments." Saying this, dad went out of the room leaving us both in awe.

With this, the destiny had brought Jenny and me together again to find Bella though.

I don't know what exactly God has in his mind. I just hope it's not worst than this.

******

Next day at exact 7'0 clock in the morning, Jenny was at my doorsteps looking beautiful as ever.

God I wish I could kiss her pink juicy blossom soft lips now.

Control Austin. My inner mind spoke.

"Take a picture it will last longer" Jenny said with a smirk.

"I know that. But I don't want to" I said with a same smirk.

Gosh I love this bold Jenny.

"Whatever, can we please start our journey now." She said faking boredom.

"Sure. After you" I said pointing at her.

"Ok. Then tell me where to go." She asked.

"How would I know that?" I said with a puzzled look.

"You were her boy friend for a long year. You must know where she stays" She stated.

"Sorry to burst your little bubble but I don't know where she stays" I informed her.

"Why, didn't you have any sources at that time?" She said in amusement.

"It's none of your business. Now just think what we can do now." I said to shut up her mouth.

Damn she is more intelligent then I had thought.

"Instead of fighting like Idiots if you go to high school, you can find Bella's address in their register book" My Mom suggested coming beside us.

"Yeah. You are right mom. Why didn't I think of this before? Damn someone is resisting my thinking capabilities." I said faking sadness.

"Excuse me? What do you mean huh?" She asked in dismal.

"I exactly mean what I said"

"Alright. That's it. You guys are not going together." My mom said getting annoyed.

"Yeah that's better."

"Weren't you guys supposed to go and look for Bella?" Very puzzled Recce asked.

"Yeah we were but Oh so intelligent friend of your doesn't have Bella's address" Jenny said in a high pitched girls voice.

"What's big deal in this we can get her address from register book." Recce said straight away.

"That's what I said exactly. But these idiots are busy in fighting" My mom pointed out.

"I will come with you guys maybe this would reduce your fights or at least I will get to have fun"

Saying this we all set out to find Bella.

Jenny was about to sit in the back seat when suddenly Recce spoke up.

"Hey Jenny I am feeling sleepy so will you please sit in the front. I would lay on backseat" Recce said making Puppy eyes for which every Girl are bound to fall except Jenny I think.

We all knew he was lying. I had thought Jenny will disagree even but surprisingly she agreed. Her anger also had seem to fade a little after yesterdays explanation.

God I hope this tension between us dissolves soon, I miss her so much.

With pin drop silence we reached the school. After talking to a few officials, we finally got one address

"Here's the address." Recce said happily.

"Note it down somewhere" Jenny told Recce handing him pen.

"Or else you can use technology like intelligent people. Just click its picture." I suggested teasingly.

"Your idea is good Austin"

"Whatever. Now can we just Go Mr. Intelligent?"

"By the address I can say that she stays nearby we can reach there in top half hour so no need to freak" Recce said examining the address.

Saying this we set again on road. Setting address in GPS device of

Car we started our Journey. The moment we reached the address, I felt a whole sea of anxiety deep down.

I was about to meet my Ex girlfriend after three long years. The girl whom I loved a lot and who have destroyed my entire life. Only God knows what he has in store for me.

We reached near doorbell. Both waited for me to press the doorbell for sometime. Luckily Jenny pressed the doorbell sensing my nervousness and fear.

God why my life has to become so unpredictable?

"Yes. Who do you want?" Said a lady in her late seventies.

"Are you Bella's grandmother?" Jenny asked kindly.

Damn her kindness can make anyone fall for her.

"No dear. I am owner of this house." The lady replied with the same tone.

"But Bella has given this address in the Register" Recce pointed out.

"Yeah she used to live here before" The lady informed.

"What do you mean?" I asked confused.

"I give students who come from far place a room on rent. Bella used to live here on rent before but she left three years back." The lady stated.

"Do you know where she must be living now?" Recce asked.

"Sorry son, I don't have any information about her now"

This was big shock for us as the only hope of finding Bella was this but it was of no use now. With dejected looks on our faces we started returning back to car.

"What do we do now?" Jenny asked again.

Sadness was quite clear on her face.

"I don't know. I don't know anything that's going in my life now please spare me" I said frustratingly joining my hands in front of her

"Hey are you Guys searching for Bella?" Said a girl in her early twenties.

She came running beside us.

Damn I felt like my entire life was now dependent in her hands.

With hopeful eyes I asked "Yeah. Do you know her?"

"Yes I know her. She was my friend. I know her parent's address you can go and check out there." Saying this girl scribbled the address on the paper and gave us.

The girl came to my rescue like knight in shining armor.

"Shit" Recce shouted.

"Now what?" I asked irritated.

"This address is of different city. It will take few hours to go there." Recce said showing me the address.

"We can't do anything else. Do we have any other option?" I asked though I knew the answer.

No we didn't have any other option. This time instead of sitting front Jenny went on backseat before Recce could protest so I had to sit with Recce.

With this our journey started again.

Damn I had never thought even such day will come in my life. Though Jenny and me were in same car we couldn't talk with each other.

Damn she wasn't even looking at me.

After few hours of driving and non sense talks of Recce we reached the destination.

"Finally here", Recce said jumping out of car.

This time he was the one who rang the doorbell without even waiting for us.

The women in her late forties opened the door. I instantly guessed that she is Bella's mother. As she reminded me a lot about Bella. They shared lot of same features.

"Yes. Who do you want?" The lady asked.

"We are Bella's friends. We have come here to meet her." Jenny replied politely.

"Then I am sorry to inform you that you have come to wrong place." The lady spoke.

"Why? This is Bella's house right then why isn't she here?" Recce asked confused and irritated.

I can tell from his face that he was fed up of traveling.

"Yeah this is her house but she doesn't stay here now"

"Is she married?" I asked all of the sudden in a low tone. I don't know where it came from but I felt an urge to ask that.

"Getting married is very far thing she hates talking about marriage even because of that Austin Parker" Her mom revealed.

Listening to my name my all senses became high alert.

"What did he do?" I asked getting curious.

"That piece of shit cheated on my daughter. My poor girl loved him and he left her forever. If I ever see him I will kill him." Bella's mom said angrily

"He took the smile away from my life" She further said with a glint of sadness.

God why am I being dragged in all the bad situations.

"I know Austin Parker. He is just a spoil brat" Jenny said with a wide smirk on his face.

"No No. She is lying just because she is in love with him and he doesn't love her back. Austin is very Good guy" I spoke up trying to clear my side.

"Really Guys are you going to start here even?" Recce said interrupting us.

"Can we know were she is now?" Recce asked Bella's Mother.

"She has warned me to not to tell about her whereabouts to anybody" Her mom informed.

"We are not anybody we are her friends. And seriously speaking my entire life is in her hands only she can help me from losing my life and love" I said with all the sincerity.

"Her life is ruined I will pray to God At least you get your back. Here is the address. She stays with her Grandmother" Her mom said handing us the address.

Damn I hope we at least find her now.

"I can't believe she has told her mom that I cheated on her" I said the moment we stepped out of the house. This was very shocking thing.

"Why do you care about that? Do you still love her?" Jenny asked trying to be cool.

I know she was just pretending it to be a casual question but from inside she was totally jealous.

"I don't know I am totally confused now maybe I still have feelings for her" I said purposely to burn her more with jealousy and my purpose was being served as I can tell she was overwhelming with jealousy. Gosh I love her so much when she is jealous of someone.

"Bad for you" Saying this she just sat back with Recce again slamming the door with anger.

Thankfully her Grandmother's house was not so far. In somewhat an hour we reached our destination.

We rang the door bell waiting for someone to open the door.

An old lady opened the door. Seeing us her facial expressions changed from happy to sour.

God why I am being suddenly hated by everyone.

"What are you doing here?" She asked with hatred.

"How do you know me?" I asked confused.

"I wont ever forget you. You ruined my Grand daughter's life." The lady said with a grudge in her voice

"I swear to God I haven't done anything. Please let me talk to Bella" I pleaded.

"No. She has just started living her life again after many years. I won't let you ruin her life again." I was startled to know this new information.

"Please try to understand Ma'am, this is very serious condition. My entire life is dependent on this. Please I promise I wont hurt her" I tried pleading, but it seemed like entire universe was turning against me.

She wasn't ready to understand anything.

"Jason" She screamed.

A tall figure few years bigger than us emerged from inside. "Throw all these people out of my house" She instructed.

Gosh what happening with me.

"Please try to understand our situation. We have came here from very far please allow us to meet Bella" This time it was Jenny who was pleading.

"Just remove them out" Saying this lady vanished inside.

"I don't know who you are but please let us talk to Bella. Its very Urgent" I pleaded to Jason even.

"I know why you are here. But this is not right time now. Come to my house. I am their neighbor and Bella's doctor." Jason spoke up.

The last sentence shocked me.

"Is she ill?" I asked concerned.

"Lets Go. I will narrate to you everything" Saying this he closed the door of Bella house and took us to his house.

Thousands of different questions were flooding in my head now. Why did Bella need a doctor? Why she was telling everyone I cheated on her? God instead of resolving, this case was getting more complicated.

After offering water and snacks the guy sat in front of us silently.

No one was speaking anything. So I took the initiative of starting the conversation.

"What has happened to Bella?" I asked again.

"She is been in depression from last few years." The man finally revealed.

I was totally flabbergasted by his words.

"What?" I and Recce shouted in unison.

"Why would she be in depression. When she left Austin she seemed to be the happiest person in the world." Recce spoke.

"Sometimes there are lots of things hidden behind the happy smile" The Jason guy tried to explain

"What do you mean?" Jenny asked.

"On the night of your anniversary party something happened that forced Bella to do few things." He spoke again.

"You mean Bella was forced to kill my sister by someone?" Jenny spoke up this time.

"Sorry I can't tell you anything about this."

"Gosh I am in damn trouble here and you are not telling us anything" I said irritated.

"Chill Austin. I can't tell you this. Its on her decision totally if she want to tell you or not but I can arrange your meeting with Bella"

"How you know so much about us?" I asked instantly.

"Luckily Bella has started talking about her past since last month. And rest the news has helped me to update" He spoke up.

"Yeah. I am very famous now" I said sarcastically.

"Don't worry everything will be all right by tomorrow. I heard you have came from very far so you guys can stay here if you want"

Jenny's POV

I couldn't sleep the entire night. The events of last few days were constantly running in my head. One more thing harassing me was the concern in Austin's eyes for Bella. The care and affection in his eyes for Bella made anger swirl like red tide within me. I had to literally curl my upper lip today evening to keep myself from speaking something stupid in front of everyone that would have confirmed my feeling for him. The feeling of jealousy was slowly growing into my skin, though I know Austin loves me and Bella was just his past, I still felt insecure and terrified.

I stirred in bed as I tried to get some sleep. The cool pillow touching my head made me fell relaxed and calm but I still wasn't falling asleep.

The soft sheets gently rubbed against my skin as I turned onto my side a third time. I sighed. This was hopeless. I opened my eyes and saw lighting flickering across my room. The light was still on, which bothered me. I took the bed sheets off me and went into hall to see who was awake.

The moment I went out I saw Austin siting on a Sofa with his back towards me. I wanted to speak to him but I couldn't gather up strength to do so I just kept staring at him thinking about all the happy times we had together. A small smile crept on my face.

"Instead of staring at me and smiling their like a creep you can come here and sit beside me, I don't bite I swear" Austin's voice brought me out of my thoughts. From back even I could tell he had a big smirk on his face my face flushed radish red and I stared at my feet, luckily he didn't noticed how embarrassed I was. His facial expression suddenly changed from grin to stoned face.

"So you couldn't sleep too?" He asked genuinely.

I couldn't form proper words, so I just shook head saying "No".

"So can you just have a talk with your sister's killer?"

"Austin, I am sorry for being suspicious. But all the evidence I had were all pointing at you" I explained

"So now you don't think I must have killed her?" He asked again.

I again shook my head saying "No"

"What made you change your mind Jenny? If it is because of what I told you yesterday then how can you trust me?"

I couldn't speak anything. I was totally wordless or you can say voiceless.

"No need to answer this. Just remember one thing, there will come a time when you will upset me and cause me unwanted anger. Cruel words you might say that will cause me hurt and bring me sadness. There are going to be unwise decisions that you will make that will disappoint me. There are going to be moments where you will make me cry and bring me to tears, but no matter what happens, I want you to know that, I will always love you, now and forever! You are worth all the pain" Saying this, he went to his room.

Tears started to stream down my cheeks freely. I sat in a sheltered corner where all thoughts roam round and round in my head. I felt guilt overwhelming me. It felt like my heart is sagging down into an empty pit of darkens. I felt guilt, I felt uneasy for doubting on Austin. Now I was hundred percent sure that Austin was innocent.

God what have I done. I just sat there crying my heart out. Though I knew crying wouldn't change anything I couldn't stop crying. I wish I could just reverse the time.

"Hey Jenny why you crying?" Recce said coming near me, rubbing his eyes to wash the sleep away

"I have done a very big mistake, Recce" I admitted.

"Woah, what happened now?" He asked concerned.

"I shouldn't have made Austin pass through so much pain. Though my heart kept on shouting that Austin is innocent I just kept on ignoring it" I spoke.

"And you now finally believe Austin is innocent"

"Yeah" I admitted again.

"What made to think this" He asked same as Austin.

"I trust on Austin. Whatever he said yesterday made me believe that he is innocent and maybe Bella must have done something to Diana".

"Thank God, finally I am hearing sensible words from you." He said with a big grin.

"You Guys must hate me now right?" I said sadly.

"Seriously speaking we did hate you before but it was Austin who made us understand that you aren't bad you just overly concerned about your sister's death which is forcing you to do such a thing. You are still our little innocent brainless Jenny".

Recce's last sentence made me chuckle though it is right.

"Now go and have good night sleep tomorrow everything will be alright" Recce said bear hugging me from one side.

I felt my heart become a lot lighter and finally I felt like sleeping.

Austin's Pov

My chat with Jenny last Night made me feel a lot Better. Now I didn't even cared what Bella has to say. Even if she says anything against me, it will be ok with me. I knew now that Jenny trusted me so I could surely prove myself right now.

Jason came in my room with a cup of coffee.

"You didn't have to do this" I said taking the coffee from his hands as it was what I needed now.

"It's my duty to serve my guests." He said with a smile.

"Thanks...For Everything" I said sincerely thanking him.

"No need buddy. I am doing this all for Bella" He Further continued" Bella will be here in an hour for her session so get ready fast"

"I am all ready" I said pointing at my outfit.

"I could see that. Tell everyone to get ready soon too. Especially Jennifer. She is still sleeping"

"She is?" I asked surprised.

Jason was Right. Jenny was still in deep sleep. She seemed calm and happy, as there was faint smile on her face. And I could even tell that she had cried yesterday because her eyes were red and fluffy. I didn't want to wake her up as I knew she must be sleeping so well after so many days but I had to. So I just shouted bomb in her ears.

Jenny instantly woke up with an huge scream.

Gosh the scared expression on her face was hilarious. I would have passed there by laughing if Jason wouldn't have called me. After little time everyone was ready in the hall waiting for Bella's arrival

Exactly at 11'0 clock Bella Arrived. She was totally stunned to see me. Even I couldn't recognize her for few minutes. She had changed totally, she looked totally dull with dark circles, long faced, lost in thoughts, pale, weary. She was a lot cheerful before but now she seemed like she get no pleasure from anything she even seemed to I cry a lot, I don't know what exactly happened but she wasn't the girl I knew and loved. My heart totally arched to see her this condition.

"So you are finally here." Bella said with a fake smile.

"You were expecting me here?" I asked confused.

"Yeah. Obviously after so much in the news I had to expect you here." She spoke lowly.

"So you know why we are here" Recce asked.

"Obviously." She said.

"I was going to come to meet you soon" she added further.

"To accept your own crime?" .Jenny asked confused

"Why did you killed her Bella? She was your best friend Right?" Recce asked in harsh tone.

"So you guys have already made up in your mind that I have killed her. Then why are you here even?" Bella asked hurt quite visible in her voice.

"To ask you the reason maybe" Recce answered.

"And what if I tell you that I haven't killed her" Bella revealed.

"What?" Jenny asked shocked.

"Then we would know you are lying" Recce spoke up again.

"Yeah you are Right .Why would you trust me you hated me even then. I don't know why" Bella said the truth.

Recce and River never liked Bella.

"That's the one reason but the other reason is that all the evidence are also against you. You going missing right after death of Diana, you telling Austin not go on Diana's funeral and you cheating on Austin right on the day of her death clearly shows that everything was planned before head" Recce spoke confidently.

"Oh. So you Guys have already labeled me villain in this story.

Then take me I am ready to accept the crime. If this is what Austin needs to be happy in his life, I am ready to do that even this time" Bella said staring directly in my eyes.

"You cant do that. You have to tell them the truth." Jason told from behind.

I don't know what she was trying to hide but I knew that it was something very important, that would change the case completely, I wanted to know it.

"I wanted to but they are not in right position to understand." Bella said staring downwards.

"Make us understand." I said with stern voice.

"You won't. You have already figured my one image in your heart now that wont change. Just keep in mind one thing I love you a lot" She said with lot sincerity.

"What are you even trying to say?" Recce interrupted her again.

"You saying that you killed Diana and cheated on Austin because you loved him. Woah! what a sacrifice" He added further.

"Yeah. You must be knowing that- the love you cant have last the longest, feels the strongest and hurts the most. That's actually true. I had to do to that for my love" Bella informed.

"Why?" Jenny asked curious.

"So that the crime of killing Diana doesn't comes on you" Bella said pointing towards me.

"Will you please try to explain in little easy words." I said.

"I haven't killed Diana I swear. You Guys suspect me as the killer as you knew me and noticed my absence after Diana's death but there was one more person who had went missing after Diana's death. Do you remember that?"

"You mean to say there is some else who have killed her?" Jenny spoke up.

"Yeah"

"Who is he?" I asked.

❄ ❄ ❄

Chapter 41- The Criminal Finally Caught

Jenny POV

"It's Nick" Bella reveled.

This was total new name for me. I had never ever heard about him ever in my entire highschool life.

"Who is Nick now?" I asked confused.

"The guy whom she really loved." Austin said sadness quite clear in his eyes.

"You mean you and your boy friend Killed Diana together?" Recce asked stunned.

I don't know what was actually happening. Was the case really unfolding or was it becoming more complicated?

Only time will tell. My inner mind said which was true. So I concentrated on their conversation.

"Why the hell you want me to be involved in the case so badly?" Bella asked heartbroken.

"Because my inner mind says that you are involved in it" Recce replied harshly.

"Recce stop it. Let her explain first whatever she has to say" Austin said looking straight into Bella's eyes.

As if to check whether she is speaking truth or not, a ping of jealousy ran through my body.

Gosh I am changing into a jealousy doll.

"Thanks" Voice of Bella distracted my thoughts, after a long silence Bella finally started speaking again.

"Only Nick killed Diana" Bella spoke in sad low voice.

"Why would he kill her?" Austin asked more confused than me.

"Because he hates you" Bella spoke all in one breath.

"What?" Austin asked shocked.

"Why?" I asked puzzled.

"What's connection between this will you please elaborate?" Recce said with rigid face again.

God I hope they don't start world war three here.

I sometimes wonder why Recce hates Bella so much. Is it just because of the cheating thing or something else?

"Nick thinks that you have snatched away from him everything whatever he deserved" Bella said staring into Austin's eyes.

"What you mean?" Recce asked a little calmed by now.

"Is he crazy?" Austin interrogated.

"Go few years back and you will understand. Do you remember the exchange program you had being given chance to go. That would have being given to Nick's if you hadn't accepted it and though for you it was just a exchange program for you, it was his dream. Also the captain of Basketball team would have being Nick if you weren't there. There are many such things and situations where if you weren't there in picture it would have been given to Nick. He even thinks that because of you he had became second option for all the girls in high school too" She explained in details.

"What the hell" I said shocked by new piece of information.

"Damn! Was he seriously getting jealous of me all these years because of such non sense things?" Austin asked frustrated.

"Austin for you these things maybe small and non sense but they meant a lot to Nick. So he was already hating you" Bella explained further.

"You added more oil into this ongoing fire when you caught him taking drugs and complained about him to the authorities because of which his parents decided to send him to a boarding school. He thinks you are responsible for destroying his life. So before going to boarding school he planned this. As he wanted or you could say he still wanted to destroy your life" Bella Revealed everything she knew.

"That still doesn't explains why he killed my sister.?" I asked in a slow tone.

"It's obvious to take Revenge of Austin" She said in duh tone.

"But Why only Diana?" I asked again.

"Because she loved Austin a lot. Nick knew she loved Austin. He took advantage of this. So he made this all plan. The fight in hall was all planned before hand by him to which we all fell prey" Bella said with a sad tone.

"What you mean?" We all asked confused.

"He wanted you to give threatening warning to Diana about killing her so that when he finally kills her doubt will automatically come to you. When his first step of plan was accomplished, he hacked into Diana's Facebook account "Bella continued.

"Oh so it is true" Austin said surprised.

"What?" Bella asked.

"That her Facebook account was hacked.". Austin replied.

"So you didn't believe on me before?" I asked Austin instantly in disbelief.

"You know you Guys are a very cute couple. You are perfect for each other" Bella said pinching my cheeks.

As if I wasn't already blushing enough by her statement that she has to further pinch my cheeks. I was blushing like an idiot and I couldn't even control my blushing.

Damn I am so crazy

"Aww look at her she is blushing" Bella said sweetly.

"She does blush a lot" Austin added.

Gosh can't they just stop talking about me? I know Austin won't stop talking about me as he loves embarrassing me. So I decided to think of something.

"Oh my God so this secret well wisher of mine is Nick?" I spoke after a while.

"What's this new piece of information?" Bella asked confused this time.

" From the death anniversary of Diana I had started receiving letters from this so called well wisher who sends me many evidences to show that Austin has killed her. In evidences there was written of this tape even" I stated.

"There maybe some photographs even" Bella spoke.

"Yeah there were, how do you know about it." I asked.

"I have been blackmailed by this evidences before" She spoke truthfully.

"What you mean?" Recce spoke this time seeming more confused.

"I was forced to leave Austin because of all this evidences" Bella said in low tone with tears filled eyes

"What?" I said with shock.

Damn this Nick guy is so cruel.

"When did this happen?" Austin asked with curiosity.

"On the day of our First year anniversary" She clarified.

"But we were at the party on that day." Recce spoke.

"Nick had come to meet me at my house before the party." She said again, from her voice anybody could tell how hard it was for her to describe her past.

Poor Girl.

I felt guilty for blaming on her.

"Why?" Recce asked uneasily.

"Will you stop speaking in the middle so that I can explain everything" Bella said in little high tone this time.

"Sorry please continue" Recce said surrendering himself.

"Nick had killed Diana after her birthday party in afternoon. Later he came to my house with the photographs and video because of which you could have been sentenced to death for killing Diana. I didn't want you to die, so I did whatever he said."

Bella confessed. Tears had now freely started to fall from her eyes.

Gosh this girl has gone through so much.

"That means the kiss and you being his girlfriend for three long year's statement were all false?" Austin asked heartbroken. I saw extreme sadness and guilt in his eyes.

At that very moment I felt I shouldn't have tried to open up this case.

"I had to do that to keep you safe and I will do this anytime for you." Bella said sincerely.

"Oh my God and all these years I kept hating you for cheating on me" Austin said hiding his face by his hands due to embarrassment "Please forgive me Bella".

"Hey no need of apologizing. I knew you must have hated me all these years. Anyone would have hated me for cheating on them. So its not your fault. It's my bad luck because of which all this happened. It's funny how things never really turn out the way you thought they would. In that entire one year together with you I had never thought that something like this will happen but it happened and my entire life took 360 degree turn.

In such conditions being an optimist is the only solution which I tried but unluckily Optimism doesn't last long in my situation Unfortunately, I had learnt that sometimes - no matter how aware you are, things may not work out - there is no such thing as sufficient mental preparation. No matter how much you try to control yourself, no matter how much you try to be positive, you get devastated at some point." Bella said with a sad sigh.

"We fall in love; we take chances, betting everything that we have for that one person, trying to make it work. But somewhere along the way, we diverge from the path. We make mistakes, and eventually grow apart. Some of us cut off ties civilly, while others just ghost away. And ghosting away is the worst way to go about it. I have experienced it. I had to ghost away from you. Let me tell you the hurt and pain that follows mars a person beyond what we can imagine. Knowing that, not all of your hopes and dreams that you have seen together are going to come true, it hurts more than you could possibly imagine.

And if that dream is a future with someone you love, your world will be turned upside down. But at some point you have to realize that some people can just stay in your heart forever not in your lives" Bella further continued with tearful eyes.

This was so much for me to take. Unbroken stream of tears started to flow from my eyes. From the corner of my eyes I saw Austin and I could sense that he was totally shocked by this information.

******

Austin's Pov

I didn't know what to say. I didn't know what to think. I didn't know how to stand. I didn't know if I should keep my hands inside or outside my pockets.

My heart was racing. The wind was knocked out of me. I couldn't spend another second talking to her, because I knew I was about to break down.

When you realize that your loved one is in love with someone else, you see that the life you thought you'd have is no longer possible. Then you do your best to figure out how to cope with it. You'll no longer feel or look at the world in the same way. You'll stop pursing the same things. Your life has just changed. YOU have just changed. You just know that you're now different.

The problem is that you don't *want* to be different. Which actually happened with me. All that I wanted then was to turn back time and figure out a way to make things work. But sadly I couldn't. I felt lot guilty now for not finding the reason behind why Bella left all of the sudden. All these years I had hated this girl for cheating on me but today that I know the truth I don't know what to feel or what to say. I was at total loss of words.

"How did he kill her? There was no marks or his fingerprints on anything". Thankfully Jenny spoke up which distracted my mind.

Damn this is what the power this girl is. She can distract me from anything just by her few words.

"He had killed her by poisoning her book." Bella clarified.

"What does this mean exactly?" Recce asked.

"Eventually Nick turned out to be a very keen observer. He had observed that Diana had the habit of putting her fingers in her mouth while reading so he had applied poison to the book that she was reading. I don't remember the name of the book, but it was her favorite maybe because she used to carry it everywhere." Bella explained further. She seemed to calm down a little after the big breakdown

"Was it 'A Walk to Remember'?" Jenny spoke.

"Yeah Exactly."

"She had told me about that book. I can't believe her such a silly habit could cause her to lose her life." Jenny said. I could tell she was about to breakdown again. At that very moment I felt like forgetting my condition and just do something that would make this girl happy but sadly I couldn't think of anything.

Gosh! I love this girl so much.

"How can we prove in court that you guys were not killer and that the killer was some body else?" Recce said thinking practically.

"Bella will tell this truth to everyone, Right Bella?" Jenny said looking at Bella with a hopeful look.

"And you think only this much is enough?" Recce spoke up again.

"What can we do else?" Jenny asked worried.

"Don't worry Jenny, we will do anything and everything to catch Nick" I spoke for the first time.

The relief on Jenny's face dissolved all my problems.

"I have an idea. Do you guys have Ashley's number?" Bela spoke up.

"Ashley the queen bee of our college?" Recce asked.

"What has she to do with this case?" I asked confused.

"Oh Gosh! Did I forget to mention, Ashley had helped Nick accomplish his plan." Bella spoke revealing another statement.

"Now why would she help him?" Recce asked.

"Well it turns out that many girls loved you to core few years back. Among those was Ashley if you remember." Bella spoke.

"Oh my Gosh! I thought she has moved on" I said stunned.

"You seriously think she would give up on you so easily?" Bella said in a duh tone.

Oh my Gosh! I never knew being the popular guy had so many disadvantages.

"There is good and bad side to everything." Jenny said this time.

"Here's Ashley's number." Recce said handling his cell to Bella.

"Woah you still keep all girl's number huh.?" Bella asked.

"Woah woah I have changed now. And I even have a girlfriend now, so don't you spoil my reputation"

"Oh my Gosh. Recce the heart breaker of the high school has a girl friend now. Am I dreaming?" Bella said sarcastically.

"I guarantee you, no. You can't afford me in your dreams even." With a devilish smirk.

"Guys will you please focus?" I said trying to end their silly discussion.

"What you gonna do with Ashley's number?" Jenny asked.

"Ashley must know where Nick would be. Now I am just going to fix our meeting." Bella stated.

"And you think he will agree to meet you?" Recce asked amused.

"No. But I know what will make him agree to meet me." Bella stated confidently.

******

Bella's Pov

I dialed Ashley's number. I totally knew that Nick would be with Ashley if he was in town. According to what Jenny says, he is in the town. So fixing a meeting with him would be easier.

After a few calls Ashley picked up the call.

"Hey bitch what made you call me after so many years?" Ashley spoke in a rude tone.

But I never got affected by her rudeness as I knew it was just her character.

"The news on the television" I said calmly.

"Oh so you know what's happening, well..." She said sarcastically.

"I want to meet Nick" I said firmly.

"Why?"

"It is for his own good. I know he is there beside you so if you guys wanna hear a brilliant idea, give him the phone." I said hoping it to work.

"What do you want to talk to me?" Nicks voice came, which proved that my plan is working.

"Hey my dear boyfriend." I spoke faking sweetness.

"Just come to the point. Why did you want to meet me?" He asked sternly.

"Because I want to know what should be my next step?"

"What are you talking about?" He asked confused.

"Don't you watch the news? They are searching for me. If I get caught, Austin will be proved innocent and you will be behind bars. Which I don't want"

"You are saying that you want me safe even after what I did to you?" Nick asked with puzzled tone again.

"No dumb I am just saying that I don't want Austin to be proved innocent as I hate Austin now. I sacrificed my love for him and he is in love again with some other girl."

"I love your spirit baby. Just come to meet me at the address I will message you. We will think of some plan together" Nick informed.

After the call ended:

"Yes! The plan was successful". I said jumping up and down crazily.

Gosh! I had never being so happy lately.

"Are you crazy. You can't go to meet Nick alone. What if he comes to know about your intentions or what if he plans to kill you too as you are the only one who knows the truth." Austin said with concern quite clear in his voice.

I don't know why, but I felt good to know that Austin still cares for me.

"Don't worry Austin. I will be safe." I assured him.

Next day we started our drive near the town early in the morning. Even Jason came along with us. As planned, I hid a camera in my clothes such that it could not be seen by anyone but it. It would record perfectly clear. To avoid risk of being caught, I told Austin, Recce and Jenny to stay in the next building so that Nick wouldn't sense any danger. So now it was just Jason and I to execute the plan. Jason was going to stay in the next floor and check the recording. If he sensed any danger he would come down, I just hoped everything went planned.

At somewhat 4.30, I reached near the building Nick had given address of. Taking a big breath. I headed forward. After many years I was finally going to do something rather then crying and sitting with grandma and having sessions with Jason.

"All the best Bella, don't worry, everything will be fine" Jason said with a big assuring smile.

This is what I liked about Jason, he always encouraged me and was always with me. No matter what I did,.he was the one who had encouraged me to live again and just because of him I am alive today or else I would I have committed suicide long back. Without Austin, my life seemed empty but it was Jason who filled some colors in my life again.

"What are you thinking?" He asked which brought me out of my thoughts.

"Nothing. I hope everything goes well" saying this, I made my way to Room No 104.

As expected, Nick along with Ashley was waiting for me. They had a big friendly smile on their face which showed that they really think I was there to help them. Good for me.

"Gosh! I am seeing you after so many years" Nick said surprised.

"You look different. Kind of sad" Ashley guessed. Damn! she is really good at reading faces.

"After what happen, you still expect me to be happy?" I interrogated.

"That's what makes me think, why were you ready to help us?"

Nick spoke.

"As I said before, I can't see Austin with anyone else. If he is not mine, he is not going to be anyone else's" I explained him again.

"So you are jealous?" He asked again.

"Yeah! Some what. And you know jealousy makes you do crazy things"

"Yeah you are right. We are on the same page now. Jealous of same person though our reasons are different" Nick said with a huge smile.

"Why did you bring up this case again?" I asked standing in such way that the camera would be directly on Nick.

"Because I can't see Austin happy. He has destroyed my life, I wont let him live happily." Nick confessed which was what I exactly wanted. I wanted to dance with happiness but I controlled my feet

"Are the rumors of his girlfriend being Diana's cousin true?" I asked to hear it from their voice

"Yeah." Ashley stated.

"That made the case easier. I had sent all evidences, which I had collected to show that Austin had killed Diana to her. She is the one who has now filed the complaint against him. Now he is going to rot in jail forever" Nick said laughing devilishly.

"But what if they find any evidences against you as they have one whole month to search?" I asked again.

"They are not gonna find any evidences. As the book on which I had applied poison by which Diana actually died, has been sealed. So there is no chance of finding that book" Nick confessed again

God this is surely my day.

"Woah! That's great. What about the Facebook account that you had hacked?"

"That Facebook account has being deleted long time ago" Nick stated.

"I must say, that was a very smart move. Do you even know hacking?"

"I am a professional Hacker." Ashley spoke up. I was stunned to know this piece of information.

"Why you hate Austin so much?" I asked again for clear proofs.

"Don't you know, he is the one because of whom I had go board school and now my parents hate me"

"By the way coming to the main point, I want you to shift here" Nick said all of sudden which totally stunned me

"What? Why?"

"Austin is searching for you, as he thinks you must have murdered Diana. So he will search all the places where he can find you but he will never look for you here"

"So?"

"You stay here for one month so that we will be safe as he has been given one month timing by the police after that he will be behind the bars" Nick Explained.

"That's great news. I will think about moving but I need to go now. It is time for me to take my medicines" I said trying to run away from the conversation as my plan was being accomplished.

❄ ❄ ❄

Chapter 42 - Criminal Caught

Jenny's Pov

Coming happily, running towards Austin, Bella hugged him tightly saying, "The plan is accomplished"

At that very moment I didn't know whether to be happy or sad. Austin and Bella both were going to be proven innocent which was a happy thing. But seeing Bella hugging Austin in such a way made something inside me uneasy.

The happiness on both of faces, forced me to think that I am coming in between something very special. Maybe Austin never stopped loving Bella.

Gosh I don't know what I am going to do now.

I really felt like a third wheel between them so I decided to get out of the room silently.

Iwasabouttopassbythemwhen Ifeltahandstightgriparoundmywrist. I thought it must be Austin but I was shocked to see Bella's hand around my wrist

"Hey! I know what you must be feeling and thinking now, but trust me it's nothing like that. I know I love Austin but I won't ever come in between you guys. Trust me. I had my chance with Austin in the past and I couldn't grab it, so I won't snatch it from you now. You are a nice girl and believe me he loves you a lot. It's just that after many years things are finally falling into their perfect places because of which I am over excited. I am sorry I got little carried away" Bella said with a sad low tone.

At that very moment I felt sad for thinking so low of Bella.

Gosh! Why I have to always think so stupidly?

"Bella, what are you saying? You don't have to say sorry you have already done a lot for me. I don't know what's happening with me. I know I shouldn't be jealous of you but my heart doesn't understands. You know it's just little overprotective. I am an Idiot" I confessed truly.

"Whoa! What I am hearing? Jenny is jealous of Bella? So, is there going to be cat fight for Austin between these two girls. What do you think Jason?" Recce said like a journalist holding a fake microphone in front of Jason. This helped me to lighten the mood a bit.

Gosh! I must confess, Recce has awesome powers to make people laugh even in their bad times. He is like the mood changer of the group. He can make anyone smile by his silly jokes. That's why I adore him. Though he speak anything most of the time, he does even speak the perfect words whenever needed.

"Shut up Champ." Austin said turning towards Bella, "Bella the days I spend with you in the past were good days of my life and they will always stay in my heart forever as good memories. But I would like it to be in past only. They are in the past for some reason you know. I want to spend my future life with Jenny. As the days I spend with Jenny were the best. They made me happy even in my sadness.

That doesn't mean I didn't love you. It's just that I love Jenny lot more than you. My definition of love for both of you is different."

"I hope you understand this too. You don't have to be jealous about anyone princess" Austin said staring deeply in eyes.

It is so difficult for me to even describe in words how I felt at that moment. It was like the most beautiful heart melting feeling that reaches all the way to your soul and it takes your breath away. I was dancing like a crazy in my head.

"I totally understand Austin" Bella spoke.

Bella's words distracted me but the distraction was for short period of time as further Austin said "And trust me Jenny I have never ever loved anyone so much in my entire life as much as I love you. My entire world now is beautiful and worth living just because of you. This Austin Parker is totally nothing without you" Austin said bowing his head down.

Gosh those were such sincere words. It took my breath away, it was a moment of awe and love and adoration and so much more.

"Ahem Ahem, I need to maybe go and call Alice now" Recce said scratching the back of his neck awkwardly.

"Even I wanted to talk with you about something important, Jason." Saying this Even Bella and Jason vacated the Room.

For a second I couldn't encounter why they all left the room together it was then it clicked me that they vacated the room to give Austin and me privacy.

Damn! these people are so thoughtful.

Austin was looking at me with hopeful eyes. He was eagerly waiting for my reply.

"Bella is a really nice girl" I said breaking his expectation.

Gosh doesn't he know in such situations I panic like hell? Austin closed his eyes in irritation as I knew he wasn't expecting this as my reply.

"I know. I only fall in love with good girls" He said directly staring into my eyes.

Gosh I love this guy so much. How could I doubt such an innocent loving guy?

I felt guilty for blaming on him. I felt lucky to still have him in my life. And I won't let him go now.

So without thinking any further, I did the first thing that came in my mind.

I knelt down in front him on my knee and without any further thinking I spoke up

"One day you had asked me to be your wife. Today I am asking you to be my Husband. So Mr. Austin Parker will you please accept my proposal?"

To say he was shocked would be an understatement. He was totally awestruck. He raised a hand to cover his fast beating heart as he took in the scene in front of him. He didn't speak for some time. Maybe he wasn't able to form correct words. As each time he would open his mouth to speak something but then would close it instantly without speaking.

"Austin, take your own time. It's not like kneeling on one knee is a painful or something" I said sarcastically.

He might have understood my sarcasm.

Scratching the back of his head he innocently spoke up "Are you serious?"

Damn! this wasn't what was I expecting.

After so much time and thinking he had only this much to say.

Great.

"Let me warn you Austin, you are never going to be proposed by a girl again" Bella said streaming inside the room with grinning Recce beside her.

"What? Why?" Austin asked confused.

What's the matter with him. How can he leave me kneeling on my one knee and start conversation with someone by completely ignoring me.

"Are you kidding me? Who the hell will propose you if you give reply after such a long time?" Bella said punching Austin lightly. Hush finally someone came to my rescue.

"Oh shit" Austin said bringing me back to standing position "Jenny I am extremely sorry. This was so out of blue that my poor brain couldn't understand what to do. And do you think I am mad to not accept such a wonderful proposal? Damn! I am even ready to marry with you now, at this very moment." Austin kept on speaking uncontrollably.

A sigh of relief escaped my mouth after hearing this. I felt extremely happy to know that the past things haven't affected our relationship at all. I involuntarily kissed Austin. Our lips met after a long time and oh my Gosh! I felt like being in total heaven. At first, I could feel the tenderness, and then I grabbed him by hair pulling him more towards me in a sudden move of passion. He opened his mouth, just enough for our tongues to interlock and do the dance. We were overwhelmed with lots of emotions.

With his hands stroking my face the moment felt perfect. I felt safe, Protected and wanted. Knowing that a guy standing here with me is mine just brought a huge smile on my face. Gosh I wish this moment remained still forever.

But sadly it had to end.

"Whoa whoa down to earth Guys. We are still here" Recce said evilly interrupting our sweet moment.

"You had to call Alice right? Then why were you guys eavesdropping on us from outside?" I asked irritated.

I really wanted more of those soft pink lips.

"Someone is in mood of eating Austin's lips today, huh?" Recce said poking me.

This was enough to bring the creepy blush back. I felt embarrassed remembering how needy I sounded.

"So you really thought that we had some work more important than your proposal? Are you serious Jenny?" Recce asked raising his eyebrow.

I was luckily saved from further embarrassment because of the call on Recce's cell.

"Whoa it's River. I had totally forgotten about him." Recce said happily.

"You three are still together, like really?" Bella asked confused.

"We are still in the high school Bella" Recce reminded her sarcastically.

"Recce stop it and pick up the call." Austin said.

"Keep it on speaker." I suggested.

"Hello brother" Recce said happily.

"You bloody Idiot. Are you nuts? Didn't you ever feel like calling us? Don't you know how much worried we are here?" River said in a high pitched voice which turned Recce's happy face into big frown.

Oh poor Guy!

"Firstly dude stop yelling at me. Secondly will you please slow down and say whatever you said before because I didn't hear a single word. Just Blah Blah Blah" Recce said teasing River.

"Are you seriously kidding me?" River asked frustrated.

"What?" Recce said puzzled.

"You are an idiot" River stated.

"I know that. If you have called to tell me that then can I keep the call now" Recce said sarcastically

"What's the matter with you?" River said further irritated.

Poor Guy.

"Nothing, just having fun talking with you" Recce said with a chuckle.

"Am I the joker to entertain you?" Now totally angry River said.

"Recce stop harassing him" Finally Austin spoke up saving Poor River.

"Thank God Austin you are here. Save me from this idiot. And tell me what's going on there." River said in a pleading voice.

"You have called at a very good timing. We are coming back. We will be there in maybe half an hour, so call the police officer and everyone one else including Jenny's parents and her Uncle, Aunt, Alec and tell them to come our home." Austin informed.

"Dude, so you finally got Bella?" River asked happily.

"Yup" Austin replied with a same tone.

"Is she ready to except her crime?" River interrogated.

"It's a very long story. I will come home and tell you" Austin said.

"Are you guys fucking kidding me? After four days of waiting, all I get to is know that it's a long story?" River said with disbelief.

"Stop being over dramatic, you will come to know everything in an hour." Austin tried explaining.

"I am not being over dramatic".

"Oh yeah Right! This is all because of Recce" Austin said pointing at Recce.

"Hell what did I do now?" Recce asked in disbelief this time.

"River stop being in company of Recce, you are turning into Recce. Total idiot and brainless" Austin said with a chuckle.

"Yeah that is right though, I think I am in bad company"

"If you guys don't know this let me tell you I am right beside you" Recce said in bitter tone.

"We surely know that" They both said in unison.

Gosh I missed this idiocy; silliness, my friends. My life would have been total mess without them.

Thank God everything is soon going to be normal soon.

Austin's POV

Though the journey back home wasn't long enough. I enjoyed

every second of it. Why wouldn't I enjoy it? I was sitting beside Jenny and the best part was that she was willingly sitting beside me with a big smile on her face and not forcibly like last time. The happiness on her face was heartwarming; the smile on her face was contagious so I had a big smile on my face too.

"Thank God you guys are finally here. I was literally fed up of facing these people's questions. Now people, spare me and ask your questions to them" River said irritated joining his hands for mercy.

He seemed totally fed up.

"Before anybody starts asking question, let me introduce someone to you" I said stopping everyone from asking questions.

"Let me guess. This is Bella right?" Beth said interrupting me.

"But who is the guy beside her?" Alice asked confused.

"Yeah this is Bella and this is Jason,. her friend" I explained

"So you are Bella. Why did you kill my Daughter?" Jenny's aunt asked all of a sudden.

Pin drop silence spread across the room. Everyone stared at Bella with expectant eyes.

"She didn't kill Bella" I disclosed breaking the silence.

"Yeah Aunt, Nick did" Jenny spoke supporting my statement.

"So you and your boyfriend killed Bella together?" River asked confused.

"Exactly my words" Recce said excitedly.

"Yeah that's why I am telling you River, to stay away from him" I said hitting Recce on head.

"Yeah whatever, you are just jealous of our closeness" Recce said teasing Austin.

Gosh these guys are going to be always childish.

"Enough with your silly talks, can I know what's the matter?" Dad said interrupting our silly fight.

"Yeah, now who is Nick?" My Mom asked.

"Nick now who is this new character. I better hope you are not trying to the fool police officers or else that will cost you a lot" Said a new voice which was of the police officer River had called.

"Why would we fool you? Will you at least listen to us?" Recce said rudely.

The officers finally calmed down which was a good thing.

I explained everything to everyone.

Right from the Bella's side to how Nick killed her.

From the expressions on everyone's faces it was damn clear that they were shocked beyond thinking. But then who wouldn't?

"How could we believe that he is saying the truth?" The officers said as expected.

"Why would everyone lie officer?" River asked angrily.

"Chill River. We knew the officers would ask questions like these. We have proof" Recce said staring directly at officers.

"And what's that?" Officer asked staring in same manner. It's when I handed over the recording to officers.

After watching the recording the officers finally agreed to what we were saying.

I must say Recce do have brains. I had thought just Bella's words would be enough. It was his idea to video record everything.

"Well job Mr. Austin Parker and sorry for harassing you and arresting you in this case" Officers finally said.

"It's ok. Officers I can understand, it's your job"

"Are you crazy? They were rude with you. That's not their job" Recce said with disbelief.

"We have to act rude with criminals or else criminals won't agree their crime." officers said which was actually true.

"Yeah yeah officer we totally understand you" River said finally forgiving the officers.

"Where will I find this Nick guy now?" One of the officers asked.

Bella handed him the address of the hotel where Nick was staying. Finally everything was falling in their right places.

In half an hour or something, the news on every Television channel was that Nick was being arrested and I was innocent. But I was happier to get Jenny Back.

* * *

Chapter 43 - The New Beginning

"Now that the problem is solved, you two also forget everything that has happened in the past few days and start a new life again. Let's get you two together again" My mom said overly joyed.

Happiness was quite evident in her eyes. Why wouldn't she? She was the one who was more excited for this marriage after Alice though. Gosh I love moments like these.

"I am afraid that can't happen Mrs. Winget" River interrupted with a serious tone.

"Why?" Mom asked shocked, there was puzzled look on everyone's face even.

"Can't you see they are already past that stage "Alice said joyfully pointing towards our intertwined hands

"Is it true?" Mom asked.

"Oh My Gosh! Yeah it's true or else why would you hold hands. How silly I am." Then she answered herself.

"How did she know? "I asked looking at Recce. "Damn even I do share thing with my girl friend" Recce said innocently.

"Even I know that" Beth retorted.

"How did she know?" I asked looking at Alice knowing about her gossiping habits but she had confused look on her face too which proved that she hasn't informed Beth.

"Well OK...Sometimes I just get over excited and tell things to everybody" Recce spoke innocently.

"Gosh! he was so excited that he had woken me in the middle of night to tell me this" Alice confessed

"Whoa me Too" Beth added.

"Don't look at me like this, I had to get it out of my system anyhow" Recce said childishly.

"Damn you are turning into a gossip king too..."Austin Teased.

"Oh my Gosh" River retorted "We can't handle two gossip mongers at a time."

"Whatever" Recce said trying to change the topic.

"Aw you Guys are too adorable when you fight" Bella said admiringly.

"I would like to interrupt your silly fight here. So it means that everyone except me knows that you guys are back together" My mom said dramatically.

"Well Recce must have forgot to call you in all the excitement" It was River who spoke up.

"Mom don't be dramatic. You were the first one to know when we were engaged for first time Remember?" I tried consoling my over dramatic mom.

"I knew that because that was my plan and I had to know it first" Mom back fired.

"Ok I am sorry."

"Sorry won't be enough. You have to inform me first when I will be grandmother" My mom said teasingly.

Damn my mom can sometimes act totally worse than small kids.

"Mom" I said awkwardly.

"Don't worry mother in law I will inform you the very moment I come to know" Austin said with a smirk.

As if my mom's words weren't embarrassing enough.

"Enough with the funny talks, tomorrow there's going to be ring exchange ceremony of Austin and Jenny" Austin's dad declared.

"Whoa why so early, how can all the decorations be completed in only one day? You should at least warn me two to three weeks before." Alice said in frenzy tone.

On this everyone shared a good laugh.

"It would be just between friends and two families so I think no need of that many arrangements" Austin's dad spoke.

"Don't worry Alice dear, there is still time for marriage. You start planning for marriage from today itself" Austin's mom spoke brightening Alice's mood again.

"Yeah. Even I promise you that I won't let these two marry until you are satisfied with all the decorations." Austin's dad said with a laugh.

******

Now I can officially declare that luck is never by my side when it comes to sleep. I don't know why everyone has problem with my sleep.

I was happily sleeping in my room peacefully, after many days I was engrossed in my fun and frolic world of dreams, when suddenly out of nowhere a gigantic balloon filled with ice-cold water burst on my face.

There is no doubt that I woke up in no time and landed myself on the ground. But, it literally took me few seconds to actually realize what just happened to me and where I have landed all of a sudden. But when I was finally awake everything started to make sense.

Three devils were laughing like maniac with ice water filled balloons in their hands, ready to attack again if I was not awake.

Devils!

"I am awake. I am awake" I cried of cold.

Gosh! Why it had to be always me.

"Now that she is awake what to do with this? "Alice asked looking at balloons.

"Damn Jenny, why do you have to wake up so easily?" Bella asked acting irritated.

"Have you guys gone crazy? How can you guys not expect me to wake up after so much torture?" I shouted still shivering with cold.

"Because you tend to lose all contacts with the world while you are asleep." Bella said as if stating a matter of fact.

"What?" I asked offended.

"Though I am saying, it's their words" Bella said pointing towards Beth and Alice.

"By the way why are you guys here so early in the morning?" I asked to know the reason for which they couldn't wait for me to wake up.

"To remind you that today is your engagement and you are getting married soon" Alice said jumping up and down.

"What? This is it? You woke me up so harshly to tell me this shit?" I asked losing my temper.

"Whoa whoa what with the shitty mood?" Beth asked sarcastically.

I am 100 percent sure this cruel idea must be of Beth only. She has mind of daemon

"You asking me this are you serious? Why can't you guys just let me sleep for once?" I asked pleadingly

"Because we are too happy today, you guys are finally getting married" Alice said excitedly putting extra force on finally.

"Guys can't we have this discussion later? You see, I am middle of something" I said pointing towards my bed.

"And this is why I told you guys to bring extra water balloons" Beth said getting thrilled.

"Ok Ok I am finally up. Just give me a second to freshen up" I said giving up my dream of sleeping.

"Devils" I said in low tone.

"We can hear that" All three shouted in unison.

"Not my fault" Saying this I rushed to washroom.

When I came out of the washroom, I saw the girls ready with tons of lists and pen.

"Didn't you guys sleep all night?" I asked astonished by seeing the length of the list.

"You are not suppose to say anything just answer what we ask" Alice ordered.

"This is the rudest thing I have ever heard after being rudely woken up" I said faking sadness.

"Whoa Thank you" Saying this Alice just blew me off.

Huh Now that was really rude.

"Just Quick questions Jenny are you really ready for marriage this time?" Beth asked sarcastically.

"Breaking up with Austin was a great mistake which won't happen again, I assure you Beth" I said putting a hand on my heart to make it sound more dramatic.

"That means there is going be a marriage right?" Alice confirmed.

"Yeah" I said in duh tone.

"Damn I am so excited for this." Alice said bouncing up and down and checking her lists she had in her hands.

"What's in that list Alice?" I asked confused.

"I have sorted out all the things necessary for wedding. Like place, dress, cakes and then all the options we can have. Like for example take cake, she said removing one page "For cake we have these many options" She said showing me the list.

They had literally sorted cakes by flavors shapes and types.

Damn this wedding is really going to be long and sleepless.

"How you want your perfect marriage to be?" Alice asked excited.

"As long as I am marrying Austin, the guy of my dreams, I don't care whenever or where ever I marry it's going to be perfect anyway" I replied honestly.

"Aw that's too sweet to hear. But sorry it's not going to happen" Alice swapped.

Whoa that was unexpected.

"Don't be a mood killer Jenny. After so much drama you guys deserve a fun wedding. There has to be parties and celebrations" Beth said.

"Yeah after all it's the marriage of the Austin Parker. The name itself demands something interesting and luxurious" Bella added.

"Yeah she is right. You agree or not it's going to be huge perfect wedding. And if you are going to be like this than I am afraid that you may not get invited" Alice said in duh tone.

"Thanks for warning me before head dear" I said sarcastically.

"Whatever Jenny. How can you be so dull about your marriage?

You marry only once in your entire life. It has to be memorable. Besides, when would you get chance to use all Austin's money" Alice said getting all serious.

"OK OK I am ready to marry by your way just try to keep it simple." I pleaded.

"We will try our best" Alice said happily.

"Gosh finally" Bella said hugging me.

Her excitement about our marriage made me happier. Bella and Jason had decided to stay here till our marriage, which was very sweet of them.

"Yayy Girl! Your marriage is going to be so awesome that no one will ever forget it in their entire lifetime. It would be the best marriage of the decade" Alice said delighted.

"Whoa whoa calm down Girl".

"How can I keep calm when it's my best friend's wedding!" Alice said playfully hitting me on head.

"Yeah the love for your best friends is clearly evident in your words and actions" I said sarcastically.

"Trust me there's lot more to come ahead" Beth added.

"Damn! Now that there's a fancy marriage, we just need to find a perfect dresses for the bride and groom, perfect cake, perfect dresses for bridesmaid perfect decoration and-" Alice started blabbering.

"Why is your excitement scaring me?" I asked.

"Because you are an idiot. It's your marriage you should get excited too" Beth said joining Alice's team.

"Look who is saying this. Are you even going to marry?" Alice said eyeing Beth up and down.

"What I was just trying to help you" Beth clarified.

"Then be more supportive and help me in wedding planning" Alice ordered.

"Gosh. Can't I just be in charge of the parties?"

"No" Me and Alice shouted in unison.

"OK whatever. But don't blame on me when you see Austin and Jenny in the party wear on their wedding day."

"Yeah whatever"

"I can't believe you are finally getting married to the man of your dreams" Bella said changing the topic

"Me Neither. Damn! It just feels like yesterday when we had met in our Math class and now Jenny is all set to marry" Beth said side hugging.

Damn I never knew that even this girl has feelings.

"What's with emotions Beth, she's just getting married not going anywhere far" Alice said hitting Beth on her head playfully.

Whoa what's with this girl and hitting today?

"Thanks for telling" Beth said arrogantly.

"Whatever, let's just think of a good marriage place. It has to be like a dream destination" Alice said turning the pages of her long list.

"Paris" Bella instantly said "the city of love"

"Whoa classy choice" Alice said shockingly.

"Or else on some island" Beth suggested.

"What you think Jenny?" Alice questioned.

"Oh even I am supposed to say? I thought I was here to just listen."

"Stop being sarcastic and speak. It's your marriage after all. You should at least get the chance to speak I think"

"Oh how sweet of you. It is the best thing I have ever heard" I said faking happiness.

"Guys don't you think even Austin should be taken into consideration while making decisions after all it's his wedding too" Beth suggested.

"Don't worry about Austin he would agree to anything Jenny says" Bella assured.

"Oh really I didn't know this" I said getting amazed.

"Gosh! Are you kidding? I have seen him for say only four days maybe but even I can say that he is totally love sick. Damn do you ever notice the way he looks at you? It says it all"

"Yeah she is right but boys won't agree I think we should discuss with them" Alice said grabbing her cell phone.

Alice instantly called Recce to told him to meet at my house next day.

She was just waiting for a reason to talk to Recce. Damn she is such a love struck too.

Just like you my inner mind spoke.

It was true.

"You could have just told him about this in the evening's program" Beth informed.

"Oh yeah I literally forget about evening's program" Alice faked.

"Don't try to fool us Alice".

"Ok. I was missing him. Happy?" Alice confessed.

"Frankly speaking, I still can't believe the flirtiest guy I have ever known is in a relationship. He must be truly loving you a lot or else he never stays in relation for more than a week, according to what knowledge I had from Austin, he hated being in relations" Bella informed.

At the end of the Bella's words Alice's cheeks flushed to the color of scarlet.

Her pale face turned as red as a rose. Red leaked into her cheeks as she nervously smiled and bit her lip trying to hide her feelings.

She looked away nervously, but she couldn't hide the red glow that came over her face.

"There is no need of hiding anything from us. We already know everything remember?" Beth teased.

"Today is Jenny's engagement, pull her leg. Why does it always have to be me?" Alice said pointing at me.

"Because this is the only way to shut you up " Beth replied.

"How dare you say that?"

With this, started the silly fight between Alice and Beth again.

Gosh I was going to miss this silliness.

******

After lots of drama and silliness, the girls finally left for getting ready for the evening program.

Oh that was relief. After Little rest, I went to the kitchen to have water.

"You seem very happy today huh?" I heard Jason's husky voice.

"Why wouldn't I? The guy for whom I have scarified my love is finally going to be happy." Bella spoke joyfully.

"You seem happy too, What's your reason Huh?" Bella said poking Jason playfully.

"Same reason" Jason said instantly.

"What?" Bella asked confused.

Even I was confused why would Jason be this happy for Austin?

There has to be some other reason for his happiness, as I must say I have never ever seen Jason so happy and smiling like this ever.

I know, I haven't known him so long but I still felt that he was hiding something or some feelings.

"I am just happy for Austin" He said with a crooked grin.

"Oh really?" Bella asked teasingly.

"Yeah! Why can't I be happy for him?" He asked raising his eyebrow.

"Yeah you can. But it's strange as you have not known him for long time." Bella clarified.

Exactly my point.

"Ok truth to be said. I am happy for you. I haven't seen you this happy in years" Jason confessed.

There was a different expression on his face something pure and clear.

The way he looked at her was so intense, it was like he approved of everything she held inside her and still loved her with all his heart.

It's truly said when girl is in love, you can see it in her smile and when the guy is in love you can see it in his eyes. That intense look in Jason's eyes just spoke it all!

At that very moment I was confirmed that he likes Bella more than a friend. There was awkward moment of silence between both of them. But their awkwardness and silence spoke a lot.

I had a deep feeling that even Bella has some feelings for Jason but wasn't ready to accept as she is scared of her past repeating itself.

I hope my gut feeling is right.

My deep thought was interrupted by an over excited Alice.

"You aren't dressed yet dumb? The boys and Austin's family is already here."

"I know that" I said pointing towards Jason.

"Oh so you saw one of the boys. Then how can you be still not dressed?" She asked irritated.

"Alice chill I will be ready in five minutes." I tried calming her down with my words.

"You have to be. We don't want Austin to wait long" Beth said coming from nowhere. "Damn the boys are looking hot in tuxedo."

"Just go and put the dress that you have bought "Alice ordered.

Now it was my time to freak out. It clicked me then that I was in charge of bringing my engagement dress from some shop where Alice had already ordered it.

Alice is right. I am an Idiot. I am good for nothing. Gosh what should I do now?

They are going to kill me but I had no other chance so I got ready to die.

"Guys I am your best friend right?"

"Whoa what with this question at this time?" Alice asked confused.

"Just felt like asking" I said with a shrug.

"Cut the emotional drama Jenny and just tell us what's wrong?" Beth asked.

"Whoa Can't I ask this question without anything being wrong?" I said trying to act innocent.

"No" Alice replied.

"You are so rude" I shouted.

"No Baby Doll I just know you so well" She fired back.

"Is something wrong?" Alice asked getting hyper.

"Umm actually yeah there's a small problem." I confessed.

"See. I am always right"

"Will you just shut up so that I can speak?".

"Stop freaking me out and just tell what the problem is?"

"It's just that I forgot to pick up the dress" I said it all in one breath.

"What?" Alice asked totally shocked.

"Whoa interesting" Beth said with a huge grin.

"This was the only thing you were supposed to do Jenny" Alice pointed out as if I didn't know that.

"I know but I forgot."

"And still you ask me why I don't involve you in your wedding preparation"

"I won't ever. From now whatever you say will be my orders just save me now" I said trying to calm Alice

"Oh my god now what are you going wear?" Alice said getting hyper again.

"Chill. We will think of something" Beth assured.

Out of nowhere Bella came and asked "What the matter guys? You seemed tensed"

"Jenny forgot to bring the dress that she's going to wear today"

"Whoa. This is weird"

"You find this weird because you don't know Jenny so well. For us its daily stuff" Beth taunted me again

"I have some good dresses in my bag which she can try. I think that dress may help" Bella spoke

"Whoo hoo" Alice rejoicing pulled us to the guest room. To our utter surprise Bella's bag was full of branded & beautiful dresses some of them were even unpacked.

I wonder why she has so many dresses.

"I am an obsessive shopper" She said looking at our puzzled faces that answered half of my question.

"Though in past few years I didn't go anywhere fancy, I still kept on shopping. It helped me distance my mind from my past" She said, this explained about the unpacked dresses.

"Whoa I must say your taste in find dresses is excellent. Thank god finally I know a girl who is really interested in girls stuff and not only parties and study".

"Stop taunting us indirectly. Let's just hunt for Jenny's dress fast we don't have much time ."

And with that, the hunt for the dress started.

To handle one over excited Alice is really a tiring job. Now that there were two Alice it was like a nightmare coming true. They had literally forced me to try on various dresses.

"I am glad you are marrying first. I don't know what people do in marriage, but now I absolutely know what I should not do for my wedding" Beth said between the dress trials.

"And what is it?" I asked curiously.

"Invite Bella and Alice. I swear to god I would message them about my wedding once everything is over"

"Ha Ha very funny." Bella said.

"Try as much as you want, I would still be at your wedding a month before" Alice said devilishly

"Oh Poor me" Beth said faking tears.

After few more dress trials and lots and lots of complaints and Drama from me and Beth they both finally agreed on one dress.

Oh my pretty Goodness.

After little makeup and hair do I was finally dressed.

* * *

Chapter 44 - Wedding preparations

Austin's POV

I was impatiently waiting for Jennifer to arrive. I haven't seen her the entire day.

Damn I was already missing her so much.

I was literally looking for her in the entire hall like an Idiot totally in Love; a girl's honey-sweet voice came from behind me. I turned leisurely and there she was, walking down the stairs laughing and talking with her friends.

The moment I saw her walking down the stairs I was totally awestruck. She wore a simple dress that suited so well on her as if it was made just for her. Her golden brown hair was long, wavy, falling brilliantly over her chest. Her face was milky white, with large dazzling beautiful eyes and kissable cherry lips.

She looked stunningly gorgeous, like a painting of a Goddess brought to life. When her eyes met mine, she smiled sweetly at me. Her eyes sparkling like stars flaunted on the night sky. I couldn't stop staring at her.

When she came down and stood beside me, the entire world beside me stood still. She is such a wonderful person, and at times it's almost unbelievable that she love me the way that she does.

"Gentlemen, if you are done staring at the lady could we please exchange the rings?" Recce said faking seriousness. It was then I came to senses and realized that I was shamelessly drooling over Jenny's beauty in front of everyone.

Everyone burst out in laughter. My face burned in embarrassment. God I have never being so embarrassed in my entire life. Jenny on the other hand was totally enjoying my uneasiness.

"Yeah Yeah Sure." I said staring at my feet, hoping no one would notice how embarrassed I was.

"Finally everything is back to normal. I wish happy and prosperous life to you two" Jenny's Mom said happily.

Luckily in exchanging rings and celebrating, everyone forgot about my silliness.

******

Jenny's POV

After the perfect ceremony and Austin's uneasiness which was the best part I must say, everyone went Home. Now only we six of friends were present in my room.

"Oh My God You Guys are Finally Engaged" Alice said shaking with excitement.

Everyone joined Alice's excitement with shouts and wishes.

"Wait a second, where's Jason and Bella?" Beth asked all of sudden.

"Oh did I forgot to tell again?" Recce said scratching his head innocently.

"What?" We all asked in Unison.

"They have gone for a long drive as Bella wanted to" Recce said with a huge grin on his face.

"Excellent" I said happily getting up.

"What's excellent in this? If they would have told us even we would have enjoyed long drive and that would have been excellent" River said confused.

"It's OK River we can go on long drive some other time. I want to tell you something very important"

"What? You still sure about marriage right?" Beth asked all of sudden.

I still can't understand why this girl thinks I am not serious about my wedding.

"When was she unsure about marriage?" Austin asked puzzled.

Then the chattering started between everyone completely ignoring my presence.

Every time. This just has to happen all the time.

"Guys would you please let me speak? I think we should play the role of cupid in Bella and Jason's life" I screamed with all the energy I had in me to stop the Idiots from chattering.

Luckily, screaming helped.

"Even you think they are in love?" Alice was first to respond.

"Who else thinks that?" I asked curious.

"Beth and I, whenever we are together Bella keeps talking about Jason. How he helped her, saved her and all" Alice explained.

"That's great. So what can we do?" I asked excitedly.

"Guys I think we should play jealous game" Recce suggested.

"I don't think this will work. It's too old trick" Austin said..

"Of all the people Dude you are saying this. How you think you and Jenny met in first place?" River said with a smirk.

"What do you mean?" Austin asked confused.

Oh my poor innocent Austin. Damn he looked so cute seeming lost.

"You seriously didn't understand our plan ever? Mr. Harshal was just our toy to make you jealous which worked pretty well I must say" River confessed.

"Are you guys serious" Austin asked with shocked Expression

Everyone Nodded with Unison.

"Don't tell me you really thought Jenny liked Mr. Harshal" Beth asked

"Whoa thanks for playing with my feeling." Austin sarcastically spoke up.

"Dude you should thank us for that or else by now you would have been still crying over the past" Recce said in duh tone as if stating matter of fact.

"Whatever" Austin said rolling his eyes.

"Guys can we focus now" I screamed again to bring everyone back on track.

"Whoa calm down girl, you are shouting in my ears" Recce said keeping hands on his ears.

Seriously this guy can get over dramatic sometimes.

"I have a great idea guys, Beth will pretend that she likes Jason which would instantly help Bella to realize her feelings if she has any" River suggested.

"Will you please elaborate why I have to do this?" Beth said staring directly at River.

"Because Jenny and Alice already have boyfriends dumb "Recce replied instead.

"What if she never realizes her feelings?" Beth asked.

"Then you marry that Jason guy. We will get rid of you" River said faking happiness.

"You bloody. ..." Beth was about to say something but was interrupted by Alice's excitement.

"Guys I think we should seriously try this, it would be fun".

"Easy for you to say" Beth said with a frown.

"Chill Beth, we are all with you" Austin tried explaining her.

This indirectly told us that he approves of our plan.

******

"Why did you have to call us so early in the morning?" Recce said lazily rubbing his eyes.

All the boys seemed sleepy. They were literally struggling with keeping their eyes open. I won't blame them it was just eight in the morning.

Poor guys.

"We are discussing about the marriage and we want even you guys to be involved in the discussion so you are here".

"Are you nuts? Who discusses about wedding so early?" Austin said irritated.

"Exactly" I said totally agreeing with Austin's words.

"If you guys really want us to be active participant in this discussion, then let us sleep for few more hours" River said with a yawn.

"No" Bella and Alice shouted in unison.

"Guys I totally understand how you are feeling but let me warn you one thing, these girls are totally rude when it comes to waking someone up" I said.

"Yeah we know about your ice balloons story" Recce confessed with a smirk.

With this said, the boys tried to suppress their giggling, but ended up bursting into loud laughter. Their guffaws echoed in the large room. If evilness could have a voice, this laugh would make it whimper in fear.

"How they know about this?" I asked staring at girls with anger and embarrassment.

"Because originally it was Austin's plan" Beth revealed.

"What?" I asked totally shocked.

With this said, the laughter on Austin's face faded, but the others started laughing more vigorously.

"You guys had promised me that you won't tell Jenny" Austin said disappointed.

"How could you do this to me?" I said staring directly into his eyes.

The fear on his face was hilarious. I wanted to laugh badly but I controlled myself.

"Chill princess. They hadn't told me that they are using this on you. They had asked me in general" Austin said stammering.

I couldn't take it anymore and finally gave up and laughed hysterically, with tears running down my face.

"Gosh your face" I said between my laughter.

"Guys I haven't called you here for cracking jokes".

"Thanks for reminding us again." River said sarcastically.

"Bella will you please sit with me? I will need you for selecting stuff?" Alice said as planned.

"Yeah sure" Saying this Bella sat beside Alice and me.

The boys occupied other three seats sofa, which meant Jason and Beth, had to sit together on the two seat sofa. I could see discomfort on Jason's face and a pit of jealously on Bella's face.

Thank God! Everything was going as planned.

Alice removed a big list from her pocket "Guys this is what we need to discuss about" She said showing the list

"Whoa, are you planning to design entire country?" River asked amused.

"Do you even know how much preparation is required for a wedding" Alice questioned.

"Obviously not this much" Recce said pointing at the list.

"Guys let Alice plan the wedding her way" Austin explained.

With a huge grin Alice spoke "Thanks Austin, now that we all have approval on this, lets discuss about the flowers needed for decoration. I think pink flowers will be more romantic"

"Oww...It would look too girly. Choose blue flowers" Recce quarreled.

"No it has to be Pink" Alice argued.

"You have called us here for opinions, so it has to be blue".

"Pink".

"Blue".

"I think flowers are girls thing so they should get to decide the color" Jason suggested.

"I agree" Bella said.

"Whoa you are so understanding than the other boys I know, you would make a great boyfriend" Beth said with a wink.

Jason shifted uncomfortably in his seat.

"Dude you are a guy you should help boys rather than girls. Even I think pink is little too girly" Austin spoke.

With that the fight started again but one thing that I didn't fail to notice was the expressions on Bella's face. They had dulled. She seemed upset by Beth's and Jason's closeness.

"Stop it guys no solution is going to come out of fighting. Let's think of other options" Bella said finally.

"Yeah she is right. What about violet flowers" River suggested.

Everyone looked at him in awe.

"Guys I only suggested, you are free to reject it. No need of staring at me like that" River said nervously.

"No dude, we are staring at you because we never expected that a solution will come from you" Recce said in awe.

"Yeah. Violets are perfect they are not too girly and nor boyish" Alice agreed.

Then the discussion about other things started.

Everyone was busy discussing about the wedding when all the sudden Austin said,

"I am hungry", patting hands over his stomach childishly to prove his word.

No one paid attention to his words. They didn't even stop their discussion.

Oh poor guy.

"Let me check what I can get for you" Saying this, I marched towards the kitchen.

I was searching for something to eat when out of nowhere two hands gripped me from behind.

I screamed by the sudden touch.

"Shh...It's me" Austin whispered getting close to my ear and hugging me tightly from behind, squeezing gently and then firmly.

It was the kind of hug through which the person tries telling how much he has missed someone or how much he cares. It was warm and comforting, my heart immediately melted in his arms. By closing my eyes I stated enjoying every moment of his presence.

Damn! I haven't met Austin for only few hours and I already missed his touch.

Gosh what is this guy doing to me?

"I missed you so much" Austin said breaking the silence.

I left a sigh of relief realizing that we both are on same page.

"Can you believe in mere two weeks we are going to be married?" I asked out of blue.

"I totally know it and I am excited for it. Out of all the moments in my life the ones I have spent with you are my favorites, now that you are going to be with me for my entire life, I know my life going to be perfect.

Let me tell you, I will Annoy you, piss you off, say stupid things at wrong times, but put that all aside and you will never find a person who cares for you loves you more than me" The love and sincerity in his voice just left me speechless.

Today I really feel like thanking my friends who encouraged me to not give up on Austin that day. That was the only best decision I had ever taken in my life.

I couldn't help but turn around and face him. That's when I saw it. Those azure eyes. Just like the ocean, so beautiful and blue. I looked deep into them as he bent down and whispered to me three very important words. I love you. I didn't have time to react, for he quickly captured my lips. It was warm, and his lips were soft. Passion burned within the kiss.

Our eyes were closed, both of us savoring the moment. His arms wrapped around my waist and my fingers intertwined with his. Who knows? Maybe fairytale really do come true.

The entire world beside me froze. I wish this stayed forever. We were totally lost in our own world.

But the clearing of throats brought us to reality.

"I knew Austin was not really hungry" Bella said clapping her hands with joy.

"You guys heard me?" Austin asked with embarrassment.

"What you think, we are five or something. We do understand everything" Beth said with a smirk.

"Dude that was hell of a kiss" Recce said blissfully.

Take free advice from me, never kiss someone when you have friends in the house. They wouldn't leave any chance of embarrassing you.

******

"Why I am here?" Beth asked puzzled.

"Because you have to find fancy suit for Jason. And yeah he shouldn't like it "Alice spoke up instantly

"Why it has to be of my choice then, pick any random fancy suit. Anyway he doesn't have to like it" Beth replied.

"Exactly for that reason you are going to choose the suit" Alice said with a smirk.

I knew where this was going. Gosh this is really going to be fun.

"What you mean?" Beth asked with a frown.

"Your choice sucks so choose whatever you like and he will definitely not like it" Alice said with a evil grin.

"Ha ha very funny."

"Now can I know why are we searching a suit for him? Aren't we here to find wedding dress for Austin and Jenny?" Beth said trying to change the topic.

"You need to find a suit for Jason because Bella is searching for a suit too"

"Damn. Why she has to be so nice" Beth said irritated..

Bella was walking towards Jason with a suit in her hands so Alice randomly gave one suit Beth's hands and literally pushed her towards Jason.

Poor Beth.

We all gathered behind the racks to watch the scene.

"Umm...Hey" Beth said awkwardly.

"Hi" Jason replied with same awkwardness.

"As I see you aren't getting anything that you like. I have selected a suit for you. I think it will look good on you, what do you think Bella" Beth asked seeing Bella beside her.

Before Bella could speak anything Jason spoke up "It's a good suit, but very fancy. It's not my style. I would rather like to wear the suit Bella has in her hands. It's simple and I like it".

"Really?" Bella said with a huge grin.

Bella further spoke "I have picked it for you only."

"I am extremely sorry Beth." Jason said sympathetically.

"No no. It's totally okay. Her choice has to be better as she knows you more than me" Beth agreed.

"Mm. I should go now" Beth said waving her bye to Bella and Jason.

"You piece of shit. You were supposed to come in between to make the situation less awkward for me" Beth said irritably hitting Recce on her head.

"Yeah I know that. But everyone was enjoying your uneasiness so much that I didn't felt like coming" Recce said with a chuckle.

"What's in your hand?" Beth asked pointing at something.

"It's called a camera, genius" Recce said with a grin.

"What are you doing with camera?"

"Just capturing few moments to make this wedding memorable" Recce said with a smirk.

"You recorded me? How could you Recce? Gosh! I am so going to kill you. Give me the camera!" Beth said boiling with anger.

"In your dreams" saying this Recce ran away from Beth. Beth ran behind Recce and in this way the cat and mouse game started in the shop itself.

"Ok so let's hunt for the perfect outfits for you guys" Alice said looking around

"What am I supposed to do now?" River asked with boredom.

"You can help me select the outfit or enjoy the Cat and Mouse chase" Alice said.

"Definitely the second one is better option" River said with a chuckle.

'Good Choice Bro" Austin said patting River's Back.

Poor Austin. He was stuck in Alice's hands. She had already removed dozens of suits for Austin to try

"Alice you know that we have to choose only one suit right?" Austin asked sarcastically.

"I do know that. I just want your outfits to be perfect"

"This is the best shop. Here all the outfits are perfectly designed so would you just pick any one?" Austin said with pleading eyes.

"Yeah he is right. All the suits are good. Don't make him to try so many outfits .He will never come shopping with you" I said backing up Austin as I knew next was my chance.

Luckily Alice stopped searching for more suits. But Austin still had to try ten outfits that she had previously selected.

Damn they all looked great on him. But Alice didn't seem too satisfied.

"They all seem just normal suits. I think I should search for some more" Alice said starting the search again.

"Whoa. Please help me" Austin said coming near me and literally begging. He seemed totally fed up.

I took one Suit from the ten which he had tried.

"Alice I think this is the best one. Austin looks so damn sexy in this" I said trying to convince her.

Luckily see seemed to be convinced.

"If you like so".

"I would never forget this favor" Austin said over dramatically.

"Now lets look for a dress for you" Alice spoke.

"Now just help me and we are even" I said to Austin.

"I would princess. But I don't want to. Enjoy Alice's madness" Austin said with an evil smirk.

Gosh how can this guy act so rude and leave me alone with Alice. Oh God save me!

"Hey Guys close your Eyes. I have found something very precious. It's Awesome. You both would love it. I swear" Bella said coming out of no where.

We didn't have any other option so we closed the eyes and waited impatiently for Bella's next words.

"Now open your eyes" Bella said.

The moment I opened my eyes, my eyes lit up. A bright smile from ear to ear spread on my lips .I couldn't believe on eyes. I rubbed my eyes severely to check whether I was day dreaming or not. In front of me Bella was standing with a gorgeous wedding dress. It was stunning, classic, traditional, simple, flowing, pure white. It was like the dress every girl dreams of for their weddings.

It was perfect but simple. We both were eagerly waiting was Alice's reply. To my utter surprise Alice gleefully said "This is what I was exactly looking for, simple but elegant at the same time. This is going to be Jenny's wedding dress" With this being said a huge smile spread on my face.

This saved me from Alice's torturous dress hunting.

"Just go and try this dress fast" Alice said pushing me towards dressing room.

"When I saw the dress it seemed like this dress was made for my body. It's like the dress is wearing me. It was a PERFECT FIT! I don't even need to have it altered! I am ridiculously happy that my new dress fits and needs minimal alterations. I am completely in love with this dress and can't wait to wear it on my wedding day".

When I stepped out of the dressing room, seven pairs of eyes were weirdly staring at me totally in awe. I checked the dress again and again to see what was wrong but I found nothing WRONG.

"Guys should I look for some other dress?" I asked getting uncomfortable by their stares.

"Whoa are you crazy? You look extremely stunning and gorgeous. This dress is totally made for you" Alice said.

"Then why are staring at me like this?".

"Because we are just shocked" Recce spoke.

"Yeah totally out of words. Damn you look totally lovely and marvelous" Austin spoke up still in state of shock.

"Seriously where you find this dress?" Beth asked now admiration clearly visible in her eyes

"Its Bella's choice".

"Whoa I must say you have good taste in clothes" Recce admired.

"Yeah Seriously Jenny, its charming. I bet Austin is going to stare at you the entire time during the wedding" Jason told.

"Dude I can't stop staring even now." Austin said directly looking into my eyes. Gosh someone help me from stop blushing.

As my face flushed bright pink, I felt like thousands of butterflies in my stomach flapping their wings to the beat of the heart. The incontrollable heat rushed to my face when I saw the love and admiration in Austin's Eyes.

I couldn't take it anymore so I broke the eye contact. After packing the dresses the boys went somewhere saying they need some time away from Alice.

******

"Hey" Austin said .

"Is something wrong?" Recce asked Alice.

"No...Why you asking like this?" She asked confused.

"Because of the expression on your face. As if you have something very difficult to decide even harder dividing 150430 by 17".

"Ha Ha so funny".

"I am not joking...".

"Whoa you guessed correct, she is deciding something very important" Beth said sarcastically.

"What's the matter?" Jason asked worried not getting Beth's sarcasm.

"What's that in your hand?" River asked noticing the list.

"It's the list of food the caterers have sent. We have to shortlist three from this and we are not able to decide any three from this" Alice said irritated.

"See! A very important topic" Beth said with a chuckle.

"Whoa that's it?" Recce said.

"Do you girls just love to complicate everything" River asked surprised.

"Not 'we', just Alice" I said pointing towards Alice.

"What! This isn't easy task. The starters has to match with main course and all" Alice said with seriousness.

"Let me decide this for you love" Recce said snatching the list from Alice's hands.

"You won't able to select" Alice pointed.

"Are you crazy. You talking about my only favorite topic , FOOD".

"Yeah. That's true" River informed.

"Hmm...Done..." Recce said after checking the list for sometime.

"So what have you shortlisted?" Alice asked curious.

"All the Six items".

"How can you select six items?" Alice asked confused.

"With pen Duh"

"Recce there were only four items in the list" Alice informed.

"Oh...Yeah I just added two more items" Recce said with a smile.

"Oh let me see what have you added extra" River said peeking at the list.
"Oh awesome bro. They are my favorite" River said with a huge grin.

"What awesome. Are you guy's nuts?" Bella said.

"Yeah she is right. Five items in wedding that too for starters... It will be too much" Alice said disagreeing.

"How can you talk about this being too much when you yourself have selected four to five different flowers for decorations? And they are of same shade"

"Hey purple and violet are totally different colors you won't get that in your little head".

"Really?" River asked surprised.

"That's not the point here. It's our friends wedding too. When you guys get to decide flowers and everything else we should at least get to decide about food" Recce said with a puppy face.

"But..." Alice tried speaking but was interrupted by Recce.

"Shhh...Back me up here guys"

"Yeah he is right. We are from grooms side even our demands should be considered" River said backing up Recce.

Gosh I must say this wedding is really going to be memorable. Me and Austin were just sitting back and enjoying the argument.

"They do have point" Bella pointed.

"But if we keep so many items, no one will look at my decorations" Alice said with a puppy face.

"That not our problem" Recce said with a smirk.

"Guys let's ask the bride and groom about what they think?" Jason suggested.

"Whoa. What a great solution .You are problem solvers" Beth said getting close to Jason.

"I think five starters is ok, if this is what the boys want" I spoke up to stop their fight.

❄ ❄ ❄

Chapter 45 - Finally together

As merely only two weeks were remaining for the wedding, the preparations were in full swing. Deciding dresses for bridesmaid, finding a good priest, deciding place for the wedding were all hectic job and as it was the responsibility of Alice, it turned out to be more hectic. She used to literally drag us to all the places to make all the small decisions even.

As it was our wedding Austin and me had to be present, Bella used to happily come with us and Recce being Alice's boyfriend had to come with us. Though the bored expression on his face had remained constant all the time.

Poor Guy.

While deciding the cake, Alice had made us to taste hundreds of different flavors. At one point all the flavors had started tasting the same.

I swear to God I won't eat cakes for next few years, neither would Austin nor Recce.

Invitation part was the worst. I won't ever forget it in my entire life. They were like nightmare. Alice had forced Austin and me for one whole day to think of our all the alive or dead relatives. Invitations were sent to each and every relative present on the planet earth. Keeping the number of invitations in mind we had no other choice but to choose beach as the wedding spot. It's not like I hate beach weddings or something, instead I always wanted beach wedding but I was scared of amount of people Alice had invited.

I just hope everything goes well. Not just because it's my wedding but also because Alice had put lots of efforts in my wedding.

Damn she used to literally be awake for whole nights to do the preparations.

Just few days before the marriage we were discussing about some final touch ups when all of sudden Beth spoke up "Jason will you come to dinner with me tonight?".

Though it was all planned we all had to fake confusion.

"Woo hoo Beth's asking someone on date huh?" Recce said poking Beth playfully.

"A Date?" Bella and Jason said in unison. Both were in total state of shock. This is what we exactly wanted.

"If that is what you want to call it" Beth said with a shrug.

Everyone was eagerly waiting for Jason's reply. Our entire plan was dependent on his one answer.

Damn why this guy has to think so much?!

"Why would he ever say no to a formal dinner?" River said, indirectly giving hint to Jason that he can't say 'no'.

That was an intelligent move I must say.

"Yeah, I would love to have dinner with Beth" Jason said nervously.

"In that case Alice would you please come to Jenny's room to help me dress up?" Saying this Beth and Alice left.

"Dude even you need to dress up come on" Recce said taking Jason to dress up, River followed them.

I could tell that Bella was in turmoil because of Jason's date.

Restlessness was all plastered on her face. She was rubbing her sweaty palms together, trying to still her breathing, but let me tell you, she was failing miserably in hiding her feeling.

Gosh everything was finally going as planned. Today was the big day.

"Bella are you OK? You seem little tense" Austin asked purposely guessing her uneasiness.

"Why would I be tensed? I am just happy for Jason" Bella said in shaky voice.

After a little silence, Alice came out with a huge grin on her face.

"Guys get ready to be surprised".

It turns out that Alice wasn't kidding at all when she said be ready to be surprised. When Beth entered the Room We all literally gasped. Beth looked marvelous in the dress. It showed her curves in perfect manner. I must say, Alice has magic in her hands.

"Who is this hot Girl?" Recce said coming out of the room.

"It's me Idiot" Beth said hitting Recce on head.

"Whoa what have you done to our tomboyish friend?" River asked stunned.

"Guys will you just shut up?" I shouted.

"Jason what you think?" Austin asked nudging Jason in with elbow.

"Whoa are you guys thinking of getting married today with all this fancy dressing?" Bella interrupted.

"Honestly speaking she looks gorgeous" Jason said with sincerity.

"You don't look bad yourself" Beth said trying to hide the blush.

"I bet she is someone different. Damn she is even blushing" River said noticing the blush

With this said, her face flushed bright pink. Oh poor Beth!

"Guys let them just go and have fun" I said stopping the idiots from speaking.

By the expression on Bella's face, anyone could tell that the fire has already ignited, now we had to just add oil to fire to make it big.

"Don't they look just perfect together?" Alice said putting extra effort on word together.

"How can they be perfect together when they are like totally opposites?" Bella said offended.

"Opposite attracts" Austin said pointing between us to prove his point.

"Guys don't you think we should stalk them" Bella said trying to act cool, but I knew from inside she wanted it too badly so we decided to fool a little.

"Stalking is not good thing" River said faking seriousness.

"Besides we will get to hear all the gossips once Beth is back" Recce said with a shrug.

"But still seeing it with our Eyes would be more fun" Bella tried reasoning.

"For that we have to know where they have gone, which we don't" Austin pointed out.

"I know where they have gone, follow me" Alice said getting excited.

"Wait won't we require to dress up?" I said purposely to test Bella's patience.

"No there is no time to dress up, it's already too late" Bella said impatiently running towards the exit.

"Whoa the plan is actually working" Austin said in disbelief.

"Jealousy game always works" Recce said proudly patting his back.

"Guys are you coming or should I leave?" Bella said irritated even though she doesn't know where to go.

Funny I know.

The restaurant which Alice had mentioned was really a classy one.

It was lit against the fading twilight, the street lamps outside it were old styled and put there to give the appearance of old city though the area wasn't stuck in the 1700's. There was a canopy above the doorway, the windows showed it was dimly lit and a man stood outside in a uniform much like a doorman of a five-star hotel, opening the door and greeting everyone who entered or exited. Despite the size of the restaurant, it still kept up a quaint appeal. The architecture of the building suggested that there were apartments stationed above the actual restaurant that seemed to be of several floors itself.

By the obvious beauty, I could see the frown on Bella's face, why wouldn't she be, the restaurant was too perfect, too romantic, and way too posh. I mean come on; 'La Morsure D'Amour' was its name. It translated to 'The Love Bite', is itself too cheesy.

"Wow," Alice exclaimed, almost breathless as we stepped into the restaurant.

"It looks amazing!" I stated.

"Please stop reminding me" Bella muttered under her breathe as I passed beside her.

The older gentleman outside tipped his hat at us as he held open the door, smiling and welcoming us into La Morsure D'Amour, "Welcome." He said.

We all muttered a "Thanks," before stepping in and letting Bella take over with the plan, I was still clueless on how we were going to get a seat because it looked like a place that people with reservation are only allowed here.

I was correct about the dimness, the room perfect for candlelight, you could see what you were doing but it was still dark and romantic.

Scattered candles of varying heights and widths were on tables covered with white cloths, wine glasses, and silverware that was aflame with reflections. I was appreciating the beauty of the room when I heard Austin saying "done".

For a moment I was confused as for what Austin was saying but when Bella stepped up near the man behind the podium with the curly mustache and big binder of names while I gazed because the man behind the podium let her scan his big book until she found Beth's and Jason's reservation, and then proceeded to find a name with a table semi-close to theirs, I got that the guys have made something up to fool the Guy. Later I came to know that their only excuse was a bad memory, the man behind the podium was nothing but polite to them, saying that it 'happens all the time', but people are never that considerate towards me. Something about their demeanor makes people trust them easily.

The table we sat down at was for six there were glasses of ice water and we were immediately offered the house wine. Everyone waited for a moment as the employees dispersed but before any waiter could come to assist us, I asked to Bella whispering nervously "What are we going to do, now?"

She shushed me harshly and pointed her lean finger across the room where a couple sat together, the man in a cut black suit and the woman in her dress, laughing at what he'd just said. I recognized the figures barely through the distance and dimness to be Beth and Jason.

"Now, we sabotage." Bella whispered. With this said we all sated at her in awe.

"Are you crazy we can't ruin anyone's date like this "Alice said shocked.

This was seriously out of blue.

"Whoa see there is Drake" Recce said out of nowhere, breaking our concentration.

"Damn! He even has girl with her" River said surprised.

"She is hot" Recce said which lead to Alice poking him with Elbow.

"Not hotter than you sweetheart" Recce said with a grin.

"This means he is finally moving on" I spoke up.

"Good for him" Austin pointed.

"I was kind of hoping to get them together" River said absentmindedly.

"What?" All shouted in unison.

"Just because I was her friend, he used to complete all my assignments, Damn" River Explained. This was some valid reason for why he wanted to hook them up.

"Whoa not getting any more free assignments is really sad thing" Recce said sympathetically patting River's Back.

"I know".

"Guys even I am here. It would be nice of you to update me" Bella said with a confused look on her face

"Oh hell yeah. Actually the Drake guy there used to have a huge crush on Beth" Alice narrated.

"Excellent. God is totally on my side today" Bella said jumping up and down.

"Whoa whoa what's going in the evil mind of your?" Austin asked knowingly.

"Nothing. I am just going to help Drake get his dream girl." Bella said with a evil grin.

"What you mean?" Recce asked confused.

"Guys just think. If Drake expresses his undying love for Beth maybe Beth would fall for him and Jason would be out of picture." Bella spoke.

"Hell no. You are not going to do anything like this. Beth hates him and Drake is finally moving on" I tried reasoning.

But the girl was not at all in mood of listening.

"I am totally going to do this" Bella said.

Before anyone could stop her Bella was already on Drake's table. Damn! This girl had lots of guts.

Luckily before any damage could have being done Recce had brought Bella back to the table. He had to literally pick her up.

"Why you want to sabotage their date so badly?" Austin asked raising his eyebrow.

"Just to have a little fun" Bella lied.

Our eyes never left her even though our waiter appeared, rattling off some sort of greeting. Bella motioned for him to come closer with her finger, a mischievous glint to her eyes. She pulled him down by the tie so he was hunched over, immediately establishing herself as the boss.

"We're not here for a normal dinner -date, but I promise if you keep your mouth quiet, we will leave quite a tip. Do you understand?" She said sounding like Godfather.

Whoa! This was totally startling.

I must say, this Girl is nothing like what I had expected.

When the frightened waiter nodded quickly, Bella smirked and wasted no time in getting started with the sabotage. "What is the most garlicky, smelly thing on your menu?" She asked the nervous waiter.

"Um, the uh hummus has garlic cloves in it." he stuttered, nearly trembling from her outward ferocity. I used to see Bella as so innocent, but even the goody-two-shoes had a dark side.

"Excellent," she cooed, releasing the grip she had on his tie again, "Make it with a lot extra garlic, and send it to that table over there." she then pointed right at Beth and Jason, "But don't tell them who it's from." He rushed away from us to go place the order in the kitchen. I had a feeling we would be receiving some very fast service for the night.

Bella started to fiddle with the glass of water and her straw, and it was then Recce asked her "So, why exactly are we ordering them hummus?"

She looked up at us and explained simply, "If their breath stinks, we can almost be sure there will be no kissing."

"Whoa that's an excellent plan" River said gladly.

"But they are not going to kiss" Recce said confidently.

"How you know? People do kiss on first date. Don't tell me you don't know that?" Bella asked shocked.

"Trust me baby, I know way much more than that" Recce said with a smirk.

"Bella! You said you wanted to just have a little fun but you are doing everything that would ruin their date what's going on?" I asked this time with little more stern voice to make her speak the truth.

"Guys actually the thing is, I think I have feelings for Jason" Bella said in a low tone.

"Seriously, you still think?" Recce asked.

"I mean I have feelings for him" Bella said more firmly this time.

"And you realized it now?" It was River who spoke up this time.

"I never thought of it before as I was scared of repeating the past.

He had asked me once before but I wasn't sure about my feelings but now, seeing Jason with someone literally kills me. I can't help but get jealous and hurt with the thought of him spending more time with this girl than me. Gosh! I am totally fucked up" Bella said resting her head in both of her hands.

"Yeah you are" River said pointing towards the table. As planned Beth placed her hands on Jason's hand but the strange thing was that Jason didn't withdraw his hands. Now this was unexpected.

"Shit. I can't see this. I am going back home" Bella said sadly.

"You can't run away from the situations" Alice said pulling her back to table.

"Then what am I supposed to do?" She asked irritated.

"We will find some way out" River consoled.

"Oh yeah, will you be my boyfriend?" Bella asked with an evil grin.

Gosh now what the hell this girl is thinking in her evil head?

"What?" We all shouted in unison.

Gosh what is this happening?

"You just confessed your love for Jason remember?" River asked puzzled.

"Yeah. I am asking you to be my fake boyfriend. You know we can play a jealousy game. It always works" Bella said excitedly.

It was my cue to say "What?" again.

"How can there be another jealously game inside jealousy game?" Recce blurt out.

"What you mean?" Bella asked dazed.

"He meant to say that the jealousy game is too old now" Alice said trying to cover Recce's words.

"Really?" This was Austin who spoke up this time.

Gosh why does this guy have to always speak at the wrong times?

"Would you just shut up and go with the flow" River whisper shouted at Austin.

"Oh yeah. It's too old. They tried playing this prank on Jenny and me but I guessed it in just few seconds. It's that easy" Austin spoke up again.

This boy is seriously going to be dead today.

Everyone one looked at Austin with wide Eyes

"What?! I am just trying to help you Guys here" Austin stated innocently.

"Guys I can't just wait here and see them like this" Bella spoke again ignoring our talks.

Which was actually good or else the guys would have totally screwed up the plans

"I think you should go there and confess your love Bella" Alice suggested Bella.

"What if he doesn't like me back?" Bella questioned.

"Are you crazy? He has came with you all the way here leaving his family and work aside just to make sure that you are safe. Why do you think someone will do this?" Austin asked.

"Then why is he dating Beth?" Bella re questioned.

"Maybe he is tired of waiting" I told sincerely.

"And what if Beth likes him. She will hate me for her entire life".

"Don't worry about Beth. I will take care of her" Austin assured Bella.

"Really Austin? Thanks a lot wish me luck guys" Saying this Bella sets out to Jason's table.

Everyone just stared at Austin with wide eyes again.

"Guys what I have said now?" Austin asked totally unaware of his deed.

"You took all the credit when you were not in the plan even previously" Recce pointed out.

"Shhh would you guys just concentrate. Our plan is finally working." I said stopping their silly fight.

"What are you doing here?" Jason asked astonished by seeing Bella beside him.

Beth just faked shock expression as we had messaged her about Bella's coming.

"Do you love Beth?" Bella asked directly. This was really unexpected. Gosh this girl is totally unpredictable.

Everyone's Eyes were fixed on Jason.

"Yeah I like her" Jason finally spoke up.

"What?" Beth asked confused.

"How can he like her?" Austin asked me confused as if I can read the minds.

"Damn the plan has backfired" Recce concluded.

"How can this plan backfire?" Austin asked me again.

I know whenever Austin gets nervous, he tends to ask lot of questions but this was not helping.

"How am I supposed to know?" I replied.

"Guys I think he is going to say something more" Alice retorted.

"How can you be so positive?" River spoke.

"There isn't any other option now" I told them.

"Are you serious?" Bella asked Jason.

"Yeah I am totally sure. She is nice and a caring girl "Jason replied looking at Beth.

I couldn't believe on my ears for a moment. I pinched the boy beside me to make sure that I wasn't daydreaming. The boy beside me turned out to be Recce.

"Whoa why are you pinching me?" Recce said rubbing his hand where I pinched.

"I just wanted to check if I was dreaming or was it reality" I said truthfully.

"You could have checked that by pinching yourself even, you know" Recce pointed out.

"Yeah I know that, but it would have hurt" I blurted out.

"And now we can say the plan has backfired" Alice confirmed finally.

"What are we going to do now?" Austin asked getting hyper nervous.

"Beth is going to kill us; Bella is going to be heartbroken again. God why is this happening" I said confused too.

"But-"Jason paused for some moment.

"Guys Guys there is a 'but', Buts are always bad so I think he has something to say" River finally spoke

"What 'But'?" Beth and Bella asked in Unison.

"As a friend" Jason said sympathetically looking at Beth.

I was literally about to pass by the high amount of nervousness, But Jason's words saved me. Damn these were the best words I had ever heard from anyone.

"Gosh you idiot! You scared a shit out of me" Bella shouted.

Before Jason could reply, Bella turned towards Beth "Do you like Jason?" Bella asked Beth.

"Does my answer really matter after what he said?" Beth said faking sadness.

I could clearly tell she was faking sadness. Damn I must say Beth acts awesomely.

"Why are you asking though?" Jason asked Bella with curiosity in his Eyes.

This was our cue to come into picture to Encourage Bella.

"Whoa Guys what's the matter? Why are you all here?" Jason asked totally confused by now.

"Because Bella want to tell you something" Recce said pushing Bella towards Jason.

"I am listening" Jason said which followed by pin drop silence.

God I hope Bella musters enough of strength to express her feelings. I hope everything goes well.

"Bella grab this chance. It's now or never" Austin explained.

"Jason I wasn't sure about what I felt being near to you but when I saw you with Beth, I knew that what I felt was love. I feel so safe and protected when I'm around you. At this moment I would give anything to be with you. You bring so much happiness and joy into my life. I can't believe it. You complete me. So Jason would you please be my boyfriend" Bella finally spoke her heart out.

Aw these were the sweetest words.

The expressions on Jason's face were priceless.

Jason's entire body was in a state of shock as I can tell he was not understanding how to react. His face got slack, with mouth open, body unmoving, and color draining from his face and was staring at Bella with wide-eyed; but when shock begins to melt away, everything started becoming normal slowly.

He let out a sudden sigh, opened his mouth to speak but snap! It shut again. Then with a little more effort, he tried saying something, but it came out raspy, barely audible.

"Dude English please; the alien language which you are speaking is going totally above our head" Recce spoke going near Jason.

"Guys I think he wants to say 'No'" Beth said purposely.

"What makes you say that? I would never say no to this. Damn this is like my wildest dream come true. This is what I dream of every night and Wish for Everyday. Even If I would have being drunk then too I would have never said no. I love you Bella. I have loved her from the moment I met her at her grandmother's house. I love her a lot. I swear" Jason answered Beth's question all in one breath.

I must say he had totally recovered from shock now.

With Jason's outburst entire table erupted into fits of laugher.

"Chill dude. We already know that. You need to tell Bella" Recce said with a smirk.

"What do you mean by you already knew?" Bella asked confused.

"We knew Jason had feelings for you from the very first day we met him. The glint of happiness in his eyes while he was talking about you said it all. Bella, we knew that this Guy is crazy about you." Austin explained.

"The thing we didn't know was about your feelings for Jason. So we made a plan" I confessed.

"What plan?" Jason asked confused.

"The jealousy trick" Recce said proudly.

"Oh my God, This date, the dress finding, flirting was all the part of this plan?" Bella asked realizing the plan now.

"Absolutely" Beth chirped happily.

"Gosh how could we be so dumb to not notice the plan?" Bella said amused.

"It's OK dear. This dumbness has made you realize your feelings." Austin said side hugging Bella.

"I am not getting proper words to thank you Guys. Seriously this means a lot to me. Thanks a lot." Jason spoke up with immense seriousness in his voice.

"You don't need to say thanks dude." River said sincerely.

"Yeah besides, we are in a very posh Restaurant. A free dinner could be a great payback" Recce said innocently.

Gosh this Guy and his love for food would never change.

In this way the perfect day ended with a grand celebration and of course a free dinner party.

❄ ❄ ❄

The Grand Wedding

"Wake up, Wake up, and Wake up" I yelled excitedly vigorously shaking my friends who were sleeping like dead beside me.

"Why the hell are you waking us up so early?" Beth asked irritated.

"Damn its just 2 am in the morning. Girl did you even sleep?" Bella asked rubbing her eyes lazily.

"I tried to, but I couldn't. I am just too excited about wedding." I replied with a huge grin.

"It's your marriage dear. Why can't we sleep?" Alice asked with pleading eyes.

"Because you didn't let me sleep on the day of my engagement" I said stubbornly.

"We woke you up because you were oversleeping. Now go to sleep we will discuss about this in morning" Beth said switching off the light.

"No. If I am not sleeping, no one is sleeping." I said turning on the light again.

"I think I should try wearing the wedding dress to check whether it's perfect or not." Saying this, I got up excitedly.

"Jenny you must have tried it for 100th time by now." Bella pointed out.

She was right, I must have actually tried the dress a lot, but they can't blame me, Damn! that dress is so beautiful!

"But what if I get fat?" I tried reasoning.

"Jenny you don't get fat in one hour." Beth spoke snatching the dress from me.

"Whatever. Alice don't you think we should practice walking down the Aisle one more time?" I said making my puppy face. I knew Alice would totally fall prey to this.

"Jenny we have practiced that too" Bella reminded me again "Stop trying to butter up Alice"

"Alice don't listen to her" Beth pleaded.

"But one more practice wouldn't harm, Guys. Let's start Jenny." Alice said getting up.

And this way we ended up doing all the rituals right from the top once again at 2 am at night.

Poor girls, I know they wanted to sleep but this was my last day being single and I wanted to have fun, so it's ok to be selfish sometimes, Right?

"Now that everything is practiced perfectly can get few hours of sleep" Beth pleaded with lots of sleep visible in her eyes.

"Guys how you can be so boring. This is my last day of being single. Cheer up "I said literally bouncing up and down the bed

"So what you want to do. Have bachelor party?" Beth spoke sarcastically.

"That would have being a great idea but we don't have much time now. So let's just chat for now" I replied in same tone.

"Jenny, are you serious?" Bella asked with a raised eyebrow.

"Yeah. Guys I want this last day with you guys to be memorable. Please just get up."

I said shaking Beth vigorously.

"OK OK let me just freshen up"

Bella finally surrendered and walked towards washroom.

Whereas Alice was already awake like an owl at night. Gossips are what made her happy as hell. At any time of day we both went down to prepare hot chocolate. With hot chocolate, cold weather and the best friends beside me, the best day or you can say night of my life started.

We laughed and shared every small big memory. We crazily danced on every song present in my play list. Drank lots of hot chocolate and did every silly thing possible.

Gosh I am going to miss them, this silliness so much.

Even though I was entering in a new world and everything would change, I know that when a tear falls or smile spreads on my face these two will come for me no matter where this crazy world will take us, nothing will ever change to point where we are not still friends. I do have that much faith in our bond.

With lots of chatting and cups of hot chocolates the time sped away really quickly but we made lots of new memories that would surely bring smile on our faces in the future

"Oh my God didn't you sleep at all entire night?" My mom asked by the amount of cups beside us.

"I must say, your guessing skills are sharp mom" I replied with a smile.

"Jenny, have you gone mad? Who stays awake whole night, just before the wedding?" My mom asked tensed.

"Mom I just wanted to make my last night memorable "I tried explaining.

"What if you feel sleepy during the wedding?" My mom spoke up still worried.

"Chill Mrs. Winget, by the amount of caffeine in our body, I assure you that we won't sleep for next whole week" Bella said pointing at the cups.

"Yeah Mom, Chill. Besides, the wedding is in the evening. I can still get a nap if I feel tired." I said to calm her down.

"Sorry to break little bubble of yours dear but we don't have much time. Remember the guests are being invited early"

"Oh shit. I completely forgot about that. We must all freshen up and get going before the guest starts arriving "Alice said getting hyper panic.

"Even Austin's parents would be there right?" I asked all of sudden ignoring all their silly talks.

"From when did you start caring about them so much?" Bella asked confused.

"Bella try to understand. She is indirectly trying to ask that would Austin be there too" Alice said nudging me with elbow.

"Yeah dear Austin would be there, waiting for you, with his arms open, thinking where the love of his life is?" Beth said dramatically spreading her both hands.

"Aren't you getting late now Alice?" I reminded Alice.

"Oh heck yeah, we will continue this topic later. Jenny you go freshen up" Alice said literally pushing me towards the bathroom.

"Choose something good to wear" Bella added while going out.

"Whoa that's too much help" I replied sarcastically.

Bella immediately guessed the tone.

"What?" She asked confused.

"For Jenny something good to wear includes just Pj's and sweatshirts" Beth informed.

"Aww you guys know me so well" I said with a fake happy smile.

"No need of buttering us. We will choose the dress for you" Alice spoke.

"Thank you Guys" I said happily hugging Alice and running towards the bathroom.

*****

"Why aren't you ready yet?" Alice said coming back to my room fully dressed.

Gosh did she have any kind of magic or something? "Because I just came out from bathroom" I pointed out.

"Damn you are too slow" Alice said with a frown.

"No you are too fast" I pointed out with pout.

"Enough. Now go get dressed" Alice said handing me the dress .

"I was just wondering since today is the wedding day shouldn't I be wearing the wedding dress?" I asked with an eyebrow raised.

"You can't wear it now."

"Why?" I asked with a pout.

"Because the wedding is in the evening" Beth spoke up coming in my room.

"Besides you can't greet the guests with the wedding dress" Bella pointed out.

"But today is the only day I get to wear this dress. And I just love this dress" I said with a frown

I was about to butter them a little but then, "Jenny stop acting like a baby and go get dressed" Alice said with the nerve popping on her forehead, this means she is on the way of getting pissed. And trust me fierce Alice is not at all good, so I silently got dressed without uttering a single word.

With this our journey to the Beach started. With lots of chattering and the girls yawning and cursing me, we finally reached our destination after an hour of driving.

"We are here finally" Alice said excitedly jumping out of the car.

"I am too excited to see the decorations" I said with same glint of happiness,

"You would definitely love the decorations" Bella added, which increased my excitement level more.

Alice purposely first took us to the hotel near the Beach where we have booked the Room to keep all our Belongings; I swear she was just testing my patience.

Later the moment when Alice opened the door to the aisle, my mouth literally hit the ground. Believe me I am not at all exaggerating, the view in front of me was so astonishing and ravish that I couldn't even believe my eyes for a moment. I felt like I had entered in some kind of a fairyland that I keep of dreaming all the nights. Everything was so perfectly and beautifully decorated that I felt like I had basically won the wedding venue lottery.

Along with blue and violet flowers the place was decorated with sea shell bouquets, with attached mini starfish to the bouquets. And various shells craft to give the Beach Effect. The crafts and bouquets made entire decorations look more marvelous. Lots of candles, candles, candles, and more candles I must say were added in the decorations, which made it look all more romantic. All different kinds of candles were chosen which totally suited the site, candles were of course electric candles keeping in mind all the air but that didn't faded its beauty even by one percent. There were candles in lanterns, hand made seashells candles, beach themed candles, candles on trays, and candles around the cake. They looked simply stunning. And I bet in the evening they will look more mind-blowing.

There were two chairs set in the sand, and to add an oceanside touch to seats there were hand-painted driftwood signs.

"It's perfect" I said hugging Alice tightly.

"I knew you would like it" Bella spoke.

"What's not to like, its way out of my expectation. Thanks lot guys, now I feel like I am going to have a best wedding ever" I said happily hugging them all happily.

****

"I can't believe my little girl is getting married" My Mother said hugging me tightly.

"I'm so happy for you. And especially happy that this bridesmaid dress is so cute, classy and sexy. It looks awesome on me. I love it and you". Bella said hugging me.

"For that you need to thank Alice" I replied pointing towards Alice.

I heard the music playing outside. I turned towards my mom, "I thought we had more time. Why are they playing music now?" I asked for which she mouth 'I don't know'.

"I am so nervous and happy at a same time. Gosh this feeling is so weird in a beautiful manner. I am finally going to marry the guy of my dreams" I said happily.

"Aw you are so lucky" Bella said hugging me again.

"Though it sounds a lot cheesy it's good" Beth said as expected.

"So you are going to say this for your vows?" Alice spoke with a cute smile on her face.

"What are you talking about?" I asked confused.

"Oh shit, don't tell me I forgot to mention about this?" Alice said with a shock on her a face. By the expression t didn't seemed good at all.

"You are scaring me Alice, just speak out what you forgot?"

"To tell you that there's going to be individual vows even" Alice said in a low tone.

"What?" Me, Beth and Bella shouted in unison.

"How can you forget this? Damn what I am going to do now? What should I say?" I said with panic quite clear in my voice.

"Don't freak out Jenny, just speak out your heart and I am sure everything will be fine" My mom tried consoling me.

"Damn this is going to be so much fun" Beth said excitedly knowing that I am going to mess up for sure

"Evil, I hope something even more worse happens at your wedding" I dramatically cursed her.

She was about to speak something but was interrupted by opening of door.

My father came through the door "It's time. Where's my little cupcake princess?" he said, at which everyone laughed.

"Right here" I said putting my hand up and my head down in embarrassment.

"Aw. You look beautiful. It's time for every father's nightmare, giving away their little girl" he said as a tear fell down his face, I wiped it and smile at him "I'll always and forever be your little cupcake. I love you, dad" he gave me a sweet smile and nodded.

Everyone awed at us, I turned to everyone and nodded my head to get ready.

"Deep breaths...Deep breaths, Jenny don't trip. Just look at Austin but don't trip" I said to myself.

Dad hooked his arm around mine as we walk towards the door, the music got louder. Suddenly, the door opened slowly. I must say, Alice had done an amazing job, it's just how I wanted it, With Lots of lights. But she had made sure to use warm lights, not cool ones, so that everyone looks like a supermodel, and not like an alien smurf when we get the photos clicked. She had bundled up strings of lights and put them underneath the tablecloths so that they glow in the pictures. Gosh this girl has really put lots of efforts in my wedding.

I've always wondered what it feels like to walk down the aisle. What goes through your mind?

Well now I knew it. Walking down the aisle is the hardest thing in weddings I must say; luckily my Dad was beside me all the time. I felt like I was floating. I was so happy and excited, I was nearly laughing down the aisle. I don't remember hearing the music after I started walking down the aisle but I heard it clearly before my first step. Keep your head up, your flowers down by your waist, and SMILE. I tried doing exactly the same, though there was constant fear of tripping, as I am not good with handling dresses. My fears and nervousness were all replaced by a totally new emotion,the moment I saw Austin.

I found him fixing his tie, then quickly looked up and made eye contact with me. He looked as nervous as I did, which was a good thing. I'm usually good with handling my emotion, but after seeing him and his breathtaking smile, it was tears of pure happiness and a radiance of love I wanted to express that to him, all I could do was smile the biggest smile and cry the happiest tears. The look on Austin's face made my heart feel like it was going to burst because I felt so full of love.

Austin's Point of View

One of the most romantic and fairy-tale like moments of the entire wedding adventure is when the ceremony doors open up and the bride begins her slow journey down the aisle with her dad and with bridesmaids behind her.

As at that moment everyone who had earlier sat in chair gets up and turns his or her head toward the bride, this is the moment when the waterworks begin. The cell phone cameras flash again and again, as if all the wedding guests have turned into mini-paparazzi, all eyes on the bride and her carefully chosen wedding dress, Its really seems like magical moment.

By seeing Jenny walking down the aisle, I felt so happy and nervous that I couldn't stop laughing. It wasn't a loud laugh, but I was smiling and laughing. I wonder if people thought I was being immature or awkward.

But I was just really happy. I felt like the luckiest guy in the world. I know that sounds lame but, in that moment, I really wondered why she picked me. I always think she looks beautiful, but on the wedding day she looked absolutely stunning. I never wanted to forget how she looked in that moment, so I closed my eyes for a second and took a mental photo. I had literally forgotten how to breathe for a second.

Jenny's Point Of View

Finally my dad and I reached the priest, he gave me a kiss on my cheek and sat down, and then everyone sat back down.

I stood staring eye to eye, hand in hand with the man I despised and then learned to love with all my heart, I'm so happy I found Austin a broken, heartless man that I fixed within time.

The priest spoke "We are gathered here in holy matrimony..." he talked for somewhat twenty minutes

"Where are the rings?" he spoke,

It's when Austin's little brother came slowly running and jumping up and down as he held the pillow with the rings.

The rings were same, which we had exchanged on engagement day but on Alice's request we decided to exchange Rings again.

We thanked him, I took Austin's ring and he took mine. We stared into each other's eyes, he grabbed the microphone and spoke first "With this ring, I wed you Jennifer Winget" he said putting the ring on then passed me the microphone.

Everything was happening so perfectly that I felt as if I was going to break down crying but instead a few tears came out, Austin looked at me and smiled while wiping away my tears.

"Beautiful woman on their wedding day should not shed tears" He whispered.

I smiled "And with this ring, I wed you Austin Parker" I said putting the ring on his finger.

"I now pronounce you Mr. and Mrs. Parker you are a couple now" Priest announced.

"Whoa that's it? Aren't they going to kiss?" Recce blurted out from behind at which everyone shared a good laugh.

Gosh this guy perfectly knows how to embarrass himself.

"Have patience young man, there is going to a kiss but after the tradition of this beach house" Priest replied calmly.

"What Tradition?" Austin asked confused.

"Aren't you aware of it?" Priest asked.

"He wouldn't act confused if he would have known about it" River said sarcastically.

The intense glare from Priest made River to stop instantly.

"What's the tradition?" Recce asked this time politely.

"Bride and groom have to say personal vows for each other"

At this the entire crowd cheered with claps and encouragement.

"What?" Austin shouted in total shock.

I don't blame him; even I was shocked for a moment. Speaking vows in front of guests that to without any preparation is not an easy thing.

"Dude forget the kiss, you are officially screwed" I heard Recce whisper to Austin.

"Be ready for embarrassment" River added patting Austin's back.

"You knew about this tradition?" Austin asked coming close to me.

"I came to know about this few minutes ago, so I am just as blank as you are" I replied honestly.

"Then who knew about this?" Recce asked the priest.

"The lady beside the bride" Priest said pointing towards Alice.

"Totally expected." Austin murmured.

"I am really sorry Guys I was so busy in decorations that I forget to inform you"

"What are we supposed to say now?" Austin said with blank face.

"Just say whatever comes in your mind" Alice suggested.

"Do we have any other choice?" Austin asked hopefully.

"Gentlemen, if the discussion is over can we continue with the ceremony?"

"Yeah Totally" Austin replied sarcastically.

Ignoring the sarcasm, the priest asked "So who will be the first to speak the vows?".

I instantly pointed finger towards Austin but unfortunately it turned out that at same time he had pointed finger toward me.

"This is New. So how we decide now?" Priest asked puzzled.

"I know, Lets the Rock Paper Scissor Game decide this" Beth said excitedly.

As strange as this may sound but we girls do make most of such decisions by playing Rock paper Scissor Game..

"Yeah that's Good Idea" Jason spoke up.

"We are here for wedding Ladies and Gentlemen so would you please stop talking about your silly game?" Priest said getting frustrated.

"Then it's up to you, you decide who will speak first" Recce said with a frown.

"Since no one is ready to speak, Jennifer Winget would first say her vows" Priest declared.

"Yay" Austin Rejoiced with joy.

I don't know why this priest hated me so much.

"Why Me?" I asked in disbelief.

"Because Austin was the first to exchange the Ring" Priest clarified.

"Yeah He is right" Austin said happily.

"Gosh I hate it, when you are right"

I felt my pulse quicken, I felt a sea of anxiety deep down ignoring the pounding of my heart, with a deep breath I turned towards Guests. I closed my Eyes and thought to myself what's the absolute worst thing that could happen? Chances are people are not going to boo me, or they are going to laugh at me. It's nothing that Serious, Personal vows are meant to make people laugh so rather than banging my head against the wall from inside I decided to give it a shot. With a final sigh I started speaking "On this day, I give you my heart, My promise, That I will walk with you, hand in hand, wherever our journey leads us, living, learning, loving, together, forever."

I heard the crowd clapping and cheering me up which gave me the encouragement to carry on

"From this day forward, I will make sure your lucky shirt is washed for every game day, and that you will have plenty of potato chips in hand. I will comfort you when your team loses and drink beer with you when they win" I said with a smile, remembering how much Austin loves football game.

From corner of my eye I saw a smile on Austin's face and even crowd shared a good laugh.

I further continued, "Today, surrounded by people who love us, I choose you, Austin Parker to be my life partner. I am proud to be your wife and to join my life with yours. I promise to always be your biggest fan and your partner in crime. I promise to create and support a family with you, in a household filled with laughter, patience, understanding, and love. I vow not just to grow old together, but also to grow together. I will love you faithfully through the difficult and the easy times. What may come, I will always be there, each one believing that love never dies. As I have given you my hand to hold, so I give you my life to keep. We shall bear together whatever trouble and sorrow life may lay upon us I marry you with no hesitation or doubt, and my commitment to you is absolute"

From the Crowd cheering and whistles from Groomsmen itself I can say that my vow wasn't that bad and it was certainly from my heart and it did touched Austin's heart as he had a huge smile on his face which in turn brought a big smile on my face too.

"Gentleman now it's your turn" Priest said to Austin.

With a big sigh he started "I take you as you, and will love who you are now and who you are yet to become. I promise to listen to you and learn from you, to support you and accept your support. I will love you and have faith in your love for me, through all our years and all that life may bring us. I vow to love you, encourage you, trust you, and respect you. As a family, we will create a home filled with learning, laughter, and compassion. Today I promise you that I will laugh with you in times of joy, and comfort you in times of sorrow. I will share your dreams and support you as you strive to achieve your goals. I will listen to you with compassion and understanding, and speak to you with encouragement. May we have many adventures and grow old together. I promise to love and care for you, and I will try in every way to be worthy of your love. From the moment you entered my world, you have filled it with life, color, and energy like never before. You are my cupcake in a salad... or a rose garden in a junkyard.

You are my rose, Jenny, and I promise to devote my life to being your dirt." With this said Austin stared directly into my eyes and continued,

"I will always be honest with you, kind, and patient and forgiving. I promise to try to be on time." He said with a chuckle, which is actually true.

"But most of all, I promise to be a true and loyal friend to you. I love you and I promise to love you. I promise to love you even when you refuse to let me watch the football, to understand you even when you are at mad at me because of something that happened in a dream. I promise to honor you with all of my actions. I will treasure you like actual treasure, but don't worry I won't burry you. I promise to keep you warm, very warm when it's cold outside. I will stand in the way of the sun when it gets hot. No matter how many books you get, or how many times we move, I promise to always carry them all every time. The way that you smile at me; the way that you speak my name with such love in your voice, touches my heart and my soul, and I wonder what did I ever do to deserve someone like you?"

This was the most honest words I had ever heard from Austin. Though I tried to control a lot I couldn't and for the second time I started crying on my wedding day.

"So princess thanks for accepting me the way I am" Austin said coming near me. Gosh! can this guy get any sweeter?

The Entire Crowd erupted in shouting and clapping expressing their happiness.

"And Now, you may now kiss the bride" the priest announced. Austin quickly grabbed me and dips me, planting his lips on mines. Everyone cheered for the fourth time today.

This is definitely the best day of my life. No event in the future would ever replace this day.

****

"Let's go he party" Beth said rejoicing with happiness, we all nodded as we exit the wedding, with people throwing rice and flowers while cheering. I hugged everyone before entering the car, but I almost forgot about the flowers I had to throw behind me for one lucky lady. But Alice won't let me forget something as important as this.

"Are you ready?" I yelled at the crowd of women behind me, they a screamed yes. I threw the flowers behind me and the lucky person to catch it was no one other but my partner in crime, Recce all the women looked at him with jealousy. Honestly I don't even know how he caught it when he was standing in the corner next to Jason and the rest of the groomsmen.

I laughed at the face he made, all the other groomsmen were laughing at him. I got into the car and noticed Recce putting his hand around Alice. She'd always prefer natural beauty which suited her perfectly, long brown hair and still the same height 5ft, standing next to Recce she looked like a smurf but a really adorable, cute smurf.

They looked like a cute couple when he kissed her; I guess my matchmaking job was over.

❄ ❄ ❄